TAPESTRY
STRANDS OF YELLOW AND BLUE

CADY ELIZABETH ARNOLD

For Bill, my rock, my home.

*For all the children who have been
sacrificed, tiny and grown,
never yield to the lure of the Beast.*

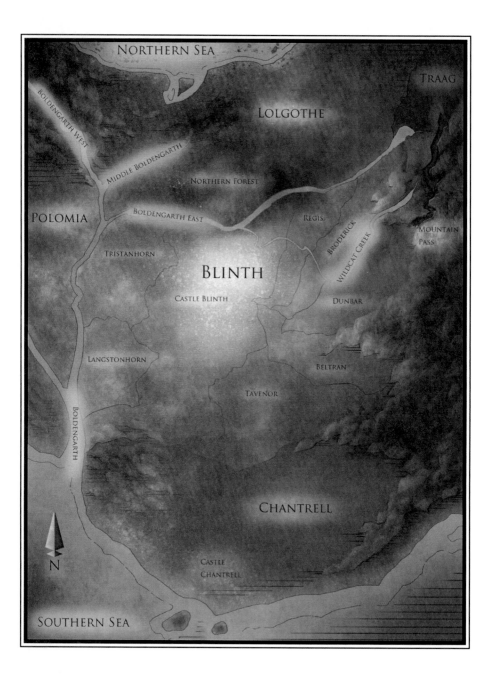

CHAPTER 1

GRACE

These are the words I cannot speak. These are the words no one knows. These are the words I carry alone.

I run through a black forest. Branches tear at my face, grabbing my hair like hands. I am breathing fierce and hard, making rasping sounds in the back of my throat, which burns with each inhalation. I focus upon one thing: speed. All other considerations are but tiny specks at the back of my mind. "Faster, faster," I chant. "Faster, faster still!" I lose myself in the motion of legs and arms and lungs. *Me* disappears, pulling away from *I*. *Me* is floating above, watching a child dressed in white running through the night.

From above, she can see the obstacles I cannot. I dodge trees and leap ravines, using her vision. She sees the gap widening. My pursuers are slowly losing me. I am running until…suddenly, I am not.

She is guiding me. How else could I stop in this ring of pines, with soft needles to cushion my falling and underbrush in which to hide? She is watching my body collapsing to the ground. Our eyes close. We see nothing.

Awakening in the grey light of early morning, I am aware of a strange warmth along one side of my body. A harsh chill numbs my other side. I am afraid of moving as the terror of the night floods my mind. Yet, strangely, I feel at peace. A rough tongue licks my forehead. A voice fills my head without flowing through my ears.

Awaken, my child; the huntsmen come.

My eyes fly open. I clutch at the body of the stag with whom I am

1

lying in the pine bed, seeking comfort. I do not wonder all the things I will wonder later: Why is he protecting me? How can I hear him speaking? I cling to him in terror. I barely notice when he stands, pulling me upright as well.

Suddenly, six bows are strung. Six arrows point at my Stag. He does not move. I am splitting myself, again. My body freezes while my mind spins upward, seating itself in the high bough of a pine.

An order is given in a language I do not understand. The men lower their bows. I wince at the leader's commanding voice, closing my eyes. When I open them, my mind and body are together on the ground with my Stag. The man with the commanding voice hands me his cloak, my Stag is still between us. The Stag seems to be speaking to the captain of the huntsmen, but words are not filling my head or my ears. The Stag turns to look full into my eyes.

They mean you no harm, Small One. The leader wants to take you to their women. I cling still more closely to the Stag.

Look into his eyes, the Stag commands me.

I cannot disobey. Turning slightly, I face a man who is tall, at least eighteen hands high. His shoulders are broad; his hands are large. His nose is prominent and straight. His chin is firm beneath sensitive lips. His eyes are somewhere between blue and grey. Concern and a strange kind of pain live in the blueness. He is speaking words I cannot understand and indicating the cloak, which he is still holding out in front of him.

Do you trust him, Small One? The Stag's question fills my head. I nod. Before I can thank him, the Stag bounds away through the pines. Bows are raised. The captain barks an order. I flinch. No arrows fly after my Stag. My heart is grateful.

I find I cannot stand alone. My knees buckle and strong arms catch me before I hit the ground. I am swaddled in a huge cloak. I like the way it smells, of smoke and of something clean and deep that I cannot describe. Water is held to my lips. I gulp until his voice speaks and the flask is moved away. Some kind of bread is offered. I bite ravenously, and the man holding me smiles; he seems pleased by my fierce appetite. The flask returns and the water flows down my throat. I am lifted upon his horse; his arms encircle me. He smells comforting, like his cloak. I try to sit upright, but I cannot. I sag against him, drifting as we ride south. No part of me is floating above watching. *Me* and *I* have come back together in the arms of this stranger who feels like home. The rocking motion of the horse is comforting and I slip into sleep.

CHAPTER 2

GRACE

Looming castle walls flood me with fear, and I can feel my eyes growing wide, my muscles tensing. He murmurs soothing words in my ear, his breath stirring my hair. I feel frozen, my hand unable to touch him, though I find myself longing for the feel of the curly, golden-brown hair covering the muscles of his forearm. Keeping my focus upon the markings on his arm keeps my fear at bay. A scar as wide as my hand runs crosswise, parallel to the crease of his elbow. A sword wound? I wonder.

Another scar looks angry. Purplish in color, it is raised and puffy. Though short in length, the wound must have been deep, caused perhaps by a dagger. Curiously, the man has no markings from animals' hooves or teeth. Pondering the arms of this huntsman, who is scarred like a warrior, keeps me still as we approach the walls of the great structure. Never have I seen such uniformly grey stones built into such an enormous edifice. How can men lift such stones?

After we pass through an archway in the outer walls, I notice solid hardwood gates. These gates are in position to be lowered, covering the opening completely. These gates are thick, with black metal latches and hinges.

Strangely, I find I cannot remember any buildings further to the north, in the land from which I come. Too many sights are meeting my eyes for me to wonder about my lack of memories.

I am lifted down when we enter a dirt courtyard. Orders are given, and the horses are led away by stable boys. Curious glances are cast my way and I fall again to studying the arms that hold me. He is carrying me down a long passage paved with flat stones. The heels of his boots make a ringing sound that bounces off the stone walls and beamed ceiling. He seems to be hurrying; I worry that I am a heavy burden.

Presently, a maidservant leads us. A door is flung open, and I am set gently upon a richly carved chair with a velvet cushion. The room seems large, with a fireplace and mullioned windows. A canopied bed is hung with purple curtains that match the seat cushion. I become aware that he is speaking with a woman of ample girth and merry eye. I study the few faint freckles visible under the tan upon his forearms. I wish those arms were still wrapping themselves around me. The woman seems kindly, but the Stag had entrusted me to him. She calls him "Sir Tristam", which seems to anger him. He repeats merely "Tristam" but she repeats both words. He shakes his head at her before turning to me. Speaking foreign words, he indicates the large woman. "Addie," he says repeatedly, "Addie."

When he places his hand upon the door latch, I feel panic rising up in me. Glancing back, he sees my widened eyes. He stops, comes back and lifts me. Addie is hovering, making soothing noises. He sends her away and lays me upon the bed. My hand brushes against his as he moves to a chair by the bed. He clasps my hand. The pressure of his fingers is reassuring, though I cannot return it; instead my hand lies limp in his. Somehow that simple act is more intimate than anything we have yet shared and I can make no sense of it. I lie on the bed, eyes wide, not moving.

We are in the same positions when Addie returns with another woman who is carrying a large tapestry bag. She places the bag on the floor and I can see the intricate needlework and the rich colors of the pattern. I lose myself in the minute stitches of blue, green, amber, and yellow. Conversation floats above my head.

The newcomer, whom Tristam calls Geneva, is pointing at my feet. He leaves my side and begins unwinding the bandages covering them. The pain of the cloth tearing away from the scabs is sharp enough to take my breath away, but I will not cry out. Tristam comes to my head again, stroking my brow. I steal a glance at his face. His eyes hold a glowing light I cannot look upon. Returning my eyes to the tapestry bag, I lose myself again in the colors. A particular shade of blue, clear as the summer sky, draws my eye. I focus on the blue. I hold my tears at bay, tears caused by kindness in the eyes of the foreigner, Tristam.

Geneva mixes herbs while Addie boils water over the fire. Tristam urges me to eat, but I do so only to please him. Fear is knotting my stomach; swallowing is difficult. I sip the herbal tea Tristam holds to my lips, and I suddenly feel incredibly tired. Sleep yawns like a beast and swallows me whole. Tristam still holds my hand.

I awake in utter darkness, my feet throbbing. A sharp intake of breath is the only concession I make to fear, though my limbs shake. I push the pain away. Tristam comes to me. He offers food and herbal tea. My arms and legs stop shaking. For a long time, I drift in sleep with brief periods of wakefulness. He is always there, keeping my fear at bay.

CHAPTER 3

TRISTAM

I will never forget the day we found Grace. The year was 1122 and the feast of the spring equinox had depleted the palace stores of meat. Game near the castle is scarce at this season. During the harsh winter, we over-hunt near our home. We were traveling far to the north for wild stag and although the creatures are lean after the long winter, they are large. Even a lean stag will fill the king's board.

Farther to the north, the forest is mostly pine, though here and there a broadleaf seedling struggles for light. On this day, our horses' hooves crush the needles of the forest floor and send the fragrance of pine upwards, masking the scent of game. We leave our horses behind after picking up the scent of a stag. I lead a party of five men.

Daniel-the-Younger is my best marksman. Torquil is my most seasoned hunter. Wee Thomas does not require dogs to track a scent. The other two are new; I watch them closely to determine their level of skill.

It is early morning, three days after the night of the equinox. Snow is still lying in patches on the moist ground, and mist rises from the snow and shows our breath as we track in utter silence. My men are ready for the kill that will allow them to return home to warm beds.

A dozen or more tall pines of equal height form a tight circle. In the clearing, a stag faces us and our bows. Though six arrows point at it, the stag stands motionless. One of the new men, Mark, draws back his arrow without waiting for my signal. Quickly and silently, I raise my right arm, giving the command to wait. Mark's breath comes out in an angry hiss as he relaxes his grip.

For a moment I hold my breath, not believing what I see. Two small, white arms cling to the stag's neck. One hand is slightly bluish in color;

the other is extremely pale. The golden head of a young girl is just visible behind the creature, her eyes wide with terror. Dropping my bow, I remove my cloak in one motion and hold it out in front of me; I face the stag. The creature seems to be assessing me, trying to read my intentions.

We mean her no harm. She will be taken to the women. The words form themselves in my head and the stag relaxes as if he hears and understands. The creature then looks deep into the eyes of the child. A silent conversation takes place between them, I know it. The small one looks deep into my eyes, as if she is reading my soul. She is older than I realized, almost a young woman, not a child. The stag suddenly bounds into the forest. I hear movement behind me and repeat my order, "Hold your arrow!"

"That is meat you are letting get away," Mark mutters as I step forward to catch the child. Her legs cannot support her without the stag to lean upon. I lift her gently; she weighs almost nothing. I wrap her in my cloak and cradle her.

"Daniel and Torquil, fetch water, food, and blankets. We need herbs and bandages," I call after them. I see lacerations upon the child's arms, legs, and feet.

"I will get them, Sir," Wee Thom says.

I nod at him.

"You others, get the horses."

Daniel returns quickly and hands me a flask. I support the girl with my left arm and I offer her the flask with my right. She drinks with relish.

"Slowly, child. Your body needs time; too much at once will cause vomiting," I caution. Daniel offers her flatbread. She snatches at it greedily when he pulls it away to prevent her from eating it too quickly. Her ferocity makes me smile. Though frail, she has some fight in her.

"Captain, her feet are bad; those cuts are deep. The green poison's setting in," Torquil informs me. "It will hurt her greatly if we touch them."

"Can you bind them gently, with the herbs that will draw out the poison?" I ask.

"Yes, Sir. I have bandaged my little sisters," Wee Thom tells me.

I look up into the face of this young man who, ironically, stands several hands taller than me. "You are poorly named. Thank you, Thomas."

His face flushes.

"Aye, that might help until we can get her to Lady Geneva," Torquil says. "She is the one to do the cleansing of the deeper wounds. If we try now, we will frighten her more."

"Captain, how did she get here? We are leagues from anywhere," Daniel interrupts.

"And why…why is she here alone, freezing, injured, and terrified?" Thomas's voice joins in.

The men have all come closer. The child's eyes have widened so that white can be seen all around the amber irises. Her tension is palpable.

"Back up, men; give the girl some room," I order. "Torquil, I will need your help to hold her while I mount."

"Yes, Sir," he replies.

"Sir, could it be that those rumors we have heard are true?" Mark asks.

"Hold your tongue, Mark," I command.

Torquil raises his eyelids and widens his eyes. "You can silence Mark, Sir, but people will wonder…and talk."

"That is not silence, Torquil. For now, let us simply get her to safety."

Torquil, wisely, responds with a nod. I heave a sigh as I lift the waif onto my horse. We have a long journey ahead of us.

CHAPTER 4

TRISTAM

The child lies in a weakened state. Fever wars with the poison in her wounds and it is too early to tell which will win. Lady Geneva's herbs are supposed to ease her pain, but even with a sleeping draught, the child tosses in the bed. Though she never cries out, she is clearly distressed. I worry. She needs all her strength to fight the green poison that fills the cuts upon her feet.

I feel responsible for the child. No…the feeling is stronger and deeper. I feel a connection forged by the fear in her eyes as she hung behind the stag. She was terrified, yet only her eyes revealed her fear. Her body was held strongly erect. She has courage, this small waif. She touches a chord in my heart I thought was dead. When she studied my face to decide if she could trust me, she read my soul. She saw my darkest deeds, yet decided I was kind. When I caught her in my arms, she sent feeling into the frozen places in my heart.

Sitting beside her sickbed, I have time to reflect. This strange child needs me. She is a gift, a grace bestowed. I think of her as "Grace."

Grace is not the first child I have nursed through sickness. I once had a wife named Constance. She bore us a daughter we named Faith. Two summers ago, they went missing. Though we searched for months, we never found anything but pieces of the fabric of their clothes. The thought of my wife and daughter lost in the woods is an ache I cannot assuage.

Had Constance and Faith been here, I would simply have taken Grace to my home, but now I am merely a huntsman, dependent upon the king for my livelihood. For the first time, I question my decision to relinquish my holdings. I have no lands or house in which to raise a child.

Thus, I need to secure Their Majesties' permission to house Grace in the castle.

Knowing I stand in need of the king's favor for Grace, I hunt alone before dawn. I return just after sunrise with a stag that had wandered south. Although smaller than Grace's stag, this creature will provide meat for several meals. I give thanks for this good fortune.

After looking in on Grace, I seek to gain an audience with the king. King Stefan and I had been raised together; he had become a page my first year as a squire. Stefan had been a good page who never took advantage of his relationship with King Leopold to ease his path through training; he had taken his share of abuse from the older pages and squires without complaint. The respect he had earned from his peers in those years had been of great benefit to him when his father died suddenly in a hunting accident. Only now, in light of the uprising, do I wonder if his death was truly accidental. King Stefan had taken over with authority, yet he displayed tact, showing respect to the older lords and ladies who looked upon him as a mere child. He had maintained peace during those first few turbulent years when the nobles were jockeying for power. When we found Grace, King Stefan was maintaining peace at home and abroad.

King Stefan had chosen a bride from Chantrell, to the south. A wise move politically, this marriage sealed our amiable relations with our southern neighbor. To the west, we are guarded by the river Boldengarth; to the east lie the mountains. To the north are vast expanses of forest through which armies cannot move quickly, but to the south we have no natural protection from invasion.

King Stefan and Queen Laurel seem genuinely happy together, their only sadness being the lack of a child. It is too early to declare the queen barren, but a longing for a child can be read in her eyes. I believe both will welcome Grace if only they do not fear her.

CHAPTER 5

TRISTAM

My audience with the king and queen has been granted and I am at Grace's bedside when Addie informs me that a page is at the door, summoning me before Their Majesties. Grateful for so quick a response to my request, I find myself smoothing my hair and straightening my tunic while following the page to the Great Hall.

I approach the dais and kneel before the king and queen.

Kin Stefan says, "My man tells me you returned from yesterday's hunt empty-handed, and with another mouth to feed."

Raising my eyes, I seek his face. Though his expression is solemn, his eyes are kindly. "Rise up, Sir Tristam. Tell us about the mysterious princess you rescued in the woods."

News travels fast in the palace; already my Grace is a princess. For once, I am grateful for servants' gossip and for Addie's kind heart and rattling tongue. Telling my tale quietly and simply, I do not speak of my heart's reaction to the girl.

"Now she is quite ill, Sire. Her feet were badly cut. The green poison is causing her fever," I finish.

It is the queen who speaks next. "You are quite concerned about this child, are you not, Sir Tristam?"

"Yes, Your Highness; I fear for her life. She must have been alone in the woods for several days. She is terribly thin to be fighting such a high fever."

"Where did you find her, Tristam?" the king asks.

"She was north of the east branch of the Boldengarth River, in a stand of pine trees."

"There are no kingdoms in that vicinity," the king replies. "She must

11

have traveled a great distance."

"The cuts on her feet and legs would indicate she ran barefoot a long way," I reply.

"Yet the nearest populated area must be at least a three-day journey to the north," King Stefan exclaims.

"Yes, Sire."

"Could she have traveled that far?"

"It seems most unlikely, Sire, but she was driven by fear. If she was frightened enough, she could travel that distance."

"Tristam, why do you say she was driven by fear? Could she not simply have cut her feet walking?"

"No, Sire. The cuts are too deep to have been caused by walking; she had to have been running. She would never have kept on unless she was too terrified to stop. Her fear must have masked her agony."

"Do you think an animal chased her?"

I shake my head. "An animal would have caught her, Sire."

"So, what is it you fear?" the king asks.

"I do not know, Your Highness." But I do, though I do not give voice to my fears.

The queen makes a startled sound in her throat, but does not speak.

I find myself nodding.

King Stefan glances back and forth between us. A look of disgust crosses his face. "Let us not imagine far-fetched conclusions. There must be some reasonable explanation. Perhaps she wandered away from a royal hunting party. Inquiries should be made."

The queen lays her hand upon the king's arm. "Please, let us proceed cautiously, My Lord, in case someone means the child harm."

"Well, Tristam?" King Stefan demands. I can tell he is not pleased.

"I believe our queen speaks wisely, Sire. We found the child alone, three days after the equinox. She was richly clad in white. She was terrified. There were leather straps upon her wrists and ankles, My Lord."

The king pauses before speaking. "It seems you may have brought us trouble, Tristam."

"Nay, My Lord," Queen Laurel interrupts, "he has merely brought us a child. All children are a gift." Her voice is wistful. "Maybe she is an answer to prayer. What do you call her, Tristam?"

"'Grace,' My Lady."

"Aye, Grace; a gift of Grace…'tis very well," the queen smiles.

Again, she lays her hand upon the king's arm and addresses him. "My Lord, may she stay? May we give her shelter?"

"I cannot say 'no' to a child in need, My Lady, or to you." Turning to me, the king continues, "You will be responsible for her, Tristam."

I kneel and say, "Thank you, My Lord...but she cannot live alone with me in a huntsman's cottage."

"You left the castle of your own free will, Tristam. No one requires you to live in that cottage."

"But I am the head huntsman, My Lord. I belong in a huntsman's cottage."

"Speaking as such, how fares my table, Sir Huntsman?"

"I had a stag this morning, My Lord."

The king's eyes brighten. "A stag? This day? Tell me!"

"I was hunting before dawn. I spied him drinking at Wildcat Creek."

"So near the castle?"

"Aye, Sire."

"That is truly amazing. It must have been seeking fresh greens. They rarely travel this far south."

"A good omen, My Lord," says the queen. "Taking in the child is already bringing us good fortune."

King Stefan laughs out loud and smiles at her. "Perhaps you are right, my dear. How many arrows did you use to bring down the stag, Tristam?"

"Just one through the neck, Sire."

"Ah, well done, Tristam....I miss the days when you called me Stefan."

"Aye, My Lord, that was before you became king."

"And when you were still a knight, Sir Tristam," the queen adds. I nod, affirming her statement. "We would welcome you back in the castle, knight or huntsman," she says. "Is that not true, Sire?"

"Of course, my dear, you are correct, as usual. I never wanted him to leave us."

I bow before speaking. "Thank you both, not only on my behalf, but also for Grace."

"We will pray for the child's recovery, Sir Tristam," the queen says, "and your own."

The king nods his agreement before dismissing me.

As I fall asleep in a chair next to Grace's bed, I ponder the queen's words.

CHAPTER 6

TRISTAM

I awake sensing danger. A deadly silence has crept into the room. Grace lies perfectly still, her breathing shallow and rapid. Gone are the restless movements I have witnessed for the past two days. Upon the battlefield, I have stood by seriously injured men; I know the look, the sounds, and the smell of death. Death is present here, filling my nostrils with its pungent sweet odor. Death is slowing her breathing. Grace opens her eyes and stares at the upper corner of the room where a ceiling beam meets the wall. The expression on her face is glowing, almost eager. She reaches out her arms to someone or something I cannot see. She smiles a shy smile of greeting.

"No!" I shout.

My voice summons Addie from the antechamber where she sleeps on a trundle bed. She assesses the situation at a glance and speaks gently. "My Lord, she is dying. You have to let her go."

"Not without a fight. We need towels, a tub, and extremely cold water."

Addie stares at me with pity in her eyes. She does not move.

"Move, Addie! Now!" I speak in my commander's voice, a voice I have not used since my days in battle.

Addie moves.

In moments, we strip Grace down to her shift and are ready to place her in the tub. Suddenly, she begins fighting against us and slips from our grasp. In her delirium, she stumbles to the fire and throws her gown and undergarments into the flames. I catch her up in my arms and force her to stare into my eyes. She seems to recognize me and grows calmer.

"Where did she get the energy to fight us, Sir Tristam? I swear she is

14

almost dead!" Addie exclaims.

Ignoring Addie's words, I bark another order, "Help me get her into the tub."

Once Grace is in the water, her eyes roll back in her head. Her pupils move back and forth rapidly under her closed eyelids, but I have no time to wonder what she is seeing. We pour water over her chest and arms and bathe her face and neck repeatedly with a cloth.

Geneva is summoned and comes to assist us. As she begins mixing her herbs, Grace's skin cools and her lips and fingernails turn blue. Geneva, gently touching my shoulder, speaks softly. "Remove her from the tub, Sir Tristam. Her body cannot handle the cold for too long."

When Grace is tucked back under her covers, Geneva comes to me with a warm flask. "This is my strongest potion. After giving her this, I can do nothing else for her. She will choose her own path."

"What does that mean," I snap, "she will choose her own path?" My voice rises. "What exactly does that mean?"

"Do you not believe we have some choice in the matter of living or dying, Sir Tristam? Surely you have seen soldiers with a strong will to live survive horrific wounds. While others, seemingly less wounded, do not survive."

"Aye," I nod.

"This child has a choice. This world has not been kind to her; perhaps the next would be better."

"No!" the word bursts from me, against my will.

The room is deathly quiet after my outburst. No one speaks. No one moves. "I am sorry," I whisper, appalled at my loss of control and embarrassed by my selfish thoughts.

"There is no need for apologies, Sir. You have suffered too many losses already. I do not wish to see you lose another person you love, and you do love this child." Geneva is not asking a question; she is making an observation.

"I do."

Geneva nods, "Very well. I shall pray for her recovery. She will need careful nursing this night. Forgive me, but I must return to assist another. Keep the water in the tub cool but not frigid. If her fever rises again, return her to the bath. Tristam, stay beside her always. Your love may ground her to this earthly life. I will brew a mixture to keep you wakeful and calm."

"I need nothing for myself, thank you."

"You need to exude peace for the sake of the child. Drink it for her,"

Geneva insists.

"Yes, my Lady. I cannot argue against you. For the sake of the child, I will drink even your nasty potions." I hope Geneva catches the teasing note in my voice.

"Take care, Sir, or I will make it nastier than is strictly necessary," comes her quick retort. It is nice to learn that Geneva has a sense of humor, even in a crisis. Turning to Addie, Geneva speaks again, "Sleep as much as you can, Nurse Addie. The child will need you tomorrow when Tristam will need to sleep."

"I pray you are right, My Lady," says Addie, shaking her head. I can tell Addie does not believe Grace will live through the night, and I am grateful she does not say as much.

I approach Grace's bed and take her hand, wrapping my other arm around her head and stroking her brow, her cheek, her nose, the sweet line of her jaw. I study the dimple of her chin, and as I smooth her hair away from her forehead, I notice she is cooler.

I begin praying as I have never prayed before. I pray not the prayer I was taught as a boy, "Thy will be done, Lord," but instead find myself praying most earnestly for my own desire, the sparing of Grace.

How long I sit praying I do not know. The night is interminable. I keep the candles burning around Grace's bed and memorize every line of her face.

CHAPTER 7

GRACE

Drifting…floating…piercing…pain…comforting hands…soothing…drink…sleep…warmth…*Him.* Always present is the huntsman with the scars of a warrior. He inhabits both my waking and my dreaming.

The Stag is also there at times, leading me through thick forests. Terror lurks in those dark woods, always at the borders of my consciousness. I follow the Stag, racing past the trees, desperate to maintain contact with him, yet he always escapes me. I awake drenched in sweat. I wake to Him, to his soothing touch and his calming presence. He calms me.

In one dream, I come very close to the Stag. Beyond the edge of the forest I see a golden-yellow meadow. Blue sky hangs above the green and amber grasses. Suddenly, I feel no fear. Arms outstretched, I race toward the sun-drenched meadow, but the Stag's voice stops me. "No, child. Run to Him." He indicates the forest from which I so long to escape. I turn and see a patch of blue sky shining through the darkness of the trees. I take a step toward the forest. I fix my eyes upon the blue patch of sky. The trees begin to spin and to whirl, and for a moment, I am caught in a vortex.

I awake, free from sweat, to Tristam's face hovering just above mine. Yellow sunlight streams through the mullioned windows, touching his face, removing the grey from his eyes. The color that remains is the exact color of the sky above the meadow in my dream.

His hand lies upon my brow, caressing my forehead, my cheeks, and my hair. His other hand he has wrapped around me, holding me in a close embrace. When he bends to kiss my forehead, I feel a drop of hot liquid land upon my cheek.

Stunned, I want to reach up a hand to wipe his tears, but I cannot.

He grasps my hand and presses a kiss into my palm.

"You have returned!" he whispers. He kisses my brow again. "I thought I had lost you."

His words I cannot understand, but I know their meaning. I remember the Stag and the enticing golden meadow. I know I have been close to death. I also know it matters greatly to this kind man that I have come back.

Chapter 8

GRACE

Dear Tristam is my first thought upon waking. *Kind Tristam* is my last thought before sleeping. His presence brings me security and something deeper, something with which I have had no previous experience. His scent calms me, pushing back my fear.

Now that I am no longer near death, Tristam is not always present upon my waking, so I sleep with his old muffler. He removed it one day at my bedside and I casually slid it under my bedclothes. When it was time for him to leave me, he had a twinkle in his eye. "I cannot seem to find my muffler; I must have left it in the stables."

Tristam loves me; I am certain of that, though I cannot understand why. I see the light in his eyes grow warmer when his glance falls upon me. When he examines my feet, he actually runs his fingers, ever so gently, along the scabs. I do not understand how he can stand to even look at my injuries, let alone touch them with such tenderness.

He is constantly touching me, petting me, hugging me, kissing my brow. I still cannot touch him, though I long to as I did on the night I almost died. My body feels frozen. I lie still and drink in his touch. His touch falls upon me like soft rain. His smile is my sunlight.

Yet I live in constant fear. I know that I do not belong to him; he is not responsible for me in any way. I know I am a girl and therefore expendable. Girls only have value for marrying into wealthy families, securing land, and creating alliances. I find this knowledge startling, for specific memories of the past are completely lacking, yet there are things I know, things that are part of my body and my soul. I know I am less than worthless, a dower-less foreign girl who is believed to be dumb. I also know I carry a secret, one which will utterly disgrace me, but I do not know what the secret is. I know someday Tristam will turn his back upon me, and I will be more alone than I was during those nights of terror in the forest. I know love can make me weak, and that to survive I have to be strong, so I revel in Tristam's love in secret, storing up his many kindnesses like treasure against future days of want. I promise myself I will never lose these memories, memories of kindness, plenty, comfort, and security. I will need them in some dim, dark, lonely future that most certainly awaits me.

Weak in body, I cannot get up. I cannot work. My mind feels trapped, so I seek activity. I begin listening intently to their foreign words, trying to make sense of the sounds. Quickly I learn the words for chair, bed, medicine, and fire. Other words with several forms are more difficult, yet soon the words for sleeping, coming, resting, and leaving are comprehensible to me. Even in my weakened state, my mind digests the words, keeping me busy…always busy.

CHAPTER 9

TRISTAM

Grace is out of danger. Her wounds improve daily. Their Majesties are content to house her in the castle, graciously granting us several rooms, including the one Grace already occupies, one normally reserved for visiting nobility. It is richly furnished with carved furniture and velvet hangings. The king and his queen are being more than generous. I cannot find the words to express my gratitude, so I hunt constantly, filling the king's storehouses with meat.

Returning to the castle is less difficult than I would have believed possible two years ago when I left, renouncing my knighthood and my nobility. Returning, even temporarily, is easy because of Grace. My every thought is for her.

I move a few of my belongings into a room two doors away from Grace's. My huntsman's cottage sits empty, awaiting my return. Addie still sleeps in the anteroom between our two chambers. She is there to provide nursing, but also to observe the proprieties. Grace is a child, but in a few years she will become a woman. I, in my thirties, am no longer young, but I am not beyond the age of marriage.

Though Grace's wounds are healing and King Stefan is being gracious, I cannot be easy in mind. I find the child's behavior baffling. According to Addie, Grace lives for my visits, refusing her sleep draught when I have not yet been to see her, but in my presence she lies perfectly still, giving no sign that my touch is welcome to her. Still, I find myself hugging her and kissing her as I would kiss my daughter. Terror and injury do strange things to soldiers, and I remind myself that Grace is a soldier in some strange, private war. I pour my love over her, hoping to unlock the mysteries of this child.

In Blinth, we adore our children. They are surrounded with love from the moment of their birth. Here, all children are precious. We do not favor sons over daughters: daughters can inherit just as sons, and not only through a dowered marriage. I know other kingdoms are different. I spent time fighting in Polomia, and have seen how the children there are scared and hesitant around adults. I attributed their behavior to our army's occupation of their land, but now I find myself wondering if perhaps that is simply how children in some cultures live.

Grace's right foot sustained the most injury. A deep gash runs lengthwise from the ball to the heel. Her arch and instep are high, so the cut is shallower there. The deep parts of the cut were packed with dirt during her travels in the forest. The green poison is receding most slowly from the places where her foot pounded the earth.

Grace's muteness worries me more than the gashes upon her feet. I have only heard Grace make one sound: on her first night in the castle, upon waking in the dark, she drew in a sharp breath. I do not know if Grace's voice works. I have never even heard her sneeze.

I would feel better if she would cry. The child is holding everything deep inside, and it is not natural. I fret. Part of me longs to ride north to discover the cause of Grace's fears. Another part of me cannot leave her for longer than is strictly necessary each day.

I organize the hunts nearer to the castle. The animals are returning with the warmth of spring and the greening of the forest. Hunting is once again possible closer to home. Torquil is leading parties into the northern forests, Daniel leads the parties to the south, and King Stefan is pleased with all our efforts. I am able to stay with Grace because I have good men.

Torquil takes an interest in Grace, always asking me about her upon his return to the castle. "Is she speaking yet, Captain?" he asks.

"No. She never cries, or laughs. I have never heard her cough or sneeze."

"No doubt she has her reasons."

Something in his manner is disturbing. "Torquil, did you find something in the north?"

"Yes, Captain." Torquil is facing away from me with only his profile visible, staring at the distant horizon. He is silent for some time.

"Torquil, are you going to tell me what you found?"

Turning back toward me, he hands me four stakes with leather straps attached. The straps have been cut.

"Where did you find these?" My voice sounds grim in my own ears.

"We were far to the north, Sir, probably three hard days' ride from here. We did not travel directly, so I cannot be certain."

"So you may have crossed into Lolgothe."

"Yes, Sir, we had crossed the east branch of the Boldengarth, following the hoof marks of a herd of deer. We were intent upon the hunt, not minding borders or boundaries. We came across those stakes pounded hard into the ground in the midst of a round clearing."

"How were they laid out?" I ask. My voice is low, as I dread the answer.

"They were in a rectangle, Sir. I know you forbade Mark to speak of it on the day we found her, but those stakes were perfectly placed for staking out a girl the size of Grace."

"I was harsh with Mark on that first day we found Grace. Since then I have done much thinking. I alluded to that theory about Grace when I first spoke to the king and queen."

"What did they say?"

"The king did not want to believe it. He acted just as I did on that day."

"Humpf."

"May I have these stakes, please?"

"Certainly, Sir."

I turn to leave but think of something else. "Torquil, be careful in the north. We may be dealing with truly godless barbarians. Watch the boundaries more carefully."

"Aye, Sir. I will protect the men; never fear."

"Thank you, Torquil…for everything."

"I wish I could do more," he says before walking away.

I stand a long time looking down at the stakes in my hand. Slowly, I walk back to the castle. When I reach the dining hall, I find I have no appetite for dinner.

CHAPTER 10

GRACE

My life has become so very easy. Delicious, warm meals are brought to my room on a tray and served to me in bed. I am bathed gently in a tub of warm water before the fire. My measurements are taken and seamstresses begin working on fine gowns for me. Geneva comes daily to change the bandages on my feet and check the progress of my healing. A few of her words I can now understand, and I know she is pleased with my recovery.

One day, when Geneva is changing the bandages, I insist upon seeing my feet. Addie tries to prevent me, but Geneva stops her. I am allowed to gaze upon the wounds that almost caused my death. Cuts cover nearly every inch of the soles of my feet. The tops of my feet and my ankles also carry a share of the injury. Some of the cuts are deep, long gashes caused, perhaps, by sharp stones. Others are more ragged, likely made by sticks upon which I trod. One cut, on the sole of my right foot, is so deep and straight it looks as if it could have been caused by a knife. The edges of the deeper wounds are dark purple, and the scabs still retain some of the green poison which I remember hearing Geneva discuss with Tristam.

As I look at my feet, my eyes glaze over. The night comes back to me, the night of running through a pitch-black forest driven by a nameless fear so great that I cannot feel the injury I am doing to my feet.

I do not remember what or who was chasing me. Nothing of my previous life is accessible; it is as if a wall, a strong, thick, grey stone wall, such as these southerners built around their castle, has been erected in my mind. My old life is completely hidden behind it. My memories begin with terror, my stag, and Tristam.

I become aware of Addie's voice, fussing, trying to draw my attention back to the present. Geneva is studying me closely. She comes to stand beside the bed, near my head, offering me her sleeping tea, but I turn away. Tristam has not yet been to see me. My heart lightens at the thought of him. I look shyly at Geneva and touch the empty place on the table next to my bed, where she places the tea. She is speaking, and I understand the words *sir* and *Tristam*. I stare. Geneva repeats, "Sir Tristam," indicating with her hands that I should try to speak the words, but I turn and face the wall.

Silence envelops me. I feel safe in my silence, always listening and never speaking. I have learned the names of the different maidservants who lay the fire and sweep in the corners of my room. From servants' conversations, I learn words Addie, Geneva, and Tristam never speak. When Addie is present, they work in silence, but servants say what they wish in front of a mute girl. Most of the time, I prefer their chatter and the variety of words they use, but sometimes their words are disturbing. From a servant called Marie, I learn of my strange behavior when the fever had me in its grip.

"It is as if she went mad, yet she was half dead. No; more dead than half. Miss Addie's saying, 'You have to let her go,' but Sir Tristam says, 'No,' frantic-like. He starts barking orders—you know his way."

"Yes, that man can be plain scary when he wants something," Bethany replied.

"Well, he was certainly scary *that* night," Marie continued. "I have never seen him like that, barking orders, expecting instant obedience. I did not dare say anything, but I thought we were wasting our time. She is dead, I think to myself. But when we started stripping off her clothes for the bath Sir Tristam ordered, she comes to life like a mad thing. No expression on her face. She is just wide-eyed, white-faced, and ferocious. She turns on me like a cornered badger. Not two seconds before, she could not lift her head, but suddenly she is grabbing at her clothes. At first, I thought she was terrified to be almost naked. Personally, I would not mind one bit being naked with that Sir Tristam. I could make that man forget his wife for at least a little while."

Marie looked for Bethany to laugh with her, but Bethany looked prim.

"Anyway," Marie continued, "instead of covering herself, she snatches at the gown in my arms. It was a white gown they found her wearing in those woods. She had not had a bath yet, even though she needed one, if you know what I mean, but Lady Geneva would not allow it because of the wounds on her feet. So I had just removed her under clothes because

I knew they would hold too much water. I was already going to have a huge mess to clean up without that much dripping. So she turns on me sudden-like. One minute she is limp, and the next she is twisting and turning and grabbing at me."

Her audience murmured appreciatively.

"Aye, at first I think she means to attack me. I mean, who really knows about these barbarians from the north? So I shrink back, but instead of clawing me, she snatches her clothes, rough-like, and rushes to the fire. Now me, I stand there with my mouth hanging open, because I cannot believe she can even move, let alone walk. But she starts with the underclothes, flinging them into the flames—the same flames we have just built up to get the room warm for this absurd cold bath Sir Tristam ordered. The flames are roaring and they gobble them clothes like they are made of paper. Then she throws in the gown. By this time, Miss Addie has stopped gawking, and she grabs the gown by the shoulder part. She pulls it out and starts scolding, but Sir Tristam barks at her, 'Never mind the gown; get the child in the tub.' So…we get her in the tub, with that gown still smoldering on the hearth. I keep an eye on it, because I don't want the furniture catching fire. When I can, I throw some water on it. It is too beautiful to let burn. I have never seen a more beautiful gown, but now all that's left is the bodice."

"What happened to her then?" Bethany asked.

"She goes back to being a limp, dead-like thing, except for her legs. She has got them tightly clamped together in that tub. I know, because I made sure I got a good view of her. I'm still gaping like a fool because she fought when I thought she was dead. I expected we would be laying her out for burial the next day. But here we are waiting on her, and she's getting stronger every day….She is strange, though. And quiet. I wonder why, so I've been thinking. You know what I think?"

"What?" Bethany replied, leaning forward with interest.

Marie lowered her voice, but I could still make out her words.

"Well," she began importantly, "I think she has been defiled. That explains everything—her clamped legs, her burning her fine gown, her not talking."

"You should not say that. She is noble!" exclaimed Bethany.

"You think nobles cannot be defiled?"

"Of course they can; we have heard about Lady Constance. I just mean that you do not know that. She deserves better than to have her life ruined by rumors."

I found myself liking this maid, Bethany.

"You are too soft," her companion replied. "She cannot even talk. I would say her life is ruined already."

"Hush, I think she is listening," Bethany said.

I had indeed stirred; I had heard enough. They did their work in silence after that, but their words gave me much to ponder. I only understood about half of them on the day they were spoken. The rest I memorized, and began seeking their meaning. It took the longest to learn the meaning of *defiled*.

After that overheard conversation, I find it difficult to be still. I want to be up and moving. Chafing at my uselessness, I long for work. Geneva's tapestry bag gives me an idea.

CHAPTER 11

GRACE

Stone walls are like fires; they require constant tending. Rocks shift with the change of season; gaps are formed by marauding hunters. The palace workmen mend our walls religiously, every spring and fall, though I did not know this when I lay upon the bed in which I almost died.

The stone wall in my mind is also a greedy fire. Not remembering, refusing to know, requires vigilance. Constant activity is needed to keep myself moving forward, away from the lurking evil. After hearing the servant girls' talk, learning the new language is no longer enough to occupy my mind, yet I am not allowed to leave my bed.

Geneva's tapestry bag is my inspiration. The memory of where and how I learned this art lies on the far side of my interior stone wall, but my fingers know what they have been taught. I pour all my concentration into the richly colored threads with which I am provided. I draw upon beauty in my recent memory for the creation of my designs. Focusing upon my needle keeps me in the present. I am not yet ready for the past.

CHAPTER 12

TRISTAM

Grace is much improved this evening. She is sitting up in bed embroidering a tapestry when I enter her room. Addie is delighted with Grace's skill, and comments, "She is an amazingly talented needlewoman, Sir Tristam."

"How did this come about?" I ask as I approach the bed for a view of Grace's handiwork.

"She picked up Geneva's bag and then made a movement with her hands imitating embroidery. We brought her some basic supplies, and when we saw what she could do, Geneva ordered more threads and a larger piece of canvas."

"Is Geneva not afraid this will tire the child?"

"No, Sir, I asked the same question. Geneva says occupation is good for her, especially an activity she enjoys. It will keep her mind from dwelling on her fears."

"How do you know she enjoys it?"

"Well, look at her."

I turn from Addie to Grace and am surprised to see her nod once, seeming to agree with Addie's words. "May I see your work, Grace?" She holds out her tapestry. The pattern is richly made, of many varied shades of green. Not a connoisseur of needlework, I start to hand the piece back to Grace, when I recognize what looks like the tops of pine trees in the threads.

"Grace, is this the circle of pines where we found you?"

This time I am not surprised when she nods.

"You understand every word I say, do you not?"

She shakes her head.

"But some; you can understand some of my words," I insist.

Again, Grace nods.

I catch her up in my arms, lifting her from the bed. I spin her around saying, "What a wonderful day this is, my Grace!"

I see Grace's eyes soften, though she does not smile. Then the beauty of the day collapses around me.

The accident happens as I am replacing Grace in her bed. The stakes Torquil gave me are still in my tunic pocket. As I place Grace back in her bed, one of the stakes falls out and lands beside her on the bedcovers. Quickly I pocket the stake, but not before she sees it. Her eyes grow wide with terror, and she shrinks before my eyes and wraps her arms around her knees. She begins rocking backward and forward in a tight ball. When I reach out for her, she scrambles away to the far side of the bed. I watch her eyes glaze over.

"No, Grace, do not go away! You have naught to fear from me."

"Addie, take these away!" I command, handing her all four stakes. "Put them somewhere safe."

"What is happening, Tristam?" Addie asks.

"I cannot explain now. Get those stakes out of here now and find Geneva."

"Aye, Sir," Addie replies.

When the door is shut behind Addie and the offending stakes, I turn back to Grace. "Grace, can you hear me?" She makes no response. I keep talking, hoping something of what I say might reach her. "Torquil found those stakes up north on his last hunting foray. He gave them to me, because ..."

Suddenly, I find it difficult to continue. I take a deep breath and make a conscious decision not to gloss over the truth. "Because...he remembered the leather on your wrists and ankles. He is afraid you were staked down. I brought the stakes here to compare the leather on them to the leather I cut off of you on your first night here. I remember cutting your bands, but I do not know where they are, and I want to compare them. Tanned leather has a unique color; we can tell if the straps are the same. That is why I have the stakes, Grace; there is no other reason. No one is going to hurt you. Do you understand?"

She makes no response, but her rocking slows.

"I would kill anyone who tried to stake you down, child!" I am surprised by the suppressed vehemence in my voice. Apparently, so is Grace. Her eyes fly to my face. I reach out to her, and this time, she allows my touch. I hold her limp hand in mine, longing to wrap my arms around her but afraid to draw nearer. We are holding hands when Geneva arrives.

Grace swallows Geneva's sleeping draught greedily. Addie, Geneva, and I stay with her until sleep finally overtakes her. When she is fully asleep, Addie unearths the leather straps. She had stored them with the charred remains of the white gown Grace had thrown into the fire.

My eyes confirm what my heart already knows: the leather on the stakes and the leather we had taken off Grace's wrists and ankles match perfectly.

I find I cannot leave her. I spend the night awake in the chair beside Grace's bed.

CHAPTER 13

TRISTAM

As a man trained for action, I chafe at my inability to ride north to the country of Lolgothe and demand an explanation of Grace's treatment. King Stefan has absolutely forbidden me to travel, unequivocally denying my request.

"Tristam, are you mad? You do not even know the child is from Lolgothe; she could be from Traag. You are assuming the worst. You do not know what events preceded her staking. Perhaps she was staked down as a punishment."

"Oh, and that makes it right?" I reply sardonically.

"No, of course not, Tristam. What happened to Grace is not right, but going up there may do more harm than good. As you and Queen Laurel reminded me the first time we discussed Grace, anything we try to do to avenge her could damage her more. We also have the rest of the country to consider. War with Lolgothe or Traag would be costly."

"I know you are right, Sire, but it is barbaric."

"I agree, but how other countries treat their children is not our concern, Tristam."

"It should be….And I suppose Grace is not our concern either," I fling at the king. But he graciously ignores this.

"Grace is very much your concern, and that is why you must stay here. She needs you. Focus on her healing. Leave vengeance for the Lord."

"Ah yes, 'Vengeance is mine saith the Lord,' is in the scriptures. Why does He get to have all the satisfaction?"

"Is it not satisfying to watch Grace heal, to see her grow stronger each day?"

"Yes, Sire, it brings me great pleasure." I want to argue that I should be doing more, but I hold my peace.

"Her tapestry is finer than any made by the queen's ladies."

"She certainly captured the scene in the woods perfectly, Sire. The circle of pines and the stag who shielded her look just as they did in life."

"And your likeness in the tapestry is quite accurate."

"I disagree. She made me look like some absurd hero."

"Well, I believe it is a fine likeness."

"What are you saying, Sire?"

"Does the glove fit, Tristam?" is all the answer I get from King Stefan.

Grace is now able to leave her room for long periods of time each day. Her favorite spot is the walled garden. I carry her there and place her in a chair along with her tapestry. She works diligently in the sunshine on her second piece of needlework. The gardeners, at first skeptical of her presence, are now accustomed to her. She is a quiet, appreciative audience for their labors.

Tobias has charge of the walled garden, a reward for years of service and a concession to his advanced years. Though many people consider him unapproachable, he smiles kindly on Grace, and I know she is safe in his presence. She grows stronger in the fresh air of late April. Her skin takes on a healthy glow. Walking is still extremely painful, but in all other ways she is functioning more as a child should, except that she is still not speaking. Geneva counsels me to give her time. "She pays attention to language and conversation," she says. "I believe she is learning our language, Sir Tristam. Strive to be less impatient."

"Patience is not in my nature," I reply.

"Perhaps that is why Grace was sent to you, My Lord."

"To teach me patience?"

"If the glove fits…" she replies, unknowingly repeating the king's earlier words to me.

"The king used those same words just the other day."

"Well, certainly I am in good company then," Geneva says teasingly. "Things happen for a reason."

"I hate that kind of talk!" I explode. "Give me one good reason for Grace's suffering or for Faith and Constance's brutal deaths!"

"I was not speaking of the death of your wife and daughter when I said things happen for a reason." Geneva's voice is soft, almost a whisper. "I was merely trying to say that Grace came into your life for a reason."

"But if some things happen for a reason, then do not *all* things happen for a reason? And if all things happen for a reason, why does a child get staked out in the woods to die?"

"I believe the priest would say because man has free will to choose evil."

"But what about storms, drought and disease? Does man choose that evil?"

"I cannot answer all your questions, Sir Tristam. I did not mean to anger you. I only meant to say that I believe Grace is good for you and that you are good for her."

Geneva turns to leave, but I stop her with a hand on her arm. "Forgive me my outburst, My Lady. I owe you so much for all you have done for Grace."

"You owe me nothing," she says placing her hand over mine and returning the pressure of my fingers. "It has been my pleasure to assist the child in her healing. It is even a pleasure to hear you rail against God; you have been silent for too long." With those words, she removes her hand and slips from my grasp.

I go in search of Grace. She is not in her chair in her usual corner of the garden. I find her on her hands and knees, planting flower seeds. She is barefoot, holding her feet up in the air behind her so that the scabs on the soles of her feet are raised to the sun.

Tobias approaches me, hat in hand, his white hair ruffling in the breeze.

"How could you allow this?" I demand of him.

"She seemed to want me to let her help. Her eyes were pleading. I could not deny her, My Lord," he replies.

I look over at Grace. She is looking at me anxiously.

"No, I suppose you could not," I respond more gently.

"May I speak freely, Sir?"

"Yes, of course, and it is no longer 'Sir.'"

"I am too old to unlearn your title, Sir Tristam; you must bear with an old man. You cannot make a plant grow by pulling on it."

I looked quizzically at the gardener.

"Nor does fretting over a seedling help it grow. Give her time."

"You are the second person today to tell me so."

"Ah…" Tobias replies, but his eyes light up.

I raise my eyebrows. "That is your only reply?"

Tobias shrugs his thin shoulders. "God speaks in human voices."

"Humpf," is my response. I have heard entirely too much talk of God for one day.

"I must return to my planting, Sir."

"Certainly, Tobias, and thank you."

Tobias's back is already turned. He raises a dismissive hand, acknowledging my words.

I shake my head and walk over to where Grace is planting. "Ah, Child, what will you do next?"

She makes no response, but her eyes hold a decided twinkle that is brighter than the April sunshine.

CHAPTER 14

GRACE

I can scarcely wait for the seeds I helped Tobias plant to sprout, so every day I go to the garden, even in inclement weather, watching for tiny green shoots to appear. Tobias laughs at my anxiety.

"Child, let nature do its work. You worry over those seeds the way Sir Tristam worries over you."

I whip my head around to stare at the gardener. He reads the expression on my face, for his next words address my fear. "Yes," he says, "Sir Tristam worries about you. Surely you know that."

I hang my head; my cheeks burn scarlet.

"There is no shame. He frets of his own free will." Tobias chuckles. "You have no idea what pleasure I take from seeing that man care about someone again."

My eyes fly back to Tobias's face, and my hands clench. Tobias notices my fists and breaks into rare outright laughter, but my temper is not appeased.

"You two are a pair. You are full of rage because I am glad Sir Tristam worries over you, are you not?"

I do not move.

Tobias repeats, "Are you not?" His eyes hold mine and he is not smiling.

I nod slowly.

"That is better." Tobias lifts my chin with one calloused finger. "You got angry at me a moment ago because I am glad to see Tristam worry over you. Well, I am equally as happy to see you fire up at me over him. Only two types of people in this world have no worries: loved infants and the dead. Sir Tristam has been walking around like a corpse for several years now. And you…you have been behind a death-like mask for as long as I have known you. I am sorry for whatever you have suffered, I truly am. Your external wounds are healing; only you can decide if your insides will also heal. Do you understand?"

I stand there frozen. As soon as I hear his words, a loud roaring fills my ears and I cannot move. I expect Tobias to get angry again at my lack of response, but he must have sensed my distress.

"Never mind, child," he says more gently. "Let us go check on the vegetables. We will leave your beloved flowers to sprout on their own."

He takes me by the hand, something he has never done before. His hand is rough from years of laboring in the garden, and it is warm. His strength seems to seep into me and I thaw. To my surprise, I find that I can walk next to Tobias without pain.

The shadows have grown long when Tristam comes to the garden looking for me. When I hear the gate opening, I glance up and then look quickly across the row of seedlings at Tobias. He seems to understand my message, that I do not want him to talk about our morning conversation, and gives a slight nod before turning to greet Tristam.

"Good evening, Tobias. How was your day?" I like the way Tristam speaks to Tobias.

"Mostly quiet, Sir, which is how I like my days," Tobias replies.

"Then you and Grace are good company for each other."

I nod my agreement.

Tristam is in front of me in two quick strides. "Did you see that, Tobias? My Grace nodded and I was not even speaking to her." Tristam lifts me and spins me around, and I cannot stop the silly grin from spreading across my face.

"Yes, I saw her," Tobias replies. "It is about time." The sparkle in his eyes takes away the gruffness of his words. I smile at Tobias over Tristam's shoulder, and he waves his hand and turns quickly away.

Something in Tobias's face is not right. As soon as Tristam sets me on my feet, I rush over to the gardener. I stand toe to toe in front of him slowly studying his face; his eyes look wrong. Without thinking, I take one of his hands in mine. I bring it up and press my lips into his palm. The wrinkled skin on the back of his hand feels surprisingly soft, and suddenly I feel embarrassed by my physical outburst, and my cheeks flame. I try to drop his hands, but he will not let me go.

Using his other hand under my chin, he urges me to look directly into his face. His eyes are solemn and full as he looks deep into mine.

"Grace, you are a treasure."

I try to lower my face, fighting to hold back tears, but his hand still holds my chin captive. "Let the words in, Grace," he commands.

"Sir Tristam, take care of your treasure," Tobias commands again. Then, stooping, Tobias places his lips upon my forehead, and I have the strange sensation of having been blessed by a priest.

Tristam nods solemnly and no one speaks. My mind is full of questions that my useless mouth cannot form.

Tobias releases me and walks away more quickly than I have ever seen him move. Tristam reaches for me and I lay my head against his chest. His arms wrap protectively around me, and I feel his lips press the top of my head. I have no defense against such tenderness, and find I can no longer contain my tears. I weep, soaking the front of Tristam's work tunic.

We stay in the garden for a long time.

CHAPTER 15

TRISTAM

Something happened in the garden between Grace and Tobias, yet neither of them has spoken of it. I wish I were not jealous that Tobias received Grace's first kiss, but I console myself with the knowledge that I am the one she clings to; she dampened my shirt front with her tears.

Perhaps I begin training her in archery because I am envious of the hours she spends with Tobias in the garden. I like to believe it is because her feet are healed enough to allow the activity. Certainly I want her to be able to defend herself, should the need arise.

Daughters of the nobility sometimes study archery to learn coordination of the hand and eye. Common girls learn archery to put food upon their families' tables, especially if there are no boys in the family. Daniel-the-Younger has been most unaccountably blessed with six daughters, and his eldest, Rebecca, is close to Grace in age. Daniel has spoken to me about her.

"That child will not listen to me; she thinks she already knows everything. Could you possibly take a look at her shooting, Sir? She worships you." The day he asked, I gave a vague reply. I suspected Daniel's request had merely been a ploy to get me around a child again. I have avoided children since Faith's death.

Now that Grace needs to learn to shoot, I can work with both girls at one time. I know enough about girls not to tell Grace she needs to learn archery; I merely invite her to go with me while I work in the target area with Rebecca. Grace nods at my invitation, and we walk in silence to the training arena. Normally this is the domain of the squires and pages, but in May, they take to the fields to receive their training.

I had come to this part of the castle myself as a child of eight years.

Until I was knighted, nearly ten years later, this was the only place within the grounds where I truly felt at home. Returning to the training arena stirs old memories, but I push them back and focus on the child in front of me. Becca is shorter and stockier than Grace, and her hair falls below her waist in a long dark plait, which shines with coppery highlights. She has eager green eyes and a gamine spirit, so I warm to my task immediately.

"Rebecca, take these three arrows, and fire them one by one at the closest target."

"Yes, Sir," she replies. "Is that Grace?" she asks, nodding toward where Grace sits upon a log.

"Yes, Rebecca, that is Grace. Now, the targets, if you please."

Rebecca blushes. Her hand shakes slightly as she draws back upon the string, but her release is clean. The arrow buries itself three inches out from the center, and Rebecca bites her lip, dissatisfied.

"Again."

This time no tremor mars her aim, and her second arrow finds the small mark at the center of the target. She flashes a smile in my direction before stringing her third arrow.

"Wait," I call out. "I am going to change your stance slightly." With my hand upon her right shoulder, I position her body completely sideways to the target. "Now try again."

She misses the center, but her rhythm is more fluid. "Did you feel the difference in your release?" I ask.

Rebecca nods. "But I missed the center."

"First we will correct your technique, then we will worry about results."

"You sound like my father…Sir." It is not a compliment.

"Thank you. He is my best marksman."

"Really?"

"Really. Now back to work, you doubter."

"He never told me that."

"How could he?"

"He has faults, but he is modest….I guess he could not."

"Exactly."

Rebecca works in silence for the next quarter of an hour, making steady progress. When I approach her to make a slight adjustment to her arrow hand, she whispers, "Somebody is not happy," inclining her head toward Grace.

I glance over at Grace, and see she has her arms folded over her chest.

"Grace, is something troubling you?"

She looks away, and I wait.

"Oh, dear," I hear Becca whisper under her breath. I pretend I have not heard her words. "Would you like to try shooting an arrow, Grace?" I ask.

Grace shrugs her shoulders, but she gets up from the log and comes toward us.

"My bow is too large for you," I tell her.

"She can try mine," Becca offers, smiling.

Grace nods her thanks and takes the bow from Becca.

"You may be surprised by the strength required to draw the bow," I tell her, handing her three arrows.

Grace does not respond but turns sideways to the target and notches her first arrow. Her draw looks strong, and her release is perfect. I could not say whether Becca or I am the more astonished when Grace's arrow buries itself in the outer rim of the target.

"Beginner's luck," I hear Becca mutter.

Grace hears her, too, and her eyes narrow in response. She notches her second arrow and lets it fly. We all watch as the arrow strikes the center of the target.

"She has done this before," Becca states flatly, and she is no longer smiling.

"Grace, have you shot before?" I ask.

Grace shrugs her shoulders, and I see her eyes get the glazed, faraway look that signals her memory is failing.

"Never mind the past, Grace; ignore my question. Would you like to have your own bow?"

Grace nods before turning to Becca and handing back the weapon. As Becca takes her bow, Grace bows with her hand over her heart. This has become her gesture for "thank you" since the day in the garden with Tobias when she began communicating unprompted.

"She is saying thank you," I inform Becca.

"Well, how does she say, 'You are welcome?'" Becca asks.

Grace shows Becca her gesture of arms held palms up, moving outward, as if offering a gift.

"You are welcome, Grace," Becca says, imitating Grace's gesture of gratitude.

I watch the two girls eye each other, pleased by both their competitiveness and their forced graciousness. My plan is working beautifully.

41

CHAPTER 16

GRACE

I hate Rebecca the first time I meet her. I sit upon a stone wall while Tristam spends all his time with this short, pert girl. When I finally have a chance to shoot, and my arrow hits the target, I hear her mutter that my shooting is the luck of a beginner. No one knows about my past, and certainly she does not, so her presumption offends me. I may have been practicing with a bow for half my life. My mind does not remember, but the feel of the bow is natural in my hand, and the draw comes easily. The release of the arrow seems to be the most difficult part of the process, yet even that is not a strain.

In my silence, I have learned to watch people closely. I observe Rebecca, or Becca, as she likes to be called, with all the concentration I have developed. I study the placement of her feet, the movement of her hands, and yet I am not prepared for the tension as I draw the arrow back. Becca is strong-muscled. As Tristam implied, I am weak from days of idleness, so I have much work to do.

I begin working alongside Tobias in earnest, lifting the heavy wooden pails of water needed to keep the ground moist for the young plants. At first, I can only lift one, using both hands, but after a time, I find I can lift two with no difficulty. Tobias watches me carefully; I will never know if he does so on his own account or at Tristam's request. I know Tobias appreciates my efforts, though he will never say so. Mostly we work in silence, for we share a bond. He is not a man who allows people to get close. We are close.

Tristam and I spend countless evenings creating my new bow from ash wood. I insist that we make a new bow for Rebecca, as well.

"It is kind of you to work so hard on a bow for Becca, Grace," Tristam comments as we sit in the common room one evening, smoothing the bows with a series of rough stones.

Hers is too short, I indicate using hand signals. I really do not want to discuss it.

"It is thoughtful of you to notice," Tristam continues, pressing his point.

I look Tristam square in his eyes, which shine almost sapphire in the firelight. When I am sure he is paying attention, I roll my eyes.

Tristam laughs out loud. "All right, I will quit playing stupid; but do admit that you do not want her to have any excuse when you beat her at the targets."

I feel my face flush and look at the ground. He comes to me, gently lifting my chin up, just as Tobias had. I keep my eyes lowered.

"Grace, look at me," his voice is soft, but I hear a command.

I obey.

"So, you think you have to be perfect and selfless?" His eyes hold a hint of steel.

I feel my brow pucker in thought, and it takes me a moment to realize that that is exactly what I feel. I nod, ever so slightly.

"You do not; you only have to be you. I love your spirit, Grace. That is what kept you alive in the woods, so do not deny it; use it. Archery is a perfect venue for a competitive spirit. Go win in a fair match."

I flash Tristam a smile, and he catches me up in his arms and gently rocks me back and forth. My hand steals up and touches the side of his face, though I feel brazen to touch him so. His cheek, above his beard, is surprisingly soft.

He sets me on my feet and orders me back to work on Becca's bow. "You cannot have any advantage now, young lady." His eyes are shining a pure blue.

Picking up the next smoothing stone, I begin working on Becca's bow with extra care.

When the bows are finished, Tobias reluctantly allows me to set up a target in a corner of the walled garden.

"Now you will be shooting arrows all day. Who will help me with the watering?"

I point at myself.

"I will hold you to that promise, My Lady, target or no target."

I stick out my hand to seal our pact with a handshake. To my surprise, Tobias raises my hand to his lips, and I feel my cheeks flame.

"Come on, Missy. The seedlings need a drink."

Scrambling to obey him, I forget my embarrassment.

From that day forward, I divide my time between gardening, archery practice, and needlework. I finish my first tapestry of the ring of pines in which Tristam found me, and begin working on an elaborate piece depicting the castle as a gift for King Stefan and Queen Laurel. Tristam takes me outside the castle walls to view the structure from different vantage points. On one of these trips, we take our bows and a supply of arrows. Tristam shoots at a target, such as a tree branch or a particular clump of grass, and then asks me to shoot as close to his arrow as possible. After several attempts, one of my arrows lands within a few inches of his.

"Good aim, Grace. I can tell you have been practicing."

I mime shooting an arrow to indicate practicing, and then make the sign I use for "Rebecca" while looking questioningly at Tristam. I have only seen her once since our first meeting.

"I do not know when we can practice with Rebecca. Her mother is not strong right now, and because Becca is the oldest, she has to help."

I make my sign for illness.

"No…she is not ill, exactly…"

I make a round sign over my belly.

"Yes, she is expecting a baby, and they are hoping for a boy this time. "

I nod my understanding. *Who would not want a boy after six daughters?* a voice in my head says. *Everyone prefers sons.* Shaking my head slightly, I furrow my brow. *Where did that thought come from?* I ask myself. The thought seems to have been planted within me as a fact, yet in Blinth, I have seen nothing but appreciation for both male and female children. Am I remembering something from my earlier life?

"Grace, what is it?" Tristam's voice penetrates my reverie. He is speaking more loudly than usual.

I do not know how to explain to him what has occurred, for my language of signs is not useful for ideas. I shrug, shaking my head slowly.

"Are you all right?" Tristam persists.

I nod.

"Are you ready to go back to the castle?"

Again, I nod, grateful that Tristam can read my moods so well. Shooting arrows seems suddenly pointless. I feel a chill, though the evening is warm.

"Satisfied with your view of the castle?"

I nod again.

The view from the crest of the southern hill is stunning. The entire castle lies spread below me, visible through a clearing. All four towers can be seen, as well as the entire southern wall. The east gate is the only view I still need for my tapestry. I memorize the proportions, my fingers itching for the needle.

That evening I work late into the night, but when I finally go to bed, sleep eludes me. Something prowls within.

CHAPTER 17

TRISTAM

I hate to waken Grace because something disturbed her yesterday evening. We had been out shooting arrows. One minute, she was concentrating on her archery and the next, she had gone away, inside herself. When we returned to the castle, she sat up late over her embroidery. She reminded me of a soldier in enemy territory, tired yet willing sleep away.

News came to me before dawn that Daniel-the-Younger's wife, Sarah, had delivered. The infant arrived seven weeks early and clings to life by a thread, and Sarah's lifeblood is draining from her. Both mother and baby face death. He had been preparing to lead one last hunting expedition before his wife's confinement. Now I will lead the men north in his stead.

I am not sorry for the opportunity to travel in the north, though I do not want to leave Grace so soon after the events of last evening. I cannot go without an explanation, so I enter her chamber as the dawning sun strikes the mullioned window. Slanting beams of light fall on the floor next to her bed, and she does not look at peace, even in repose. Her brow is wrinkled and grey circles lie beneath her eyes. I sit watching her as precious minutes tick by.

"Grace," I call out softly. She startles awake; she knows something is wrong. "It is Sarah, Becca's mother. The baby came early."

Grace makes a cradling motion, and asks a question with her eyes.

"The little boy is still alive but in danger, as is Sarah. I must take Daniel's trip north, as he is needed here."

Grace nods.

"We expect to be gone a fortnight, but we have to take a wagon for supplies and for the meat on the return journey. If we have to clear the road of fallen trees, our journey could take as long as three weeks."

Grace nods again.

"I want you to keep doing exactly what you are doing—gardening, archery practice, and needlework—but stay inside the castle walls."

Grace's brow furrows. Her next two questions should have alerted me to her intentions, but I was not attending.

"Yes, Grace?"

May I visit Becca's family? Grace signs.

I pause for a moment before nodding. "Yes, but only at midday. I want you inside the castle well after dawn and well before dusk."

May I take a basket to Becca's family? Grace asks, indicating a basket near her bed filled with her needlework.

"Yes, of course. I have left money with Addie for your needs, so you may use some of it. Do not go into the market alone; take Addie with you. She will be good at helping you pick out what the family might need."

Grace rolls her eyes and touches her stomach.

"Yes, of course, you know they need food. I meant that Addie might know if any of the children have particular needs."

Grace points to her feet while lifting her brow.

"Exactly, such as shoes."

Grace looks thoughtful, and I answer her next question before she asks it.

"I do not know how Addie knows these things. She just does."

Grace nods and smiles. She makes talking signs with both her hands.

I nod, smiling at Grace's imitation of Addie's predilection for gossip. Addie's knowledge frequently comes in handy. I do not want to end our conversation.

"I have to leave now, child. The men are gathering."

Again, Grace nods, without the smile. I take her in my arms, lifting her out of the bed. I spin her around, as has become our custom. Before I set her on her feet, she reaches her hand up to lay it upon my cheek. She so rarely touches me that I am deeply moved. I lay my hand over hers for a moment. When I set her down, I kiss the palm of her right hand. She lays that palm against her own cheek, savoring my kiss. This is the image I carry north with me; Grace in a white nightgown, standing in the slanting light of dawn, her left hand laid over her right, pressing my kiss into her cheek.

The king is talking with the men when I arrive at the west gate.

Torquil is my second in command, and together we lead a band of ten men, one wagon, and half a dozen horses. This is one of the largest hunting expeditions of the summer season, but I suspect the king is here for other reasons. When he speaks, my fears are confirmed.

"Tristam, a word in private, please."

"Yes, Sire."

We walk several paces away from the others before King Stefan speaks again.

"Daniel's misfortune has created exactly the situation I have been hoping to avoid."

I keep quiet.

"This is a hunting party, Tristam. These are not soldiers, and their safety is in your hands."

I nod.

"I am not going to forbid you to cross into Lolgothe, for that would simply tempt you further."

I find myself grinning at the young king.

"At this time, you are a huntsman."

I nod.

"Go, and hunt well."

I smile at him, for his order is ambiguous. I can hunt for clues about Grace under such an order.

King Stefan understands me all too well. "Hunt for animals, Tristam...for meat. This is not a time to try to discover more of Grace's past."

"Yes, Sire. We most certainly will hunt for game." I do not give him time to forbid me from hunting for anything other than meat. "With your leave, we will depart."

He nods and we return to where the men are gathered.

"Godspeed on your journey. Good hunting." The king uses his regal voice to send us off.

"God protect you, Sire, and the sovereign country of Blinth," we respond in unison as the wagon begins to roll.

In fourteen days, we have loaded the wagon with game, most of which is skinned and prepared for the drying racks. We have a handsome stack of pelts as well, for the northern woods have been gracious to us. We load our cooking supplies after eating our last supper at camp. When everything we do not need for the night is packed, I take Torquil aside.

"How far is it to the clearing where you found the stakes?"

"From here, I would guess several hours' riding, Sir."

"I have to go, and I am leaving you in charge."

"Should I not come with you? You may not find it in the dark."

"No, Torquil, I need you here. Break camp at first light and head south, whether I am back or not."

"But Sir…" Torquil begins.

I interrupt. "I am a difficult man to kill, and I travel quickly alone. Rufus and I are old friends and he carries me well; we can catch you if we get delayed."

"Just what are you planning?"

"I am not planning anything, but I want to see that clearing. I want to know how far Grace traveled alone before she collapsed in the ring of pines. "

"A long way," Torquil replies.

"I have to see it for myself, if I can. If I have not found it by the time the moon is high, I will turn around."

"Will you?"

"Yes, I will."

"Why do I not believe you? You are like a man possessed."

"I know, Torquil. I am sorry, but I may never have this chance again."

"Well, then you need to know the landmarks."

"Thank you, Torquil."

"I wish I could say you are welcome."

His directions are good, and I find the clearing just before midnight. I know I am in the right place, because four fresh stakes are pounded into the cleared earth. I tether Rufus to a tree and peer into the clearing from the cover of the forest. A ring of stones encircles the stakes, and another ring of stones encircles the charred remains of some logs. I wait several minutes, listening, before I step into the open space.

The stakes are laid out in such a way that the victim's head would be to the south. The southernmost stakes are set further to the east and west for the hands. The northern stakes are not as wide apart. I lie down in the position I believe Grace would have been tethered in and find I have a clear view of the sky. I wonder which stars would be visible if the moon was not directly overhead. The stakes are set so they touch my legs at mid-calf and my forearms, and I realize they are perfectly set for a child of Grace's size. My stomach lurches, and a wave of nausea sweeps over me. I control my reactions just before I hear footsteps approaching from the north northeast.

I dodge to the southern edge of the clearing, near where Rufus is tethered. Two soldiers, fully armed, enter the circle carelessly. They obviously did not hear me scramble into the trees; if these men had been trained like my own guards had been in my soldiering days, they would have captured me.

I do not understand their language, although I know it to be the language of Lolgothe. Unfortunately, the guards stay in the circle chatting, and one even lounges on the ground. These men lack respect for their mission. Time crawls by, and I cannot move without giving myself away. I swear vengeance on every biting insect that uses my situation to its own advantage.

The guards are not fifteen feet from me, and I can see the back of the one who stands. He is tall and slender. His responses are brief when the stocky one who lounges speaks. I judge the tall guard to be no more than twenty years of age, perhaps much younger. He peers around in a nervous fashion. I cannot see much of the other guard, but his voice is deeper. He is probably the more experienced soldier, though he is sloppy. Perhaps he has spent countless nights guarding a clearing from invisible invaders. Perhaps the circle has been guarded ever since Torquil pulled up the stakes in early spring. I think of Grace.

I have an urge to attack and stake these guards to the ground. I think of my men, our stores of meat, and my promise to the king, and control my rage.

I hear Rufus growing restless long before either of the inattentive guards do. The younger guard hears him first. He freezes, turns and looks south, directly toward my hiding place. I see he is so young that he scarcely has facial hair. The older guard waves a careless hand until Rufus's nickers grow louder.

They choose to explore rather than go for help. The older guard leads the way, and I silently reach for my dagger. The natural path to the south comes directly past the oak I am using for cover. I decide to deal with the older man first and hope the anxious youngster does not overreact.

I spring as soon as the older guard is abreast of me, and the hilt of my dagger to his temple drops him in his tracks. I flip the blade over in my hand and have it pressed to the young guard's throat before he can draw a weapon.

His eyes are wide, and a sharp blow just below his rib cage doubles him over. I strike the back of his neck, sending him to the ground on top of his partner.

Working stealthily, I strip them of their weapons and their clothing. Using their garments and belts, I tie them with their backs against two different trees, and I long for more stakes and the time to use them. Now

I am grateful that the woods harbor such a large population of biting insects.

Rufus greets me with pleasure, and I pat his nose and take him to where the guards' weapons and remaining clothes lie. I mount with laden arms and head west, scattering first clothes and then weapons. When I come to a stream, I force Rufus into it, and we head north in the stream-bed a short distance and then ride up the western bank. We travel several miles on the path, leaving tracks. Then we turn aside and I keep Rufus to the pine paths, where he leaves no hoofprints. We make our way back to the stream and head south in the water for many miles, before climbing out on rocky ground.

I ride into camp in the last full hour of night. Torquil sits vigilant at the fire, his weapons at the ready.

"Sir?"

"I ran into a trouble. We have to break camp now."

Torquil shakes his head. "Of course you did," is all he says, grinning. He does not waste time asking questions, but rouses the men from sleep.

I keep to the rear of our party, certain we are being followed. Torquil and I make several forays back to the north as the wagon and men head south, but we find no evidence to support my theory. I send ahead for troop protection anyway. King Stefan is already going to be displeased with my actions; I will not risk our winter stores, as well.

The trip south takes several days longer than our trip north. Though the road is clear of debris, the wagons are heavily laden, and there have been rains. The wheels become stuck countless times, and I chafe at every delay. We finally reach the castle late on the fourth day, just as the gates are being closed for the night.

Grace is not in the castle.

CHAPTER 18

GRACE

I sling Becca's new bow over my shoulder. The basket Addie and I filled takes two hands for me to carry. We enjoyed picking out the best-looking delicacies from the market, and meat pies, breads, rolls, and pasties full of potatoes and sausages weigh down the basket. Addie and I argued about a cherry pie or a blueberry one, so we settled on both. Numerous sweet rolls and small cakes, and a soft blue blanket that I could not resist, are tucked in there as well. The baby deserves something special, even if he does not stay with us very long. I understand not wanting to stay on this earth.

I feel nervous after knocking on the cottage door and wish Addie had been able to accompany me. I straighten my shoulders and take a deep breath as Becca opens the door.

"What are you doing here?" she demands. She has never been friendly, but she has never before been openly hostile.

I indicate the basket in my arms, and I see her eyes flicker over the bow before returning to my face.

"We do not need charity."

Setting the basket down, I make my symbol for Sir Tristam, indicating the basket is a gift from him.

"If you have something to say, just say it. I have no time for games."

"Rebecca," a reproving voice murmurs from inside the cottage, "who is our guest?" Geneva pulls the door open wider. "Why, Grace, what a pleasure."

Becca rolls her eyes.

I sign rapidly to Geneva.

"So, this basket is from Sir Tristam, and you brought it because he had to leave?"

I nod and hold out the bow, indicating Becca, who is still standing there barring the door.

"Rebecca, the bow is for you. Also a gift from Tristam, but I suspect Grace helped make it."

I do not sign.

"Grace," Geneva's voice is reproving me now, "did you help make the bow?"

I nod.

By this time, several smaller girls have gathered around the basket that Geneva is holding.

"Look at all this bread! Becca, you will not have to bake today, and I will not have to help." The child looks to be perhaps eight or nine years of age. She is a fairer version of Becca, with auburn hair and green eyes; she bobs a curtsy when she sees me peeking at her. "Thank you most kindly, Miss Grace."

I smile and hold out my hand, and she takes it.

"My name is Sally,"

I smile again.

"Becca, look at this bow."

"I cannot. I have chores to do," Becca says.

Geneva intervenes again. "Sally is right. Becca, you no longer need to bake. I think you have time to look at your gift and even go try it out. Some outdoor time will be good for you; you have been doing the work of a grown woman all day and half of last night."

"I cannot leave…my mother," Becca responds, but I can tell she is tempted, and so can Geneva.

"Your father is tending your mother, and I am going to feed the baby. Grace and Sally can help the younger girls. Go outside and try out that new bow. You will be called upon to put meat on the table soon."

"If you think I should…" Becca says.

"I do. I am ordering you: go."

I hold out the bow again, and this time Becca takes it. Her eyes meet mine for a brief moment.

"Thank you," she murmurs.

I make my sign for Tristam.

"What did she say?" Becca asks Geneva.

"Grace said she will tell Tristam of your gratitude."

"How did you learn what her signs mean?" Becca asks Geneva.

"It simply takes a bit of time. Most of Grace's signs are easy to understand."

"If I remember, this is the sign for 'thank you'?" Becca says, cupping her hands and moving them towards me at the height of her heart.

I nod.

"Thank you, Grace," Becca says. "Uh, what is the sign for Grace?"

I shrug.

"There is not one," Geneva responds. "Grace just points to herself."

"Well, that just will not do." Suddenly Becca squares her shoulders and lifts her head higher. "This should be the symbol for Grace."

I realize Becca is holding her body in an exact imitation of mine, so I take a deep breath and relax my shoulders. I grin at Becca and make my sign for *all right*. Then I point at Becca and frown.

"Well, that might be a good sign for Becca, Grace. But I think the sign for Grace should be this," Geneva said, placing both hands over her mouth. "And the sign for Becca should be this," she continues, making her right hand "talk" by holding her fingers together and closing them against her thumb. "And if opposites attract, then you two should be good friends," Geneva finishes.

I look at Becca and catch her stealing a glance at me. Our eyes lock. I make the talking sign for Becca and frown. She squares her shoulders, raises her chin, and covers her mouth with both hands, and we burst into laughter at the same time. She has a rich, throaty laugh, but mine is silent. Geneva is nodding her head.

"Go on, Becca; get some practice time in with that new bow. Grace, come in. There are some folks I want you to meet."

I stay until late afternoon wiping noses, washing dishes, and helping with whatever chores I can. A screen is set up between the main part of the cottage and the bed that holds Sarah and her infant son. Sally and I try to keep the younger children busy and away from their parents. The youngest child is not yet two; her name is Lydia, or Lyddie, and mostly she just wants to be held. She does not talk very much but walks quickly. If we set her down, she heads straight for the screen, wanting her mother, so I carry her as long as I can and then hand her over to Sally until her arms get tired. Priscilla is three and wholly adorable; she wants to be grown up, yet is quite tiny. The twins are nearly seven, and I cannot tell them apart.

Geneva is with the baby, who has not yet been given a name. I find myself silently praying to the god of Blinth for the life of these children's mother; they need her. I pray also for the tiny boy. I do not know why, but in my heart his name is Benjamin.

I pray as we gather vegetables from the garden and as we wash clothes. I pray as I wipe cherry pie from Lyddie's face after the midday meal.

Becca returns after an hour of practice. She is not exactly beaming, but she is as close as a girl can be, whose mother and brother are terribly ill. "This bow is quite fine!" she exclaims. "Did you try it?"

I shake my head.

"It is well balanced. Did you make one for yourself?"

I nod.

"Good, now we will have some shooting matches, you and me."

I grin, nodding enthusiastically, before returning to the task of washing dishes.

"Wait, you should not be washing my family's dishes. How do you even know how to wash dishes? You are noble."

I can tell by the way she speaks that she holds nobles in contempt, but before I can answer her question, Sally pipes up.

"Rebecca, Grace has been helping the whole time you were playing, and she is no stranger to hard work. Lyddie loves her." Sally indicates the child who is sleeping in her arms.

"Lyddie loves anyone who will hold her," Becca says.

"Well Prissy does not, and she let Grace help her sweep the floor."

"Really..." Becca replies, raising her brows, "she does not take to just anybody."

"Neither do you, but that new bow sure made you grin."

Becca has the grace to blush.

Sally pushes her point. "A great many nobles work; look at Sir Tristam and Lady Geneva."

"For every one like those two, there are ten who sit around gossiping and plying their needles on worthless tapestries," Becca says.

It is my turn to blush.

Becca looks at me and pounces. "I bet you sit making tapestries."

I nod and make my sign for *in the evening*.

"What did she say?" Becca demands.

"She said she makes tapestries in the evening, imbecile. Her fist is the sun going down. Is that not right, Grace?" Sally asks.

I nod.

"What does it matter?" Sally continues. "Grace would never gossip even if she could talk, and there is work to do. Take Lyddie and I will dry those dishes."

"No, do not risk waking her. I will dry," Becca says.

We work in silence for a time. Only when the dishes are all dried and put away does Becca speak. "Thank you, Grace," she both signs and speaks, and her eyes hold mine.

You are welcome, I sign back. *It is a pleasure.*

Becca looks puzzled. Sally pipes up, "I think that sign means something like 'she is glad to be of service.'"

I nod, smiling at Sally. She has learned so quickly to read my signs.

Also, it is fun working together, I sign.

Now Sally looks puzzled.

"What did she say?" Becca demands.

"I do not know that sign yet," Sally responds.

I repeat the sign, spinning on my heels, raising my hands toward the sky, while smiling.

"Well, she looks happy," Becca says. "Is that it, Grace?"

I hold my forefinger and thumb close together.

"You are close, Becca," Sally says.

"Grace, you must learn to talk," Becca says, turning to me.

I feel the smile disappear from my face.

Sally says, "Grace, you talk beautifully. You do not assault my ears like Becca does. And besides, it is fun to figure out what you're saying. It is like playing a game."

I point at Sally and make my spinning sign again.

"Sally, what did you just say?" Becca asks.

"A game?" Sally questions me.

I shake my head.

"It is fun to figure out..." Becca begins slowly repeating Sally's words.

I point at her, spinning yet again.

"*Fun!* That is it!" Sally grins.

Becca grins, too. "Only a noble would think chores are fun," she says, but her eyes hold warmth.

I shake my head; I cannot tell her that being with her family is the fun part—holding a child, being useful and being needed. There are not enough signs for those concepts.

"What is it, Grace?" Sally's voice is kind.

I shrug my shoulders and sign, *I must learn to talk.*

Becca and Sally burst out laughing.

Geneva peeks out from behind the makeshift divider. "Speak softly, your mother is sleeping." But she is smiling, too.

For a moment I had forgotten that two lives hang in the balance. Becca and Sally look stricken.

"Sorry, ma'am," Becca curtsies as she speaks.

"There is no need for formal talk, Becca. You are old enough to simply call me Geneva. Your laughter will not harm your mother or the baby, but they both need sleep."

"We will take the young ones outside," Becca replies.

"I will put Lyddie on her pallet," Sally adds.

"Yes, I will hear her when she wakes. Thank you, girls."

As we head outside to tend the garden, I become aware of a cold place in my heart that the sun cannot warm. I am afraid for Benjamin.

CHAPTER 19

GRACE

From that day forward, I spend the largest portion of my days immersed in Rebecca's family. Rising at dawn, I help Tobias in the garden, and when the sun is high enough, he sends me to Rebecca's laden with vegetables and cheerful flowers. Some days, Addie comes with me to attend to baby Benjamin, but I can tell she does not hold out much hope for the tiny infant.

Becca's mother still bleeds freely. Someone washes out the rags before I arrive, but I see them hanging on the line, and their rusty stains sicken me. Sarah should be feeling better after this many days, but she lies weak and pale in her bed. Addie has taught Benjamin to suckle through the tip of a leather glove attached to a bottle. When he can suckle easily from the bottle, Geneva demands cabbage leaves of us.

"I will also need long strips of cloth. Get them from Addie's basket."

Sally covers her face with her hands.

I glance at Becca, asking for an explanation.

"Geneva is drying up mother's milk, because she is not strong enough to nurse."

"That will kill Momma, not to be able to nurse him," Sally wails.

"Hush! Do not use the word 'kill' in the same breath with 'Momma,'" Becca hisses ferociously.

Sally runs from the cabin. I look at Becca, and in that instant, I can see her fear. Becca not only stands to lose her mother; her own life and her freedom also hang in the balance. Without a mother, Becca will become a mother to all the younger ones without ever having been a wife. I nod at her with understanding and then go find Sally to console her.

Becca's family and the chores keep my mind occupied during the daylight hours. In the evening, while working on my tapestry, the longing for Sir Tristam engulfs me. Becca has so many relatives—uncles, aunts, and cousins—who come to the cabin daily, bringing whatever they can to ease the burden in Daniel's house. Sir Tristam and I only have each other. I fear for him in the northern woods. Sleep eludes me.

On the fourteenth night that Tristam is gone, I cannot sleep at all, so I sit by the narrow window in my room. I cannot see the moon traveling across the sky, but I can watch the shadows in the courtyard below. When the shadows are their smallest, I am gripped by fear which clutches my chest. My heart is pounding as if I have run a great distance, and my breathing is shallow and rapid. A terrible panic grips me, and I cannot be still. I pace the floor until my movements awaken Addie.

During Tristam's absence, Addie has returned to sleep in the small antechamber by my room. I thought the precaution unnecessary, but I cannot fight Addie and Tristam when they are in agreement. When she stumbles into the room with her nightcap askew, I am glad to see her.

She takes a long look at me before speaking. "You need Geneva's sleeping draught, or perhaps something stronger. I will send for her."

I shake my head and make the sign for sleeping. Geneva needs her rest, and if she is not sleeping but attending Sarah, I do not want to interrupt her.

I am fine, I sign, expecting Addie to argue.

Addie studies my face. "Will you at least let me administer the sleeping draught Geneva left here for you?"

I nod and resume my pacing. When Addie has mixed the herbs with hot water, I sip the draught.

"Drink it all," Addie commands. "Tristam would not want you to suffer."

I do as she bids before resuming my pacing. Even with the medicine, I cannot rest. In the hour before dawn, the panic subsides as abruptly as it had begun. I am left with a nagging fear for Tristam and a deep exhaustion. I fall asleep just after the yellow sunlight breaks over the trees, casting long shadows in the courtyard beneath my window. In my dreams, the sun chases the moon across the midnight sky.

I arrive at Becca's as she is cleaning up after the midday meal. Their home seems especially quiet. I find a cloth and begin drying a clay bowl.

"I am glad to see you could come today," Becca whispers, her words dripping with sarcasm. "Too busy celebrating the pagan solstice to remember someone needs you?"

I feel a roaring in my ears, and my vision whitens. The fog spreads and I see nothing.

"Quick, make her sit down," Geneva's voice seems far away, and barely penetrates my clouded mind. I am forced into a chair while strong hands on my back bend me forward. My head is below my knees. The roaring passes and I am dripping with sweat.

"What is wrong with her?" I hear Sally ask.

"How I wish I knew," Geneva replies. "Addie told me she had a bad night."

"It was the solstice," I hear Becca say. I manage to pry open my eyes and see Becca standing over me. Our eyes lock, and I give a tiny, almost imperceptible nod.

Geneva wants to send me back to the castle, but I plead with my eyes to be allowed to stay and she relents.

"There is really no one to go with you and you cannot go alone in your condition. Take her out in the garden, Sally and Becca. She can watch over the little ones while you two work," Geneva says.

I expect Becca to make a caustic remark about another invalid, but instead, she places a bench against a tree and gently leads me to it. Sally hands Lyddie to me, and the child curls up in my arms and places her thumb in her mouth. Prissy sits next to me, patting my arm.

"Poor Grace, poor, poor Grace," she murmurs.

I try to smile reassuringly at her, but I am fighting tears. She lays her head against my shoulder and all three of us sleep while the twins work in the garden.

When the evening meal is prepared, Geneva takes Becca and me aside. "I will be staying here tonight. Grace, I want you to stay and eat. After supper, Becca will accompany you to the castle. Find Addie and ask her for my other herb basket. I also need the other glove, as Benjamin is wearing this one out."

"That is good, is it not?" I have never heard Becca's voice sound so small.

"Yes, he is doing well. He is still tiny, however."

"It is mother's fever…that is why you are staying, is it not?

Geneva nods.

"You are afraid her fever will mount again, as it did last night." It is not really a question.

Geneva nods again. "Becca, when you have gathered my things, have one of the huntsmen walk you home. They will be happy to be of service to Daniel's daughter."

"I will be fine."

"Yes, because you will have an escort."

"I meant I will be fine alone."

"Becca, you will mind me."

I add entreaties to Geneva's order, making my sign for *please.*

"Becca, if anything happens to you, Grace will never forgive herself, and your family needs you."

I nod.

"Oh, fine, I give in." Becca rolls her eyes at me. "I will suffer an escort for Lady Geneva and Princess Grace."

Geneva gives her a mock curtsy.

I incline my head slightly, as I have seen the queen do.

Becca raises her eyebrows.

"Supper is getting cold," Sally calls.

After we have eaten, we start toward the castle in silence. I can tell Becca has something on her mind, and it is not like her not to speak freely. We are more than halfway to the castle when she finally speaks.

"We almost lost mother last night. Geneva does not know I was awake, but I heard everything. Her fever was highest just before dawn, and I kept thinking everything would be all right by the time you arrived with your flowers and vegetables. I do not know why..."

I stop walking.

"Then, you did not come."

I reach out and touch her arm, and she leans against my shoulder. I put my arms around her, causing her tears to flow.

"I am so afraid," she continues, when she can talk.

Me, too, I sign.

We finish our walk in silence. After we find Addie and collect Geneva's things, I walk with Becca to find the huntsmen.

"You do not have to go with me," Becca says, "I am certain to find at least one of them near the stables."

I know, I sign and continue walking beside her.

I want to go back to her home, but my promise to Tristam holds me back.

We find the men and they greet Becca warmly and fight in a playful manner over who will be her escort. I stand a little apart from the group, watching, and see Mark take a swig of ale.

"Ho, Grace, cat got your tongue?" asks a young man I have never seen before.

"You leave her alone, William," Becca says, her eyes flashing fire. "She has worked as hard as anyone these past few weeks."

I am surprised at her vehemence.

"Calm down, Spitfire. Grace can take a joke. Can you not, Grace?"

I nod, studying William. I like the look in his eyes.

"That is not the point, Will. You are just plain mean."

"Calm yourself, Becca, cry truce. I guess it is good that Grace does not speak, since you talk enough for two."

"Not to you anymore," Becca concludes the conversation, turning her back pointedly on William.

"Touché, eh Grace?" William touches his heart in a fencing gesture of surrender. I nod, shrug my shoulders and give him a slight smile.

"Grace agrees with me, Becca; you win," William calls to her, and she turns from her conversation with Mark to reply, "Of course she does."

William lowers his voice conspiratorially. "I love to tease that girl. She has so much spunk, do you not agree, Grace?"

I nod.

"I would marry her in a few years, only—"

"—Only Hollace would kill you," a young man who looks familiar finishes for him. "Hollace is his wife," the other man says, laughing.

"Yes, she would indeed, for Holly is a spunky girl herself. Never marry a redhead, Grace. You will never know a moment's peace, but neither will your life be boring," William grins at me.

"I am Thomas," the younger man introduces himself.

I cannot help but grin back at him, and I sign my gesture of greeting.

"What did she say?"

"She is greeting you." Becca is back at my side, explaining.

You look so familiar, I sign. Becca speaks my words.

"I was there the day we found you."

I remember, I sign the wrapping of bandages around my feet.

He nods. "Yes, I did the bandages…fancy you remembering that. It is wonderful to see you looking so well."

"Watch out, Grace. Do not let him sweet-talk you; all the girls love Thomas."

Thomas's face turns red.

I hold my hand close to the ground and then raise it over his head to change the subject.

Thomas is nodding. "Yes, they used to call me Wee Thom. You have a very good memory."

I do not know what to say.

Becca breaks the silence.

"Grace, I have to go. Mark is taking me back."

My heart goes with you, I sign. It is too difficult to sign *I wish I could go with you.* I want to grab her and hug her. Instead, we shake hands in the accepted manner. I do not release her hand immediately.

"I have to go," she insists.

I nod, touching my heart.

I watch her walking away with Mark, until the path turns and their image is lost in the darkening forest.

"Why so friendly with the Princess?" I hear Mark ask Becca, but I cannot make out her response.

Thomas and William stand on either side of me.

"Do not worry about him, Grace. He is still sore over that enormous stag Tristam would not let him kill," Thomas explains.

"Yes, that stag gets bigger every time he tells the story, but I think he is really angry because Tristam is no longer as sour as he is himself. You are a blessing to Tristam and also to Becca's family." William's words are kind, and I feel color rush to my cheeks. "Come along, Grace. I will walk you back to the nobles' quarters."

"No, you will not. You are married. I shall escort Grace, if she will have me," Thomas says.

I smile at him and hold out my hand; he tucks it into his arm and leads me toward the castle. I understand why he is a favorite of the maidens.

"Have a good night," he says, when he leaves me.

I can only smile in return and wave farewell. I watch his back until his curly hair disappears into the night.

I do not expect to have a good night. In fact, I do not expect to sleep at all, but I also did not expect Geneva to find the time to send Addie one of her strongest sleeping concoctions.

I awake at dawn. Panic grips me. I must get to Benjamin and Sarah.

CHAPTER 20

GRACE

I pull my cloak up over my hair and almost slip past the guard at the gate.

"Lady Grace, you are not to leave the castle walls until midmorning. Tristam's orders," the man exclaims.

I look toward the path that leads to Becca's house and back at the guard.

"You do not want to disobey Tristam's orders, little lady."

"Of course she does not," Thomas's voice comes out of nowhere. "But she was also told to help Daniel's family. If I accompany her, will you allow her to pass?"

"If you want to take responsibility when Sir Tristam comes asking questions, it can be on your head. He is not a man I would disobey."

Thomas turns to study my face. "It is important that you get there soon, is it not?"

I nod vigorously.

Thomas turns back to the guard. "I will be responsible."

The guard shrugs and allows us to pass.

I run toward Becca's and Thomas huffs along beside me. His breathing is labored.

When we reach the cabin door, he manages, "You are really fast," through gulps of air.

I touch my heart.

"I understand," he replies. "Shall I stay and see if they need anything?"

I nod emphatically.

"I am going to find water for both of us; if you are not thirsty, you should be. Then I will wait here."

I touch his hand before slipping into the cabin.

I know something is terribly wrong. Becca is at the basin wringing out rags. Her aunt is holding the baby and his face is flushed a bright scarlet. The house is strangely silent, and I notice none of the other children are present.

Becca turns when the door opens.

"Grace, the baby has the fever, and Geneva sent all the children away. My mother's fever is not the birthing fever. Geneva thinks Benjamin caught it from her."

"Grace, you should not be here. You must go!" Geneva barks from behind the screen that shields Sarah from view.

I see the wash basin in front of the fire, and I know what Geneva needs.

On the way back to the castle, Thomas cannot keep pace with me.

I enter Tobias's garden alone.

"You are late, Missy. Did you oversleep?" Tobias asks. Then he sees my face. "Grace, what is it?" Tobias demands.

I do not waste time explaining but begin gathering buckets. I know of a stream that flows from the ice on the top of the mountains before it drains into the eastern branch of the Boldengarth River. Unfortunately, it is quite a distance from Becca's cabin, and we need a steady stream of water to lower Sarah's and the baby's fevers.

"Thomas, what is wrong?" I hear Tobias ask.

"Daniel's wife and the baby have the fever. Geneva ordered Grace to leave, and then she ran so fast that she practically flew here."

We need men, I sign to Tobias, *and buckets.*

They both look at me with expressions of puzzlement and concern. When Tobias speaks, it is clear he thinks I am addled.

"What are you doing, Child? Geneva will know what to do. You can only wait and pray."

No! I am practically screaming with my hands. *Geneva needs water! Cold water!*

I see understanding dawn on Tobias's face. "Thomas, was there a washtub in front of Daniel's fire?"

"I did not go into the house."

Yes, I sign, nodding my head with my full force.

"Lead on, Grace," Tobias says.

I give him a quick, grateful smile, before loading my arms with buckets.

Almost an hour has passed before the first buckets of water arrive at the cabin. Geneva is not pleased to see me, until she sees what I carry.

"Grace, that is sweet, but it will not be enough," she explains.

I point out the door at the line of men behind me, and Geneva begins organizing.

"Becca, move the screen in front of the tub. Daniel, get your wife in the bath. Becca, Grace, you take the buckets at the door and pour them in the tub. The men are not to enter, as we cannot risk spreading this fever."

My existence is reduced to the repetitive motion of taking a full bucket, moving to the tub, emptying it, returning to the door, handing off the empty bucket, and receiving a full one. I see arms but not faces. I hear noise, but only one voice is discernible to me; I listen to every order Geneva gives. From her voice alone I know Becca's Aunt Sharon is bathing the infant in the small basin closest to the fire. I know Daniel and Sarah's sister are bathing Sarah. From her tone, I know Geneva has not given up on saving these lives, but I also know that she does not expect our efforts to succeed.

I pray with my arms. I pray with my legs. I pray with every bucket I pour. I have been going to church with Tristam, but I do not understand the God which people in Blinth worship. He is one God but in three forms. He is love yet people still sicken and die in Blinth. I hope he loves Sarah and the baby enough to make them well.

After the tubs are full, Geneva alters our routine.

"Becca, you need to drain off the old water from the tub without harming your mother."

I do not hear Becca's reply.

"Grace, take the water away from the tub, and do not let anyone use it. I do not want it anywhere near a garden; see that it is dumped off in the woods."

I do not know how to communicate her order. She must have seen my distress.

"Who is at the door?" she barks.

"Huntsman Thomas, My Lady." I am surprised to hear his reply.

"Did you hear my order about the disposal of the water?"

"Yes, ma'am."

"See to it!"

"Yes, ma'am."

After that exchange, the rhythm of our routine is not altered again. I lose all sense of time. I will my arms and back to keep the rhythm, and refuse to think of my tiring muscles. I hear no sound in that noisy room until Geneva's voice orders, "Halt the water."

In a few moments, Geneva goes to the door. I stand behind her in the room, listening.

"Good friends, thank you. Sarah and the baby are sleeping; you have lowered their fevers."

Someone asks a question that I cannot hear.

"It is too early to tell," Geneva replies.

We have won a battle, but the war is not yet over. Becca flops on a bench, her hands over her face, and only then do I realize how parched my throat is and that my arms feel heavy as lead. When I can move, I begin preparing food and drink for Becca and the rest of us. I have been working for a few minutes when I feel a gentle touch on my shoulder. Becca is standing behind me.

"I am sorry," she says, hanging her head.

I make a puzzled face and wait.

"When Geneva told you that you should not be here and you flew from the cabin, I thought…well, I thought that you…"

That I was scared of the fever? I sign.

Becca nods.

Oh, Becca, I sign, *it is all right.* I reach out for her, but she backs away.

"I called you some terrible names."

Like what? I say with my expression.

"Drunken pig, um….cowardly ferret."

At least you did not call me "spoiled princess," I try to sign. I am not certain she will understand, but she does.

"I called you that one, too."

In your mind, I deserved it, I try to sign.

"But you did not deserve it. You came back."

I shrug. I am hurt that Becca thought I could leave her family in their darkest hour, yet somehow, I cannot blame her. Something, or someone, had taught her not to trust the nobility, and I am noble, foreign, and mute as well. I am grateful she trusts me enough to tell me the names she called me.

A drunken pig? I sign. *Is that the best you can do?* I catch her eye and grin.

She bursts into laughter, which she quickly squelches.

The princess is hungry, I sign.

"My life is but to serve," she replies.

I roll my eyes.

After we serve the adults and eat, Geneva takes me aside.

"Grace, you have been an amazing help, but you cannot stay here."

Geneva rushes on. "And how are your feet?"

They are fine, I sign back. I am not willing to admit to Geneva how much my scars are aching. All the running is surely the cause.

"Tonight, you need to bathe them and use the salve for the next three days."

I want to stay here, I sign, *and help*.

"Grace, I do not know what this fever is. When I thought Sarah's fever was from birthing, I could let you stay here in good conscience. Now the baby is ill..."

He needs a name, I sign.

"Sarah is too weak to name him. Daniel is too distraught."

The priest, Father Gregory, has read about the twelve tribes of Israel in church. I hold up ten fingers, and add two more.

"Twelve, Grace?"

I nod and try to sign *tribes*.

Geneva catches on quickly. "Tribes? The twelve tribes of Israel?"

I give an emphatic nod and point to the finger that represented Benjamin. I watch Geneva calculating in her head.

"Benjamin?" she asks.

I nod again.

"Well, for now, I will ask Daniel if we can call him Benjamin, but Sarah and Daniel may have other ideas."

Fine, I sign.

"The baby is ill, and the fever may spread. Becca held him most of the night, so she is already exposed, so she will be staying here to help."

I should, too.

"Sir Tristam would be enraged with me if I let you stay, and he would be right. I know you do not think that you matter..."

I am looking away, but at her words, my head snaps back around.

"But you do," she continues. "You have changed Tristam's world. I have to protect you, not only for your own sake, but also for his."

I want to help, I sign, but I can no longer really argue with her.

"Good; here is my plan. According to her aunt, Priscilla is inconsolable without Sarah, Becca, or you. I am going to ask William and Thomas to watch over the home where Lyddie and Priscilla are staying. You will stay with them and care for the children. The children's aunts will help you during the day, but they need their sleep at night, as they both have children of their own. Do you think you can calm Prissy?"

I nod.

"I will send word to Addie with William. He or Thomas will bring your salve and a change of clothes. I have taken it upon myself to disobey Sir Tristam. I am taking every precaution for your safety, but we really need you. You are not to leave the home where I am sending you, without letting someone know where you are going, even during the day. Do you understand?"

I nod.

"Is that a promise?"

I nod again and place my hand over my heart.

"God save us from Sir Tristam," she mutters under her breath.

I grin and nod.

Geneva smiles and we part.

Tristam is not pleased when he finds me, two nights later, in a cabin with Lyddie curled up on my left and Prissy on my right.

CHAPTER 21

TRISTAM

The men and I work quickly, storing the meat, hanging the skins, and caring for the horses. My huntsmen are as eager to see their families as I am to see Grace. But when I creep into her chamber, just before midnight, her bed is empty. There is no sign she has been there.

I am terse when rousting Addie, and she lays the blame for Grace's absence at Geneva's door. Addie tries to tell me what has been happening with Daniel's family, but I am only partially listening.

"Do not go rousting Lady Geneva at this hour of the night. She is staying with Daniel, Sarah, and the baby; besides, Grace is not there."

"Where is she?"

"She is at Sarah's sister's house, caring for Daniel's youngest girls."

"Is there no one else who can do that? I left specific instructions she is not to be out of the castle after dark!" I am practically yelling.

Addie gives me an appraising look. "Did something happen up north?"

I sometimes forget Addie has known me since birth.

"Later, Addie. Right now, it is what is happening here that concerns me." I can barely control my tone.

"William and Thomas are keeping watch over the house, so approach cautiously. Be gentle with Grace, for she has been working hard in the presence of death. She is tired and her feet are sore."

"What is wrong with her feet?"

Addie takes a deep breath.

"Explanations can wait," I say, changing my mind.

I have no trouble exiting the castle, since the guard on duty knows both me and the trouble plaguing Daniel's house.

"Grace is quite the little heroine, Sir," he says.

"Humpf, Grace is a disobedient child."

"With all due respect, Sir, Lady Geneva credits her with saving two lives."

His words give me something to ponder as I hasten to the cottage. Using our hunting signals, I warn the guard of my approach.

"I was hoping Thomas would be on duty when you arrived," William complains good-naturedly. "Go and see her before you start chewing on me."

I do not reply but enter the cottage as quietly as I can and I exhale as I catch sight of Grace on a pallet near the embers of the fire. A tiny girl of maybe three years is lying in the crook of her right arm. An even younger child sprawls on Grace's left side; she lies face down, sleeping almost on top of Grace. Grace's hair fans out around her head, for she did not take time to braid it for sleep. The light of the embers plays with the gold in her hair.

"Who is there?" Sarah's sister asks from the corner.

"Tristam," I whisper. "I needed a glimpse of my Grace."

"She is surely gracing us, My Lord."

"I was worried when she was not in the castle. Is she well?"

"Yes, Sir, she is well, though she is tired. The young ones adore her and she is good with them, but everyone here is exhausted, My Lord."

I hear her husband stirring. "Pardon my intrusion, I will return in the morning."

"You are always welcome here," she replies.

"Thank you. Rest well," I say slipping out the door and walking over to William.

"Well?" he queries.

"It is not well; she should be in the castle."

"By all means, take her there. Prissy will cry all night and none of those good folks will be rested tomorrow, but yes, you should definitely take her to the castle."

I grin and feel my temper wane.

"As bad as all that, is it?"

"Worse."

"Why Grace? Why does the child cling to her?"

"How much do you know?"

"Almost nothing. Enlighten me."

By the time William has filled me in on the events of the last two and a half weeks, Thomas has arrived for a changing of the guard.

"I want to thank you both for guarding her."

"It has been a pleasure," William replies. "She is an amazing girl."

"She certainly is," Thomas adds. His voice is a little too enthusiastic for my taste.

"Go, get some rest, Tristam," William suggests.

"No, I will stay here."

"By all means stay; I will bring you a bedroll. Thomas is rested so he can keep watch. If I know you, you have been traveling since dawn."

"Longer than that."

"It would be an honor to keep watch, Sir," Thomas adds.

"Thomas, how old are you?"

"Eighteen, Sir."

"Do you know how old Grace is?"

"No, Sir."

"Neither do I, but she is too young for you."

"Spoken like a true father," William says.

"I see that your redheaded wife has not taught you to mind your tongue," I reply.

I keep my face earnest for just long enough to frighten William. When I grin, we all break into laughter.

"I could use some rest. Thank you, Thomas."

I wish my homecoming with Grace could have occurred in private. Instead, we hug under the watchful eyes of most of Sarah and Daniel's families. She runs to me and I catch her in my arms, spin her around, and set her on her feet.

"Let me look at you," I say.

She stands before me, beaming. Her face is radiant as she smiles up at me, and I bend down to kiss her forehead.

Welcome back, she signs. *Good hunting?*

"Excellent hunting, thank you, and I hear you have been busy."

Grace nods and suddenly looks scared.

Are you angry? she signs.

"No, Grace, I am proud of you."

Are you sure? she signs. She seems to be growing younger before my eyes.

"I am sure," I smile at her and turn to Becca's uncle. "Can you spare her for a few moments?"

"Certainly, Sir."

"Come, Grace, let us take a walk."

Grace turns, signing rapidly to the small girl tugging at her skirt. I catch *back soon* in her signs.

"Promise?" the child asks.

I promise, Grace signs.

"I will not keep her away too long," I tell the child.

"Come, Priscilla, we are having flat cakes for breakfast. Can you stir the batter?"

I appreciate her aunt's assistance in distracting Prissy.

Grace kisses Priscilla on top of her curls before turning to me. I hold out my hand and she places her hand in it; we walk in silence until we are well away from the cottage.

"Grace, are you afraid of me?" I finally ask.

She shakes her head too vigorously.

"Grace?"

I disobeyed you, she signs.

"For good reason," I add.

She nods.

"You were careful," I continue.

She nods again. *You are really not angry?*

"I was last night when I opened the door to your chamber and found it empty."

I am sorry, she signs, looking at the ground.

I raise her chin and look into her eyes. "But I am not angry now that I understand why you were gone. I am proud of you."

She smiles and blushes adorably. I pull her to me and hold her for a long time. Eventually, she pulls away and signs, *I was afraid for you.*

"I am fine, Grace."

No! I was really scared for you…four nights ago. What happened?

"Nothing," I tell her.

You are lying, she signs. She is becoming agitated, for my lies are not soothing her. Though how she knows I am lying, I cannot tell.

"I had a run-in with two foreign guards."

Were you hurt?

"No, and I did not hurt them very much either."

She gives a small smile.

Were you followed traveling back?

I do not like the way her mind works.

"There is no reason to believe we were."

But you think you were followed.

She can read me better than Addie. I nod.

Were you near the ring of pines?
"Yes."
So the guards were from my country?
"Probably, but Grace, you are safe here, and this is your country now."
Yet, you worry, she signs.
The child has a point.

Later that day, I am summoned to a private meeting with King Stefan.
"Tell me, Tristam, why did your messenger request me to send troops to protect a hunting expedition? What did you do to make that necessary?"
I tell him of my run-in with the guards.
"So next I will be receiving an ambassador from Lolgothe demanding to know why you attacked their guards?"
"It is quite possible, Sire. I am sorry."
"I can handle our northern neighbors, but I do not want them to come looking for Grace."
"Neither do I."
"Did you get any satisfaction for your troubles?"
"Yes, Sire. There was a clearing with a ring of stones, and stakes were laid out for a child of Grace's size. The victim's head would be facing due south, and the legs would be strapped apart, not together."
"And you found this alone in the dark, without assistance?"
"Torquil found the stakes while hunting there in April. He brought them to me and I compared the leather to the straps we cut from Grace's wrists and ankles."
"Why did I not know of this?"
"Forgive me, Your Majesty, I should have done so."
"Have you told anyone?"
"No, Sire, and Torquil will keep silent."
"Good. She is safer if no one knows."
"Yes, Sire."
"Tristam, I am sorry."
"Thank you, Your Majesty."
"Perhaps she will never remember and will simply learn to live and belong here. At some point, we must discuss her future and your own, but for now that can wait. You are dismissed."
I turn to leave.
"Oh, and Tristam, try to stay out of trouble." His face is grave but his

eyes are smiling.

"Yes, Sire." I want to ask about Grace's future, but the king's private guards are already opening the door for me to exit.

CHAPTER 22

TRISTAM

Thankfully, Daniel's wife and new son both overcame the fever. The baby is doing well, but Sarah continues to be weak. Grace spends her days helping Tobias in the garden and assisting Daniel's family. None of her time is spent amongst the nobility.

My decision to relinquish my holdings leaves Grace in an unclear position. By birth, she is clearly noble, but I have nothing with which to dower her. Without a dowry, she will never marry into our nobility. Thomas is clearly smitten with her, although he keeps his distance. She could have a future amongst the people with whom she is spending her time; she is no stranger to hard work. I, too, found solace among these good, hardworking folk. Yet, though I admire Thomas, I would not have wanted Faith to marry a huntsman and work constantly.

Addie watches me closely. One evening, when I exit Grace's chamber, she is waiting for me.

"Sir, you said you would tell me what happened up north."

"The king has forbidden me to speak of it."

"Which confirms my belief that it was not good."

I raise my eyebrows involuntarily, but I do not speak.

"Sir, you are watching her like a hen with one chick. I want to help, but I do not know what I am watching for."

"Signs of distress, same as before."

"She is doing quite well, Sir, in spite of her lack of voice."

"That is what worries me."

"Sir?"

I look at Addie appraisingly. She continues.

"I have a reputation for gossip, which I cultivate. In my work as a nurse, there are secrets I can never tell. They weigh heavy on me, so I discourage people from confiding in me. Secrets about Grace would not be a burden, Sir."

"Addie, please quit calling me 'Sir.' We are the same, you and I. We both serve at the pleasure of the king."

"But you were born noble, as was Grace. That is part of what worries you."

I nod.

"The other part is 'The Sacrifice,'" she says.

"Addie, I swear, if you ever use those words in relation to Grace…"

"I never would, Sir, not to anyone but you. That has not stopped rumors from spreading, though. People are curious."

"And malicious," I interject, speaking vehemently.

"That too, Sir, and do not forget jealous. She is beautiful and kind. She is also living in the part of the castle normally reserved for visiting dignitaries."

"You are not easing my mind."

"I am sorry, Sir, but you stopped paying attention to the social intrigues here when you gave up your holdings."

"And you have no idea what a relief that was."

"Depending on what you want for Grace's future, it might be time to take your head out of the dirt."

I sigh. "You are right. Thank you, Miss Addie."

"Miss Addie?"

"Well, you keep calling me 'Sir.'"

"That is because you are, Sir. You still have not told me what concerns you about Grace. It will stay between us."

"It had better."

She nods.

"Sometimes, when soldiers are seriously wounded in battle, they cannot remember what happened. I have noticed that the ones who take longest to remember usually have the worst stories. Grace is pushing her memories away. She will not even speak."

"Perhaps she never could," Addie suggests.

"She can speak."

"How do you know that, Sir?"

"They only choose perfect children to sacrifice."

"Oh, my…" Addie's voice trails off.

"Exactly."

A few weeks later Grace and I along with Geneva are the guests of honor at Daniel's son's christening. We sit together just behind the family.

I am surprised to hear Daniel's reply, "Benjamin Tristam," when the priest asks for the child's name.

I look at Grace. She is smiling. Later in the service, when the priest takes the child from Sarah's arms, I feel Grace grow tense beside me.

Father Gregory is a huge man, the tallest I have ever seen. He must weigh close to nineteen stone, but there is no fat on him. I am moved watching him cradle the infant, who seems even tinier in his arms. He lifts the child with great tenderness in his enormous hands, so all who are gathered can see the infant. He walks toward the font of water, and Grace takes a quick breath. I reach for her hand, but she pulls away. Her eyes are glued to the ritual in front of us. I watch as Father Gregory raises his hand, filled with water, to sprinkle over Benjamin.

"Benjamin Tristam, I baptize thee in the name of the Father, the Son, and the Holy Ghost."

Benjamin cries when the water touches his crown. The priest then anoints him with oil, making the sign of the cross on his forehead.

"You are sealed as Christ's own, forever." The ritual continues. "Precious child of the Most High God…"

Father Gregory hands the child back to Sarah. Grace's posture becomes less rigid, but her eyes still hold a faraway look. This time, when I reach for her, she lets me take her hand. It is cold in mine. I chafe her hands with both of mine, trying to get blood flowing back into her fingertips.

"And now, renew with me your baptismal vows," Father Gregory continues. It is then that I hear King Stefan's voice ring out his responses. The words wash over me. I have heard them so many times, but Grace sits riveted, taking in each word. Watching her, I find myself listening as if the words are new to me.

"All praise and thanks to you, most merciful Father, for adopting us as Your own children, for incorporating us into Your Holy Church, and for making us worthy to share in Your inheritance of the saints of light through Jesus Christ, Your son, our Lord who lives and reigns with You and the Holy Spirit, one God, for ever and ever. Amen."

When the priest finishes speaking, Grace's hand is relaxed in mine. After the service, no one moves until King Stefan and Queen Laurel make their way to the front of the church to congratulate the parents.

Royalty does not attend every child's christening.

"Congratulations on your son and his health," I hear King Stefan say, "and your own."

Sarah curtsies low.

"Thank you most kindly, Your Majesty. We are truly honored," Daniel replies.

Lady Geneva follows after the royal couple, offering her congratulations. Then it is our turn. Grace reaches out, gently touching Benjamin's feet. She is smiling at Sarah. Her tension is completely gone.

"Could you not think of a better name than Tristam?" I tease Daniel.

Daniel smiles. "It seems appropriate. Grace saved his life and Sarah's."

"I heard Lady Geneva had something to do with it."

"Of course she did, and we owe her greatly, but Grace's quick thinking and hard work gave us hope when hope had almost extinguished."

Beside me Grace blushes a fiery red. "Thank you," I reply.

Grace lingers, signing to Sarah. I walk outside where I find King Stefan waiting for me.

"Tristam, a word."

"Yes, Sire."

"Grace needs to spend more time amongst the nobility. I will give her the summer, but in the fall she needs to enroll in the instruction classes for children of the nobility."

"Are rumors spreading, Sire?"

"Sources tell me they are. People need to know *her*, not the rumors about her."

"Thank you for your concern for her welfare. I do not see how it is to be accomplished." I do not have money for the expensive classes offered to noble girls, though I do not give voice to this thought.

"We will arrange the details later."

"I cannot accept charity for her..." I begin, but the king raises his hand to silence me.

"Tristam, the details can wait."

I open my mouth, but do not speak. If he were anyone but the king, I would argue my point.

The king understands my dilemma. "Good choice, Sir Tristam," he says, smiling at me. Then his attention is claimed by another.

I ponder his plans for Grace's future. I do not see a clear path.

CHAPTER 23

GRACE

I get to meet the queen at Benjamin's christening. One minute, I am congratulating Sarah and Daniel while playing with the baby's feet. The next, I am alone facing Her Majesty, Queen Laurel.

"Grace, I am Queen Laurel," she says. Her voice is deep and melodic.

I sink into my deepest curtsy, and stay bent low, looking at the ground.

"Rise, my dear. I wish to thank you for the beautiful tapestry you created."

It was my pleasure, I sign.

"Oh, dear, I am going to need some help," she replies. "Sarah, can you spare your daughter? Rebecca, will you assist me?"

"Yes, Your Highness," they reply in unison.

I appreciate her asking politely when she could have commanded. I only have a moment to wonder if there is a reason I find consideration from royalty noteworthy before my attention is needed in the present, rather than the past.

"Can you tell me what Grace said?"

"Yes, ma'am."

I repeat my sign.

"She says it was her pleasure," Becca tells the queen.

"You have some skills with the needle, Grace."

I sign *Thank you,* and Becca speaks my words.

"How did you learn her signs, Becca?"

"Lady Geneva helped me, at first. Grace and I have spent a great deal of time together, Your Highness, since my mother delivered Benjamin."

"Did Grace truly save their lives?"

"Lady Geneva says so, ma'am. Lady Geneva said she had given up hope. Grace's knowledge of Wildcat Creek and her willingness to enlist help saved their lives."

"Lady Geneva, no doubt, did her part as well."

"Yes, ma'am. We owe much to both of them."

I sign to Becca without thinking, *You do not owe me anything.*

"What did she say?" the queen asks.

"She said we do not owe her anything," Becca replies.

"Really, Grace?" the queen addresses me.

Really, ma'am, I try to express my thoughts in signs. *You have given me a home, taken me in. I can never repay you. I owe you my life. Whatever I can give back to the people of Blinth, it is an honor.*

"Rebecca?"

"I am not certain of all the signs, Your Highness. But I think she is expressing her gratitude for giving her a home."

I nod. *You saved my life,* I sign.

The queen looks at Becca. "She said we saved her life."

"It is a pleasure to have you amongst us, Grace. I hope to be seeing more of you. Rebecca, thank you for your assistance today. Take good care of your mother; she still looks tired."

"Yes, ma'am," Becca says as we both curtsy.

Tristam and I take a walk after the ceremony and celebration are over. I like having him all to myself.

"So, Grace, now you have met King Stefan and spoken with Queen Laurel. Do you like them?"

Very much, I sign. *The queen did not reprimand me for speaking without permission.*

"She has a good heart," he continues. "Our monarchs do not restrict the speech of their subjects."

Again, I find myself wondering why I thought they would.

We walk on in silence until Tristam says, "It was a beautiful ceremony."

I nod, thinking of the words of the baptismal ritual: "Sealed as Christ's own forever."

"Grace..." I hear Tristam's voice, as if from far away, "what is it?"

I do not know how to say it, I sign.

"Please try," he replies.

The priest says Christ loves everyone. I make the sign for Christ by touching my palms in succession with the opposite index finger.

"Is this Lord Jesus Christ?" Tristam asks, repeating the sign.

I nod, giving him a smile.

"See, I am a clever lad," he teases.

I smile. My shoulder touches his arm as we walk side by side. I am aware of his closeness and his warmth.

"Yes, Christ loves everyone," he finally responds to my question.

Even sinners? I want to ask. It takes me a moment to remember the two thieves that were executed with Jesus. I make a sign for three crosses and then point to the two outside ones.

"Are you asking about the thieves who were killed with Jesus?"

I nod and spread my arms wide and then point to myself.

"I do not understand."

I sigh heavily. Glancing across the path I see several stones the size of a man's hand. I gather two and hand them to Tristam. Then I huddle on the ground.

"Are you being stoned?"

I nod.

"Are you an adulteress?"

I shake my head.

"Are you a sinner?"

I nod. Using my signs, I ask the question, *Does Jesus love sinners?*

"I think Jesus loves sinners the most, Grace."

Why? I thought sinners were punished with eternal damnation. I am struggling with my own signs, but Tristam seems to understand.

"Christ loves sinners most because they have gone astray. He knows how hard it is for them to turn to him, so he welcomes them with open arms."

I shake my head.

"Grace, I am not a very good person to talk to about God. I have been angry at Him since Constance and Faith were abducted. That means I am a sinner. Perhaps you should talk to Father Gregory."

I vigorously shake my head.

"He is a good man, Grace. He can explain."

I stamp my foot. *You are not a sinner!* I sign.

"Of course I am, Grace. I have not loved God with my whole heart. I have not loved my neighbor as myself."

Tristam is quoting the ritual. I long to quote the Bible: "Jesus says, 'Whatever you have done unto the least of these, my brethren, you have done it unto me.'" I am one of the least of these. Tristam loves me.

You love me, I sign.

"Yes, I love you."

So you are not a sinner, I try to sign but I cannot. A lump rises in my throat.

"Grace, are you all right?"

I can barely hear him; my ears feel full of goose down. I feel his arms go around me and I lay my face against his chest. I do not deserve this love. I am the worst sinner of all. Christ cannot possibly love me. Tristam would not love me if he knew the things I cannot remember about my-self. I feel certain of this. The tears I long for will not come.

CHAPTER 24

TRISTAM

Grace's sadness troubles me. It is sadness that goes beyond words. Tears fall sometimes, but only silent ones. I find myself longing for the day she will cry aloud almost as much as the day she will talk.

I pour love over her. I constantly touch her and hold her as one does with a much younger child. Grace rarely touches me back, yet she seems to relax in my embrace. If she cannot feel God's love, I want to make certain she can feel mine. My heart is thawing. I feel both joy and fear at this realization.

King Stefan sends for me three weeks after the christening. Emissaries from the north have arrived, and I am on my guard when I enter the king's chamber. I bow low to King Stefan and, on rising, I search his face. He gives me a certain look, so I know to follow his lead.

"Tristam, rise. These good men from Lolgothe were sent here on a double mission. They wish to know why two of their guards were found bound near their southern border, and they are seeking information about a lost child."

I look at my king inquiringly, as if I am asking permission to speak. "Go on, tell them how you saw a child in the woods and later went looking for another glimpse of her."

"Yes, Sire. There is not much to tell. I was hunting with a group in our northern woods back in—"

"What month?" The taller one interrupts me. He speaks with an accent.

"What month did you lose a child?" I ask. My manner is not friendly.

"I apologize that my comrade interrupted you. Please continue," the shorter, stockier of the two men says.

"It was probably late March or sometime in early April, because there was still a bit of snow on the ground. My men and I were hunting in northern Blinth, when we spotted a child."

"What did she look like?" the tall one demands.

"I did not get a very good look at her. We wanted to help the child, but she ran from us."

"Surely you, a grown man, could have caught the girl," the tall one says.

"She was swift. She ran like the devil himself chased her," I reply.

The two men exchange glances.

"We had no cause for pursuit, and it seemed cruel to chase her when she was clearly terrified. We left food and blankets. I pray she made use of them."

"Do you remember which direction she was heading?" the stockier emissary asks.

"Due west," I cheerfully lie. "What do you think terrified her so?" I ask, feigning ignorance.

"How should we know? Perhaps she had been chased by a wild animal. She was lost from a hunting party."

"Is it common practice to take young girls on hunting parties? She acted more like *she* had been hunted." Even as I say these words, I know it is unwise.

The king sends a warning look my way, when no one is looking. I try to apologize with my eyes.

Again, the men eye one another.

King Stefan reenters the conversation. "Forgive Sir Tristam's rudeness. He has worried over that child."

"Why should you care about a girl, a foreigner, in the woods?" the tall one asks.

"I would be concerned for any child, indeed, any person, alone in the woods. Have you inquired at the western kingdoms?"

"No one but you has seen a child in the woods."

"Tristam, explain to these men why you bound their guards," the king demands, changing the subject.

"I wanted to go back toward the place where I had seen the child, where we had left the blankets and food. I did not expect to see her, but I felt a need to try."

"You left the blankets on Lolgothe's land?"

"No, the child I spotted back in the spring was on Blinthian soil. This summer, I must have overshot my goal; I had no intention of trespassing on your land. I was shocked when I ran into your guards."

"Why did you not simply declare yourself?"

"When I trespassed on Lolgothe soil, searching for my lost wife and child, I was detained for some period of time and sent home under armed guard. It was not an experience I cared to repeat," I say with hostility. "I had large stores of meat and I had left my men. My king would not have been pleased if I were detained."

"So you harmed our guards on our own soil?"

"Only slightly. My wife and daughter were abducted on Blinthian soil while picking berries in the north. Their clothes were found much farther north, in Lolgothe, but they never were. The woods can be mightily inhospitable."

"Our guards' clothes were found much farther to the west."

"Then you should be visiting Polomia," King Stefan interrupts. "Tell your king I am sorry he lost a child, and even sorrier she has not yet been found. Any child found in my kingdom will certainly be returned to the place they tell us is home. Assure your monarch that none of my subjects will cross the border in the future without punishment. It is not my wish for my people to trespass. My guards will have gifts for your king in the morning when they lead you to the border. You are dismissed."

The two foreign guards bow and are escorted from the Great Hall. King Stefan catches my eye, and I can see he is not pleased.

I do not know who told Grace that we had visitors from Lolgothe, but that evening I find her pacing in her room. Sleep is far from her. Her arms are wrapped tightly across her chest, and every muscle is tense.

Have the foreign guards left? she signs.

"No, Grace. They will be escorted to Lolgothe in the morning."

Why did King Stefan not give me to them? she signs.

"King Stefan would never do that."

But he said that any foreign child would be returned to their home.

"How do you know that?"

People talk, Tristam.

"I was there. He said, 'Any child found here will be returned to the place they tell us is home.'"

So, if the king is being honest, he should send me back.

"Do you wish to leave?"

Grace shakes her head. Her pupils grow large, as though she is terrified at the thought.

"The King is honest, Grace. You cannot tell us of your home. You believe you are from Lolgothe, but you do not remember. Our king is very clever with his words."

Grace nods her head very slightly but does not relax her arms away from her chest.

"Grace, you are holding yourself. Would you like me to hold you?" I say impulsively.

She eyes me for a moment before nodding.

"Come here, little one," I say, seating myself in a chair.

She walks over and climbs up in my lap. It takes a long time for her to relax and fall asleep.

CHAPTER 25

GRACE

Something shifts in me the day I wake up in Tristam's arms. His touch creates a chink in my interior walls. I could not explain this to anyone, for I do not understand it myself. Father Gregory talks about God's love, but I used to think God loves everyone else but me. Somehow I thought I was not good enough or pure enough to be loved by God, but when I wake up in Tristam's arms, I wonder if perhaps this is what it feels like to be enfolded in the arms of God. Father says God uses people in our lives to be His messenger. Mostly, the priest says that when he wants us to be God's messenger to someone else, but perhaps Tristam is God's messenger to me. What if God really does care about me?

I do not want Tristam to know I am awake. I want him to go on holding me forever. I also know he must be tired, so I begin climbing down from his lap, but his grip on me tightens.

"Whoa, Child, where do you think you're going?"

I thought your arms must be tired, I sign.

"No, but my legs are asleep," he replies.

I am sorry, I sign, jumping up.

"Oh Grace, I am only teasing you. I love holding you."

Thank you, I sign. I feel the color rising to my cheeks.

"Grace, what is it?" he asks, reaching for my hand.

I stare out the window, noting the darkening sky. The shadows tell me it is late in the evening. Finally I take a deep breath. *I do not want to cause problems for Blinth.*

"I wish you would not think that way. The king is not worried about his northern neighbors."

I shake my head.

"I do not think anyone cares, Grace. We do not believe in harming the young."

We are not certain they harmed me. What if I just got lost, as they said?

"Grace, someone tied you up by your wrists and ankles. Someone released you. Until you can remember what happened and figure out where you want to live, we will harbor you here."

I find myself staring out of the window. I feel pressure on my wrists and ankles.

"Grace?"

Tristam's voice comes from far away. He places his hand on my shoulder. I want to reach up and hold it, but I cannot move.

CHAPTER 26

GRACE

July becomes August. Becca's family allows me to come and help them, but they do not really need me anymore. Sarah is almost back to her usual level of strength, and Benjamin is growing rapidly. I feel like an intruder in their home, although they welcome me graciously. I help the most with Prissy and Lyddie. With the children, sometimes, I lose the feeling of being hunted. That feeling is the reason I spend so much time in the garden with Tobias. I feel safer with walls around me.

Tristam notices I am spending most of my time inside the castle walls, and comments upon it, but he has very little free time. All day, he works with his men on the meat stores. He has multiple groups out hunting all over Blinth, and he is overseeing the skinning, butchering, and storing of the meat. He is staying close to home because of me, but I only see him in the evening. We walk together, collecting sticks to make arrows; we practice our shooting, and sometimes we shoot small game. He is also teaching me all he can about the plants found in the woods. I am learning what our warriors learn so they can survive if they are cut off from the troops in battle.

Addie thinks it is a waste of time. She fusses when I return to my chamber with sticks and seeds stuck to my skirt.

"You do not need to know the properties of all the plants in the wilderness. You are damaging your finery," she complains.

I keep silent, not even signing a reply. I know why Tristam is teaching me about survival. Addie does not know how much I know about Constance and Faith's disappearance. Addie has also never been lost in the woods, alone and hungry. I soak up Tristam's teachings like the flowers soak up the water that Tobias and I pour on them.

My favorite evenings, however, are the ones during which Tristam talks about himself. These times are rare, but occasionally he will get lost in reverie, talking almost as if I am not present. On one such evening, he talks about the upcoming ball for the dignitaries of Chantrell. While serving as Head Huntsman and living in a cottage, he had been excused from such social events for the nobility. Now that he lives in the castle, though, his attendance is required. This will be his first public appearance in his old role as "Sir Tristam."

"I am not looking forward to returning to court life, even for one evening. I hate the maneuvering, the gossiping, especially of the ladies. I feel like prey." He pauses, looking out over the trees.

Was it like that before? I sign.

"When I was young, I had Constance."

What about before you married?

"It was different. I was the younger son. My father was not about to divide his holdings between us."

I frown.

"I did not blame him; the property would have been weakened if divided. Father gave me my start in life, my equipment, weapons, horses, and training. It was up to me to make something of myself. Constance was always there, always encouraging. She believed in me. She was thirteen when we met, not too much older than you are, I imagine. I was fifteen, a squire to one of the leading knights. He never treated his squires very well, as he was ruthless, and not only in battle. He showed me who I did not want to be, and I learned a great deal. He also taught me to be ruthless when necessary. Oh, Grace, I am sorry. Why am I rambling on? This cannot interest you."

Tell me more, I sign eagerly.

"Are you sure?"

I give a definite nod.

Tristam resumes talking. "Warfare is not pretty. Blinth was defending our western border from Polomia. The casualties were high. We were taught to be ruthless in battle and gentlemen everywhere else. Often, it is difficult to go from being a warrior to being a gentleman. Constance was my…I guess she was like a touchstone. She kept me human. I could be a ferocious warrior, but when I came home to her, she changed me back into Tristam. When I lost her…I lost a part of me. I lost my way. Losing Faith at the same time—it was too much.

"Suddenly, I was the grieving widower. By then, I had lost my brother. My father was gone, and I was wealthy beyond any dream I had ever had in my youth. And Grace…it meant nothing. Everything that mattered—nay, every*one* that mattered was gone. I was alone. There were many people who wanted to comfort me, widows and mothers with marriageable daughters. I found the situation intolerable. My older brother had complained of feeling hunted at court before he married. I laughed at him when the ladies flocked, but I was not laughing when it happened to me."

So you gave it up? I sign.

"Yes, I did."

Have you found yourself?

"What do you mean?"

You said you felt lost without Constance and Faith. Your touchstone was gone. I have difficulty signing these thoughts, but Tristam understands.

"I guess I found a different me, older, battle-scarred. I feel a mission amongst the huntsmen. We have a job. We provide the meat. It is simple and straightforward. I am no longer looking for joy or fulfillment, I only want to serve."

To serve and be left alone.

Tristam stares at me intently. "Yes, Grace, that is exactly what I want. I never saw that so clearly before."

I am sorry, I sign, hanging my head.

Tristam traces my face with his forefinger. His brow is furrowed. "Sorry for what?"

For not leaving you alone…for bringing changes to your life. I am sorry that you have to attend this ball, I sign, hoping some of the concepts are intelligible to him. I find myself longing for words, for speech.

"Oh, Grace, slow down, now stop. I am filled with gratitude for you. You bring me joy I never thought to know again in this lifetime. You are a treasure, a gift of Grace."

But the ball…the ladies.

"One ball is a small price to pay for having you in my life. The ladies only flock when there is money. Forgive an old man's ramblings at the end of the day. I should not talk so. Do not take this to heart, Grace. All will be well at court. Perhaps we should walk back. It is getting dark."

Tristam, will you marry again?

"I cannot imagine that. Right now, you are all the woman I need, girl Child. Somehow we must establish you amongst the nobility. Are you prepared for that?"

I shake my head.

"Well, I am counting on you to stir things up a bit at court. The young men will be flocking. You are so beautiful."

I shake my head, making my sign for money.

"So, you know about dowries?"

I nod.

"Do not worry, Grace. I will take care of you. I have started from nothing before."

I am silent for a long time, thinking.

"Grace?"

I shake my head slightly; my ideas are jumbled.

"What is it?"

You hate warfare. You should not have to fight to provide for me.

"It would be an honor," he replies, going down on one knee, in the courtly manner.

I am serious! I sign, stamping my foot.

"So am I. I will do whatever it takes to provide for you."

I do not need much, I sign.

"You ease my mind of a great care, for if all else fails, I will marry you, when you are older, and we can be poor together."

His tone is teasing, but I can imagine no greater happiness than to truly belong to Tristam forever. To hide my feelings, I sink into my deepest curtsy, pretending to accept his offer of marriage.

Tristam laughs and reaches out to me. He raises me to my feet and gallantly kisses my hand. The softness of his lips sends a shiver into parts of my body that I did not know were capable of feeling. I feel even more unbalanced as we head back toward the western gate.

I know I will probably never marry, as I am damaged wares. I cannot speak, and I have probably been defiled. I do not really belong in Blinth. I feel the black hole in me yawn wide. Tristam might be the only man who would marry me if I have been defiled.

Defiled? Have I been? Why can I not remember?

CHAPTER 27

GRACE

I love the flowers. I cannot believe our effort with the seeds has become this lush fairyland of color. I have begun working on a tapestry of the flowers to capture their beauty forever.

One day Tobias will not allow me to help in the garden, but sends me to get my tapestry instead. Though it is morning, I ply my needle in a corner of the garden. Suddenly, the gardeners swarm over the flowers, cutting all the choicest blooms. I leap from my chair and rush over to Tobias. I tug on his arm and force him to stop. I plead with my eyes for the life of each precious blossom. I feel as though my children are being murdered each time a stem is separated from its roots.

Tobias takes my hand. "Miss Grace, it is the queen's orders. She wants two dozen large arrangements at the ball tonight. I am sorry, child."

I hang my head.

"Do not worry, Grace. We will leave the buds. These plants will bloom again before the frosts of autumn."

I sigh heavily, resigning myself to the loss of our flowers.

Tobias halts all the gardeners. They all look at me as I take a long last look, memorizing the scene for my tapestry and for myself.

Tobias waits.

I take a deep breath, and nod. Tobias signals the men to resume working.

May I? I sign, reaching for Tobias's shears.

"Be my guest," he replies.

I use an angled cut on the stems so the blooms will last as long as possible. My mind wanders to Sir Tristam as I cut flowers I do not want to cut for a ball he does not wish to attend.

I become lost in a mindless haze, sorting, selecting, and cutting flowers with the longest possible stems. Eventually, Tobias touches me on the shoulder and I look up. All the gardeners are staring at me, again.

"We have enough, Grace. Did you not hear me?"

I shake my head.

"We will carry them to the arranging room. Would you like to come?"

I nod and pick up the basket I have just filled. I follow Tobias and another man into a part of the castle I have never seen. The walls are made of rough stones and the air is cool. Tables are covered with vases of all shapes and sizes. One in particular catches my eye. It is tall, flaring from a square base to a rectangular opening. I begin selecting the blossoms for this arrangement without thought.

Tobias dismisses the gardeners, as the arrangement takes shape in my hands. When I finish, I have created a display that can be viewed from all four sides. The flowers grow out of a square base and became a round whorl of color. I use dark blue irises for the largest blossoms, yellow lilies, and some small green flowers whose name I do not know.

"Grace, it is lovely. Possibly the most beautiful I have ever seen," Tobias says wonderingly. "How did you learn to do that?"

I shrug. A sudden chill sweeps through me and I wrap my arms protectively around myself. I hear footsteps and voices approaching.

"It is the ladies. They have come to arrange the flowers," Tobias explains.

"For my mother, there must always be roses," I hear Queen Laurel say. "But I prefer the wilder blossoms myself. Roses seem too...cultivated." She enters the room on those words.

Tobias touches my shoulder. He bows and I sink into a low, deep, curtsy.

"Please rise," Queen Laurel says. We obey. She opens her mouth to speak, but her eyes travel past us to the arrangement I have just completed.

"Grace, is this your work?"

I nod, while making the sign for *yes*.

"You saw her do this, Tobias?"

"Yes, Your Majesty."

"It is absolutely stunning." The queen is smiling. I see two ladies behind her exchange glances and I can feel their displeasure.

Thank you, ma'am, I sign, curtsying again.

"Grace, you must stay and help us arrange the rest of these. You have a delicate touch."

Yes, ma'am, I sign again. *Thank you.* I cannot say no to her, but I can already feel myself shrinking inside. At least two of her ladies are clearly displeased with me.

"Permission to speak, My Queen?" I hear Tobias say.

"Of course, Tobias. Your flowers are as beautiful as ever."

"Thank you, Your Highness. It is about Grace…"

"Pray, continue."

"She gets agitated if there are too many gardeners in the garden. She wants to obey you, but she may not be able to."

"Tobias, thank you for speaking freely."

Tobias nods, bowing again.

"Grace, when I said you must stay and help us, it was not a royal command. I meant that you would be *welcome* to stay and help us. We would be pleased to see your arrangements. This one is as beautiful as your tapestries. You may leave now, or whenever you wish. Do you understand?"

Yes, Your Majesty, I sign. The tightness in my chest loosens, but I still feel the hostility from some of the others.

"Good," Queen Laurel says, smiling. "Now, to work." She moves toward the flowers and vases at the far end of the table. The ladies swarm around her, chattering.

Tobias bends toward me speaking softly. "Will you be able to stay?"

I look past him over his shoulder. After a moment, I nod.

"That is the spirit. I must get back to the garden."

Thank you, I sign, *for everything.*

He gives his quick nod and slips out the door.

I stand rooted to the floor, watching the doorway through which he disappeared. The noise of voices bouncing off the stone walls feels sharp, like blows to the head. I take a deep breath and go into myself. The ladies' voices sink to the level of a hum like the bees in the garden. I am far away. I ignore everything except my fingers and the flowers and I begin to work.

I complete three more arrangements before I hear the queen speak my name.

"Grace, Lady Beltran is asking you a question."

Forgive me, I sign. *I did not hear.*

"Are you apologizing?" Queen Laurel asks.

I nod.

"You were lost in your work, were you not?"

I nod again.

"Lady Beltran has a question for you."

I turn to look at the woman she indicates. I do not like what I see. Lady Beltran's face is hard, like the stone of the castle walls. Her lips smile, but her grey eyes do not. Her voice is falsely sweet.

"Dear child, where did you learn to arrange flowers so well?" she asks.

I do not know, I sign. I also lift my shoulders and let them fall.

"My Lady, Grace does not remember her life before she came here." Queen Laurel rescues me. "What colors shall we work with next?"

"Anything you like, Your Highness," says Lady Beltran as she follows the queen away from me. "I just find it curious that her fingers remember how to embroider and arrange flowers. Perhaps she remembers more than she is telling us."

I bend over my arrangement of pink, blue, purple, and yellow flowers, but I hear the queen's response. Her voice holds a hint of steel. "What are you suggesting?"

"Nothing, My Queen. I mean no offense."

"Yet, I am offended. Grace is our guest for as long as she wishes to reside with us. It matters not where she came from, nor what her past contains. She has saved Blinthian lives, and we are in her debt. You would do well to remember it. She has never given us any reason to suspect her of deceit. I wish I could say the same of all our subjects."

I dare to peek at Lady Beltran. She blanches visibly, and the entire room is suddenly quiet.

"Shall we let bygones be bygones, My Lady?" the queen asks.

Lady Beltran sinks into a low curtsy. "If you please, Your Majesty." Her voice sounds small.

I want to know the story of Lady Beltran's deceit, as some of the ladies' eyes are merry. They are clearly enjoying her discomfort.

"I do please," the queen says. "Rise up and select some flowers for this brown vase. I think oranges and yellows would do nicely. What do you think?"

"I agree, Your Highness, and perhaps a touch of red."

"Excellent choice," the queen replies.

I stop following their conversation. Other voices resume. I slip away when I finish my fourth floral display. I feel something as I approach the door and, looking up, I see Lady Beltran's cold eyes following me. I have made another enemy in Blinth, but unlike Becca, I will not win this one over. I shiver on the other side of the door and hurry back to the warm yellow sunshine of the garden.

CHAPTER 28

TRISTAM

On the evening of the ball, I go to Grace's chamber to tell her good-night. She sits on the chair by the window. The fading evening light touches her golden hair; such a beauty she is. She is becoming a young woman right before my eyes. She looks up from her needlework as I approach; her face is solemn. She is frightened.

"What is it, Grace?"

She shakes her head as if to ward off a memory. Her eyes have a far-away look. I wait, watching her until she seems to come back to herself.

Turn around, she signs, indicating a full circle turn with her forefinger.

I turn slowly, keeping my eyes upon her face as long as possible. My fine new garments make a swishing sound as I turn.

You look so different, she signs. She is not smiling.

"But I am still me," I reply. "I thought you would say I look handsome. I was expecting compliments galore, young lady."

She responds to my teasing tone with a slight smile. *You look magnificent, but you do not look like my Tristam.*

"Well, I am your Tristam. Clothes do not make the man, Grace…"

The man makes the clothes, she signs, finishing my sentence for me.

"Well…we agree on that." I wonder where she has heard that phrase but I know better than to ask.

"I do not believe I quite make these clothes; they seem too fine for me. But I could not go to the ball in huntsman's attire."

Are you dreading it?

"No, you place too much weight on my words that night when I was tired. I look forward to mingling with my old friends."

Really?

"Really, truly. I do not miss the maneuvering, but court is more than that. I have missed my old friends, and the food. Shall I bring you back pastries?"

Yes, please.

"Do not wait up for me. I will wrap them so they will keep until morning."

Thank you. Try to enjoy yourself. And you do look wonderful, so like a noble Sir.

"A penniless noble Sir, in finery provided by my king. This may be more fun than I thought. No one will be pursuing me, that is certain."

Grace smiles and I kiss her forehead. I find it ironic that my last words to her are about being penniless. Her demeanor worries me. She is afraid of me in noble attire. What, if anything, does that signify? I want answers. I realize, in that moment, that I want more than answers; I finally acknowledge to myself that I want to avenge every wrong that has been done to Grace. I thought I had given up on revenge. It seems I have not.

While standing in the receiving line, I ponder avenging Grace. My battle skills are rusty, if I still have any at all; getting myself killed certainly would not be helpful to her. However, she has yet to remember anything. If I start training, I could be in shape when she begins to retrieve her past. Deep in thought, I simply nod hello to acquaintances as I wait in line.

A loud voice breaks into my reverie. "Well, as I live and breathe! If it is not the long-lost Sir Tristam!"

Broderick's hand claps me so hard on the back that I nearly stumble into the couple standing in line ahead of me. Heads turn to look at us. A few whispers begin behind cupped hands.

"Brody, I see you have not changed a bit. I wish to thank you for helping me remain quietly in the shadows."

"It is time for you to come out into the light. You have been absent for too long."

"I find it interesting that you should come along right at this moment and say so. I may need your help with a little project I am contemplating."

"The more crazy and daring the project, the more committed I am."

"Considering some of your exploits, I am frankly surprised you have not been 'committed' along with the other lunatics."

Broderick's boisterous laugh turns heads for a second time.

"The king needs a crazy knight too much to lock me up. Besides, with you hunting nothing but game, I am his only man for the daring missions."

"Well, we may not want the king to know about this mission," I reply, lowering my voice. "We should talk about it later."

"First day back at court, you are, and already heading for trouble. I thought they said you changed."

"I thought I had, but maybe not."

"Tristam, at least give me a hint."

"Well, you have heard of this child I adopted?"

"Oh, yes, everywhere I go. She is the object of much discussion."

"Really?"

"Yes, you cannot bring a beautiful foreign girl into the castle and not set tongues wagging."

"What is being said about her?"

"Easy Tristam, no need to look so grim."

"Well?"

"They say she is beautiful beyond compare. That she has you eating out of her hand."

I chuckle. "Well, that part is true. What else do they say?"

"They say she could talk if she wanted to and that she is only pretending not to remember."

"Why would she do that?"

"So she does not have to go back home or tell anyone she was defiled."

My eyes flash. I clench my jaw.

"Tris, it is not like you to be concerned about gossip. What is really on your mind?"

"I do not know how I am going to establish her in society."

"Rumors say she wants to marry you."

"Brody, she is a child, near in age to Faith. I have no intention of marrying her."

Brody raises his eyebrows. "Whatever you say, Tris. Look, Lady Tavenor is summoning you. It is good to see you." He grips my shoulder and is gone.

Before I can gather my thoughts or move to greet Lady Tavenor, Lady Beltran approaches me. She must have been waiting for an opening. "Ah, dear Tristam, so good to see you back where you belong."

"Why thank you, Lady Beltran." I bow.

"I suppose Grace told you how she won over the queen this afternoon with her flower arranging?"

"She did not mention it."

"Really?" The lady raises her eyebrows.

"Really," my reply is cool.

"Well, look around. The arrangements in the most prominent places are the ones Grace made. She did that one in the main entryway, and that one on the table by the queen. She is quite a talented child."

"Thank you." I bow again. I want her to leave.

"I have seen the needlework piece she gave Their Majesties. It is also quite lovely."

I bow again without speaking.

"Really...if my Melanie were not already betrothed, I could find it in my heart to be quite jealous."

"How old is Melanie?" I remember a short child of nine or ten years, with fawn-colored hair.

"She is turning twelve," the lady replies.

I raise my eyebrows.

"But the wedding will not take place for at least two years," she continues.

"I think that is wise. I think children deserve a chance to actually be children. Who is the lucky groom to be?"

"Lord Dunbar," Lady Beltran announces proudly.

Lord Dunbar is at least fifteen years my senior. He has three sons and one daughter, all of whom are married with children of their own. I become aware that Lady Beltran is still speaking.

"He lost his dear wife shortly after you lost Lady Constance. He has not looked at another, until he met my Melanie."

"Congratulations," I manage to say without choking on the words. "Is she happy?"

"Quite ecstatic. She is looking forward to being Lady Dunbar. She will be seated higher up the table at state dinners than her parents. She can barely wait."

"Well, that is marvelous."

"Yes, it truly is. So you see, I have no reason to be jealous of the favor your Grace finds with the king and queen. But be aware that other mothers may have."

"My dear Lady Beltran," the courtly words flow off my tongue, "with all due respect, I will heed your kind warning. But I hardly think a penniless, mute child will be the object of envy. Pity is more likely."

"She will not be penniless for long with you as her sponsor. Surely you mean to dower her. Her muteness is part of her charm. I think she is smart enough to realize that. I predict she will never speak."

The hair on my scalp prickles. Fire leaps from my belly to my throat and I control myself with effort. "My dear lady, please explain. First, how am I to dower her when I myself am destitute? Is there a noble family who would accept a stag or two as a dowry?"

"Lord Tristam, you are the third largest landholder in Blinth behind only the Tavenors and the Dunbars. Surely you are tired of playing the huntsman by now?" Her voice has an edge.

"My dear Lady, you are always well-informed. Has it slipped your notice that I gave away my holdings?"

"You gave them to the king," she replies.

"To do with as he pleased."

"Well, you should ask him what his pleasure is. I must go, I see Lady—"

"Not quite so fast," I say, grasping her wrist as she turns to leave. Her eyes travel from my hand on her wrist to my face, and there is not an ounce of warmth in her gaze. I release my grip. She smooths the skin of the wrist I have been holding.

"You forget yourself." It is a statement, a rebuke.

"Pray, forgive me," I reply. "I merely wish to know what it is that you know."

"The king is holding your land in trust for you. You are the only one who believes you are penniless. I doubt even Grace believes it."

"You do not know Grace."

"Do you?" she asks, slipping away.

CHAPTER 29

TRISTAM

I stand fuming as the line snakes slowly toward the dais at the front of the room. An alto voice speaks in my ear. "That was quite an exchange between you and our dear friend, Lady Beltran."

"Why Lady Tavenor, a pleasure to see you." My face lights up in a genuine smile.

"Yes, I thought I might be a welcome relief after spending time with dear Lady Beltran. Why do you let her upset you?"

"I do not know. She implied that Grace is mute by choice and that she is manipulating me. The queen…"

"Tristam, Lady Beltran is jealous of Grace. The dear lady made the same implications this afternoon, and the queen ruthlessly set her in her place. I confess it was a pleasure to observe."

"Why be jealous of a penniless, voiceless foreigner?"

"She is really jealous of you. She and that spineless husband of hers tried to get the king to give them the portion of your land that adjoins their estate. Not only did they not get the land, Lord Beltran spent six months at the border on guard patrol, as punishment for his greed."

"So what has the king done with the land?"

"I believe he is holding it in trust for his best knight."

"I thought Lady Beltran was lying."

"Not this time."

"I…I do not know what to say."

"You do not have to say anything. I can stand here and do all the talking. People will leave you alone and you can have a moment to grow accustomed."

"I think it is going to take more than a moment. I am not resigned to this. I gave away my lands in good faith."

"Yes, Tristam, you did. But put yourself in King Stefan's position. How could he parcel out your land as favors to his nobles when your wife and daughter were abducted on Blinthian soil while you were away serving at King Leopold's pleasure? King Leopold held on to your land for you. How could King Stefan then do otherwise?"

"I must talk with him."

"Yes, but not tonight. You are still an impetuous youth, despite your thirty-odd years. Proceed slowly. That is good advice from an old woman."

"You are not an old woman."

"I am the same age your sainted mother would be if she had not succumbed to the fever. In her absence, I am offering advice which you are, of course, free not to follow."

"I will try to follow it."

"Excellent. While you are in an agreeable mood, I will offer further advice. Put Grace in the company of the nobility. The rumors about her run rampant because no one knows her. She seems like a sweet child."

"I certainly think so, but Lady Beltran thinks Grace is deceitful."

"Oh, for goodness sake, Tristam! Lady Beltran is a most manipulative woman; it colors how she sees everyone. Why are you letting her words annoy you?"

"I do not really know. Grace is so…vulnerable."

"She is not the only one."

"Who else is vulnerable?"

"You are coming back to us, Tristam. You went through some difficult times and made some unusual choices. Your father is not here anymore. You are still fairly young for all the lands you hold. I like you; I always have. Your dear mother was my closest friend. So please, take care of yourself."

"How do you suggest I do that?"

"You also need to spend time amongst the nobles. The alliances have shifted."

"How so?"

"I could not begin to put it into words and do not want my perceptions to color your own. You will figure it out—you were always very good at strategic thinking. You are almost to the front of the line, so I will take my leave of you. Farewell, my dear."

"Thank you, My Lady."

She shakes her head, waves her hand and disappears into the crowd.

Eventually I make my way to the front of the line. "Sir Tristam of

Langstonhorn," is how I am announced to the royal party.

Queen Laurel greets me graciously and introduces me to her mother. As I take my leave of her, she leans toward me and lowers her voice. "Grace did a wonderful job with the flowers today. Lady Beltran is quite jealous."

"Thank you most sincerely, Your Majesty."

"Sir Tristam, it is truly a pleasure."

I can tell by the look in her eye that she means what she says. I receive the impression she enjoys sparring with Lady Beltran. I am grateful the queen has bestowed her favor upon Grace.

"Well, Sir Tristam of Langstonhorn, how are you this fine evening?" The king greets me jovially.

"I am shocked to find that I am still Sir Tristam of Langstonhorn, Sire."

"So the word has leaked to you; you do not seem pleased."

"That is correct, Your Highness. I am not reconciled to taking back what I gave into your father's keeping. I would rather start over again."

"Tristam, this is neither the time nor the place for this discussion. Besides, I need you."

I raise my eyebrows.

"We will talk soon. I have my reasons. Oh, and my queen is most pleased with Grace."

"I am delighted," I reply.

"Well, I am glad something pleases you, even if it is not me. Go talk, dance, and eat something. There is a great deal of food."

"That is an order I can joyfully obey. Thank you, Your Majesty. I have missed the royal pastry chef's delicacies."

"Well, go and enjoy. Come see me on the sixth day of the next week. Come early. We will ride and discuss that other matter."

"As you wish, Sire."

I bow deeply and leave the dais, heading for the food tables. I am quietly munching on my delicacies when I notice Lady Geneva across the room, deep in conversation with a rather portly gentleman. The man keeps moving toward her and she surreptitiously takes a step back. Pretty soon, however, the gentleman is going to have her cornered. I decide to take matters into my own hands. I finish my plate and set it aside.

I approach Lady Geneva and make my finest bow. "There you are, good Lady, you cannot escape me. We are promised for this dance."

"Please forgive me, good Sir; I did not mean to slight you. I was deep in conversation with Lord Dunbar. Are you acquainted with Sir Tristam of Langstonhorn, My Lord?"

"I knew your father well. Sorry we lost him so young. He was a good man."

"Thank you, sir. I understand that congratulations are in order."

Lord Dunbar looks puzzled, "Eh?"

"On your betrothal to the Beltrans' daughter, Melanie."

"Oh, well…It is in the early stages of discussion. Nothing formal has yet been announced. The child seems a bit young to me, but the mother seems quite set on it. Where did you hear that bit of news?"

"I heard it from the child's mother, of course. Look, she approaches now. We will leave you, Lord Dunbar. Lady Geneva, shall we?" Geneva's eyes look gratefully up into mine as she takes my arm.

"Lord Dunbar did not look pleased to relinquish you to me," I whisper to Geneva, while leading her to the dance floor.

"Well, I am delighted to have escaped even though you lied about having asked for this dance."

"I know."

"How could you know?"

"I watched him move a step forward and you move a step backward for a while. It was an unusual dance, but you did not have many more steps until you would have been driven against the wall. I decided it was time for a rescue."

"That lecherous old goat. Is he really engaged? He was wooing me, dreadfully."

"Oh, had he promised you marriage?" I ask, mercilessly teasing Geneva. "He is the wealthiest landowner in Blinth, other than the king. Have I done you a disservice? Shall I take you back to him?"

Geneva slaps my arm. "Do not dare take me back! No amount of money would make marriage with him acceptable to me. Where did you learn that anyway? That does not sound like something you would know."

"Dear Lady Beltran, of course."

"Talking to her is worse than talking to him. Do you really think that poor Melanie Beltran is betrothed to that fat old man? She is not much older than Grace."

"I neither know nor care," I reply.

"Well, if she is, I think it is criminal. He was going to make me a proposal tonight but not of marriage. He is horrid."

Lady Geneva momentarily lapses into silence as I maneuver us into a place on the dance floor.

"That explains Lady Beltran's comment about the moral laxness of widowed ladies," Geneva continues.

"Oh, really? Did she make such a comment?"

Geneva nods, and I burst out laughing.

"Yes, and I could not figure out what in the world she was talking about."

"Of course, it made no sense. She is making it up to protect her daughter's dubious claim to Lord Dunbar."

"Yes, but she will tarnish my reputation if she can."

"Well, she cannot. Everyone knows she is a spiteful gossip; Lady Tavenor just reminded me of that fact."

"Yes. What I cannot understand is why people believe her. She is scheming and transparent."

"Geneva, have you not figured out that far too many people are fools?"

This time Geneva bursts into laughter. "I guess you are right. I never really thought about it, not like that, anyway."

"That is because you are so much kinder than I am."

When we finish our dance, I get a plate for her and find a quiet place where we can talk. "Geneva, may I ask you a question?"

"Of course."

"It is rather personal."

"Well, we have already discussed my morals and Lord Dunbar's indecent intentions; I have no further secrets to hide."

"Well...I want to talk to you about that proposal. Do men bother you, since..."

"Since my husband died?" she finishes for me.

"Yes, that is what I am asking."

"Sometimes, but I can handle myself."

"I know you can; you are an amazing woman. Just know that if you ever need anyone..."

"If I need a man, you mean?"

"Yes, that is what I mean. I owe you so much. It would be a pleasure to assist you in any way possible, especially if it meant fighting a lecher like Dunbar."

Geneva smiles and looks away. She takes a deep breath before replying. "Tristam, thank you, but you owe me nothing. I assure you, I am a woman who can handle herself."

"But still, just a young woman. How long were you and your husband married?"

"Six weeks, three days, and fourteen hours. Only I feel like we are still married."

"How long since he died?"

"Three years, two months, and twelve days."

"What, you are not counting hours and minutes?"

I watch Lady Geneva's face as she does some calculating. "Six hours and thirty minutes."

"I remember your husband. He was a promising squire when I last saw him. He would have made a fine knight."

Geneva does not reply. She is looking off into the main hall. "Thank you," she finally says. "My parents wanted us to wait to marry until he was knighted. Had we waited, we would never have wed."

"Do you wish you had heeded their advice?"

"Never!"

"Even though your life is not easy?"

"My life is fine, Tristam. I fulfill a unique role. I feel blessed to serve Their Majesties with my healing abilities."

"We are fortunate to have you."

At that moment we are interrupted by a page. "Excuse me, Lady Geneva."

"Yes, Page John?"

"Nurse Addie is asking for you. There is a sick infant in need of your help."

"Right on cue," I add.

Geneva casts me a reproachful look.

"Sir?" the page inquires.

"Ignore him, John. Will you take me to Addie?"

"Yes, ma'am."

"Goodnight, Sir Tristam. Thank you for the dance."

"No, Geneva, I will walk with you to Nurse Addie."

"That is not necessary."

"But it will please me. I can check on Grace. If Addie is occupied, I should be close by."

"Well, then, I appreciate your escort."

She rises and gives me her arm. "Lead on, Page John."

CHAPTER 30

TRISTAM

My meeting with King Stefan takes place three days after the departure of the party from Chantrell. The king is riding a great black stallion and I am mounted upon my trusty Rufus.

King Stefan begins in much the same way he spoke during the ball. "Be reasonable, Tristam. My father could not have given your family's holdings away while you were in the depths of your grief. Had either your father or your brother still been alive, I have no doubt he would have given your holdings to one of them with the understanding they would return your lands to you at the appropriate time. But as you are the last of your name, that was not an option. I chose to continue to follow my father's direction is this matter. My hope is that you will remarry and carry on your family name. Langstonhorns have been serving the royal family for generations; it is not a tradition I am eager to see end. Frankly, we could use your solid support amongst the nobility. Few are as loyal as Langstonhorns."

"My family owes you much, Sire, even if I am the only one left."

"I would like to see that change; I wish for your family to grow," he replies.

"Well, you will be glad to know that Grace wishes to marry me," I reply. "I teased her about it and she played along, accepting my proposal."

"You could become betrothed. She is not too young for that," the king replies.

"Do be serious. I am an old man compared to her."

"She is between eleven and thirteen years old, and you are thirty. Many of our nobles have an even greater age difference in their marriages."

"And you approve of such marriages?"

"It is not for me to approve or disapprove a particular union. Who but God knows what really goes on inside a marriage?"

"Would you want your daughter to marry a man twenty or thirty years older than she is?"

"If I had a daughter, I suppose it would depend upon the man himself."

"But it would not depend upon the dowry, would it?"

"Do you ask that to insult me?"

"No, Sire, but to make my point. I am set against marriages that are basically nothing but the selling of a daughter for material gain."

"Not all disparate age marriages are based on economics, Tristam. Some are based on love."

"Really, Sire. Love may grow, but how can a child love a man old enough to be her father? How can marital relations not be disgusting to her?"

"Oh, and all young men are gentle with their brides, never causing disgust or fear." His sarcasm is biting.

"I see your point," I reply.

"How old were you when you married Lady Constance?"

"I was eighteen."

"How old was she?"

"She was fifteen."

"And you two were very happy. That was obvious to everyone, but that is not the only type of marriage that can work. Do you know Lady Tavenor's age?

"No, Sire."

"Neither do I, but I know twenty-five years separate her and her Lord. They always seem happy together."

I make no reply.

"Grace loves you. You would husband her well. She may not have another opportunity," the king continues.

"Oh, she will have plenty of opportunity when I dower her with Tristenhorn," I reply.

"So, she will be married for your money?"

"No, Sir. She will not be forbidden from marrying her true love by his greedy parents. They will be pleased with her dowry and will ignore her lineage."

"What if you are her true love?"

"Right now, I love her as a father. I trust it will always be so."

"She loves you and you are not her father, you are her hero."

"Well, I have feet of clay, so that will not last."

"You cannot know that. At any rate, I am delighted to learn you are taking your holdings back so you can dower Grace. When do you wish to assume control?"

"Not yet, Sire, if it pleases you. I do not wish to make any great changes until Grace is more secure, perhaps until she begins talking. I also have a job to do, gathering the winter stores of meat. That will keep me occupied well into the fall."

"Another leader could be appointed."

I keep silent.

"But I can wait. I admire your work with the child, Sir Tristam. It is nice to have you back in the castle. I am in no hurry for you to move out to your estates just yet."

"Thank you, Sire."

"I miss the days when you called me Stefan."

"You were an excellent page when I met you as Stefan. Now that you are king, you will always be my Sire."

"Have it your way, Tristam. It is good to have you back, even if you call me Sire."

I bow as low as possible while riding. "Thank you most kindly, your Revered Majesty, King Stefan, of the bountiful country of Blinth." My eyes are twinkling merrily when I rise.

King Stefan slaps me with his gloves. "Oh, do go away, you irritating Sir Tristam of Langstonhorn."

"What, and leave you alone in the forest? I think not."

"Are you disobeying a direct order from your king?"

"I am guarding my Sovereign," I reply.

"Then gallop with me."

I obey. I wonder if he has any idea how grateful I am for his care of me, of my lands, and especially of my Grace.

CHAPTER 31

GRACE

I knew something had happened at the ball to disturb Tristam. He did not speak to me of it until after he had ridden out with the king on a morning in early August. The next day, we left the castle by the western gate, supposedly to practice our archery. When we were well away from the gate, Tristam's demeanor became serious.

"Grace, come sit with me," he commands, spreading his coat over a log and indicating I should sit.

I cast him an apprehensive glance and obey.

"King Stefan has returned both my estate and the estate of my fore-fathers to me."

You found that out at the ball, I sign.

"How did you know that?" he asks.

I shrug my shoulders. I do not know how I knew that something had been bothering him.

"You are no longer the ward of a penniless man. I shall be able to provide for you as befits your station in life."

Is this what you want? I sign.

"King Stefan needs me. You need me. I have hidden from my place in the world for too long."

You did not answer the question, I insist.

"Grace, you care more for my happiness than for your own, do you not?"

All I really need is to know Tristam is nearby. Whether I live in the castle, on an estate, or in a cottage is not important. It is impossible to sign my thoughts. I try to explain. *I need to be near you.... That is all I need.*

Tristam studies me carefully. "I do not understand your signs. Would you try again, please?"

It was difficult to attempt to sign it the first time. I am scared to admit I need anyone. I make the sign for money and shake my head.

"You do not care about money?" Tristam asks.

I nod.

"What do you care about?"

I point at him, while studying the ground.

He slides his arm around my shoulder and pulls me to him. "I need you, also. I want to provide you with a good life."

I want you to be happy, I sign emphatically.

"I am happy, happier than I ever expected I could be again in this life."

I point at his furrowed brow.

"Oh, child, you keep reminding me that I am allowed no secrets. I do not see my way clearly, that is all. There will be a great deal of change for both of us."

I make the sign for *school*.

"You would have begun school, even had this not occurred. The king commanded it." He speaks gently while studying my face.

I know, I sign.

"Grace, it is classes with other girls and a few classes with boys. How bad can it be?"

I shake my head. He knows so little. Dread settles in my gut. I can no longer sit. I stand, taking aim at a squirrel that came out of hiding as we talked.

I use the coordination of my hand and eye, drawing the bowstring taut and releasing the arrow cleanly. My arrow finds its target and pierces the right eye of the squirrel. The horror of blood oozing around my arrow where seconds before there was a seeing eye is indescribable.

Tristam moves forward to bag the carcass. I do not wait for him, but begin walking back to the castle immediately.

The nightmares return. At first, the dreams are impossible to remember. I simply waken with clenched teeth and a tight stomach. I never feel rested. I never feel calm. I know how to keep busy.

Just as I can lose myself in the setting of a stitch, in the tiny details of creating something beautiful, so can I lose myself in the stringing of the arrow. Every facet of archery requires concentration. The placement of the feet, the height of the shoulder, the grip of the hands, and especially the release of the arrow require all of me. I am not certain if it is Tristam's news or the horror of that dead squirrel that releases the nightmares from their hiding place, but after that day, I only practice archery on objects that do not have life.

CHAPTER 32

GRACE

August ends much too quickly. Noble classes are worse than I had expected and I had expected them to be horrid.

Being surrounded by people and completely alone is worse than being surrounded only by dark pines. At school, I pretend to be in a forest. The chatter of noble children is only the wind rattling dead branches or the chirruping of the fat black squirrels that eat pine seeds from cones.

The classes I take with just the girls are the most difficult. We study deportment, etiquette, and other feminine arts, sequestered well away from our male counterparts. The young men are studying heraldry, falconry, and the etiquette of knighthood. I would much prefer to study with them.

The short stout dame who teaches us is neither intelligent nor compassionate. She seems frightened of me, and I am largely ignored, except by the girls around me. I am more often teased and taunted in the classes that have no male students. When the boys are with us, the girls ignore me.

The classes we take with the boys are reading, writing, figuring with numbers, and formal dancing. No one wants me for their partner.

My teachers treat me like some particularly dimwitted child. They speak loudly and slowly when addressing me. When we turn in written assignments, they accuse me of cheating. Kept inside from the autumn sunshine, I redo my assignment under the watchful eye of the junior teacher. The next day it is a senior teacher. In October, I am taken before the headmaster of the school.

"She writes our language, Blinthian, better than any other child in the school, yet she cannot speak," my teacher relates.

114

"Thank you," Headmaster replies, "that will be all."

Silence fills the chamber. I raise my eyes from the floor to glance at Headmaster's face. He is looking directly at me.

"Do they always talk about you as if you are not in the room?"

I nod with my eyes on the floor.

"I suspect you write well because you have much to say and no other voice."

I raise my eyes to his for a quick moment.

"I see we understand one another." There is an intelligent gleam in his deep blue eyes. He looks much younger for a moment. "Shall we work on this gift of yours together?" I make the sign for please without thinking. He mimics my movement.

"What is this?" he asks, pushing a piece of parchment, a quill, and ink toward me.

"Please," I write.

"Good. Will you be kind enough to teach me your language?"

"Certainly," I write.

"Because I like to learn new things," he replies to my unasked question. His lips do not curve, but his eyes are sparkling. I give him a small smile.

"Do the children tease you?" he asks.

I look out the window. My smile is gone.

"I see."

I send a question with my eyes.

"I have been teaching for a long time. Many times I have seen children turn upon those who are different."

My eyes look back out the window.

"Yet many times those who are different are indeed our brightest."

My eyes return to his face.

"I have seen your writing and your tapestries. You have much work to do with your gifts."

I do not know what to say, but apparently no response is necessary.

"You will come each week to work with me, here. For now, you are dismissed."

After my weekly meetings with Headmaster begin, school becomes a bit more pleasant. He makes learning interesting, and he challenges me.

"Tristam found you to the north, so perhaps the language of Lolgothe is your native tongue." He then says something in a language other than Blinthian. "Can you understand those words?" he asks.

The words stir something inside me, and I wrap my arms across my chest.

"Never mind, Grace. We will learn foreign languages when your Blinthian improves."

Eventually, he teaches me to write the languages of Lolgothe and Traag, in addition to Blinthian. At first, this special instruction is one more thing the other children tease me about, but by December, my weekly meetings with Headmaster no longer hold anyone's interest. By January, I have become invisible.

CHAPTER 33

TRISTAM

All fall, I suspect that King Stefan's plan for Grace's socialization is failing. At Christmas Festival, my suspicions are confirmed. The few children who speak to Grace do so in formal tones. Grace never smiles amongst her peers. No one signs as Becca does.

I am surprised when Headmaster approaches, greets me, and signs to Grace. I watch their conversation. After an exchange of pleasantries, he sends her off to procure some mulled wine.

"She is a remarkable girl," he says to me.

"She is remarkably isolated," I reply.

"The special children always are, unless they shine at the games, as you did."

"That was a long time ago."

"Yes, but nothing really changes, does it?" He pauses before continuing. "Tell me, is she as good at archery as rumors claim?"

"I have not heard the rumors." My response sounds surly in my own ears.

"Nevertheless, I feel certain you can answer the question."

I feel suitably chastised. "She will outshoot me someday."

"Your record from your last spring games still stands."

"Perhaps it is time it fell," I reply.

"Ah, Tristam, your wit never disappoints me. Have a nice evening." He ends the conversation by walking away.

In January and February, I train Grace with the bow in the relative warmth of the stables. In March, we move to the forests. Soon, her aim and distance rival that of my former huntsmen. Her arms, shoulders, and legs grow strong. To me, she looks like a goddess when her arrow is drawn back against the bowstring.

More importantly, she seems happy during her training. Becca joins us when she can, and together the girls supply Daniel's family with much-needed game in the last months of winter. Grace will only shoot at live targets if the meat and skins are used, and she never aims at an animal's head. I notice that the girls' competition at archery does not seem to affect their friendship. I am more grateful to Becca than she will ever know; Grace seems almost like any other girl when she is with Becca.

My days are full of plans for the two estates. I often ride out to Langstonhorn or Tristenhorn after Grace leaves for classes in the morning. I return in the late afternoon and use the last hour of daylight for training the girls in archery. After supper, Grace works at her studies while I go over account books. We work at the same table in companionable silence. The rhythm of the days is pleasant and I am lulled into a false sense of security.

CHAPTER 34

GRACE

I do not remember exactly when the nightmares return. We are still practicing archery in the stables because the weather has not warmed much. Sometimes we see one or two of the huntsmen, though Thomas seems to be assigned to the task of checking on the hunting horses and their tack often. He watches us carefully, once offering Becca a pointer on her stance while Tristam nodded his approval. I find I miss Thomas's friendly face when our training moves outside.

I know I was having nightmares by the end of February, but I barely remember their content beyond a flash of the night sky through the pines. I remember running and the panicky feelings I have upon waking. Sometimes I awake sweat-drenched and panting. I keep a cup of water by my bed to soothe my parched throat.

In March, the dream comes more frequently, until nights without the visitation are rare. Perhaps I should have asked for Geneva's sleeping herbs, but I want to know what the dream has to tell me. I am frightened by it, but I want to know about my past.

CHAPTER 35

TRISTAM

I wake to pounding on the door of my room. "It is open," I call out.

A young guard bursts through the door. I do not know his name.

"It is Grace, My Lord. She has fled the castle."

I leap up, reaching for my coat. "What happened?" I demand.

"I do not know. We were guarding the main gate when a swift figure approached. We called for her to stop, but she slipped through the side and ran into the forest."

"Why did you not stop her?"

"The other guard tried, My Lord, but she ran like the devil himself was after her. We could not abandon our post."

I nod. "You had best return."

"I am sorry, Sir," his voice trails off.

"You did your job and I thank you. Please give orders for my horse to be saddled."

I take time to gather a blanket, knife, bow and arrows, a flask of water, and my flint. At the gate, I speak to the other guard, the one who had followed her.

"She went due west, Sir," he replies to my query. "I turned back at the large stones, halfway to the Boldengarth. She cannot ford that river, My Lord."

I nod, turning toward the stable. Thomas appears out of dark leading two saddle horses.

"Are you not simply the man of the hour?" I say.

He shrugs off my compliment. "I was putting ointment on a graze on Mark's horse when your order was delivered. It is Grace, is it not?"

"Yes."

"May I come? I want to help."

"Let us go."

We swing up into our saddles and the guards open the main gates for us to pass. "Godspeed," they call out.

"God's peace," we reply from the liturgy.

We cannot travel fast; Grace left a barely discernible trail that is difficult to follow on the well-worn western trail. At the Boldengarth, she turned southward along a lesser trail. Here her tracks are easier to follow, even before they are marked by blood.

Her trail ends in a partially open clearing where some large bushes grow. She has pulled dry leaves and pine boughs into a heap in which to hide. I approach her cautiously, signaling Thomas to stay back with the horses.

When I am several paces from the pile, I begin talking to her in a normal voice.

"Grace, it is Tristam. Thomas is behind me, with the horses. Rufus is here, and Timber. We are going to take you home. Do you understand, Grace?"

I wait, but not a leaf rustles in her pile.

"Grace, I am coming closer. I know your feet are bleeding. I need to see if you have other wounds. I am going to uncover you." I reach out and touch the pile. She cowers back further under the bushes, raising herself to a crouch. Her eyes are wide and riveted on mine. There is no recognition in them.

"Grace, it is me, Tristam. Remember me?"

She does not move.

"I am going to touch your foot," I say, reaching out.

Her hand shoots out and punches my arm away. She crouches, her eyes darting, as if she is going to run.

I back up several paces. Her eyes stop their frantic movement. She watches me intently and I begin to sign.

Grace, wake up. It is me, Tristam. I love you. I want to take you home to the castle in Blinth. Remember the castle? Remember Addie, Geneva, and Becca? I want to hold you, my precious Grace.

She watches my hands in the light of an early grey dawn.

I keep signing. *Do you remember your tapestry? Do you remember Tobias in the garden? All of these people love you, Grace. I love you. I want you to come home, please. Please, will you come home?*

Her eyes look more alive as she watches my hands. Her shoulders relax and lower away from her ears. She begins to stand up.

121

"No, Grace. Do not stand on your feet," I speak without thinking. She freezes. Her eyes begin to dart back and forth. *I am sorry*, I sign. *I did not mean to startle you.* I ramble on for a while. Her eyes focus on my hands. *Do you see Thomas behind me with the horses?*

She gives a barely perceptible nod.

He is going to bring them over.

I turn and motion to Thomas. He comes immediately, holding out the blanket. I take it from him and hold it out toward Grace, laying it on the ground between us.

Shall we go home? I sign.

This time she gives a small, distinct nod and rises to her feet. I catch her as she begins to fall and she shivers in my arms. Thomas wraps the blanket around her without speaking. He leads me to a stump and helps me mount Rufus so I do not have to set Grace down. I cradle her in front of me as Thomas leads the way home. Grace neither moves nor signs. She does not help me, but neither does she struggle. Her eyes have lost their wildness, but she still looks hunted. My heart is heavy within my chest.

The morning routine of the castle is fully underway when we arrive. The guards have not changed, which is fortunate. One of them helps us enter the stables by opening a side gate.

"I will take care of the horses," Thomas assures me.

I smile my thanks, afraid to startle Grace by speaking. I carry her to her room. By some miraculous coincidence, the only person I see is Addie.

"Fetch Geneva," I quietly command her.

"Yes, Sir. Right away," she whispers back.

I feel as though I have been transported back to the previous March, when we first found Grace. She is taller and stronger and her braid is longer, but she is the same ghostly white. She acts as terrified as when we were strangers and just as distant.

Geneva arrives and brings with her basins, bandages, herbs, and salves. She gives orders in her calm, reassuring way. She doses Grace with sleeping herb, then studies her feet but does not touch them. Her feet are not as badly damaged as they had been a year ago. I sit in a chair by the head of Grace's bed and watch as Addie lays blankets over Grace and then wraps one around me while placing a mug of hot cider in my hands. Maidservants build up a roaring fire.

Geneva boils rags in a pot over the fire to clean them. Addie follows Geneva's instructions. I finish my cider before Geneva touches Grace's right foot, at the same time she is telling Grace everything she is going to do.

"Grace, I need to bathe your feet. Are you ready?"

Grace does not sign.

"Grace, come back. I need your permission. May I bathe your feet?"

Grace gives a tiny nod.

In time, Geneva bandages Grace's feet and moves on to the cuts on her face. One, near her right eye, is deep and jagged, surrounded by a purplish bruise. Grace gives no sign of pain as Geneva nurses her. It is as if Grace does not inhabit her own body. I rage at my helplessness in the face of this child's pain, and fear that all her gains have been lost.

Eventually, the bustle around Grace calms. One by one, people exit the room. Before she leaves, Geneva whispers instructions for me about the herbal medicine.

Grace still has her eyes open, staring at the ceiling, though I know Geneva has given her a strong dose of the sleeping draught. I draw her attention to me and try signing.

Grace, can you understand me? I ask. She is completely unresponsive, yet her eyes follow the movement of my hands.

Grace, I am so sorry you are hurt, I sign. *I love you and will protect you. I am going to stay right here beside you in this chair for the rest of the night. Will that make you feel safer?*

She looks into my eyes and there is a spark of recognition. She gives me a tiny nod.

Would you like me to hold your hand, dear?

Her eyes looked frightened and she draws her hands under the coverlet.

Then I will not do so, I reply. *Do you think you can rest?*

Her shoulders give a tiny shrug.

Try, my darling, and I will watch over you.

I watch her until her breathing evens and her eyes close, but I do not sleep at all.

CHAPTER 36

GRACE

I fight my way up from a drugged sleep, as a sense of panic grips my chest. Breathing is difficult. I rise to a sitting position and swing my feet toward the floor.

"Grace," a voice calls out. Why "Grace"? That is not my name. I reach for my name, but nothing comes.

"You cannot walk," the voice continues, and a hand grips my forearm. I throw it off. Panic rises in my throat.

Hands grip my shoulders. "It is me, Tristam. Look at me."

I know that voice. The panic eases and I obey.

"Grace, you are safe. The danger is over." Tristam's eyes bore into mine. His grip on my shoulders is strong. I see pain in his eyes, and love.

My mind feels jumbled. I look around the room, seeing the washstand, the fireplace, and the familiar high, narrow window. I shake my head, attempting to clear my mind. I remember darkness, a forest, and running.

"The danger is over…" he repeats.

I nod, slowly.

"I think you had a dream."

I nod. His words seem true.

"It was only a nightmare."

I shake my head.

"What are you saying?" he asks. "Do you remember anything?"

No, I sign, *no details. But the dream is real.*

Tristam's mouth becomes a straight line. His brow furrows. He looks away and then back before nodding.

"I guess we both knew that." He squeezes my shoulders and kisses the top of my head before returning to his chair.

I make the discovery that my feet are bandaged. *What happened to me?*

"What do you remember?"

I remember falling asleep and waking up right here...afraid.

"Do you remember any dreams or nightmares?"

I remember being terrified and running through a forest. I was being chased in my dream. But what happened to me? How did I get injured? I demand with my signs.

He tells me.

I do not like what I hear. I remember nothing. What is wrong with me? I have to find out.

Life becomes the routine I remember so well from the previous March. Geneva comes and goes, changing bandages and doling out herbal potions. Tristam spends large amounts of time working on his accounts in my room. I work on a tapestry of Tobias's garden in full bloom under a summer sky. The bright colors cheer me.

I have visitors. This is a change from the previous year. Becca comes, fussing over me and calling me an idiot.

I feel like an idiot, I sign.

"Well, you really scared Thomas."

Thomas?

"Yes, Thomas. He saddled the horses and went with Tristam."

I search my memory.

"You really do not remember anything, do you?"

I shake my head.

"What has Tristam told you?"

That I ran out of the castle, past the guards and into the forest. That he tracked me and brought me back on Rufus.

"Thomas helped him," Becca says. "Tristam has sworn him to secrecy. But he had already told me," she amended, "before Tristam made him swear."

Why secrecy?

"So no one gossips."

You can never stop people from gossiping.

"Grace, how can you be so pessimistic? Tristam is doing everything he can to protect you!"

I blink at Becca. I cannot stop tears from pooling in my eyes. I write what I cannot say.

"I am not ungrateful to Tristam. I owe him everything. I just meant that those who gossip will always talk about me, and I keep giving them more to talk about. I really am an idiot."

"You could not help it. You did not know what you were doing. It is not your fault."

"Well, whose fault is it?"

"I wish I knew. There are a lot of us who would like to find out. There are some horrible people somewhere who have a lot to answer for."

I draw my knees to my chest. I never want to see anyone who hurt me ever again. I want them to stay in the past.

I have never thought of revenge, I sign.

"Well, I have, and I would bet all our land that Tristam has, as well. You did not know him before, but he was the fiercest of the knights. He has thought of revenge, I am certain of it."

I smile.

"What is that grin about?" Becca demands.

I do not want anyone to avenge me. I do not want anyone to risk getting hurt, but it is nice to think that someone wants to. I do not want to say that to Becca, so I just shake my head.

"All right, keep your grinning secrets. Laugh at me all you want."

I am not laughing at you, I sign. *I am smiling because you care.*

"Of course I care! You really are an idiot. A lot of people care. Thomas was so upset by what he saw, he is vowing revenge, and he is not even a soldier."

What did he say?

"I am not supposed to talk about it," Becca says; her face looks set.

But you already have, I remind her with squinting eyes.

Becca gives me an appraising look.

It is my life. Why can you not tell me about my own life?

"It has something to do with evil things and memory. They want you to remember, but only when you are ready."

Who are "they"?

"Geneva and Tristam."

But it is my life. Help me remember, Becca. Tell me what Thomas said, please. I watch her face as she makes her decision.

"You cannot tell anyone I told you."

Certainly not.

She lowers her voice before beginning. "Thomas said he did not know that a human being could run as fast as you must have done. You were well hidden when they finally tracked you down. He said you were like a wild animal striking out at Tristam when he reached for you."

I look out the window.

"Thomas was frightened for you...and *of* you."

I wrap my arms across my chest.

"Do you want me to stop?"

No, I sign. *How did they get me to come back?*

"Tristam began signing."

That was well done of him, I say.

"Yes, they did not want to force you..."

A shadow crosses her face. We are both thinking the same thing. Neither of us speaks for a moment.

"Grace, may I ask you something?"

Yes, but I probably will not remember, though. This situation needs humor, but my joke is weak.

However, it makes Becca smile a small smile. "Of course you will not, but I must ask. Did you know that two nights ago was the equinox? It was the night you ran."

I shake my head.

"It was. And last fall, that night you did not sleep...remember?"

I nod.

"That was the equinox, too. Do you think it means anything?"

Before I can answer, Tristam's knock sounds on the door. He enters with Headmaster.

"Grace, you have a visitor," he begins. "I see I should say 'another' visitor. Hello, Rebecca. I would like you to meet Headmaster."

Becca curtsies. While she does, I steal a look at Tristam. He glances at me and then back at Becca. His eyes tell me he knows that we were talking about my past. I turn my attention back to Becca.

"It is a pleasure to meet you, young lady," says Headmaster. "Why do we not have you in our instructional classes?"

Becca blushes.

Tristam speaks up. "A very good question, Sir. I have always wondered why only our noble children get the chance for an education."

"Well, Rebecca is most welcome in our classes," Headmaster replies.

"Thank you, Sir," Becca stammers, curtsying again. "My family needs me to work. I am truly grateful for your kind offer, however."

"Might you not be able to assist them more fully with an education?"

Becca shifts her weight from one foot to the other, keeping her head down. She takes a deep breath. "Sir, I am not noble...and there are fees."

"I care for none of that. Do you want to learn to read and write?"

"Yes, Sir. More than anything."

Becca's words surprise me. I did not know of this wish of hers.

"Very well. I will speak to your parents. I will tutor you in the evenings, if necessary. Can you read at all?"

"Yes, Sir. Mother teaches us, when she can."

"Tell me, why are you keen to learn?"

"My grandfather was cheated out of his land. He could not read the contract the noble had drawn up. He set his mark on it, trusting it stated their agreement. It did not. Because he signed his mark, the noble won in court."

My chest tightened. That certainly explained Becca's distrust of nobles.

Headmaster nods. "I remember when that happened." He and Tristam exchange glances.

"If you work hard, you can make sure that never happens to anyone in your family again, if your parents approve."

"They will, Sir," Becca replies.

"Tristam, will you introduce me to Rebecca's parents?"

"Yes, Sir. I will make the arrangements."

"Grace, you will help Becca and also do this work," he says, handing me several parchments. "You shall use this time to study, while your feet are healing."

"Yes, Sir," I reply.

"Rebecca, I am a taskmaster. Grace will tell you I demand hard work and perfection. Now, if you will excuse us, Grace and I need to go over these assignments."

I try to thank Headmaster when Becca has gone, but he refuses to accept.

"She will be working harder than she has ever worked in her life. You should not thank me. She may end up hating you for this introduction."

No, Sir, she will not, I contradict him, surprising myself.

"Well, your appreciation bores me. There is work to be done."

Later, when we are alone, I ask Tristam about Headmaster. *Why does he hide his kind heart behind all that gruffness?*

"I never thought about it. Perhaps his gruffness is how he keeps order among the students."

It is easy to see how kind he is, if you pay attention.

"Yes, but most people do not look below the surface, now, do they?"

No, they do not. I don't understand that.

"That is because you live so far below the surface. You have depth, child."

I just want to be normal. I want to be like everyone else.

"Would you really want to give up being extraordinary so you could be ordinary?" He asks, smiling and flicking my cheek.

He does not expect an answer. I could not give him one.

CHAPTER 37

GRACE

My feet heal quickly and Geneva is delighted that infection has not set in. I would have preferred infection to going back to school. The other children still treat me as if I am not there, or tease me without mercy. No doubt word will have spread of my strange behavior and I will be taunted with new phrases about running away.

I am surprised when Trinicia greets me and asks about my feet. Headmaster has given me a flat grey tablet made of porous stone and a rough pinkish rock to leave marks on it. These marks can be wiped away with a cloth. I carry it to write my answers to questions that are asked of me. Usually, only teachers ask me questions. I dig the tablet out of my bag while Trinicia waits.

I hate lying. Tristam and I have agreed that I will simply tell part of the truth. He trained me at deflecting questions.

"I hurt them in the woods," I write. "Thank you for asking."

"I hear you are an archer. Is that how you got hurt?" Trinicia asks.

"I do love archery and spend a lot of time in the woods. That is where I got hurt," I write. "Do you shoot?"

"A little," she replies, "but I am probably not as good as you are."

"What makes you think that?" I write.

"Rumor says you are very good."

"Well, you should not listen to rumors. I just began last summer."

"She is good," a male voice chimes in. It is a boy named Peter.

"How do you know?" I write.

"I watched you and that huntsman's daughter practicing one day."

"Her name is Rebecca," I write in large letters.

"Rebecca, so that is her name. I watched you and Rebecca shooting one day. You are a good shot."

"Thank you," I write. "I think Rebecca shoots very well."

"Peter is better, no doubt." His friend Coltrane pipes up. "Come on, Peter, or we will have to sit in the front."

"I am not sure I am better, Coltrane. Good-bye, Grace and Trinicia." He bows slightly before walking away.

"Would you like to sit with me and Catherine?" Trinicia asks.

I nod and write, "If Catherine does not mind."

"I will go ask her, if you prefer, but I am certain she will approve."

I nod, not sure at all that Catherine will agree. I am not moving very fast, so I send Trinicia on ahead. When I get to class, she and Catherine beckon me to sit with them.

It is a strange day for me. For the first time, I am not completely isolated at school. No one makes snide comments about my bandaged feet or my absences from class. I have two people to sit with. I do not know what is happening and I do not trust the change.

That night, Tristam asks me about school. "How was it to be back in class?"

Very strange, I reply, stealing a glance at Tristam. I notice a certain knowing look in his eyes.

"In what way?" he asks.

No one whispered about me, I sign.

"Really?" He wears an odd little grin. "Was that the only difference?"

No. Trinicia spoke with me. I sat with her and Catherine in class.

Tristam is smiling. "That is wonderful, Grace."

Tristam, why are you smiling like that?

"I am happy for you."

And…? I prompt, looking at him with suspicion.

"And what?" He is the picture of innocence.

And what do you have to do with this? I demand.

"How can I possibly have anything to do with your school friends?" he asks. He tries to make his face look blank, but I know his expressions.

I do not know, but I know you are behind this.

"Perhaps you are finally winning them over."

Tristam, if you do not wish to tell me what you did, that is your choice, but stop being dishonest.

"What makes you think I am being dishonest?"

Your face. I always know when you are lying.

He sighs heavily. "A plague on all women…and girls," he adds. He takes a deep breath. "Well… I just happened to mention your dowry to

131

Lady Beltran, in strictest confidence."

Melanie's mother?

"That's right."

So Trinicia and Catherine only talked to me because of gossip about your money?

"No, Grace. Trinicia is a nice girl. You already told me that when you said she did not tease you. But the reality is that two things make people acceptable in our culture: birth and money. We can only control one of those, and I suspect you have the other."

That is horrid, I sign. *It is wrong.*

"I did not say I like it, just that it is the way of the world."

So you started rumors that I am an heiress?

"You *are* an heiress."

What if you marry and have legitimate heirs?

"You are my legitimate heir right now. That will not change."

Your wife might have something to say to that.

"I am not married. I do not plan to marry. You are my only family."

Tears sting my eyelids. I turn away.

"Grace, why are we arguing? I do not understand. I thought we could share this joke. Talk to me!"

I shake my head and move quickly toward the door. He grabs my wrist. "You are not running out on me."

I look at his hand on my wrist. Then I look into his face. He lets me go.

"Please, Grace…I am sorry. I know it upset you and I am sorry. I want to understand."

I cannot explain, I sign. *I need time to sort my thoughts.*

"How much time?"

I shrug.

"As you wish. I will leave. You stay here where you are safe. I will come back after a time."

I nod.

"Grace, you have to promise me you will not run away." He says this gently, but the words touch a raw place. I glare at him. "Promise?" he prompts.

I have no intention of running, I sign. *But if I fall asleep…I may not be able to keep my promise,* I say to remind him that I do not always have control of my actions.

"If you do not let me back before nightfall, I will sleep on the floor outside the door and catch you if you run. So promise…"

I promise, I sign. I have a surly impulse to go to bed and make him sleep on the floor all night.

CHAPTER 38

TRISTAM

Grace is tortured. She seems utterly convinced that she will lose her place in my affections. My love has never before been doubted by anyone upon whom I have bestowed it, and I try to tell myself it is her past, not me, that causes her doubts. I only marginally believe this, however.

"I have been alone too long," I mutter.

"What did you say?" a voice replies.

I spin around in the corridor. Geneva is just behind me.

"Nothing of any importance. I was merely talking to myself. I did not realize you were there."

"I just came from down that hallway," she points.

"Is someone ill?"

"A minor injury, a cut finger," she replies. "Are you well?"

"For the most part, I am, but I have upset Grace somehow."

"I see."

We walk along the corridor in silence. I like that she does not ask prying questions, especially since I have no answers. When we reach the common room, I ask her if she would like to join me in a cup of tea.

"That would be nice," she replies.

She does not speak until we are seated across from one another, stirring our tea. "I have tried to imagine what life is like for Grace. It must be so difficult."

I nod. "Go on…"

"How can she trust anyone or anything? To know nothing of one's own past must be terrifying. How could I trust the present with no history?"

"I do not understand what you are saying."

"That is because I am not saying it well. If I lost my past and suddenly found myself in another country with no security…I would be afraid it could happen again."

"What do you mean, no security? She has me."

"Oh, Tristam, forgive me, but that is a thing only a man could say."

"Enlighten me, oh Wise Female, I beg of thee." I give her an exaggerated formal bow.

She laughs and slaps my arm. "Are you ever serious?"

"Sometimes," I grin at her. "Please try to explain what you mean."

"Of course. You see, you have your lands, your holdings, and your title. People know who you are, where you came from, your parents, your grandparents, and your history. Grace has none of that. She has your love, but it must be hard for her to trust that anything is permanent. If you had not found her when she had her nightmare and ran into the woods…"

"I would have found her. I would never give up."

"Yes, I know that and you know that, but what does Grace know? What does she trust? Has she known love before? Does she know she will never be abandoned by you? Someone abandoned her. Maybe it was her mother or father or someone else who has more claim upon her than you. She must suspect it will happen again. It causes my heart to ache."

"When I told her I would adopt her, she asked what my fictitious wife would say. I did not understand, but you are saying she feels she has no right to my wealth, no claim?"

"Yes, and legally, she does not."

"But…"

"If you died tomorrow, do you think your estates would be given to her?"

"That is what I assume, as it is my wish, and I have made a will."

Geneva shakes her head. "She would have to marry quickly or go into a convent. Your land would be fought over," she finishes.

"King Stefan would protect her."

"He would try, but to some extent his hands would be tied. She is not your heir by blood. She is foreign. Your holdings are vast and nobles would be jockeying to find legal claim to ownership before your body was cold. You know this, Tristam," she scolds. "This should not come as a surprise to you."

"And Grace…does she know this?"

"She is an astute young lady. There are ways in which she was more secure as a huntsman's adopted daughter."

"I could adopt her."

"You could marry her. That would give her the most protection."

"She is a child…a frightened child. She is much too young."

"I honor your scruples, Tristam, but be careful. Watch behind you and cover your drink glass."

"This is Blinth, Geneva, not Polomia. Why are you taking such a dark view?"

"Tristam, you were gone a long time. Now that you are back, you are avoiding the intrigues of court. Is that wise?"

"Clearly you think it is not, and you are not the first to tell me so."

"You should listen to us."

"What is afoot, Geneva?"

She glances around and lowers her voice. "Your family was always in King Leopold's camp, and now you are in King Stefan's, but there is a disgruntled faction to the east that supports the heir of Richard, Duke of Tragoltha."

"You cannot be serious. The heir of Richard is but a legend told to children as a bedtime story and a warning to obey their king."

"He is not a legend to these men, and they claim he is a more direct descendant of the great King George."

"Are you talking about George-the-Founder who established Blinth?"

"Yes, and they claim there is a flesh-and-blood heir," she replies.

"Is there any truth to it?"

"I have studied the bloodlines…"

I raise my eyebrows. "I am impressed."

"Do not be, this is purely self-serving. These followers of Richard's heir want to remove the rights of women to own property, to inherit, and to work unless they are attached to a patron."

"That is barbaric."

Geneva simply raises her eyebrows and cocks her head.

"Why have I not heard of this?"

"Few people have, but my work takes me many places. People say things in front of me, unknowingly, as they do with servants. I have pieced scraps together."

"What would happen to a woman…" I begin.

"Like me?" she says. "I would have to marry and give my house and garden over to my husband. If I did not, I would lose it outright."

"Who would get it?"

"The closest male relative. In my case, my husband's brother."

"What would become of you?"

"I would be dependent on the generosity of family."

"And those who have none?"

"These people do not care."

"I see."

"I am sorry to be the bearer of bad news. I know your concern is completely for Grace, but you are the largest western landholder in the country. The king needs your support."

"He has it."

"It needs to be a more active support, Tristam. It is not my place to censure your actions, but this movement frightens me. They talk about placing an emphasis on the family. They mean bloodlines, kin, caring for their own. It sounds well and good, but what it covers up is that the rich will get richer and more and more people will be without land, deprived of any legal rights."

"Who is involved?"

"It is difficult to discern. They speak in whispers while paying lip service to the king. It is treasonous."

"Who is this 'heir of Richard'?"

"Richard had four sons. All are married with children. I do not know which one is considered to be the heir. I only know that whoever he is, he is residing in Traag."

"How are King Stefan's spirits?"

"He is young, but he is astute. He brought you back into the fold. He is using tasters to test his food, though he hates putting others at risk. That weighs heavily on his spirit. He has me researching poison antidotes, more on his tasters' behalf than on his own."

"Geneva, tell me you are joking!"

"I do so wish I could. Queen Laurel is desperate for an heir. She longs to be pregnant."

"It has not been that long, has it?"

"They married just before your tragedy. King Stefan's father died within a few months of the wedding. You have been absorbed in your own troubles."

"That is no excuse."

"No, it is simply a reality. But now you are in a position to help the king."

"Now I wish he really had given my land away," I tease, reaching for a lighter note.

"The followers of Richard's heir brought the king a proposal for the closest heir of King George to take over your estates. They trace that descendant to the Beltrans."

"Using what lines?"

"I am not certain; I have not seen it."

"My God."

"Exactly….Grace would be lucky to be kept as a chambermaid. Or she would be sold in marriage to the highest bidder."

I feel my hands clench. "I should legally adopt her, settle lands on her."

"That would not hurt her cause, but what I am telling you is they will not necessarily honor such claims, if these traitors have their way."

"King Stefan will not be deposed; he is a good man."

"And when good men and bad men fight, good always prevails?" I have never heard Geneva sound so sarcastic.

"Geneva, this is a dark side of you I have not seen before."

"Protect Grace, Tristam." Her tone is strident.

"What about you?"

"I will be fine. I started an herb garden in a meadow to the north, but the property is not mine. I would like to plant a garden somewhere where I am certain it cannot be taken from me."

"How many acres do you need?"

Geneva laughs, though not unkindly. "My needs are small; I currently own half an acre. Fortunately, I have both sun and shade."

"I can provide you with land for both sun and shade gardens."

"I accept your most generous offer." She gives me an exaggerated curtsy. "Now there are *two* orphan women dependent upon you. Watch your back, Tristam, please."

"Thank you, My Lady, but is your concern for me or for you?" I sweep her a grand bow.

"Now that you have become my benefactor, your welfare is of grave importance to me," she speaks in a serious tone, but her eyes are smiling.

"Whereas yesterday you had no concern for me?" I query.

"I must, sadly, admit you are correct, good Sir."

"Oh, My Lady, I protest! You pain my heart and I will spar with you no more," I reply laughing.

"How wise of you, good Sir," she replies in the same formal tones. Then her face grows grave. "Tristam, in all seriousness, Grace is the most vulnerable of us."

CHAPTER 39

GRACE

Becca has to help her mother get the garden planted before she can begin school. She attends as many days as possible after that. Sarah is delighted that Becca has the opportunity to learn to read and write properly.

"Mother said that she never regretted her family's change in status for herself, but she hates that her children do not have the opportunities to learn that she had when she was very young. She teaches us what she can, but she is always working."

What happened exactly? I ask.

"I do not know much more than I told Headmaster when we were in your room. Her father was a younger son. He had poor eyesight, so he could not be a knight. He was a scholar, always using a huge magnifying glass. He was a good teacher. He saved his wages slowly, over many years, to buy land. The plot he intended to buy had a brook and plenty of level farmland. He was swindled by a person he trusted. He could not read the contract; it was written small—on purpose, no doubt. He took this man's word, and ended up with land much farther to the east. It is in the foothills of the mountains and is full of rocks. There is no running water on the property. He protested, but the contract he had signed was valid. There was no help for him. He never really recovered after that. He spent his last years clearing rocks out of his fields. He died at a young age.

"My mother had one brother. He was killed in the war with Polomia. He sold his father's rock-filled farm but could not afford a fast horse or sound armor. Mother says he never stood a chance in battle.

"My father's family lived in the village near Mother's home. He always loved her, but knew they could never be married. But Momma went back and traced them both to Lillian and Chalmer Geddes, three generations back."

I find my mind wandering as Becca tells me more of her family's past. Her voice goes on and on.

"Grace, are you listening?"

Yes. So your mother convinced your father he was not beneath her station.

"Correct, and Momma is a hard worker. She has adapted well to her new station in life, but I still think it is wrong that she had to."

I nod my agreement.

"I am going to make the most of this opportunity. I promised Momma I will study hard."

Of course you will, I reply. *Come along now, or we will have to sit in the front.*

"I would prefer to sit in the front, to make sure I hear it all."

"Of course you would," Coltrane's voice interrupts our conversation. "Sit right up front where we all have to look at you...you, who do not belong here," he continues.

"She belongs," I write rapidly on my slate. "She was invited."

"Oh, so is Tristam going to dower her, also? First a mute foreigner, now a peasant? What next; will we have female dogs in class?"

Becca's fists clench. Before I can do anything, Peter walks over to us. "Coltrane, you are acting like a ferret. What do you care if Grace's friend learns to read?"

"That is how it starts, Peter. If you educate the lower classes, it is harder to keep them in their place." Coltrane turns on his heels and walks away.

We are left in awkward silence.

Peter is the first to speak. "Hello, my name is Peter. It is a pleasure to meet you," he says, extending his hand to Becca.

Becca stares after Coltrane. At first it seems she has not heard Peter's introduction. Finally she pulls herself back with visible effort. "I am Rebecca," she replies. "I am pleased to meet you. What is his last name?" she asks, nodding at Coltrane's retreating back.

"Tragoltha," Peter replies.

"I thought so," Becca says. "Do they own land to the east, near Traag?"

"Yes, do you know his family?" Peter appears to be trying to figure out Becca's interest in Coltrane.

"I know of them," is all she says. The tone of her response does not encourage Peter to pursue the subject.

I fill the void in the conversation. *We better get to class,* I sign.

"What did she say?" Peter asks Becca.

Becca translates.

We begin walking. "How did you learn her signs?" Peter asks.

"Well, since she will not learn to talk, I had to learn to sign." Becca indicates me with an exaggerated movement of her head, while winking at me to ease the sting of her words. "It is quite easy."

"Can you teach me?"

"Certainly."

By the time we reach the classroom, Peter is attempting to speak to me in my own language.

"Are you going to sign to woo the heiress?" Coltrane asks him.

Peter blushes.

"You better be certain that fortune is really going to her before you waste all that effort."

"Coltrane, what is wrong with you?" Peter asks.

"Nothing," Coltrane replies. "I just hate to see you lower yourself. Get over here."

"Thank you, but I prefer to sit right here," Peter replies, indicating a chair next to Rebecca's.

"I hope you do not live to regret that decision."

"I hope you wake up on the more congenial side of the bed tomorrow," Peter tries for a teasing note.

"I always wake up on the nobleman's side."

"But not the gentleman's side," Becca says.

"She won that round, Coltrane!" Peter says, laughing.

Coltrane flushes and does not laugh; instead a flash of hatred shoots from his eyes.

Becca meets his anger with eyes of steel. My stomach begins to ache and I cover it with my hands, while Peter gives me a reassuring look. The teacher enters the room and the class falls silent.

CHAPTER 40

GRACE

Rebecca comes early to walk me to class the next day. She is full of repressed excitement. "You will never guess what I learned last night!" She does not stop to let me try.

"Coltrane and I share the same great-great-great grandfather! Coltrane is the great-great-grandson of the oldest son, Regis. Both my mother and father are descended from the second son, Chalmers."

So Sarah and Daniel are second cousins? I ask.

"Yes, I already told you that. But I just learned that I am related to Coltrane."

So how did Coltrane end up so wealthy?

"He is descended from the oldest son, Regis. Chalmers, his little brother, came along seventeen months later. Their family is so wealthy because they are directly descended from the oldest son in every generation. Coltrane's father is the fifth Regis. The best part is that Coltrane has an older brother, exactly seventeen months older. Coltrane could be the beginning of a line that slips down into the peasantry. I cannot wait to tell him where he is going to end up!"

Becca, be careful, I sign.

"You are not afraid of Coltrane, are you?"

I shake my head. I do not have the signs to tell Becca what I am thinking. It is not even a thought really; I just have the sense that Coltrane is evil. I sense it, even then.

I change the subject. *How did you learn all this?* I sign.

"I offered to help Mother clean up after the evening meal. By asking questions, I managed to get her talking about her ancestry. It really is fascinating. I wrote it all down on my slate, but I need to transfer it to parchment."

I can help with that, I reply.

"I would be most grateful."

I will enjoy practicing my writing. I can work on it while I am soaking my feet this afternoon.

Three days later, I hand the parchment to Becca at the start of our first class. She loses no time in searching for an opportunity to lay it before Coltrane.

"Coltrane, did you know we are related?"

"Have you lost your mind?" he replies. "No, but you best be careful not to lose your future!"

"That will never happen," he replies smugly.

"It happens to younger sons quite often. You could learn a lesson from our great-great-grandfather. By the way, how old is Regis, your brother?"

"He is seventeen." Coltrane practically spits his answer.

"And you are fifteen and a half, am I correct?" Becca's face looks thoughtful

"Why do you care?"

"I just wonder," Becca replies, trying to look innocent.

She begins studying the chart I made, tracing lines and counting on her fingers.

"Let me see that," Coltrane commands. He snatches the parchment from Becca, just as our history instructor enters the room.

"Lord Coltrane," he says, "what is on that parchment that you feel you must rip it away from Mistress Rebecca?"

The room grows silent.

"Mistress Rebecca, since Lord Coltrane is showing reluctance, perhaps you can enlighten me?"

Rebecca pauses a moment before answering. "Yes, Sir. It is a genealogy. I was showing Coltrane how our families are related."

All eyes in the classroom move back and forth between Becca and Coltrane. Coltrane's eyes shoot daggers at Becca, but she smiles sweetly back at him.

"Bring it to me, Lord Coltrane."

"Yes, Sir."

"This is a fine piece of work, Mistress Rebecca. It is both historically accurate and beautiful to look upon."

"Thank you, Sir, but Lady Grace copied it onto the parchment."

"Well done, Lady Grace."

Thank you, I sign, blushing.

I feel something and turn to see Coltrane glaring at me.

The teacher says, "Rebecca, your grandfather, Arthur, had an incredible mind. He was one of my instructors."

"Thank you, Sir," she replies.

"It was a great sadness to me when his life was cut short." He pauses. "Seeing this genealogy written out…there is much that is enlightening here." He shakes his head, as if shaking off a bad memory.

"Now, class," he begins, "we must learn from history or be doomed to repeat the failings of our forefathers. That thought leads us back to our discussion of King George the Second. Does anyone remember who he married?"

I am only vaguely aware of someone answering the teacher's question and of the rest of his lecture. No more is said about the genealogy until the end of class.

"Mistress Rebecca, you may retrieve your chart at the end of the school day."

"Thank you, Sir," she replies.

But when she goes to get her parchment at the end of the day, the instructor cannot find it. It has vanished.

CHAPTER 41

TRISTAM

After my conversation with Geneva, I begin paying close attention to the political environment. She did not exaggerate the threat to King Stefan. I begin stepping in at strategic moments with support for my king. He and I have an unspoken understanding; I am his man.

Grace's second spring in Blinth is a busy time; overseeing the planting at Langstonhorn and Tristenhorn occupy most of my daylight hours. I still sleep in the castle, to be near Grace, so I ride at least eight leagues each day.

I look forward to the Spring Festival for several reasons. The nobles gather from across the land for three days of feasting, games, and celebration, and this is my first opportunity to observe them together since Geneva raised my awareness of possible rebellion. I am also looking forward to a few days of recreation and the chance to spend time with Grace.

Our time together this spring has been limited, and though she seems to have recovered nicely from her terror in March, I now realize she cannot have been perfectly at ease. She is very good at portraying herself as composed, and I did not know she had new worries, not just worries from her past.

I look forward to showing Grace the pageantry of the Spring Festival. Last year, she was too frail to attend and I was a mere huntsman. Much has changed.

Overtly, I learn nothing of the uprising. However, I observe which groups of nobles fall silent at my approach. I begin to learn which families need to be watched more closely in my secret effort to protect my king.

CHAPTER 42

GRACE

There is a great spring celebration in Blinth. The children run around dressed in white with wreaths of flowers on their heads. Even the boys have flowers tucked behind their ears and ivy trailing behind them as they prance amongst the throng.

The great ladies are dressed to dazzle the eye. Yellows, blues, greens, and pinks fill the crowd with the colors of spring. The noblemen wear more muted tones, mainly mauves, golds, dusty blues, and various greens. Everyone looks festive and alive. The peasants add what color they can to their drab brown tunics. Here and there, a colorful scarf or a bunch of wildflowers adorn their clothing. The working women have braided rapidly wilting flowers into their hair.

The scent of food is everywhere. Huge fire pits with roasting boar, stag, and elk are gathered near the western gate of the castle. The pits are tended by huntsmen and cooks alike. Wood smoke and sizzling fat fill everyone's nostrils.

Loaves of bread, sweet buns, cakes, and pies line the merchants' stalls. A brisk business causes money to be handed over and pies to leave their baker's hands. Tables are set out on the lawn for the nobility. The massive carved furniture looks out of place against the green grasses of the meadow, and the tables are laden with food of every variety. The peasants sit upon blankets, but their food is no less plentiful or lavish.

The king and queen's dais is set upon a slight hill overlooking the western castle gate to their left and Wildcat Creek to their right, but the king and queen themselves are moving freely amongst the throng, speaking, smiling, and nodding at every subject who comes forward to greet them.

I notice that the queen is especially gracious to the mothers who bring their infants forward for her blessings, which she freely gives. I wonder if anyone else notices the wistfulness of her gaze or her hungry eyes following each child as it is carried away by its mother.

I have never seen Blinth in the throes of such revelry. I feel crushed by the crowd and long to withdraw to the creek and its soothing babble. Tristam leads me by the hand as if I am a small child rather than a girl on the verge of womanhood, but I am grateful for his care of me. He greets friends of all varieties. The huntsmen call out greetings to their "Captain." The nobles clap him on the back and make much of his presence. I notice that although he is greeted by everyone, he is not fully of any group.

By evening, I am exhausted, but Tristam cannot seem to escape the crowd; he is much sought-after. He has not attended the celebration since the abduction of his wife and daughter.

Tristam is absorbed in conversation, so I wander on ahead. As I approach open farmland, I see a child being dragged toward a barn by a large man. She is perhaps six or seven years of age.

I freeze in terror, until her cries propel me to action.

"No, no! I will not!" she screams, pulling and twisting in his grip.

I race toward her.

"*No!*" I shout. The sound of my own voice is a strange thing in my ears, but my focus is upon assisting the child to escape the man's grasp. To my surprise, she cowers away from me. She goes to him, wrapping her arms around his waist.

"Papa, Papa!" she repeats, hiding her face from me.

My face flames and I feel rooted in place, watching him soothe his daughter. I am an outsider as he strokes her hair and whispers into her ear. Bewilderment must show on my face. His face changes, and I see concern in his eyes for me.

Tristam appears at my side, panting.

"What is happening here?" he demands.

"My daughter would not help with the milking, Sir. Too excited by the celebration, no doubt. I was taking her to the barn when young Lady Grace came flying at me. She is hollering 'No!' just like my daughter. She frightened my Sadie here, but she meant no harm."

"You are certain Grace spoke?" Tristam asks. The man nods, and only then am I certain I have heard my own voice. He is telling the truth. His eyes do not lie.

A roaring fills my ears. I close my eyes as something rips through my mind like a fierce storm. The wall cracks and I am fighting for control.

Opening my eyes, I look into this father's face. "Please accept my apology," I manage to whisper. Then I flee.

The roaring in my ears grows louder. The storm pursues me. I must get to the safety of the creek. My vision blurs and my entire being is focused upon the movement of my feet. "Faster, faster," I chant. "Faster, faster, still!"

When hands catch me from behind, I do not stop. I feel more than hear my gown tearing.

"Grace, Grace…it is me, your Tristam," he says.

Recognition pierces my mind. I fight him still. "Must escape…the storm is coming," I pant.

He dodges the hand I aim for his face, my nails extended. Pinning my arms to my sides, he lifts me off the ground, though I thrash and fight, grunting out loud.

"Grace! Grace, calm yourself. It is all right. You are here. You are safe."

"No!" I insist. "Let me go! Let me go!"

"I cannot," he whispers. "I cannot lose you."

The love in his eyes stops me cold. I quit fighting.

The storm engulfs me. I squeeze my eyes tight, rocking myself back and forth, back and forth. I hear a roar like a mighty wind as I pass through a black tunnel of trees. At its far end, I see a child, like me at six or seven, being dragged toward a barn. The scene changes. I see her thrown to the ground, naked. I see the man climb on top of her. She is not screaming…

I am.

CHAPTER 43

TRISTAM

Her wailing draws a crowd. People are walking home from the celebration with sleepy children in their arms. I know some of these farmers.

"Get Lady Geneva, someone…please!"

A woman steps forward, her eyes full of compassion.

"My son, Will, can fetch her, Sir." She nods at a boy of twelve or thirteen, and at her signal he runs back toward the castle.

"Child, what do you see?" this mother asks Grace.

Grace only shakes her head in huge exaggerated motions. She continues her rocking motion, her arms wrapped around her chest.

"Child, you do not have to tell me. Just look at it. See it!" the woman says.

Grace squeezes her eyes tight.

"See it?" she repeats.

Grace nods.

"Now, let it go, child…it is over. It is over now. You are safe. You are here, safe with me and the good Sir Tristam."

Grace breaks. She draws a gasping breath, buries her face in my chest and begins a ragged weeping. She cries silently at first, but slowly her sobs grow louder. She keeps rocking back and forth with enough force that I am moving, too. I hold on tightly and begin cradling her. She weeps more loudly still as I fight back tears of my own.

Dimly, I am aware of this kind woman dispersing the crowd. She waits a respectful distance from us, only approaching with Geneva. I look up as Geneva touches my shoulder.

She is nodding. "This is good," she whispers through her own tears.

"Keep holding her tightly."

The other woman melts away. I want to thank her…to know who she is. That can wait, however; Grace cannot.

She sobs inconsolably as I rock and croon to her mindless words that one would use with a baby. "Um-hmm…I have you." Geneva watches over us as darkness falls and the moon rises. Geneva lights a lantern.

After much time, Grace's sobs slow to a soft steady cry. Eventually, her cries cease.

Geneva waits a few more minutes before speaking. "Grace, darkness is upon us. Shall we return to the castle?"

Grace catches her breath, nods, and quickly tries to rise to her feet. She would have fallen had I not been there to steady her.

"Slowly, child, there is no hurry," I tell her. "Can you look at me?"

She shakes her head and again buries her face against my wet shirt front. I kiss the top of her head.

"Are you here with us, Grace, in the present?" Geneva asks.

Grace slowly nods, her face still hidden.

"Take Tristam's hand, child. Let us begin walking back. Can you manage that?"

Grace nods again, stepping away from me. Even in the flickering lantern light, I can see her face is changed. She is less tense and infinitely sadder. I want to carry her, but when I stoop to lift her, Geneva touches my shoulder and shakes her head.

Grace begins walking.

Geneva talks softly about the path we travel…the crescent moon rising in the sky…the chirping of the crickets. Banalities. She keeps asking Grace questions: "Do those five stars not look like the letter 'w'?" or "Does that tree not look like a good place for an owl to roost?"

I want Geneva to be quiet, but Grace responds, answering her questions and looking at the things Geneva indicates. Geneva's wisdom pierces my ignorance. She is grounding Grace in the present.

CHAPTER 44

GRACE

I know not whether I am awake or dreaming. I put my hand to my throat, which feels raw and foreign as if it and my screams belong to another and are not mine. The vision I have seen of the child in the barn takes my mind down a dark path. I feel shaken, disoriented, and utterly confused. What is real? Which is the dream? Why do I want to immerse myself in a hot bath and scrub my skin raw? Why do I feel unclean?

I jump at every sound the woods make in the darkness. Tristam has his arm around my shoulders, and he pats me every time I startle in fright.

Geneva keeps asking me questions…on and on. I try to be polite and focus on the present, as she wants me to do.

Tristam and Geneva insist that I eat something and drink steamed milk with honey before I am allowed to have my bath. I have no energy with which to fight them.

"I will have your bath prepared while you are eating," Geneva insists. "It will take time to heat enough water, and the hour is advanced; many of the servants are asleep."

I feel badly for the trouble I am causing, but I cannot imagine sleeping without cleansing myself.

Geneva reads my mind. "I will help them, child. An herbal bath will soothe you."

I nod and give her a small smile.

Tristam never leaves me. He sits across the table while I force food down my throat. He speaks encouraging words as I struggle, for I want nothing but my bath and the oblivion of sleep. The milk with honey is not as difficult to swallow as the food. Tristam removes my plate without a word and brings a second cup of warm, sweet milk. He sits beside me on the bench.

"I will not tell Geneva," he says, winking at me.

I make the sign for *thank you* without thinking.

"You are most welcome, my Grace."

"Tristam, I love you," my words are a whisper. I steal a glance at his face, I cannot read his expression. He swallows a lump in his throat and places a hand on either side of my face, looking deep into my eyes.

"I love you, Grace. My precious one, I love you." His voice is husky. He kisses my forehead and pulls me to him and I rest in his embrace. More tears come for both of us.

When Tristam and I enter my chamber, Bethany, the servant who often waits upon me, and Geneva are pouring a cauldron of steaming water into the tub. They have built a fine fire. Their faces are flushed and their dress sleeves are rolled back.

"Thank you both," I say in a soft voice.

Bethany looks at me swiftly. I see surprise in her face before she turns away.

"You are most welcome, child," Geneva replies, smiling at me.

"Tristam, bring that screen over to shield Grace as she bathes. I will remain with her, but she shall have her privacy. You may wait outside the door."

"Certainly, Lady Geneva, I will do as I am bid." There is a mischievous gleam in Tristam's eye.

"If you please, Sir," Geneva replies, acknowledging her masterful ways.

"And Bethany, you may seek your bed. You are tired, no doubt."

"No, ma'am, I am not sleepy. May I stay and serve Lady Grace?"

Everyone turns, looking at me. I nod. "If you truly wish it," I say shyly.

"Thank you, it is my pleasure to serve you."

My throat tightens. Her caring catches me by surprise. "Thank you," I whisper.

The water feels silken as I slip into my bath. I scrub my skin until it shines pink. Even with the dirt removed, I feel unclean. Despite the herbs floating in the water and the warm steam in my nostrils, I cannot be calm.

After my bath, Geneva brings the sleeping draught and Bethany empties the tub. When I am dressed in my nightclothes, Tristam enters the room and takes the heavy buckets from Bethany, emptying them himself down the chute in the antechamber.

I pace.

"Drink this, child. You need rest," Geneva says.

"Not yet. I must write," I reply, "I must."

"Can that not wait?"

I shake my head.

Tristam comes to my rescue. "Geneva, you look exhausted. You and Bethany have worked hard at the end of an already long day. Go rest, both of you. I will stay here while Grace does her writing, and then see she takes the draught. Can you trust me?"

"Of course," Geneva replies.

Tristam ushers Bethany to the door. I do not hear the words he speaks to her.

I approach Geneva and take her hands in mine. "Thank you, thank you for everything." I pause and draw a deep breath. "I love you," I whisper.

"Oh, my darling, I love you as well." She enfolds me in her strong arms. In a moment, wiping her eyes, she reverts to her usual brisk manner.

"Now, do not let her stay up all night, Tristam. Her body desperately needs rest."

"Yes, My Lady," Tristam says, bowing his head in a servant-like fashion.

Geneva hits his arm with the cloth she is holding, but she is smiling.

"Good night, Sir," she replies.

He walks her to the door and bids her a good night, thanking her again for helping me.

When he returns, he says, "How about if I rest in this chair over here," indicating a chair that has been pushed into the corner, "while you sort out your thoughts?"

"That is perfect," I reply.

Taking up my slate and chalk, I seat myself at the table. I write down the flashes I have seen. It is not a great deal, merely two scenes, yet the bile rises in my throat. The details are so clear. I can feel the roughness of the man's touch upon the child's arm, his poorly woven tunic is filthy and in tatters, his features are coarse and his eyes are flat.

The child's features I cannot see, because I am behind her eyes. I see the rafters as she does, looking past the man's head as it looms over her. I follow her eyes as they go to the crack of fading sunlight, visible in the open place between two slats above the hayloft. Then her vision shifts and I see the man's back and the child's hair spread upon the earthen floor, as if I am sitting on the rafters, looking down. Yet, even from this angle, I can feel the searing pain between her legs.

I think I know, in that moment, that these things are real and that the child is me, but I do not want to believe it. I rebel against what my mind's eye is showing me. I erase the slates and wish I could wipe the vision from my mind, as well. I do not want this to be true, nor do I want anyone to know what I have seen. I drink the sleeping draught greedily when Tristam brings it.

"Do not leave me," I beg. "Please…will you stay until I fall asleep?"

"Of course," he replies. I cling to his hand. He walks me over to the bed, and I climb in. Then he pulls his chair right up next to me and I fall asleep with his arm cradling my head…his scent filling my nostrils.

CHAPTER 45

GRACE

A chink has appeared in the wall in my mind and I pile stones against it to shore it up. What I saw disgusts me. I do not want it to be true. It feels both true and like a vivid dream. I refuse to speak of it, although I am grateful I can speak again. With the return of my voice, I will become less of an oddity in Blinth.

Tristam and Geneva want to know what I have seen. I only shake my head when they press me, withdrawing into my silence. I become aware that my silence is greatly feared and I am not proud to say that I play upon their fears to get my way.

The only person I feel drawn to is the woman who assumed charge of me last night when my voice returned. She knew so clearly what to do, and I sense she knows this from deep within herself; it is not merely learned.

When Geneva comes to visit me the next morning, I ask her about the woman.

"Her name is Lucinda, and her son, Will, came to fetch me."

"I would like to meet her and thank her for her kindness."

Geneva casts me a knowing glance before responding, "Do you feel a special closeness to her?"

"How did you know?" I hear the surprise in my voice.

"It makes sense to me. I must go to a cottage near hers later today; would you like to come with me? We can stop and you can meet Lucinda."

I start to nod, and then remember I can talk. "Yes, thank you," I reply.

Lucinda's cottage is no larger than Becca's home, but it is situated in a field, not the forest. The garden surrounds the house itself. Not only vegetables, but flowers as well, grow in abundance. I recognize them by their names, thanks to Tobias.

Geneva knocks upon the gate. It is whitewashed and fits tightly into its post. The thatching on the house has been repaired already this spring. Everything is tidy and in order.

Lucinda herself comes through the doorway, wiping her hands upon a cloth tucked into her apron. "Lady Geneva, what a lovely surprise. Lady Grace," she nods in my direction. I nod back.

"Lucinda, how are you? How is your family?" Geneva asks.

"We are quite well, I thank you. How are you?"

"I am also well, I thank you."

"What brings you to my gate?" Lucinda asks, looking at me. I look down at my shoes poking out from beneath my skirts.

"Grace came to thank you for your assistance yesterday. Grace, this is Mistress Whittier. Mistress Whittier, this is Grace."

I raise my eyes once again into her face. She is smiling and holding out her hand. "Please, call me Lucinda. My husband's mother is Mistress Whittier. Will you ladies not come in?"

"Thank you, but I need to call upon Mistress Levin and the new baby. Grace, would you like to stay here?"

I nod. "Yes, please, if I may."

"Certainly," Lucinda smiles, "come in. It is baking day, so the cottage is warm."

"I love baking day," I say. "May I please help?"

"Where did a young lady such as yourself learn about baking day?"

"Last summer, at the home of my friend Becca."

"Oh, yes, after Benjamin was born."

I nod.

"I hear you were of much help to them."

I blush.

"She was a very great help," Geneva says. "Grace, I will return for you after a time."

"While you are gone, I will put this child to work. An extra pair of hands is always welcome, especially female hands. My boys are wonderful, but they can eat a whole loaf of bread in one sitting and think it beneath them to knead the dough." Lucinda shakes her head.

Stepping into the cottage is like stepping into high summer. Lucinda's baking ovens are out in back of her home, but she has a fire going in the hearth and dough, rising in bowls, fills her kitchen. I detect sage and rosemary amongst the aromas that fill the room.

"The dough in that bowl with the blue stripe needs to be worked, if you please."

"Certainly," I reply.

She is rolling out dough. I watch as she flattens it and spreads honey and butter over the top. She rolls it expertly and begins cutting it into slices. "These are Will's favorite," she says, catching my eye.

"Would you please thank him for his trouble yesterday? I want to thank you, also."

"You are most welcome, child. My Will would say the same."

I look down at my hands, working the dough, then take a deep breath and look up. "How did you know...?" I falter. "You knew exactly what to say..."

There is a long silence.

"I am sorry," I begin, "I do not mean to pry."

"No apology, my dear. You can ask me anything. I pause because I am not sure I understand what it is you want to know. I would like to answer the right question."

"Well, yesterday...it is just...you seemed to know what was happening to me. It felt almost as if you knew what was happening inside me. I felt like..." I find I cannot go on. When I look up, she is nodding.

"You are asking if I have memories also?"

"It is too bold a question. Forgive me."

She holds up her hand, palm facing me. "No apologies. Your instincts are right. I do have memories. I grew up in Polomia. Children, especially girl children, are expendable there."

I wait, hoping she will go on. She does not disappoint me.

"The details of my past are not important. Right now, the details of your past still are."

"Why are yours not important?"

"There was a time when it was important for me to know, to remember my past fully, but that was long ago on my journey. Now, all of those memories are just a part of me, and they are not even the most important part. But you do not yet know your past, do you?"

"No...I just saw flashes yesterday, like one sees things at night when lightning illuminates the landscape."

"And those flashes frightened you." It is not a question.

I nod. "Are they real?"

"Reality is a trickster. The flashes are real. They are in your mind."

"But did they really happen?"

"You are the only one who can discover that."

I squeeze the dough in my hands roughly. "How…how will I know?"

"Do you really want to know these things are real, or are you hoping you are simply unwell in your mind?"

"I think I would prefer to be crazy than to know that what I saw really happened to me."

"Use caution, Child, in what you wish."

"I do not understand."

"Grace, everyone deals with the pain of life differently. Some people need to know everything, to remember the details. Some people just need to know something happened. Others never remember anything. They get sick or go crazy instead."

"Which kind are you?"

"I needed to know everything…to remember it all."

"How did you remember?"

"A nightmare caused me to remember. I was older than you are. James and I had just started our family. James's mother was a godsend. She listened."

"You did not tell James?"

"Not the details. It would not have been fair to him. I am his wife, and he would have wanted to run off to Polomia and kill people. I needed him here." She smiles.

"How did Mistress Whittier know what to do?"

"She was old, even then. She had seen everything."

"Had she been…?" I cannot finish my question.

"No, she did not have memories like mine. She had suffered in other ways, though. Her vision was never good. I think it made her heart better able to hear…"

"How did you remember?" I ask.

"For me, something would happen that would remind me of the past, or I would have a nightmare that was like a memory. At first, when that happened, the memories would come in a rush, as yours seemed to do yesterday. Later, I learned I could take more control. I started to feel when the memories were about to come. I would see a picture, a scene in my mind. I could hold it back for a little while. I could get the children safely to their aunt's house first, so they did not see their mama crying."

"So there were many memories?"

"For me, yes."

I shake my head and look away from Lucinda.

"Part of you is saying no to these flashes that are unfolding, but some part of you is saying yes. Yesterday, you could not talk. You remembered something. Now you can speak. That is a big gain."

"But is what I remembered *real*?" I do not like the demanding tone in my voice.

"No one can be certain, but I would say probably so."

"Why? Maybe I am merely making up a story."

"Perhaps. Some people do make up stories about their past. Most people that I have talked to do not."

"How can you tell?"

"The ones with real memories do not wish to speak of them."

"Like me?"

She nods. "Have you told anyone what you saw yesterday outside of Tucker's barn?"

I shake my head. "Do I have to tell?"

"I do not know what you must do. I only know I had to tell someone. If I did not tell Mistress Whittier, I would grow more disturbed. The flashes would come more often and I could not sleep. Even though I did not wish to speak of these things, I had to. After I told her, there were always gains. Nothing as dramatic is getting my voice back. My gains were smaller, like sleeping better. After the first memory came, for example, I saw colors more clearly."

I nod. "Was it difficult to tell her what you had seen?"

"Yes, because all the feelings I had held back came out when I told her. I felt as though the horrible things had just happened."

I nod slowly.

"That is how you feel today, is it not?"

Tears pool in my eyes and I wrap my arms across my chest. I am grateful that she does not say anything while I fight for some control over my feelings.

"After I told Mistress Whittier what I saw, she would comfort me with sweet bread rolls. Just like these here," she says, indicating the hot rolls she is taking out of the oven.

"They smell delicious."

An awkward silence falls.

"Grace?"

"Yes?" I reply, not looking up.

"Would you like a sweet roll?"

"But…I did not tell you what I saw." I glance at her shyly.

She smiles. "No, I do not believe you are ready. Perhaps I am not the person you should tell. You can still have sweet bread, though."

I look at her in surprise.

"Truly," she says, nodding, "my boys eat this bread as often as they can and they never tell me anything of importance."

We laugh together.

"That is not what surprises me," I say.

Lucinda looks into my eyes.

"It is that you know I am not ready. How do you know that?"

"Grace, we just met. I do not expect you to tell me anything, but I do have a favor to ask."

"Yes?"

"I want you to promise that if other questions come to mind, you will ask me…in your own time. Will you do that?"

I nod.

"Do you have any more questions now?"

"No…none that I am ready to ask."

"So are you ready for sweet rolls and milk?"

"Most definitely."

That night, when the questions I could not ask keep me from sleep, I begin working on a tapestry of Lucinda's cottage.

CHAPTER 46

GRACE

I do not want to remember, and I cannot seem to forget. Flashes of the child being forced into the barn come to me at the strangest times. Sometimes I see the scene with my mind's eye. Sometimes the feeling of terror descends unaccompanied by visions.

Lucinda was already married when she discovered her past. Her husband, James, did not leave her because he already loved her. They already had a child. Would he have married her if he had known about her past earlier? I wonder.

I wonder if what I saw is real. I wonder if I was defiled. If so, I wonder how that will affect my future.

Curiously, no sounds or smells accompany my visions. No doubt the man reeked of ale, or pipe smoke, or sour cabbage. I could feel and see the nasty tunic, but not smell it. I could see his movements, but sound did not accompany them. The child made no sound; she suffered in complete silence, and I follow her lead.

I push the vision and conversation with Lucinda back behind the stone wall in my mind. I send it where it belongs.

I fling myself into gardening, archery, my studies, and my tapestry with zest. If I had escaped into activity before, now I am desperate for it. I cannot be still. My needle flies at the cloth when I must be seated. Food is not appealing, yet I force myself to eat. Bread and fruit are the easiest things to swallow; meat is almost impossible to choke down.

Tristam worries. He watches me pretending to myself that I am fine. To escape his watchful eye, I spend time in the garden with Tobias.

Now that I can talk, most people expect it of me, but speech is exhausting. Tobias is quiet himself; he neither asks questions nor presses me to talk. Spring is a busy time in the garden, and I am able to help Tobias, stay busy, and be silent within his walled kingdom of flowers and vegetables. Curiously, permission to be silent leads me into conversation.

I am on my knees weeding when I ask my question. "Tobias, do you think the flowers drink the sunlight?"

"Looks to me like *you* drink the sunlight."

"I do. I also drink in all this great blue sky."

"Tell me."

I pause, searching for just the right words. Tobias stops working and leans on his shovel.

"There are places inside me that are dark…like the forest at night. But today, the sun is pouring out pure yellow light and the sky is a clear blue color. I want to bathe in the light, but when I breathe in the yellow and blue, it does not reach all the dark places in me. But the places it reaches get filled up, at least for a little while. I do not feel completely hollow, or quite so lost."

Tobias does not speak.

"You have dark places in you, also." It is not a question. "Is that why you work in the garden?" I ask.

Tobias smiles. "I like the feel of the earth and the green of the new shoots."

"And the yellow light and the blue sky?"

"Yes, child. And every flower that drinks in the sun in my garden."

He brushes my cheek with his forefinger. I smell earth and goodness.

"Some of us have work to do," he says, picking up his shovel.

I turn back to my weeding, but he stops me.

"No, child; you need to drink the sun. Get full so you can go back to those classes of yours."

That is the only time Tobias ever mentions instruction to me. He knows how hard it is for me. He has already turned away, but turns back to ask a question.

"Grace, is it only the spring sunlight that fills you up?"

I must think before I can reply.

"No, there are days of yellow and blue in all seasons: in the fall, when the sky is clear and the leaves are tinged with red; in the winter when the sun is blinding on the snow; and in summer, the yellow and blue bring a dark green to the landscape."

"You have the soul of a poet and the wisdom of an old woman."

I blush.

"You are a rose in my garden."

"Could I be a daisy instead?"

He casts me a look.

"Roses are too fussy. They need too much care. I like the simplicity of a daisy with white petals and a yellow center."

He shakes his head but does not speak. He walks over to the rose garden and cuts a single yellow rose. He does not smile when he presents it to me.

I feel my throat tighten, but it does not matter. The conversation is over.

CHAPTER 47

TRISTAM

In order to tell Grace's story, it becomes necessary to tell a bit of my own, as they have become intertwined. The summer following the return of Grace's voice is not an easy time. Grace and I are leaving the castle for Tristenhorn as soon as classes are released for the summer months.

Lucinda counsels Geneva—and through her, me—not to press Grace to speak about her visions. According to Lucinda, Grace has been forced in the past; we are not to force her now. She will be forthcoming in her own time.

I watch her frantic activity, and her constant busyness exhausts me. One day in early August, when she is rearranging the decorations in the front hallway yet again, I break and ask her to tell me what she saw in her vision back in May.

She looks away from me in silence, and draws a deep breath before turning to look straight into my eyes. "Tell me what happened to Constance and Faith." Her tone is demanding.

I shake my head. It is my turn to look away. When I look back, her eyes have softened. "It is not so easy to talk about what hurts, is it?" she says.

"No, my dear, it is not," I reply.

We are both silent until she slips her hand into mine.

"I am sorry."

"For what?" I ask.

"For sending you there…into your sadness."

I have to smile, "Grace, I have been trying to send you into your past. You asked your question to make a point."

"But it was unkind. I was angry."

164

"You have a right to be."

"So do you."

"I am. Believe me, I am."

"Tell me."

"It is not an edifying story. It will not help you sleep at night."

"Tell me."

"What if I promise to speak to someone else, to tell them the full story? Would that satisfy you?" Geneva comes to mind as I say this.

Grace shakes her head. "Tell *me*," she insists.

This is the first time her formidable will is directed at me. For good or for ill, I tell her.

"I was in Polomia. The border skirmishes had been settled, but we were still occupying their easternmost lands, protecting our western border. The battle had been going on for several years, although we were only at war from the fall of 1116 until early summer of 1117. Most of the army had returned home. I was commander in the Polomian province of Chrispaken. The area was war-ravaged, people were starving. I wanted to come home, but duty prevented it. I was caring for the starving women and children of Chrispaken when my own wife and daughter were captured.

"Constance was the type of person who needed time alone. She loved people, and yet could become overburdened if constantly surrounded. During the war, it was necessary for my family to live in the castle because Tristenhorn is near the western border; it was too near the fighting for my comfort.

"As soon as the war officially ended, Constance begged me, in a letter, to allow her to return home with Faith. She wanted to begin getting things in order for my return. I encouraged her to wait; though I had no proof, I feared raiding parties were still crossing into Blinth. We could not catch them and care for the people at the same time. We focused upon the refugees, hoping kindness toward our former enemies would lead to a complete end of hostilities."

"Did it?" Grace asked.

"Eventually, but not soon enough for Constance and Faith. I should have insisted they remain within the castle walls, but when she begged to escape those confines, I relented." I feel my fists clench and my jaw tighten.

"You think it is your fault." Grace is not asking a question.

"They were my responsibility. I failed them."

"You could not have known..." Grace begins, but I hold up my hand.

"I did know. I simply did not want to say no to Constance. I was a fool."

Grace does not argue. "Go on," is all she says.

I pause in my narration, selecting my next words carefully. "Grace, you only see the best in me, but I am a different man in battle. I do what has to be done."

"I have heard tell of your heroics in battle."

"Heroics for Blinth are seen in a different light in Polomia. I was much hated by the men and I cannot blame them. They felt helpless, humiliated, and many were wounded. They found it difficult to watch me feed their families."

"The women liked you because you are not one of those warriors who hurt women and children."

Her words capture my attention. "How would you know anything about that?"

"I know you. You could not."

"You are right. So, the women liked me. That only fueled the fire of hatred amongst the weaponless Polomian soldiers. I was threatened by a man who had lost an arm to my sword in battle. He was twisted in his pain. He had a wife and several children, but they did not seem to love him, so perhaps he was twisted before he lost his arm, I do not know. I did not take his threats seriously."

"What did he threaten?"

"That he would get revenge somehow; he did not elaborate. I thought him deranged, but I did write home to tell Constance that she needed to return to the castle. I took every precaution, but the letter arrived after…"

"After they were gone?" Grace asks.

I nod and keep silent.

Grace waits.

"A messenger was sent to me, just two days later, telling me of their disappearance. I was relieved of my command so I could go home and search for my wife and child. When I arrived home, the household was grieving and unsettled.

"It was the ninth celebration of Faith's birth, June the twenty-seventh. The housekeeper told me Faith had badgered her mother for a birthday picnic. Constance agreed to go on an excursion into the forest north of home. They had a favorite spot near a brook that was magical to them. According to Faith, the fairies only visited her there. She made up stories about them and entertained us in the evenings with her imaginings." A smile lingers as I remember those cozy evenings. "Across the brook, the meadow is full of raspberry brambles and blackberry thickets. Faith loved them. The thorn canes and their fruit were often part of her stories. So, of course Faith had to gather berries on her birthday.

"The laborer told me that Constance and Faith spread out as they were gathering berries. He was nearer to Faith when four armed men came out of the forest. He ran to Faith, but two of the men held Constance with a knife to her throat. He did not have time to string an arrow before the other two were upon him. They slashed his right arm to the bone and left him to die. He told me they spoke a foreign language. Their accents were heavy, but the young man thought he heard the words 'Tristam, Constance, and Faith.' He said the men laughed after they spoke."

Grace gasps.

I nod at her. "Yes, it was personal. Very few people know that."

"So that is why—" she begins, then stops abruptly.

"It is my fault," I finish for her.

"I was going to say, 'why you think it is your fault.'"

"That distinction is too minute to be meaningful. I am to blame." My face is set and hard.

"You made a mistake. So did Constance."

I am surprised to hear her say so.

"But your mistake was born of kindness. So was your wife's. You are not responsible. Those evil men are."

"And what of the evil done to those men by our army?"

"They should not have crossed the border. They started the war."

"But their families were starving. They needed food."

"Why are you defending them?" Grace asks.

"I am not defending what they did; taking revenge upon a mother and her child is evil. But once I start blaming, how do I decide where it ends? Who is responsible for the storm that destroyed Polomia's crops? Would Blinth have shared her food if Polomia had made such a request as opposed to raiding us? I have pondered these questions these past three years."

"So you decided it ends with you? That you are responsible?"

"Yes, I am responsible, along with a whole host of others. I could blame others, rage against them, and refuse to look at my mistakes, but that is not my way."

Grace is silent for a while. Eventually, she says, "And they were never found."

"Correct. The laborer made it back to Tristenhorn and told his tale. He had lost so much blood that it is a miracle he walked so far. Word was sent to the castle and armed guards were dispatched, but the marauders had at least a three-hour lead. The trail was lost four days' ride to the north."

"That is where you found me!" Grace exclaims.

"Yes, but you were much farther east, due north of the castle. My family was traveling closer to our western border. Constance and Faith must have been leaving clues and gotten caught. Our guards found bits of cloth and a shoe along the trail. Then they found a pile of women's clothes near the western branch of the Boldengarth River. Those clothes were the ones the maidservant said they had been wearing that day. After that, if they were still alive, they had no means of leaving a definite trail.

"I spent weeks combing those woods. I did find a place where it appeared five or six horses had climbed out of the river headed toward Lolgothe. That trail was lost in the pines. In my grief, I was careless. I was captured in Lolgothe.

"I was escorted, under armed guard, back to Blinth after I made them understand my trespassing. That could have gone much worse for me; I was grateful for their compassion."

"The attackers were never found?"

"No. I returned to Polomia seeking answers, and was told some people from Lolgothe must have taken my wife and daughter, arguing that that is where the trail ended. I wanted to question my one-armed friend, but he had died of his injuries. Every trail I followed went cold.

"I was crazed, and my behavior was not assisting the fragile peace between Polomia and Blinth, so King Leopold ordered me home. I put my estates in order and gave them over to the King just before he was killed. That was during the autumn of 1117. I thought King Stefan must have had to deal with the distribution of my lands. But of course, he did not." I shake my head.

"But that is not important. After that, I wanted no part of killing, but that is all I was trained for," I continue.

"So you began hunting?"

I nod. "I was still in the business of killing, but at least I did not kill people."

Grace slips her hand in mine. "Tell me about your wife and daughter."

"What exactly do you want to know?" I ask impatiently. "That Constance had chestnut hair, thick and wavy, which she wore in braided bands around her head? That her smile was full of sunlight and her brown eyes glistened? Do you want to know that Faith was born with curly black hair that all fell out when she was six weeks old?" My tone changes as I reminisce.

"She was nearly bald for two years. We thought she would never have hair. But finally it grew in straight and much lighter than mine or Constance's. Her eyes were a mixture of blue and green. The sun rose and set on her. Is that what you want to know?"

"Yes, that is exactly what I want to know." Grace is not deterred by my attitude. "What did Faith like to do?"

"Besides telling stories, she loved horses and could ride any horse in our stable. Even the great black stallion, the one I had forbidden her to ride, carried her. She made pets of chickens, kittens, any wounded creature. She tamed a squirrel once."

I tell Grace all about Faith and a good bit about Constance. That day, I talk for hours. She is an attentive listener. She seems to really want to know, so I unburden myself. At the end of the conversation, I feel lighter than I have in years.

I fear I have burdened Grace, however. That night she weeps in my arms for Faith and Constance. I believe she also weeps for what happens to girls in the woods.

CHAPTER 48

GRACE

I weep in Tristam's arms the night he tells me about Constance and Faith. He thinks I weep for him, and I do, but I also weep for myself. I am ashamed to say that I am jealous of his wife and daughter. Not of their deaths, but of their lives. They had known security and love. They had belonged to Tristam. They were his. They had a place, a right to him, which I lack.

But we are bound together somehow, the three of us. Had they not perished, would I have been found, or would I too have died in the woods? Had they been alive, would Tristam still love me? I wonder if they are alive somewhere as captives and I shudder, as I can imagine no worse fate.

I carry another guilty secret from that day besides my jealousy. That night is the first night I feel something other than comfort in Tristam's arms. When he finishes speaking about Constance and Faith, the glow on his face dies. His eyes grow sad and distant. He looks suddenly much older. His pain brings tears to my eyes and for the first time, I seek to give him comfort. I go to him and wrap him in my arms as best I can. I stroke his hair. I kiss his brow, as he has kissed mine so often before. As I do, a tear of mine falls upon his cheek. He reaches out, touching my face. Both our eyes are full of tears. He cradles my head in his hands.

"Oh, Grace," he murmurs, as he holds me close. Something in my stomach flutters. I feel light and my heart leaps into my throat. I do not know if he feels it, too. I am shocked, so I pull back, though I long to press closer.

"Are you all right, Small One?" he asks.

"It is so sad. It is so terribly sad…" I reply, unwilling to talk about those other feelings.

"I told you it is not an edifying story," he says in his teasing tone.

"Are you sorry I made you tell me?" I ask.

"First of all, young lady, you did not make me tell you."

"You did not exactly offer willingly," I reply.

"No, but you did not force me. Secondly, no; I am not the least bit sorry that I told you. It was good medicine, my healing Grace."

"I hope it did not taste as nasty as Geneva's medicines taste," I tease.

"Let me see," he says bending over to kiss my lips. "No, not nasty... sweet...you taste deliciously sweet."

His lips are soft and gentle. My senses fill and my heart again rises into my throat. My stomach lifts to the space vacated by my heart and my breath is quick and shallow. I want more, so I turn away quickly.

"Grace, what is it?" Tristam asks.

I use the same excuse I have used before. "I am full of sadness..."

"It is a sad tale and it always will be. And yet, now I have you to bring joy into my life."

I smile. I do not say, "joy and a great deal of trouble is what I bring into your life."

He seems unconcerned by the problems my presence causes him. Perhaps I am troubled enough for both of us.

CHAPTER 49

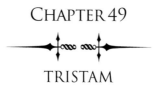

TRISTAM

We are both closer and further away from each other after I tell Grace about Constance and Faith. I find her watching me, assessing me. She has always been tuned to every nuance of my changing moods. Now, she seems doubly so. I do not want her worrying about me; it is my place to watch over her.

Though I have shared deeply with her, she now pulls back from my touch. I am saddened, but I respect her wishes. I tell myself she is maturing and that less touching is appropriate. I do not probe deeper, nor do I ask her about this change. I simply follow her lead. I still hug her, of course, and sometimes I kiss her forehead. She never recoils from my touch, but she seems stiffer in my embrace than she did before. I worry.

My sharing does not lead to her telling me what she has remembered. Looking back, I see that I should have made a distinction between making her talk to me about the past and making her talk to me about the present. Perhaps if I had known more about her fears, I could have been more helpful. I like to think we could have avoided the pit into which we both fell, but perhaps that is only wishful thinking.

We move back into our rooms in the castle just before Grace resumes classes in the fall.

CHAPTER 50

GRACE

When autumn comes, Tristam and I leave Tristenhorn and return to our rooms at the castle. I still remember seeing myself dragged to a barn as a young child, but it feels more like the memory of a dream than the memory of a real event. Staying busy through the summer months has helped to pile new stones upon the wall in my mind. I do not want to remember or feel.

Just before the equinox, I seek out Geneva and ask her for a sleeping potion. I tell her I have struggled falling asleep since our return to the castle and, gratefully, she does not question me, as I am more likely to avoid her potions than seek them out. I take the full amount for three nights on either side of the equinox. I am not disturbed by dreams of any kind.

Tristam rides back and forth to his estates several times each week, but he always sleeps in his chamber at the castle. I wish I could be less aware of where he sleeps. I am always conscious of his presence or his absence.

I throw myself into my studies to avoid thinking about both my past and my newfound feelings for Tristam. We are being instructed in the history of Blinth and the countries surrounding her. Headmaster and I continue to work on foreign languages. I work hard, and my stone wall remains strong.

By this time Peter, Becca, Trinicia, Catherine, and I have become good friends. Peter's friendship with us ended his friendship with Coltrane and I ask him about that change one day.

He and I are the only two left eating at the table. The others, including Peter's shy friend, James, have gone to join in a noisy game of

Beebrong.

"Do you miss your friendship with Coltrane?" I ask Peter.

"Not really. We were close as children; our estates border one another. He was the only boy near my age within an hour's ride of my home, so we were thrown together a great deal."

"It must be strange not to be close now."

"Actually, it is something of a relief."

"How so?"

"Well, look at him," Peter indicates the rough game of Beebrong in which Coltrane and Becca are both engaged. "He is much rougher than is necessary."

"Was he rough when you were growing up?"

"Not usually to me. It was always someone, though; a servant, a farmhand, or anyone he thought beneath himself."

"Like Becca?"

Peter shoots me an appraising glance. "Yes, like Becca."

I nod slightly.

We lapse into silence, studying the game the others are playing.

Becca is good at Beebrong, as she is at all things athletic; she is always one of the first chosen for the teams. Coltrane's ferocity toward Becca in these games frightens me. Even when they are chosen for the same side, Coltrane passes the ball roughly and seems to jostle Becca at every opportunity. Becca gives back as good as she gets, but she comes away more battered every time.

Coltrane is more than two years our senior. At almost sixteen, one can practically watch him change daily from a boy into a man. Becca, too, is changing, but she is growing softer and rounder while Coltrane grows more muscular. Becca is not losing her muscles, nor is she getting fat; she is simply acquiring the curves of a woman.

For all his roughness, though, Becca seems to thrive on her bouts with Coltrane. "I have him," she crows. "He hates that we are related; he cannot bear it that I stand up to him. A bruise or two is worth my while simply to cause annoyance to that pompous pus-pit."

"Pus-pit? Really?" I comment.

"It fits," she replies. "You cannot tell me that under his regal looks and ash-blond hair he is not seething with pus."

"He is seething with venom, I think," I reply. "I wish you would be more careful around him. He is dangerous."

"What can he do to me? Our paths never cross except here near the classrooms."

"I do not know, Becca. It is simply…"

"Grace, Sweet One, you worry too much. I would like to have a go at the pus-pits who made you so frightened."

"Well, I would not bet against you extracting a pound or two of flesh from them, if that ever did happen."

"I would take a pound right out of their black hearts." Becca is quite serious as she speaks.

"I believe you would," I reply, deeply touched. I turn away for a moment to collect myself. When I feel ready, I return to the subject of Coltrane. "Still, I wish you would be careful around Coltrane. He is like a snake; he will strike when he thinks he can get away with it. He has the genealogy, I am sure of it, and he is waiting to make you pay for humiliating him. If he hurt you, I would have to kill him."

"Oh ho!" twinkles Becca. "And how would you set about doing that?" she teases.

"I do not know," I reply, not teasing.

"Well, Sir Tristam is the man to teach you, if you are serious."

I discover that I am serious.

That very evening, I speak with Tristam as soon as he returns from his daily trip to his estates. We are fortunate that Langstonhorn and Tristenhorn are both within riding distance of the castle. Most of the noble children live away from their families during the months when classes meet.

The students are housed in a different wing of the castle than the one Tristam and I still occupy. The girls are on the hall above the boys. Catherine and Trinicia share a room. I have been there to visit. The room they share is about one-quarter the size of my room and I feel guilty about my luxurious life.

Tristam is one of the king's favored ones and that is why we live well. That evening, I barely wait until Tristam has dismounted from Rufus before asking my question.

"Tristam, if I needed to kill someone, what would be the best way?"

"Good evening to you, Grace." I blush when he reminds me of my manners.

"Good evening to you. Are things well at Tristenhorn?" I reply.

"Yes, my dear. Now, why so bloodthirsty? Who is the object of your wrath?"

"No one." I blush again.

"Grace, you are a terrible liar."

I take a deep breath. "There is a rivalry between Becca and Coltrane."

"Yes, I remember the genealogy," he replies.

"Well, today I warned Becca to be careful. She and Coltrane compete in everything: marks in class, archery, and games. I think…no, I *feel*, that Coltrane is just waiting, like a snake, to strike at her."

"So you are going to strike first?"

"No. I just told Becca to be careful. I said if Coltrane hurt her, I would have to kill him. I did not really mean it seriously, but she said I would not know how. She is right, so I began thinking."

"So, you want to learn to kill a man?"

"Yes and no. I would like to know how, if the need ever arose. I would never really want to kill someone. I was joking with Becca, but…"

"I see," he pauses a long time before continuing. "Taking a man's life is a very serious thing. They did not teach us that when we were training to be knights. Or perhaps not everyone experiences it the same way I do…" His voice trails off.

"How do you experience it?"

"Do you really wish to know?"

I nod.

"I remember the face of every man I have killed. I remember their shocked expressions as the weapon penetrated. I remember seeing the life draining out of their eyes. I thought those images would fade as I aged. Instead, they have grown stronger."

"But they would have killed you, if they could have. They were enemies."

"Father Gregory would say our enemies are still our neighbors."

"But you were doing your job," I insist. My voice is plaintive.

"Yes, dear, I was, but I am no sainted hero. War is ugly business, as is killing. If I am going to train you to kill, you had better know that."

"Yes, Sir," I reply.

"Do you really want to learn?"

"I think I do. I hope I never *have* to know how to kill. But if…"

"Better to know and not need to, than the other way 'round?"

"Exactly," I reply.

"Well, I am traveling to the east to examine some crops tomorrow. I will consider your request."

CHAPTER 51

TRISTAM

As I ride east, I ponder Grace's request of the previous evening. I do not want to think of her in a situation in which she might need to kill a man. I prefer to think Blinth is safe. However, my current activities make her less safe. An image of Faith and Constance picking berries flashes through my mind. Would things have been different if they had been armed? Training Grace in self-defense is probably wise, though I do not relish the task.

I dislike lying to Grace, so I tell her part of the truth. I am, in fact, gathering information about crops from the various estates I visit; however, my primary purpose is to gather what information I can about the uprising. If my work ever becomes known to the rebels, hurting Grace would be their quickest revenge upon me.

My mind continues to wander back to Grace. If she ever needs to defend herself, it will probably be at close range. For close-range defense, a knife with a three- to four-inch blade is the best choice. Grace would have to be proficient or her own weapon could be turned against her. She will need a good deal of training. Her movements will have to be swift and accurate. The element of surprise would be helpful. I decide that her training with the knife must be a secret, unlike her prowess in archery, which has become well known. In the spring, she will compete in archery at the May Day games. So skilled has she become that I am already looking forward to the event.

The lands to the immediate north of the castle are owned by small farmers. Thomas's family owns such a farm. Farther to the northeast are a number of smaller properties owned by various noble families. The first large estate I come to belongs to Sir Regis Tragoltha. His second son,

Coltrane, is Grace's nemesis at noble classes.

I am welcomed cordially, if not warmly, by my host. "Ah, Tristam, come in. November seems such an odd month for inquiries about agriculture."

"Spring, summer, and autumn, I am too busy overseeing the crops to be able to learn more about them."

"And you lacked this education in your youth?" He asks.

"As you know, Sir, I was the younger son. I would have paid more attention to agriculture and less to warfare had I had any premonition of my brother's early demise."

"You are certainly the reluctant landowner, are you not?"

"No, I am fully reconciled to the king's wishes."

"So docile?" he asks.

"I prefer to think of myself as loyal," I reply, looking directly into his eyes. He is the first to look away.

I change the subject. "I hear you are getting good wheat yield from the land you cleared near the borders of Traag and Lolgothe."

"Yes, I cleared the meadows of rocks and planted around the hilltops."

"Is the yield covering the cost of clearing the land?"

"It has not yet done so, but I expect to recover my expenses this year, my third season of planting."

"That is excellent," I reply.

"I am rather pleased. My bailiff predicted at least five seasons would pass before we would see profits. What land are you considering clearing?" he asks.

"The hills to the north of Tristenhorn, near the Lolgothe border. Have you had any issues with your neighbors to the north since clearing your hills?"

"No. Unlike your friend Broderick, I am on excellent terms with my neighbors in Traag."

"Is Brody having difficulties?" I ask.

"Ask him when you see the young hothead."

"I most certainly will, but I am more concerned about our Lolgothe neighbors."

"Their land is so heavily forested that I do not fear a crossing of my boundaries."

"So, you have had no raiding parties or visitations?"

"Not one in the two years—excuse me, now three years—since you lost your wife and daughter. Such a tragedy." The light in his eyes does not match the sympathy of his words. "Too bad there is no young Tristam to introduce to my oldest son, Regis, at dinner tonight, or better still, a daughter for him to woo. Marriage within pure noble families is so important."

I feel my jaw clench. I try to steer the conversation back to crops, but my host will not allow it.

"Yes, yes, back to agriculture in a moment. What are your plans for the foreign girl? My second son, Coltrane, says she is quite beautiful."

"Grace also speaks well of your son's archery," I reply in an attempt at politeness.

"Did I say Coltrane spoke well of her beauty? How careless of me. He merely spoke of it, but not well, if I recall. She is foreign, after all."

"As is the queen," I remind him.

"Yes, but that is different. Her lineage is well known."

"What are you saying?"

"Only that the king indulges you. The girl has no future amongst the nobles in Blinth. Bed her if you wish, but you would be best served by seeking a second wife amongst the nobility."

I pause, take a sip of the mead my host has offered, and work at controlling my temper. If I alienate this man, my king will not be well served. If he knows he can arouse my anger, he will continue to do so. I choose to keep the focus on him. "Seek a second wife from the nobility as you did, My Lord?"

"My second marriage did expand my estates to the north and west. You could do worse than to follow my example."

"And how is your lovely wife?" I ask, knowing full well that his wife is known for the unattractiveness that kept her single for more than twenty years in spite of her enormous dowry. "Will I see her this evening?"

He flushes. "No," he spits. "She is indisposed. Women are tiresome creatures, but they serve a need."

"Do you hold them so cheaply?" I ask.

"Do you not?" is his reply.

I no longer question Grace's judgment in wishing to be trained in self-defense. I make his wife's purported illness my excuse to ride on to Brody's estate that afternoon.

Over wine later in the evening, Brody reads my mood, asking, "What troubles you, my friend?"

I tell him of my encounter with Regis.

"Ah, yes. Such a charming man," Brody replies. "I would apologize for him, but there is really no excuse for his crudeness."

"I feel sorry for his wife. Do you see much of her?"

"Very little. Of course Regis and I do not visit often. I know his oldest son, Regis-the-Younger, slightly better. We are closer in age."

"How old is he?" I ask.

"Well…Regis-the-Younger, is nearing twenty. But Regis has three daughters who are all married, so he must be at least forty-five."

"He does not look it," I reply, "and he has a son a little older than Grace."

"His second wife is much younger than he is himself."

"Is she Coltrane's mother?"

"Yes; he and Regis-the-Younger are her two children. Regis's first wife had three daughters before dying in childbirth along with her stillborn son. The daughters all married well."

"Sold to the highest bidder?" I ask.

Brody shoots me a look. "Something like that."

There is a lull in the conversation.

Finally Brody asks, "Why so curious about my neighbor?"

"The king has sent me to ask for your assistance."

"I am his to command."

"The same is not true for your neighbor."

Brody raises his eyebrows. "This is newsworthy; fill me in!"

I proceed to tell him about our secret mission for the king.

CHAPTER 52

GRACE

When Tristam is away and I need comfort, I slip into his room. Usually, I hug his pillow and breathe in the scent of him. To me, he is the scent of home.

Becca and Coltrane have been especially annoying to one another lately. Her taunting of him seems foolhardy and I leave after classes angry at Becca for ignoring my warnings.

I enter Tristam's chamber in the early darkness of a November afternoon. Instantly, I am aware that I am not alone.

"Who is there?" I demand.

I hear a slight sniff and then a soft voice says, "It is I, Lady Grace; Bethany."

I light the candle next to Tristam's bed. Turning, I see she has been crying. "What are you doing here?" I ask.

She opens her mouth to speak, then stops. Various expressions sweep across her face.

I wait.

Finally, she speaks. "I guess I…I knew Sir Tristam was away. I needed a place to…" she begins.

"To cry?" I finish.

Tears spill over and run down her cheeks. "I am sorry, My Lady. I promise never to do it again," she says, heading for the door.

"Bethany, I do the same thing. I come here for comfort."

"Yes, but you are allowed to be here. Please do not tell anyone. I would be in a great deal of trouble."

"I will not tell anyone, but I would like to know what the matter is."

"Thank you, most earnestly, My Lady, but it is nothing," she replies.

"Bethany, I remember when I first came here, before I could talk. You defended me when the other maids were talking about me. And the day my voice returned, you prepared my bath. I would appreciate the opportunity to assist you."

"There is nothing you can do, but it means a great deal to me that you want to. I must get back to work."

"Bethany, perhaps I will have to tell Tristam you were in his room." I am using unfair tactics, but I sense she is in some type of danger.

"Please do not!"

"Tell me what is wrong and I will not."

I watch her inner struggle for several minutes before relenting. "Bethany, I will not tell a soul you were here. You may keep your secret."

She bursts into tears. "Thank you, thank you," she says between sobs.

I hand her a handkerchief, gently touching her shoulder as I do so. She clasps my hand and squeezes it.

"Can it be all that bad?" I ask gently.

"It is just…I was supposed to go home. I have served here for two years; my time is up. But father has taken sick and Mother needs my wages. Lord Dunbar asked me to serve at his estate. It is far to the east, and…" She stops.

"Go on…"

"Well, Lady Grace, a few of the lords take liberties."

"Does he touch you?" I demand, enraged.

She winces at my tone. "It is all right. We get used to it. Here in the castle we maids watch out for one another. But, on his estate…"

"Bethany, that is horrid! I will tell Sir Tristam and he will…" I begin.

"You must not! Please, please do not! Lord Dunbar is paying a very high wage. My family needs every penny I can earn. I am afraid…" her voice trails off.

"You are afraid the high wage will be used to buy your silence about the liberties he takes," I finish angrily.

She nods.

"Can you keep working here?"

"No, ma'am. We serve for two years and then it is someone else's turn."

"I see." I let out a great sigh. "And please, call me Grace."

"I cannot, ma'am, though I thank you. I am an honest girl. My man and I planned to marry when I came home."

"Can he help your mother?"

"He would if he could, but he is just getting his small plot of land yielding enough to support his own ailing father and two younger sisters."

"I see," I reply, sighing again.

"Never mind, miss. I will be all right. I am merely disappointed; I just learned of these plans today. I best get back to work and not be found here."

"Bethany, where is your home?"

"It is over toward Polomia," she replies, "not far from Langstonhorn. My granny worked for Sir Tristam's father before she passed."

"I would like to talk to Tristam about hiring you. May I do that?"

"No, miss, please do not trouble him about me. It is already settled."

"Please, just let me try."

"Why would you do that for me?"

I do not know what to say, for she has been kind to me. Also, I do not wish her to be touched by someone she does not love. Before I can form my thoughts into a response, she begins talking again.

"Most of the ladies do not care about maids. They would just be angry that I was here crying."

"I am not like that."

"No, you are different."

"I am often reminded of that," I reply.

"It is a good thing."

"Thank you, Bethany. Will you let me try to help you?"

"All right, but please do not tell him about Lord Dunbar. If I have to go to work for him, and he knew I told…"

"I will not mention that part. May I tell him I am fond of you and would like to have you near me at Langstonhorn?"

"That would be most kind," she replies. I see relief and apprehension in her eyes.

"Thank you for telling me. Tristam comes home the day after tomorrow, so come see me the day after that."

"Yes, My Lady, I will."

I can tell she is not hopeful.

"My name is Grace, and you need to have hope," I tell her firmly.

She smiles a weak smile, curtsies and slips from the room.

CHAPTER 53

TRISTAM

Riding to the castle from the east, my mind turns to Grace and her request. Dagger training involves much physical contact, and Grace has become a young woman. I would be forced to pretend to attack her during training. I worry about how she might respond, but I do not want her to remain unskilled at defense. The more I learn of the rebellion, the more frightened I become on her behalf. I decide training her is a task I must undertake.

Immediately upon my return to the castle, Grace comes to me with another unusual request.

"There is a maid named Bethany. She was there the night you brought me to the castle. She is good and kind. Her grandmother worked at Langstonhorn."

Grace pauses.

"Yes?" I encourage.

"Her time of service at the castle is complete. Her betrothed lives in the village between your two estates. I wonder if there might be work for her upon one of them."

"Child, think of my home as your home. If you wish Bethany to work there, I have no qualms."

Grace does not speak immediately. I wait.

"You will have to speak to Lord Dunbar."

"For what purpose?"

"Bethany's family hired her to him, but she is most unhappy. She will be far away from the man she loves."

"If her family has made a promise—"

"They do not know Lord Dunbar," she interrupts.

"What do you know of Lord Dunbar?" I ask. A memory of Geneva, backed against a wall at the queen's ball, flashes through my mind.

"Nothing," she replies looking away, and I know she is lying.

"Grace?"

She clenches her hands together in front of her and turns to face me. "I promised Bethany I would not tell."

I study her face.

"Can you promise me that this arrangement between Bethany's parents and Lord Dunbar needs to be changed?"

"Yes, Sir."

"Very well. I will see what I can do."

She throws her arms around me, giving me a quick hug. "I have to go tell Bethany."

"You should wait until this is settled."

"You will settle it. You always attain your goal."

"Nevertheless, I am requesting that you wait."

"Yes, Sir....May I tell her I have spoken to you?"

"This is very important to you, is it not?"

"Yes, she has been so unhappy and afraid, I think."

I relent. "You may tell her I will speak to Lord Dunbar, but tell her nothing is settled."

Grace is beaming and I receive another, even stronger hug before she departs in search of Bethany.

I seek out Lord Dunbar soon after Grace leaves. I do not expect to enjoy our conversation, but I have made a promise. I find him just before supper, sipping on mead.

"Good day, Lord Dunbar," I greet him with a smile. "How are you?"

"Fine, fine; and yourself?" he blusters.

"I am well."

"Just returned from a trip to the east, I hear."

"You are well informed, Sir." I feel my eyebrows rise.

"Well, you cannot travel in my part of the country without thinking someone will write to tell me of it."

"So you had a letter?"

"Yes, Lord Regis happened to mention it. So, you are interested in clearing land to the north of Langstonhorn?"

"Yes."

"Have you not enough fields to manage already?" he asks, taking a large swallow of his mead.

"Like Lord Regis, I believe in gaining the greatest yield from my estates."

"Yes, Lord Regis is always seeking improvements. Me, I find I am content with my lot."

I incline my head.

"You are young yet, Tristam. At my time of life, one has other interests."

"In fact, I came to speak with you about another matter, or interest," I reply.

"Speak then." His tone remains friendly and I realize he has consumed more mead than I had first supposed.

"There is a maid, Bethany, who has waited upon Grace. She has been kind to her and they have grown close. I wish to employ her at Langstonhorn, but learned you had already secured her services. I came to request that she be allowed to work for me."

"The arrangements have already been made." His smile fades.

"Surely, they can be changed."

"She is a good worker. I have a fancy to have her at my estate."

"But you do not wish her to be unhappy, I feel certain."

His face flushes. "What has she told you?" he demands.

"I have not spoken with the maid. Grace tells of a betrothed in the village near my home and of Bethany's sadness to be moving still further away from him."

"Ah, well, hearts do not really break. She will do well to accustom herself. As a serving maid, her life is not her own. She is required to serve the needs of her lord."

It takes effort to continue in a congenial tone, "But you could make two girls happy if you would but relinquish your claim. I myself will make all the arrangement and find a maid to fill Bethany's place."

"You need not trouble yourself."

"It is no trouble, I assure you."

"You misunderstand: I will not relinquish my claim."

"Very well. If you will excuse me, I will go and speak with Bethany."

"You are going to speak with her?" For the first time in our conversation, he seems alarmed.

"Of course. She will be disappointed," I reply innocently.

"Why must you meddle? She is but a servant."

"Servants have feelings, no less than nobles, and their lives are more difficult."

"Ah, yes, that is what comes of working among the common people, as you have done. You believe their wishes matter."

"I believe everyone's wishes matter. Did you miss Father Gregory's sermon on the Sabbath? 'In Christ there is neither Greek nor Jew, male nor female, slave nor free, but all are one in Christ Jesus.'"

"Well, he does not say there is neither noble nor peasant."

"No, but such distinctions are implied as being erased. You must excuse me; two young ladies await my return, if you feel your decision is wise."

"Are you questioning the wisdom of my decision?"

I nod.

"On what grounds?" he huffs.

"I feel certain there is more to this request of theirs than they have spoken of. They have not told me as yet, but they will."

His face grows scarlet. "Servants tell lies; you know they do, especially female ones."

"How odd that you should say so; that has not been my experience. Bethany does not strike me as someone who would tell a lie, and she certainly will not lie to me when we talk."

I watch Lord Dunbar struggle with himself and know that I have won.

"If it matters so much to you, have it your way," he flings at me.

He is no longer jovial, but I continue speaking in a cordial fashion. "You are most kind," I reply. "I will employ another maid for you."

I search my memory for a female servant to hire for Dunbar; one who will stand up to him and rid him of his lecherous habits.

It seems as if he can read my mind when he replies, "I prefer to employ my own servants."

"Very well. Again, I thank you." I hold out my hand. He does not take it but instead spits upon the ground and turns away.

I have made an enemy of yet another eastern landholder, but his hatred does not concern me, at least not at the moment.

CHAPTER 54

GRACE

Tristam returns from his trip changed somehow. I cannot help but notice the intangible shift within him, even though my first conversation with him is about Bethany. I am reminded of the time he came home from the ball after learning about his restored fortune. If he had learned something on his travels, he does not share it and I do not ask.

When he left on his journey, I felt certain he would not train me to kill. I am surprised that he has decided to train me in the art of dagger defense, and I suspect his activities in the east have affected his decision. As is Tristam's way, once he determines a course of action, he is ready to act immediately. We start training on his first full day back.

"I have arranged for us to train in the portion of the stables that houses the huntsmen's horses, during times when Thomas will be caring for the horses."

I nod.

"He is discreet and trustworthy."

I make no reply.

"You will train in the use of the dagger. If you are ever attacked from a distance, you will defend yourself with your bow, but you need to know how to defend yourself if your attacker is this close," he says, stepping within an arm's length of me.

I start to step back but he grips my shoulder. "No, Grace, pretend there is a wall behind you. What are you going to do?"

"Well…I could raise my knee to your…" I do not finish my sentence.

"Do it."

"But…"

"Now!"

I tentatively raise my knee. He sidesteps and places his right arm across my throat; with his left he wields an imaginary dagger to my breast.

"Every boy ever born has been defending that part of his body since he could walk. Pick a different target," he says releasing me. "What comes to mind?"

I massage my throat and gather my thoughts. "The throat...the stomach..."

"Good choices. See if you can come up with some more by this evening."

"Yes, Sir."

"And do not ask anyone for help." His eyes are sparkling now and he seems more like my Tristam.

"I was planning to ask Becca and Peter."

"I want to keep this between us, Grace."

"Why?"

"The element of surprise is most useful in this art. If it becomes known that you are proficient with a dagger, you lose that advantage and someone may test you, just for fun. Things could get out of hand."

"Will I become proficient?"

"You will have to or you had better not use one at all. If your dagger can be wrested from your grasp, your assailant will turn it on you. And he will be angry."

"That sounds like something you have experienced."

Tristam lifts his eyebrow and cocks his head.

"Tell me."

He glances down at the scar that runs parallel to the crease in his elbow. I can tell he is remembering something and I wait for him to speak. Instead, he shakes his head and changes the subject. "It is time for class."

In the evening, Tristam begins where we left off in our morning discussion. "What targets have you thought of?" he asks.

"I think the heart and perhaps the eye."

"Good choices, but the heart is protected by the ribs. You have to know exactly how to slip the blade through. The eye is good, but also requires precise aim. You may not have that in hand-to-hand fighting." He is deadly serious.

"Tristam, this is a little..."

"Yes?" he asks more gently.

"I do not know," I begin. "It is simply that...you seem so serious... and scary."

"This is very serious business. I do not want to frighten you, but you must respect this training and your weapon."

"I do respect the dagger, and I am not frightened of you, but you seem different. You are so…intense. That is the word, intense."

He nods. "I have heard that from my students before. Shall we continue?"

It is my turn to nod.

"I want you to remember this."

"Yes, Sir," my tone mimics that of the squires I have heard during their training.

He smiles briefly and then launches into speech. "The first target you mentioned this morning is a good one for a fatal wound. The throat is one of our most vulnerable areas. The best place to strike it is just below the Adam's apple. Also below the ear, just behind the jaw is a good target. If the blade enters there, thrust it back toward the spine. Another good choice is piercing the eardrum, but like the eye, it is surrounded by bone. If your aim is not true, your blow will glance off."

I do not speak.

"Straight up through the armpit will also kill a man. There is an artery there. Sever it and your target will rapidly lose his life's blood. There is another artery in the inner thigh. Sometimes, if a man's leg is fully broken there, the bone will pierce the artery. He dies very quickly.

"On the torso, aim for this soft place, right here," he says, pushing his fingers into that spot. "I call this the center; it lies just below the breastbone, between the ribs. Those are the seven targets to remember. The three best choices are the Adam's apple, the center, and under the arm. That one is very useful if your opponent raises his arm to strike you."

"Again, I detect the voice of experience," I say.

"Combat is not pretty, Grace."

"I believe you have mentioned that before."

"If you strike at close range, you must be prepared to be bathed in blood. Can you handle that?"

"I do not know," I answer, trying to imagine such an event.

"Good answer. Those who immediately answer 'yes' have not given the question enough thought. Think it over."

I nod again.

"Remember, only use these skills if you must kill to stay alive. You have to be ruthless in hand-to-hand warfare. If you cannot be, you are better off untrained. You will die more quickly and easily that way."

I shudder.

"Precisely," he says.

"It is also good to know the amount of force required." He produces a tuber root. "It takes about as much force to kill a man as it does to pierce this root. We will practice that in a moment. First, let me show you how to hold the blade.

"There are really only two ways to hold a dagger. The best way is to have the blade protruding from between your thumb and first finger, the hilt firmly in your fist. In certain situations, the blade protruding from the other side of your palm is the better choice. One can use gravity and strike with a hard downward motion that engages the upper arm and shoulder muscles, but this only works if your opponent is below you.

"I tend to prefer overhand to underhand no matter which direction my blade is protruding." He shows me the difference between the former with the palm down and the latter with the palm up. He continues, "I prefer to strike overhand because the arm has more power in that position. Also, underhand strikes are more likely to end in self-injury if your opponent moves." He demonstrates the motions.

"That is logical," I say.

"Practice all the grips," he orders.

I obey, striking with a dull wooden practice dagger that he provides.

"Which feels more natural?" he asks.

I try each movement again, stepping into each strike with my feet.

"Good footwork, Grace. You can add power with your lower body."

"I think I prefer the overhand strike with the blade this way." I indicate the practice blade protruding from between my thumb and forefinger.

"Most people do. It is a good choice. I also want you proficient with its opposite." He demonstrates the underhand move with the blade extending from the other side of the palm. "It would be a better choice if someone were this close." He steps forward until our foreheads are almost touching.

"Best target here?" he demands.

"Just below the ear. I cannot reach your Adam's apple."

"Good," he replies. "Now, we will use this root."

We practice hand-to-hand combat every day except Sunday. "This has to become part of you, something you can do in your sleep. You must be able to move without thinking in combat. Your muscles have to know exactly what to do."

"Like my fingers just know what to do when I am working on tapestry?"

"Tell me more."

"Well…sometimes, if I think too much, I cannot make proper stitches, but if I relax, my fingers know what to do. It is almost as though I have to get my mind out of the way."

"Yes, that is exactly what I mean."

We practice until I can anticipate Tristam's every move.

CHAPTER 55

TRISTAM

Training Grace in archery brings me much joy. She has an innate understanding of the weapon and is able to join with her bow as if it is simply an extension of her arm. Such ability is rare. When I was a young page, the archery trainer who taught the squires and knights was rumored to be such a man. He passed before I became a squire, so I do not know if the rumors are true.

Training Grace in the use of the dagger, though, is most unpleasant. She does not lack understanding of the movements and can practice them alone, but when she and I come into contact during practice, she is unable to use the movements against me. The fluidity of her archery is gone. In its place, she seems to have only stiffness.

I force myself to continue the work. When I trained the squires, I made a rule for myself: Never question a young one's ability in the first six weeks of training. Every boy was given six weeks before I judged his capacity. Grace deserves as much consideration.

On the sixth day of the sixth week, I see a flash of fight in her. I push her hard. I have to know if she should continue her training, but neither of us comes away from the encounter unscathed.

CHAPTER 56

GRACE

It takes six weeks of training before I manage to break through Tristam's guard and lay my wooden blade across his throat.

"I did it! I killed you!" I exclaim. I am panting from exertion.

"It was sloppy, Grace. Try again," he barks.

He proceeds with a full frontal assault, actually knocking me to the floor. His face is looming over mine. His hands pin my wrists. A flash of another face replaces Tristam's. I feel myself shrinking, becoming smaller and younger. I cannot move.

"Grace, stay with me," Tristam demands. "Look at me. Do something…anything."

I do not think. I just move. My right knee flies up, wedging itself into the space between our bodies. I throw my head forward, smashing Tristam's Adams apple with my forehead. He rears back, a hand to his throat. My right hand flies upward and my dagger finds its mark, just below his left ear.

I scramble to my feet, watching Tristam as he lies upon the earthen floor with his eyes watering. I glare at him. "How could you do that to me?" I gasp.

His voice is a hoarse whisper. "To get you past the freezing." He reaches a hand toward me. I pull back.

"Grace, it is me, Tristam. Look at me."

I obey. There is such tenderness in his eyes that I look away instantly.

My heart races and blood pounds in my ears. My breath is shallow and fast. Slowly, I begin to calm. I find myself nodding. "I did freeze. I could not move."

"Some people can never unfreeze. They cannot be warriors. I had to know if you could push through your fear."

"Does everyone freeze in battle?"

"No, but someone who has been injured in the past often does."

"I see." My eyes travel and do not focus. I think of the little girl on the floor of the barn. Tristam gently pulls me into his arms and I weep.

A long time later, we are seated on the ground. Tristam's back is against the partition of Rufus's stall. He is totally supporting my weight; his chest is wet with my tears. Mucus drips from my nose. I try to sit up, but he still holds me ever so gently.

"Slowly, child. There is no rush."

"But your shirt," I begin.

"It matters not. Look at me."

I cover my face with my hands. "I cannot," I whisper.

He takes my face in his hands, gently prying my hands out of the way. He kisses my dampened cheek, my nose, and my forehead. My eyes are downcast, glued to his darkened shirt front.

"I am sorry, Grace. I had to do it. Do you understand?"

I nod.

"Can you forgive me?"

"There is nothing to forgive. You had to test me," I whisper. "And besides, your Adam's apple will be sore for a week."

He throws back his head and roars with laughter. I smile and steal a glance at his face. His eyes are moist when he says, "I love you."

I bury my face in his shoulder. The words "I love you" stick in my throat.

CHAPTER 57

GRACE

Spring comes early in the fourth year of King Stefan's reign. No deep snows fall during the month of March, and none at all after the equinox. I again request sleeping herbs of Geneva to assist me; but this time I am honest and explain to her my desire to avoid the nightmare that plagued me the previous March.

Throughout the winter, I have been training in archery and knife combat. I greatly prefer the arrow to the blade. In archery, I lose myself, mesmerized by the fluid motion of sighting my target, stringing my arrow, and letting it fly. Blade work requires me to stay present in my body and fight at close quarters. Tristam is an excellent and demanding teacher. I believe he also prefers training me in archery, though he never ends our blade training sessions early. I do not like the close physical combat, and I know Tristam does not like to imitate an attacker. The days we practice archery are both a relief and a pleasure.

My abilities with the bow far surpass my abilities with the blade. Tristam still makes corrections to my archery stance and positioning, but I am increasingly able to anticipate his coaching and make the corrections myself. Becca joins us when she can, but between her chores and her studies, she has little time to spare. I do not like that I have now surpassed her in archery skills.

"I do not care which one of us is the better archer," she insists. "When you beat Coltrane at the May games, I will be just as happy is if I had done it myself."

"You do not know for certain that I will beat him," I reply.

Becca cast me a glance of impatience. "You do not realize how skilled you are."

Her words are true. "I feel I have much yet to learn."

"You outshoot Tristam consistently at the closer range targets. Your reach will never rival that of a full-grown man, but your technique is flawless and enables you to be accurate at a much greater distance than is to be expected of one of your stature."

I stare at Becca.

"That is what Tristam told my father the other day in the market-place," Becca grins. "If he had said that about me, I would be beaming with pride. Why are you not?"

I shake my head. "I do not feel as if I deserve such praise."

"You do not recognize your worth."

"At least I never overestimate my skill," I reply.

Becca blushes and grins. She recently took a rattling fall during a game of Beebrong. "I thought I could leap up and catch it."

"You might have been able to, had Coltrane not been guarding you."

"I took a risk," she replies, shrugging her shoulders.

"And he never misses an opportunity to hurt you."

"Nor I, him."

"True, your comments about your shared ancestors hurt him more than the bruises he inflicts hurt you."

Becca nods and grins. "That is very true."

I shake my head but do not speak.

"You will beat him at the archery competition and that will hurt him, too," she predicts.

The first round of the competition is in late March. The ten of us with the greatest accuracy will compete again at the end of April. Peter, Coltrane, Becca, and I are amongst the ten. I am in first place, with Coltrane in second. Becca is in fifth place and Peter takes eighth.

Peter is most complimentary to Becca and me, praising our skill. Coltrane storms off, complaining about cloud cover, sunlight, and unfair advantages. I watch him hurry away. At the edge of the crowd, I see him bow to a man who scolds him for placing second. After a moment, Coltrane speaks and turns to point his finger at me. I return his gaze steadily. He hunches his shoulder and walks away from the man.

"That is his father," Peter informs me.

"He did not compliment his son's skill."

"No, Regis believes that he and his family are above all others in Blinth."

"On what basis?"

"Bloodlines. They claim theirs are the purest in our fair country. Any evidence that they are not the best is unwelcome."

"So second place counts for nothing?"

"That's right. When we played as children, he had to come in first at all costs. He would cheat at games and trip me during races if I ever got ahead. Usually, though, he could beat me fairly. As you see, I placed eighth to his second."

"You do not sound as if you care greatly."

"No, there are more important things in life than winning competitions." He glances over at Becca and his expression softens. "Becca did very well today," he says.

"Especially when you consider how little time she has for practice," I say. "She will do better at the April competition, with live targets. Most of her practice is to help feed her family."

"I admire her hard work. It will be a pleasure to see her demonstrate her skill," he replies.

His parents come over at that moment and Tristam appears. We stand quietly as the adults make conversation. I pay little attention to their words as they discuss crops and land in the east of Blinth. I should be listening more carefully, but I am pondering my discovery that Peter cares about Becca.

CHAPTER 58

TRISTAM

I deliberately seek out the parents of Grace's friend Peter after the first level of the spring archery competition ends, and use the children's friendship as an excuse to introduce myself. I hope to learn that Peter's parents are Loyalists; unfortunately, Peter is the grandson of Lord Dunbar. Dunbar is a weak man who has been persuaded by his western neighbor, Regis, to join the rebel cause. Dunbar must traverse Regis's estate to travel west to the castle. For Dunbar it is easier to agree with Regis and continue on friendly terms with his neighbor than to remain loyal to the king. For Grace's sake, I hope Peter's parents are not involved in the rebellion.

Through my servant informants, I have learned that Regis is the leader of the rebellion and has joined forces with the neighboring country of Traag. Our ring of Loyalists suspect the heir of Richard is in hiding there. Only Broderick's family's relatively small estate prevents the entire northeast corner of Blinth from belonging to the rebels. I am concerned for my friend whose family estate is bordered by three rebel nobles and the country of Traag.

"You need not fear for me," Brody insists. "My father and brother manage the estate. I am still a knight, well trained in battle."

"Well trained?" I chide him.

"Very well trained, and you know it," he shoots back. "Most of my training came from you and we have fought our way out of some tough corners. Remember when we were pinned up against the barn, five Polomians against the two of us?"

I nod, a smile on my lips. "We fought well that day."

"Yes, we did. They did not believe me when I told them five on two was not fair odds for them."

"Not then, they did not," I agree.

"Well, they could not agree afterward, for all five were dead."

"Had they been able, I feel certain they would have conceded your point."

"Impossible to argue against us after we proved our mettle."

"Brody, I fear we may land in yet another tight corner. Keep watchful."

"As always, Tristam....You did not used to be such a man for worrying."

The thought *back then, I did not know how much I stood to lose* flashes through my mind, but I do not speak the words.

"As usual, you are correct, Lord Broderick."

Peter's mother is Lord Dunbar's oldest child. She married young and delivered her lord of an heir, Peter's older brother, within one year of her marriage. Her husband is of the family of Tavenor. The Tavenors have a long and loyal history with King Leopold, and now they maintain those ties with King Stefan. They clearly have aspirations for Peter to marry Grace and are inclined to be gracious, though I see no bond between Peter and Grace save the bond of friendship.

In late April, the ten archery contestants gather once again. This time a squirrel is released at thirty paces for each archer. Only the archers who kill their squirrel will compete at the games in May. Though Becca excels at hunting game, Grace never shoots at living targets, unless I force her and we use the meat. She has a distaste for bloodshed of any kind. The tenth-place archer will shoot first, followed by the ninth. Grace will have to wait, watch, and compete last. She wears an expression of one whose thoughts are far away, as the tenth archer misses his squirrel and I am not sure she even notices.

Peter is the first to hit his target, and although the squirrel is barely wounded and escapes quickly into the underbrush, much clapping follows his attempt. Becca is the first to make a clean kill, but she receives less applause than had Peter. I note that those families which I know to be rebels applaud her not at all. The third-place archer is the second to make a clean kill and receives a burst of hearty applause. He is a chubby lad, Timothy. I know him to be distantly related to Lady Tavenor.

Coltrane appears nervous as he takes his place on the line. He glances over at Regis before giving the signal he is ready. When the squirrel runs from its cage, Coltrane's stance is incorrect. He cannot maintain his balance for a clean release. The squirrel is pierced through its left haunch and gives a shrieking cry. Anxiously, I glance toward Grace. And see that her face is white. She averts her eyes from the squirrel, which has been pinned to the ground in agony.

Coltrane walks forward, delivers the squirrel its death blow, and walks to the place where the contestants with clean kills stand. The judges call a halt to the competition to discuss a ruling.

Coltrane's assumption of success displeases the crowd. Only Regis and Dunbar clap as he stands next to Timothy. Every year that I have attended these competitions, rulings are handed down concerning mortally wounded squirrels. Usually the contestant stands humbly with those who missed their shot entirely, until a ruling is determined. Coltrane's presumption makes many in the crowd uneasy.

What I had witnessed in prior years was that a wounded squirrel, which could be captured and killed easily, usually admitted the archer to the final competition. A wounded squirrel that escaped destined its shooter to join the losers. In this case, the judges deliberate longer than usual before declaring that Coltrane may remain with Becca and the other winner.

Although Grace stands poised at the line, her face looks blank. As she gives the signal for her squirrel to be released, Coltrane lets out a sharp cry. Grace flinches, and her arrow rips through the left shoulder of the squirrel, missing its heart. Grace does not spring forward to deliver the death blow. The squirrel cowers until one of the judges clubs it.

A cry of "foul!" goes up from several members of the assembly. Coltrane is called before the judges and a discussion ensues.

At the judges' request, Grace remains poised at the line. Time seems to move slowly.

Later, I learn that Coltrane claimed to have been stung by a bee, though Becca swears it is a lie. I see Coltrane approach Grace. His eyes look cold as the two speak, then I watch him return to the winners' circle ahead of Grace, who is escorted to the winners' circle by the head judge. Coltrane moves to the other side of the group as Grace approaches. Becca casts him a glance of loathing and I find myself in full agreement with her.

CHAPTER 59

GRACE

I dread the final archery competition in May and beg Becca to avoid Beebrong until after the competition. For once, she does not laugh at my fears. "If he could break my arm, he would," she concedes. "He will stop at nothing to win."

I remain silent.

"There was no bee," she comments for at least the tenth time.

I smile but do not speak.

"Oh, very well, we will not discuss the matter again. But I will always believe he should have had to show the sting or be disqualified."

"He said it was on his backside," I say.

"So he claims," Becca replies. "I stood next to him and heard no buzzing."

"I thought we were not going to discuss this."

"Admit that you think he cheated," she demands.

"I do," I reply, just as Coltrane steps out from behind a tree.

"Are you questioning my honor?" He demands of me, ignoring Becca altogether.

I shake my head. Becca's jaw drops.

"No, I question your truthfulness. I fear you have no honor." I hear the words as if they have been spoken by another.

Rage registers on Coltrane's face and he raises his fist. Becca steps forward and leads me away to where Peter and Catherine stand talking.

"What was that about?" Peter asks, nodding at Coltrane's retreating back.

I hear Becca's response as though from under a woolen blanket. My eyes follow Coltrane and I feel my throat closing.

Catherine takes my hand. "Come, Grace, sit down. You are trembling."

I am embarrassed by my weakness. "I am fine," I reply, willing the trembling to cease. "I should not have said that I thought he cheated."

"Well…not within his hearing," Peter chuckles, "but we all think it. You need not be afraid of him. We will guard you."

"I am not afraid of him, but rather of the evil that resides in him," I reply.

Peter nods. No one laughs at me.

Trinicia, Catherine, and Peter work together to see that I am never alone in the vicinity of Coltrane, and I am deeply touched. I stay close to Becca, too, as I also fear for her safety.

CHAPTER 60

GRACE

The final round of the archery competition has three parts. The first is target shooting at a circular target and each of us four shooters has three arrows for the round. We receive points for each arrow that hits the target, with more points being awarded for the arrows that land closer to the center. In the second round, a human-shaped target will suddenly be revealed. Each of the four shooters will have one arrow marked with a different colored band, and we will all fire as soon as the target appears. Only arrows that pierce the heart drawn on the target will score points.

The points of the first two rounds will then be totaled. The two shooters with the most points will compete at a distance round. A hawk will be released at one hundred paces. Both shooters will take aim with their color-banded arrow. If both shooters hit the hawk, which I am told rarely happens, the cleanest kill shot wins the competition.

This is the part of the competition I dread. Hawks are regal birds that we do not hunt in Blinth. Their meat is not edible; killing the hawk will be only for sport. If I make it into the final round, I do not plan to aim at the hawk. I do not like to kill, though killing for food is essential.

I think about this because I am expected to be one of the finalists. Indeed, Peter and Becca talk of nothing else. As friends, we stay close together and away from Coltrane and his minions. He will have an advantage at the distance shooting; he is taller and stronger than the rest of the competitors. Many people make it clear to me that they expect him to win. If I make it to the final round and do not fire at the hawk, they will be right.

I tell no one about my reluctance to kill a hawk. Tristam is as excited as if he were competing himself. He seems younger and more joyous, and

I catch a glimpse of the young man he once was as I practice with him every day. We shoot at targets, squirrels, and the crows that raid the gardens of seeds. We shoot at birds which are good to eat, including pigeons, ducks, and geese. My aim and quickness improve, and Tristam is full of praise.

"Grace, that was marvelous! When I flushed that pigeon, you did not hesitate. Your motion was completely fluid. Let us go find the bird."

"Thank you. Shall we try to get another and give them to Geneva as a gift?" I ask.

"If it would please you," he replies.

"Yes, a slain animal should feed someone."

"The hawk will be stuffed and preserved as a trophy. How do you feel about that?"

"Ill at ease. It seems wrong. Do you not agree?"

"I confess I have never given the matter much thought. Your respect for nature is deeper than my own."

"I think it is because of the stag that kept me warm in the forest on the morning you found me. He was wise and kind. To me, he seemed as human as you did on that day."

"You have never mentioned that to me before."

"There was no need. I think animals have spirits and feelings. I do not wish to kill a hawk."

"What will you do when you are a finalist?"

"*If* I am a finalist," I correct him, "I do not know."

Tristam does not reply.

"If I do not shoot, will you be disappointed?"

"Of course, Grace…I want you to win. I believe you are the best young archer Blinth has seen in many years."

I look at the ground.

"But I think I would also be proud of you for standing up for your beliefs and convictions. That is a different kind of winning."

"Thank you," I whisper. "I wish this were over."

"It soon will be, and then we can go to Tristenhorn for the summer months."

I find myself smiling as I give a large sigh. "I love it there."

"I know you do. This summer you need not work so hard to bring order to the manor."

"That is true. My task this summer is the flower gardens. They are in dire need of restoration."

"You need to rest and be restored yourself."

"Working in the garden will rest me."

"Sitting in the garden would be better."

"But you know I can never be still."

"Yes, Grace, I do," he replies. His eyes are smiling into mine.

CHAPTER 61

GRACE

The day of the contest dawns bright and clear. Not a cloud can be seen in all of the sky and only a rustle of wind plays in the trees. The entire day is for feasting and games. There will be footraces for the younger children, and eight Beebrong teams will be playing throughout the day to determine which is the best.

Thomas, Torquil, and several other huntsmen play on a team. Becca knows where and when their first match is being held and she, Peter, and I watch from the edges of the field. Peter calls loud cheers when Thomas's team scores. Becca and I wave ribbons in the accepted manner. I can tell Becca longs to yell like Peter, but she maintains her ladylike dignity.

After the game, Thomas approaches us. "You are the reason we played so well; you cheered us on to victory."

He spoke to all of us, but his eyes rest the longest on me. I blush.

"When is your next match?" Becca asks.

"At midday. If we win that one, we will play in the final round at the third hour. Will you be there?"

"Most certainly," Becca replies.

"I will be there at the hour of your archery competition. I wish you both good luck."

"Thank you," Becca and I reply in unison.

The four of us walk toward the center of town. The merchants' stalls are set up, as if for market day, but the wares are more festive than usual. Garlands of flowers and ivy are being sold, woven with many colors of ribbon. Special cakes, meat pies, breads, and berries are also for sale. The market is crowded.

Peter buys a wreath of flowers with a bright green ribbon and places it upon Becca's head. The ribbon matches the color of her eyes.

"For the Lady Rebecca, daughter of Sir Daniel-the-Younger," he says bending down on one knee. His voice is teasing, but his eyes look earnest.

"Hush," Becca scolds. "What if someone hears you? I cannot claim the title 'Lady.'"

"Nonetheless, it should be yours," he replies.

"Well, I do not mind being 'Mistress,' so it need not concern you." She turns away and speaks to Thomas. She misses the look of sadness in Peter's eyes. I know he cares for her and that his parents want him to care for me. His eyes give me the first inkling that his caring for my friend might be love.

I catch his eye and smile.

"Grace, you need a wreath also," he exclaims, reaching into his pocket for money.

"No, young Peter, I will place this wreath," Thomas says.

While placing a garland of white daisies with a pale blue ribbon upon my head, he whispers, "You deserve that it should be roses."

"Daisies are much better for a wreath," I reply, thinking of my conversation with Tobias. "Thank you most kindly."

"You are most kindly welcome," he replies. "It will bring you luck today."

"She does not need luck," Peter says. "She only needs Coltrane not to cheat and she will easily win."

I think about the hawk that I do not want to kill and look away.

"Grace, you are not losing your confidence, are you?" Becca asks.

"No…I will do the best I can," I reply.

"I do not care if it is not your very best, as long as you win," she says.

"You should be concentrating on winning yourself," I say.

"I will do my best, but you will win."

I bite my lower lip. Thomas is looking directly at me. I look away.

Thomas says, "Any archer can have a good or bad day, just as in Beebrong—teams have good games and bad."

"He is not acquainted with our friend Coltrane," Becca pipes up, rolling her eyes.

"If he wins, he will talk of it forever," Peter says.

"If he loses, he will give excuses forever," Becca agrees.

"Are they telling the truth, Grace?" Thomas asks.

I shrug my shoulders, nod, and change the subject. "Which team do you play next?" I ask Thomas.

"They call themselves the Foxes," he replies.

"I do not know anyone on that team. If you win, will you play the Lions? I know some of those players," Peter says.

"The Lions could make it to the final round," Thomas replies.

"That team is made up of all noblemen from the east," Peter says.

"How do the teams get selected?" I ask.

"Usually, a team consists of all classes. Nobles, peasants, small land-owners, soldiers, and merchants can all be on the same team. It is best to have it so, because the more a team practices together, the better they will play," Thomas answers. "So most of the teams are made up of people who live close to one another."

"That team, the Lions, wants to be all nobles," Peter says. "I heard my grandfather and my mother arguing about it."

"Tell us about the argument," Becca demands.

"Grandfather liked the idea of an all-noble team, but Mother argued against it. My grandfather, Lord Dunbar, has been acting odd lately. He has been talking about pure-blood noble families as if they are better than other people. My mother argued that the best Beebrong teams are the ones that practice together all the time, and she feels Grandfather is treating those he thinks are beneath him badly."

"Who did you side with?" Thomas asks.

"I choose my friends by their character, not their class," Peter replies.

"Yes, he is good enough to befriend the peasant girl at noble classes," Becca says.

"Did someone actually call you that?" Thomas asks Becca.

"Only Coltrane, and not to her face," Peter says. "I spoke to him about it, but it did no good."

Thomas raises his eyebrows. "Well, even a humble huntsman such as myself is smart enough not to insult Mistress Rebecca."

Becca curtsies and we all laugh together. The subject is dropped.

CHAPTER 62

GRACE

Watching Thomas's team keeps my mind off archery. They win by one point, at midday, against the Foxes. At the final game, I find myself focusing upon Thomas as his team takes the field. He is tall, lean, and well-muscled, with loosely curling brown hair. He is older than we are by several years.

Thomas has been a constant in my life since my arrival in Blinth. He seems to always be at hand when he is most needed. He guarded me when Becca's mother was ill and I stayed with her sister. He was in the stables the night I ran away in March, and he helped Tristam bring me home. I think of him as a dear friend, almost a brother, but the look on his face was not brotherly when he placed the wreath of daisies on my head.

He is an exceptional Beebrong player. His considerable height enables him to catch the ball above the heads of most other players. He is skilled at throwing the ball accurately to his teammates so they can score. He scores himself, but only when there is no one to pass to. His play is clean and he moves easily amongst the opposing team's players, without jostling or bumping them.

The Lions are clearly not as skilled as Thomas's team, the Harvesters. Each member of the Harvesters seems to know exactly where the other ten team members are on the field at any moment. They make quick passes and score four points in the first few minutes of the game.

The Lions become frustrated and begin playing harder, though not better. They get rough and aggressive. The Harvesters do not match their roughness. If anything, their play becomes more polite and more focused. The Lions score one point, but the Harvesters score three more points, leaving them one point short of a victory.

As Thomas catches the ball and leaps to throw it, a black-haired player pushes him from behind with both hands. Thomas sprawls on the ground, face down. When he stands up, blood runs from his nose. His fists are clenched.

"Clumsy huntsman!" the aggressive player calls out.

"That is Coltrane's older brother, Regis-the-Younger," Peter informs us.

"Of course it is," Becca replies in her sarcastic voice.

"They look nothing alike," I comment as Thomas's teammate puts an arm around him and tries to lead him away. Thomas shakes his head, wipes his nose, and the game resumes.

Thomas catches the first pass and stands as if daring Coltrane's brother to take it from him. When Regis-the-Younger charges, Thomas leaps into the air, dodges the attack, and scores the final point. The crowd cheers his beautiful movement, just as Coltrane's brother grasps Thomas from behind and slams him to the ground. Thomas flings up his arm to defend himself and most of the other Lions surround him, calling on the judges to witness Thomas's violence toward a nobleman. The crowd lets out a roar of disapproval and the judges, including Tristam, walk onto the playing field. The Harvesters are sent off the field as Lady Geneva comes forward to assist Thomas. He appears unsteady on his feet.

The Lions are kept talking to the judges for some time. Finally, the judges rule an extra point to the Harvesters, who have already won the game, declaring them the unquestioned champions. I see Thomas thank Geneva before running over to join his teammates as they receive their prizes.

The Lions leave the field without shaking hands with their opponents and I feel a chill creep over my skin, as a single grey cloud momentarily blocks out the sun.

"Grace, Rebecca, Peter, it is time," Tristam calls to us. I shake my head to clear away the chill and walk with my friends toward the archery field.

Most of our classmates are already gathered, along with a larger crowd of adults than I had expected. Headmaster beckons to us, and Becca and I join Coltrane and Timothy for a reading of the rules of the contest.

"The ruling of the judges shall be final," Headmaster announces, his voice carrying across the crowd. "Do you understand?" he asks us.

"Yes, Sir," we respond as one.

"Do you understand?" he asks the crowd. Much laughter meets this sally.

I see Becca's family gathered, including all her uncles, aunts, and cousins. I see Thomas walk over and sit with them. Geneva and Tristam sit amongst the nobility, as does Coltrane's father. Peter is with his grandmother, Lady Tavenor. He has a green ribbon tied on his sleeve.

I notice young Timothy seems nervous, and I talk with him to distract his mind. Becca is constantly moving. She keeps herself between me and Coltrane. I doubt her efforts are necessary, but I appreciate them. Coltrane has completely ignored me since the day I questioned his character. If he thinks he is punishing me, he is mistaken.

We draw numbers to determine the order in which we will shoot at the targets. I draw number one. All three of my arrows pierce the center and I earn 45 points. Timothy shoots second and scores 15. Coltrane misses the center with one of his arrows and scores 40. Becca is the last to shoot. Her first two arrows pierce the center and I see her look of concentration as she notches her third arrow; she wants to score another perfect hit. As she draws, Coltrane makes a movement. Becca lowers her bow and stares at him. Headmaster approaches and leads the three of us away from the line, leaving Becca to stand alone. I will her arrow to find its mark.

Becca takes a deep breath and notches her arrow while biting her lower lip. Watching her clean release, I do not have to look at the target to know her arrow found the mark. We are in first place together.

Coltrane lets out an angry hiss. Headmaster leans over and whispers in his ear and I watch Coltrane's face flush. I wish I knew what Headmaster said.

A rope is strung across the archery field and blankets hang across it. We four contestants are lined up behind another rope at the near end of the field. One human-shaped target will be placed somewhere on the field. When the rope with the blankets is lowered, we sight and shoot at will. Judges watch to see which arrow hits the target first; the first arrow to land within the heart will receive 20 points, the second 15, the third 10. Only arrows landing within the heart will score.

The target could be set up at any distance. Various distances require different stances and bow tensions. This will be a truer test of our skill than ordinary target shooting.

I keep my eye upon the top of the blankets, as Tristam has taught me. As the blankets fall, I will first see the target's head. Knowing the distance, I can set my stance before taking aim and releasing. I lose awareness of the crowd and the other archers. My entire world becomes the blankets and what lies beyond them.

I notice a grey sliver of the head and remember nothing else. My body does what it is trained to do. My arrow finds the mark. I believe it is the first.

I see Timothy's arrow go wide. I hold out my hand to him. "You are the youngest competitor. This experience will help you win the finals someday, when you are older."

He raises his head. "Thank you, Lady Grace. You are most kind," he says and then lowers his voice. "I hope you win," he whispers.

The judges swarm upon the target.

"Becca, did you make your shot?" I ask.

"I think so, but not the center of the heart, I fear."

"Did you release quickly?"

She nods and looks to where the judges are doing their work. Coltrane stands apart, in silence. His body is held erect and his chest is pushed forward. He believes he has hit the mark.

We are called before the judges.

"Please congratulate all of the contestants." Headmaster addresses the crowd and a cheer goes up.

"Master Timothy, our youngest archer, has finished his competition. His skill is impressive in one so young, and he will undoubtedly return to compete again in another year."

The crowd cheers. Timothy bows, waves at the crowd, and leaves the field. He is smiling now and holding up his head.

"Our final three contestants scored a very close first two rounds. Mistress Rebecca and Lady Grace began the second round with forty-five points each. Lord Coltrane had forty points. In this second round, Lady Grace's arrow pierced the heart first, thus giving her twenty additional points and the highest score of sixty-five. Lord Coltrane's was second to pierce the heart, giving him an additional fifteen points for a total of fifty-five points."

A gasp goes up from the crowd, as the meaning of his words sinks in. Headmaster's formal announcement is unnecessary. Becca and Coltrane are tied for second.

Headmaster raises his arms and the crowd grows quiet.

"It is the ruling of the judges that since Lord Coltrane's arrow is closer to the center and reached the target first, he will proceed to the final round."

Much of the crowd is grumbling. Headmaster again raises his hands for quiet.

"Let us show our appreciation for Mistress Rebecca's fine shooting."

A great cheer erupts from the crowd, and I notice most of the nobles are cheering loudly. I dare not look Becca in the eye, for I can feel her anger wash over me in waves.

I look over at the three judges. Lord Dunbar, Lord Tavenor, and a man I do not know are judging. Lord Tavenor looks disgruntled. I vow to find out who the third judge is. I guess him to be from the east.

I reach toward Becca and pull her over to shake her hand, though I long to hug her. Coltrane looks away. Headmaster approaches, again whispering in Coltrane's ear. Coltrane extends his hand to Becca but does not speak.

I watch her leave the field, my stomach knotted with rage. I feel certain that had she been noble, three of us would be competing in the finals instead of two.

I glance over at Sir Tristam and he gives a slight nod. His face is set in harsh lines. I watch him leave his seat and greet Becca, walking with her to where her family is seated.

I am full of feelings. I find I am of two minds; I want to kill the hawk and win the competition for Becca, but I am also full of feeling for the hawk, hooded and tied to its perch. He will soon face death and does not know it. As I approach the line, I feel malevolence radiating from Coltrane. His hatred is like a pool around him, pushing wave after wave of animosity outward in ever-widening rings. I feel myself shrinking inside as fear begins to take hold of me.

I reach into my heart, looking for protection from the hatred that surrounds me and for some answer to my dilemma. I try to picture the face of the hawk. Instead, I see the face of the stag, my Stag. I know he is only a vision I conjure, but I close my eyes, willing him to speak to me and tell me what to do. He looks deep into my eyes and seems satisfied. He nods to me and bounds away. I look into my heart and find no hatred for the hawk, only compassion. I do not believe Coltrane can hit him. I know I can, but I will not. The knot in my stomach softens and I open my eyes.

The order is given for the contestants to string their bows. The hawk's head is unhooded. He strikes at the gloved hand of the handler. On the count of five, the hawk is released and soars into the air.

I watch, mesmerized by the beauty of his flight. I lower my bow, my arrow points at the ground. I hear Coltrane's arrow leave his bowstring. I see the hawk halt its flight, as an arrow pierces its right wing and passes through. Coltrane gives a cry of triumph. The hawk spirals, falling from the sky, screeching its cry of anguish and fear. As I watch the odd spiral pattern, I raise my bow and release my arrow. My aim is true and the hawk falls straight from the sky. I know I have freed him from fear and pain.

A gasp goes up from the assembled company. Coltrane turns to face me, and involuntarily I take a step backward from his open hostility. His eyes blaze, his lips are drawn back from his teeth, and the snarl he makes is almost a growl.

Headmaster appears suddenly, taking Coltrane by the hand and shaking it in the usual manner before grasping mine.

"Wonderful shooting, both of you! This is a rather unusual situation. We must await the ruling of the judges."

"Did the hawk suffer?" I ask.

"Only in the brief moment between the two arrows," Headmaster replies. He is looking at me with his piercing gaze.

I let go a sigh of relief.

Coltrane casts me a look of disgust before walking away. In a moment, I alone am called before the judges.

"Why did you not release your arrow when the signal was given?" the unknown judge demands.

"I was struck by the beauty of the hawk," I reply.

"I do not understand your answer," the judge states.

"The hawk was full of beauty. It is not needed for food."

"So you did not wish to kill it?" he asks.

"That is correct," I reply.

"So you forfeited the contest?"

"Had Coltrane's arrow missed, I would not have fired."

"So you shot to ease the bird's pain?"

"Yes, Sir."

"That will be all, Grace," he says, dismissing me.

I am not surprised when Coltrane is declared the winner. I am surprised when the crowd encircles me, lifting me onto their shoulders. I feel Coltrane's icy glare as he stands with his prize and a handful of members of noble families from the east.

CHAPTER 63

TRISTAM

Grace seems oblivious to the feat of archery she has demonstrated. To shoot a falling bird from the sky is something only a rare archer can ever hope to accomplish. She refuses to take credit, nor is she upset that Coltrane is declared the winner of the contest. She is the only one who is not upset by the judges' ruling, other than Coltrane, his family, and their few close friends. I am furious at the gross injustice of the contest.

"The judges' ruling is just," Grace tells me the following morning.

"How can you say so when you are clearly the better archer?"

"I told them I had no intention of shooting the hawk. I would have preferred to forfeit. I only shot him because he was suffering."

"It was an amazing shot. How did you know where to aim?"

"I did not think, Tristam; I simply reacted to the Hawk's pain. I think some greater force guided the arrow."

"God?"

"Well…it could be God, I suppose. I saw the Stag in my mind, just before the hawk was released."

"Did he speak to you?"

"No, but he seemed to be telling me to listen to my heart. He did not tell me whether to shoot or not."

I nod and wait for her to say more.

"God made the Stag. Perhaps God guides me through the Stag's spirit. We are connected, he and I, just as you and I are connected. Father Gregory speaks of God using people around us to be His voice. Why could God's creatures not also speak His voice?"

"I know of no reason why they could not, but I do not know many people with the sensitivity to listen."

Grace looks away. "I know I am different."

"But you see that as only a bad thing. You do not appreciate how special and talented you are."

"The talent is not mine. It belongs to God," she argues.

"If God gave you the talent but you never practiced with your bow, you could not have made that shot yesterday. Your muscles could not have responded quickly enough, nor been strong enough to send an arrow that far."

Grace tilts her head, weighing my words.

"God gave you a talent which you have developed. When God's creature needed help, you were able to send mercy. It was not a miracle yesterday, but rather a partnership between you and God. You have the right to feel pride in your shooting."

Grace's eyes light up. "But you have more than enough pride in me for both of us."

When I finish laughing, I joke, "Well, I *am* a magnificent teacher of archery."

"Yes, you trained two of the finalists. I am so angry that Becca was not allowed to compete. Had she been noble, she would also have shot at the hawk."

"Who told you so?"

"No one; but it was clear. Lord Tavenor did not like the ruling. I am guessing the other judge and Lord Dunbar are both from the east."

"You are perceptive."

"Thank you for sitting with Becca after she left the field."

"It was where I wanted to be."

"Yes, it was where you belonged. I hope other nobles took notice."

"They did. Becca received many compliments yesterday. Coltrane's victory is hollow."

"Yes, I fear that Becca or I will pay for that one day."

"What do you mean?"

"Coltrane is full of hatred. His father speaks harshly to him. He is like a snake with a long memory. My fear is that he will target Becca, as he considers her beneath him. But then, he also considers me beneath him, as I am foreign."

"I hope you are wrong, but I fear you are not."

"I am not wrong." Grace speaks with a certainty I have never heard before.

I move our departure for Tristenhorn forward by a fortnight. I also seek out the silversmith and the blacksmith and commission a piece of work.

CHAPTER 64

GRACE

We are tested upon our learning before being released from noble classes for the summer. I only see Coltrane from a distance because Peter continues his precaution of never allowing Becca or me to be alone in Coltrane's vicinity. Becca is furious about the competition; if Coltrane accosts her, she will use her anger against him. I do not wish that encounter to take place. Because of this, I want to remove Becca to Tristenhorn with us for the summer months, but Tristam will not agree.

"Her family needs her, Grace. You know how hard they must work in the summer months."

"Could you not hire a servant to take her place?"

"Grace, such speech is unworthy of you. You know it would greatly offend Daniel were I to make such an offer."

I hang my head, knowing he is right.

"You are very worried about her safety."

"Yes, I am. Peter watches over her, but he will be gone, as well. Thomas will be here, except when he is sent out on long hunting expeditions."

"May I speak to Daniel of your fears?"

"Yes, please do so; Becca will never tell him herself. She does not take Coltrane's evil seriously."

"You can trust Daniel to take care of his daughter."

I am silent.

"You would still prefer to take her to Tristenhorn, would you not?"

"Yes, I would."

"It may not matter. No doubt Coltrane is going to his estates for the summer months."

"I do not know his plans."

218

"I will find out."

"Thank you."

When Tristam tells me Coltrane has already gone east and will not return until the squires gather in the fall, I feel only slightly better about leaving Becca.

I broach the subject directly with her. "You must be careful. Coltrane would willingly murder us both, or worse."

"Well, I could just as willingly murder him, so do not expect me to cower all summer in fear," she snaps. "And what could be worse than murder?"

I pause before speaking. "I think Coltrane is capable of inflicting great pain. He would have no mercy."

"Forgive me, Grace. I forget how you have suffered." Becca's voice has softened and she reaches for my hand.

I return the clasp of her hand and look into her eyes. "I would suffer more greatly still if he hurt you."

"For your sake, I will be cautious."

"Thank you," I reply. A lump grows in my throat. "I miss you already," I whisper.

"But I am right here, Oh, foolish Sweet One."

I pull her into my arms. I will not see her again until autumn.

Life at Tristenhorn is easy. I am treated as the Lady of the Manor and must grow accustomed to my orders being obeyed, though I do not like to tell others what they must do. Bethany is my personal maid. She is happily married now and travels each night to her home in the village. It brings me joy to see her so happy. Tristam's housekeeper teaches me what I need to know in order to fulfill my role. I learn to order the supplies needed for the manor and to arrange the formal seating when Tristam entertains.

The gardens are my special pleasure. Tobias and I had discussed them at length; he had suggested certain flowers, shrubs, and trees that would grow well in the landscape I had described to him. I send messages to him as the gardens develop. I also keep Geneva's herb garden in order. Tristam said she did not have enough land of her own to grow all she needs, but he is lying; there is a deeper reason which he does not disclose.

It is Tristam who carries my messages to Tobias; he is restless. He often travels to the castle and beyond. He never speaks of his travels and I do not pry, but I know that he has secrets and burdens unknown to me.

The summer is more than half gone when Tristam returns from yet another of his trips with a gift for me. He presents it to me after dinner, when the plates have been removed. He sits sipping his wine while the candles glow. His eyes are full of anticipation as he says, "Grace, I have something for you. I have been waiting for it since the day after you competed in the archery contest. This is my award to you, as you should have received the prize."

He draws a parcel from under the table, tied up with a clumsy bow.

"I wrapped it myself. Can you tell?"

I smile into his eyes. "Yes, indeed I can."

He reaches for my hand. "Come here, child." His tone is serious.

I obey.

Tristam has given me many things in the years we have been together, and though these things are rarely presented as gifts unless it is a holiday, I feel everything he gives me is a present. He acts as if it is my due; however, he has never before made such a formal presentation.

"I cannot imagine what this is," I say.

"Open it."

When I untie the bow and remove the cloth, a jeweled belt lies in my hands.

"Tristam, it is beautiful!"

"Study it closely, Grace."

I do as he tells me.

The chain of the belt is wrought with silver links. At one end is a clasp which can be used on any link of the chain. Off-center, to the left if the belt is being worn, is a fairly large but delicately wrought medallion. On it, aquamarine stones are set in a flowerlike design. The medallion seems strangely thick for such a delicate piece. Upon careful inspection, I notice a seam near the top of the jewel work. The medallion is in the shape of an inverted drop of water, much wider at the top, narrowing to a point that curves slightly to the left. When I insert my thumb along the seam, the wide part of the medallion slides out, revealing a curving, two-edged dagger. I glance at Tristam in surprise.

"I had it made for you."

"It is beautiful. And deadly," I reply.

"You are proficient with the dagger and have earned the right to be armed. Yet no one need know you carry a dagger. They will see only a beautiful belt."

"How did you think of such a thing?" I ask.

"I saw something like it many years ago, in Polomia. It was much larger and clumsier, but the idea is the same. Our artisans have never made such a belt; it took some time for them to fashion it to my liking."

"Tristam, thank you. It is lovely, but…" I do not know how to continue.

"Yes?"

"You travel with secrets. You seem burdened. I do not wish to pry into what you do not want to tell me, but can you tell me…am I in danger?"

Tristam looks away and takes a sip of his wine. The dark liquid reflects the candlelight.

"I am engaged upon business for the king; of that I can say no more. If my enemies wished to hurt me…"

"They would harm me," I finish for him.

"Yes, if they could. I doubt this is necessary, but the idea came to me when you spoke of Coltrane's evil."

"I see."

"We must continue your training."

"Yes, I have grown lazy over the summer months."

"The skills are within you. They will return rapidly," his tone is matter-of-fact, "and it is time to begin."

"Yes, I must remain strong. There may be another hawk that needs me," I reply.

"Perhaps so. I believe my enemies would find you are not an easy target for them."

I nod.

"I will protect you in every way I can. I will lay down my life for you. But I cannot keep you locked away here."

"And Constance and Faith were not safe, even here."

Tristam sighs and nods in silence. His eyes hold a faraway look. I take his hand.

"I will keep myself safe," I vow.

"If I cannot, you must."

We stay hand-in-hand, with me standing beside his chair, for a long time. Each of us is lost in our own thoughts.

I begin practicing with the new dagger that very night. It feels as if it has been made to fit my hand. The thought strikes me that, of course, it has been.

CHAPTER 65

GRACE

In autumn, Coltrane does not return for noble classes. He begins train-ing full-time as a squire. Peter is also training as a squire, but continues to learn dancing, writing, and history with us.

Becca asks Peter why Coltrane's studies are different from everyone else's.

"I do not know. Most of the squires are here with us in these classes. Only Coltrane does not join us."

"Perhaps he is too good for us," Becca states.

"Or not good enough," Peter replies. "He likes to excel and he does not excel at any of these arts."

I believe Peter speaks the truth, but I do not say so.

My life becomes much easier without daily contact with Coltrane. My archery skills earn me a new respect amongst even the noble children who do not think I belong in their classes. Time moves swiftly and the months pass.

Every year that I attend classes, I compete in the archery competi-tion. It means a great deal to Tristam. I love seeing his face beaming with pride. The second year I compete, I place second to Becca. She refuses to accept her prize because I have again lost by refusing to shoot the hawk.

The third year, the year Becca celebrates sixteen years of life, the bird to be shot is a small, quick duck. All ducks are a delicacy in Blinth, and this shy duck is no exception. It hides from humans and roosts in trees, so hunters rarely bother hunting them. I win this competition. I try to thank Headmaster, for I am certain he requested this change. He refuses to accept my thanks, merely saying the judges could not capture a hawk.

The year Becca and Peter both turn seventeen is the final year we will attend classes. Much emphasis is placed on etiquette and deportment. We attend all the nobles' gatherings. Becca tries to avoid them, but Headmaster will not allow it. The first ball is during Christmastide.

"I am not noble," she insists, as I pull the sash tight around her waist. The emerald green color of the gown makes her skin appear white and draws out the red highlights in her hair. Her eyes are magnificent, shooting fire at the indignity of being dressed as a member of the class she hates.

Tristam and I had schemed together, knowing Becca would never have allowed him to pay for her ball gown. We selected the rich green fabric knowing it would not suit me.

At the first fitting, I said, "Tristam, this color makes me look pale and insignificant." We had agreed I would start this conversation.

"But I thought it was the color you most admired when we were looking at fabrics," he replies on cue.

"It is a beautiful color, but not a color I should wear. It would look beautiful on someone with dark hair," I say, continuing our deception.

"Forgive me, my dear. I chose poorly. You shall choose a different fabric."

"Oh, no," I reply, watching the seamstress's face, as she takes in my every word. "I could not ask that of you. I shall wear this emerald gown to please you."

"But it will not please me to see you looking less than your best." He turns, addressing the seamstress. "Do you have time before the ball to make a new gown?"

"Certainly, My Lord, though it will need to be done quickly."

"You shall have the fabric within the hour and I will pay you double."

She nods graciously. "What shall I do with this gown?"

"Grace has no use for it," Tristam replies.

I pretend an idea has struck me. "Mistress, would you have time to finish this gown as well?"

"What are you thinking, Grace?" Tristam asks, though he knows full well what I am thinking, as we had hatched this plan over dinner the previous evening.

"Rebecca has nothing to wear and Headmaster has made her attendance a requirement to staying in classes. She is planning to attend in her Sabbath dress."

"That will not do," he says emphatically.

"I cannot convince her otherwise."

"Would she wear this green gown?" He is doing a wonderful job of acting and the seamstress is soaking in every word.

"I believe she might, if you explain to her what happened."

Tristam had Becca fitted for the dress that very day.

As I had expected, she questioned the seamstress mercilessly. Our acting had fooled the woman and she unknowingly convinced Becca to accept a gift intended for her all along.

Now, a fortnight later, all our trickery is rewarded when I see Peter's face as Becca enters the Great Hall. His parents' faces are polite, though not effusive, when they approach in his wake. Peter has eyes for no one but Becca, though Becca will not take his attentions seriously.

Becca never puts herself forward or expects to be treated as noble, but she learns every lesson perfectly. If she harbors secret dreams of becoming Peter's lady, she never speaks of them to me. I think she has good reason to be cautious, but watching her dance with Peter convinces me they belong together. As a younger son, he will have to make his way in the world. Becca is hardworking. They would be happy.

"Watching the peasant girl pretending to be nobility, I see." Lady Beltran's voice penetrates my reverie. "She forgets herself."

I glance over at Tristam hoping he will rescue me, but he is deep in conversation with an elderly gentleman who is unknown to me.

"But of course, you do not belong here, either. Come, Melanie," she beckons her daughter.

Melanie lifts her nose in the air and promptly trips over an uneven floor stone. Tristam catches her, and I can barely suppress the laughter that rises to my throat.

After she and her mother have departed, Tristam whispers in my ear, "It is not polite to laugh at others' misfortunes."

"She is not deserving of politeness."

He looks at me and asks the question without speaking.

"Melanie has not spoken to me in the five years we have been in class together."

Tristam watches the retreating backs of mother and daughter. "She does not concern me. Laugh at her all you wish in private, but you are under scrutiny here; do not disappoint me."

I blush scarlet. "I am sorry," I whisper.

"You need not be. But for now, we must be polite to our enemies. Come, dance with me."

I do as he bids me though I cannot forget his rebuke. When the rebellion unfolds, I understand the meaning of his words more fully.

CHAPTER 66

GRACE

The following spring, during another ball, I learn that Thomas and Becca have been keeping a secret from me. Once again, I am standing and watching Peter dance with Becca as one of the servants approaches.

"Excuse me, Lady Grace."

"Yes?"

"I was asked to deliver this note to Mistress Rebecca, but she is dancing. I am needed in the kitchen."

"I will see that she gets it as soon as this dance is over."

"Thank you," the man replies.

Before he turns to leave I ask, "Who gave you this?"

"One of the huntsmen, My Lady. I do not know his name."

"Is he waiting for a response?"

"Yes, he waits in the hallway to the kitchen."

"Will you take me to him?"

"Yes, My Lady."

I am not surprised when the servant leads me to Thomas.

"Thomas, good evening. Is something amiss?"

"Yes, Becca's grandmother is asking for her."

"The one who has been so very ill?"

"Yes, they think her time is near."

"I will fetch her at the end of this dance."

"Thank you."

I glance down at the note in my hand and am surprised to see a handwriting I do not recognize. "Thomas, this is not Sarah's writing. Who sent this note?"

The light in the hallway is dim, but I see Thomas's face flush. "I was sent to fetch her," he finally says, "and I did not wish to enter the ball-room."

"So, who wrote this note?"

"I did," he replies. He is looking toward the ballroom. "How soon will this dance end?"

"In just a few moments. Would you like me to interrupt her?"

"No, her grandmother has some time."

An awkward silence falls. I study the note in my hand.

"Your writing looks just as I would expect it to."

"What do you mean?"

"The letters are large and well formed. A certain boldness characterizes the style."

"Well, I am large, but I do not see myself as either well-formed or bold," he says making light of my compliment.

A few moments pass in silence before Thomas takes a deep breath and says, "I have never seen you dressed for a ball. That shade of pale blue is most becoming."

I feel myself blush and turn the conversation back to writing. "When did you learn to write?"

"My mother began teaching me when I was still Wee Thom, but," he pauses and then continues, "she could not continue after my sisters were born."

"That is not what you were going to say."

"How do you know that?" he asks.

"I can tell. But I shall not pry."

He smiles and nods. "Lately, Becca has been helping me."

"That is wonderful. If I can help, please tell me."

He nods, blushing. "Thank you, My Lady."

I give him a searching look, feeling strangely hurt. He has never called me "My Lady" before.

"My name is Grace."

He does not speak and the music ceases, so I go in search of Becca.

Tristam and I attend the funeral of Becca's grandmother. Several more days pass before Becca returns to class. Finally, I am able to ask her about teaching Thomas to write.

"Why did you not tell me you were helping Thomas?"

"He does not wish anyone to know."

"But he is my friend. I want to help."

"He does not want your help."

"I do not understand." I am trying to keep the hurt out of my voice.

"Put yourself in Thomas's place. You are wealthy, noble, beautiful, and much younger than he is. Why would he ask for your help?"

"I do not care about such differences. Thomas is my friend."

"Perhaps. Or perhaps you are blind."

Becca's words give me much to ponder. It makes me feel uncomfortable to think of Thomas caring for me. He has been a true friend and I do not want that to change.

CHAPTER 67

TRISTAM

Grace is hurt. She cannot understand Thomas's refusal to allow her to teach him to read and write. Nor does she wish to understand Becca's accusation that she is blind. I do not enlighten her that Thomas's interest in her began on the day we found her, the day he went from being "Wee Thom" to "Thomas."

Thomas's character, kindness, and the fact that he is hardworking make him just the type of man I would choose for my Grace to marry. The lad has a good heart, though I still have reservations about Grace marrying a huntsman. If he is improving himself to become an acceptable suitor, he will need money in addition to an education. I may be able to help Thomas and fulfill the needs of the king at the same time.

In this, the eighth year of Stefan's reign, the rebellion is heating rapidly. The king has asked me to find a trustworthy man who travels silently and swiftly through the woods. He also requires the man to be able to read and write Blinthian.

Once I learn of Thomas's education, I lose no time in speaking with him. At Becca's grandmother's funeral, I ask him to ride out with me three days hence. We travel several miles from the castle before I begin the conversation.

"Thomas, the king is looking for a loyal man to serve him."

"I am his to command," he replies.

"This is a dangerous undertaking and the rewards will be great."

"Go on," Thomas says.

"How would your mother fare if you did not return?"

"She is getting married."

"To a good man?"

"He is very good," Thomas smiles.

"She would receive your reward if you did not return. She would not have to worry about money the rest of her days, though I am certain she would prefer to have her son."

"What does the king require?"

"I am not fully in his confidence, but I know you have the skills he asks for."

"And they are?"

"The man must be familiar with the woods to the east, a swift and silent traveler, and able to read and write."

Enlightenment dawns on Thomas's face. "I understand why you are asking me now: Grace must have told you that I have learned to read and write."

I nod.

"The king must need some type of messenger."

"Yes, and perhaps more. He cautions that the man's life will be in danger if he is captured."

"Which enemies does he fear?"

"Enemies both within and outside the kingdom."

Thomas casts me a swift glance. "Then the rumors I am hearing are true."

"What have you heard?"

"Rumblings of a rebellion."

"The king will tell you what he wants you to know." Thomas looks abashed and remains silent. "Take time to make your decision."

"The decision is made."

"Are you certain?"

"My king needs me, My Lord."

"This is an excellent opportunity for just such advancement as you seek."

"Sir?"

"Grace is blind," I tell him gently, "but I am not."

Thomas's face burns. He looks at the ground. A few moments pass before he raises his eyes to mine. "Forgive my impertinence, Sir."

"There is nothing to forgive."

"Sir?"

"Thomas, you are a good man. Grace's future is in her own hands. She is well dowered and I will force no man upon her. She calls you her friend. Perhaps she will grow to love you."

"So you would not disapprove?"

"I would not."

"But Grace loves *you*, Sir." His hazel eyes look directly into mine. He has grown so tall, I must look up to meet his gaze.

"My relationship with Grace is complicated," I tell him.

"No. It is simple. You adore her."

"I wish it were simple. I must be certain I am not taking advantage of her position before I am free to marry her. I have been like a father to her, and it is too soon to become her suitor."

"It is not your way to take advantage."

"Yet I might so easily do so without wishing to. I cannot see my path. Until Grace remembers her past, I can only wait."

"So you wish to marry her, but you do not discourage me from seeking her hand?"

"My only desire is for her happiness. She may need me as her father, her protector, her husband, or her friend. I am hers in whatever way she needs me."

"I, too, want her to be happy."

"Then take my advice, treat her as a friend."

"Thank you, Sir." Thomas holds out his hand and I take it in my own. His grip is strong.

"You are to go to the king's chamber tonight at midnight. His guards will be expecting you."

"Thank you for your trust, Sir."

"You may not thank me if things go badly."

"You are not responsible for the outcome, I am. I thank you for the opportunity."

"Godspeed, lad. Keep your skin whole."

"And you as well," he replies.

In the end, only one of us will be able to do so.

CHAPTER 68

GRACE

Becca and I remain close, but as we approach the end of classes we are keenly aware that our lives will soon take separate paths. We train for our last archery competition, and again place first and second. I wonder if Becca will return to her former life or if, someday, Peter's wishes will prevail. I cannot see my own future; it is as walled off as my past.

I find Thomas often in my thoughts and occasionally in my dreams. He is polite and respectful when our paths cross, but he seems different. Perhaps I am dwelling too much on his not wanting my help to learn to write. I do not know how to bridge the gap between us. Perhaps the summer months apart will change things.

We move to Tristam's estates as soon as classes end, but he is always gone. I find myself missing Becca, Peter, Catherine, and Trinicia much more than I have in other summers. It does not help that we will not be returning to classes together in the fall. I find that being away from Thomas does not help me think of him less often.

In the fall, to my surprise, we return to the castle. Tristam's work requires this. I feel hemmed in and stifled because Tristam has made me promise never to ride alone or leave the castle walls unattended. I am restless and I worry for his safety. He still tells me nothing, but I know what is happening.

One day, after Michaelmas, I go to the stables. The weather is glorious, without a cloud to mar the beauty of the clear blue sky. A gentle breeze rustles the trees. I long to gallop through the open fields, but Tristam is away on one of his trips to the east and I am mindful of my promise.

Rufus and Firefly, the young mare Tristam gave me, are stabled near the huntsmen's horses. Rufus likes it so. He had grown agitated when an attempt had been made to stable him with the other noblemen's steeds, so he had been returned to his humbler lodging and has been quite satisfied. Firefly is stabled with him. She is a delicate black horse with a white blaze between her eyes, which seems to light up in the dark. She is named for that mark. She is young and skittish and when Rufus is gone, she is unhappy.

I go to her stall with apples to soothe her. I brush her and talk to her as one speaks to a young child. I do not notice Thomas until he speaks.

"Good day," he says, holding his hat in his hands.

I jump. Firefly whinnies.

"Oh, Thomas, good day. You startled me."

"I am sorry. I came to check on one of the horses. He grazed his forelock yesterday."

"May I look at the wound?"

"Certainly. I am applying an ointment."

I have become somewhat skilled in the use of herbs because of Geneva. I ask her questions about the herbs in the garden when she visits us at Tristenhorn, and when I see her mix her medicines, I ask more questions. She is a good teacher.

"This is Storm," Thomas says, indicating a beautiful grey stallion with a dappled coat.

I begin talking to the horse, letting him grow accustomed to me, before examining the wound on his leg.

"There is some green poison here, just along the center of the graze."

"I know."

"Was it there yesterday?"

"Yes, but there was less of it."

"What is in the ointment?"

"I do not know. I was told to use it by the head huntsman."

"That would be Daniel, Becca's father."

"Yes, yes, of course you know Daniel. Forgive me." Thomas's face grows red.

"Would you ask him if I can provide an herbal mixture that will draw out the poison?"

"Of course. He will say yes. He wants what is best for the horse."

"It will take some time to prepare. I can bring it back in the late morning."

"I will gladly fetch it."

"No, thank you. Firefly is lonely. I need to come back and visit her, so it is not a bother to bring the salve."

I glance out of the stable at the clear blue sky. "How I would like to ride today," I say aloud, without thinking.

"If you will accept my escort, we can ride upon your return."

"I was not asking you to accommodate me. I spoke without thinking."

"Is my escort unacceptable to you?" There is a sudden stiffness in his manner.

"Your escort is most welcome if you are certain you can spare the time." I glance at his face and am glad to see it soften.

"You worry too much. Of course I am certain." He smiles down at me and his dimples appear. My stomach feels odd. I drop my gaze.

"I accept your escort with pleasure and I thank you most kindly." I curtsy.

"The pleasure will be mine," he replies with a formal bow. He winks and I grin up at the young giant. It is the first time he has seemed happy to see me since the night I learned he could write.

Later that day, Thomas sits astride a beautiful bay. I keep Firefly in hand until we reach an open meadow, then I let her break into a gallop. Thomas's horse thunders along behind us. We pull up at the far end of the meadow.

"I do not know who enjoys this more, Firefly or me!" I am grinning.

"That is quite a pace you set," Thomas says, grinning back to me.

"I will race you back," I say, not waiting for his response but urging Firefly to a gallop.

He and his bay catch us just before we rein in at the edge of the forest.

"How did you learn to ride like that?" Thomas asks.

"At Tristenhorn, during the summer months."

"Is there no end to your talents?"

I blush.

"You are a famous archer. Your tapestries are the most beautiful I have ever seen. You ride fast and strong. You are fluent in three languages."

"How do you know that?"

"Becca told me of your special classes with Headmaster."

"Oh," I respond in a flat tone.

"Grace, were your classes supposed to be a secret? Should I not have been told?"

"Not necessarily. I am merely surprised you know of them." I strive to sound as if nothing is bothering me, but I do not succeed in fooling him.

"Grace, what is it?"

"Did she tell you about my classes during your special classes with her?" My voice has a sarcastic edge.

"Perhaps. I do not recall. Are you still upset that I did not ask for your help learning to read?"

"What makes you think I was ever upset about that?" I pretend to be nonchalant.

"Becca told me."

"So she keeps your secrets, but not mine," I say, rolling my eyes.

"She thought it was important that I knew I had hurt you. I am sorry. I should have told you sooner."

His directness catches me off guard. I do not know what to say.

"Will you forgive me?"

"Why did you not want my help?"

"There are reasons."

"Tell me."

"Someday I will."

"But not today?"

"Not today," he affirms.

"But we are still friends?"

"Grace, you will never lose my friendship."

I look up into his eyes. They look brown yet also green. "Promise?" I ask.

"I promise."

"Then you are forgiven."

"Thank you, My Lady," he says with a grand bow.

"I hate it when you call me that."

"I know; that is why I do it," he teases. "Come on." He leads and Firefly and I follow.

After we rein in again, he asks, "Which languages has Headmaster taught you?"

"Well, Blinthian, of course," I smile, as it is the language we are speaking. "Headmaster also taught me the language of Lolgothe. I learned it so rapidly, we both suspect I already knew it. The language of Traag is closely related to it, so it was not difficult."

"You are talented and humble."

I blush. "You make too much of me."

"You make too little of yourself."

"You sound like Tristam."

"He is a wise man."

I steer the conversation in another direction. "Tell me about your family."

Thomas looks as if he wants to say something, but changes his mind and answers my question. "My mother is a widow. My father passed when I was but six years of age."

"What happened?"

"He was a huntsman. He was gored by a wild boar."

"Through the thigh?" I ask.

Thomas turns his head to look at me. "How did you know that?"

"It was a guess. A man bleeds to death quickly if a wound goes deep there."

"He died in a quarter of an hour, I am told."

"How you and your mother must have suffered."

"My sisters also. They were too young to even remember him, but they remember that our lives changed."

"Oh, dear." I can think of nothing else to say.

Thomas continues, "It would have been much worse for us if it were not for the kindness of the huntsmen and my mother's brother. We never lacked for food, but I kept outgrowing my shoes," he laughs, indicting his enormous feet. "I was a severe trial to my mother."

"I am sure you were her support."

Thomas casts me an appraising glance. "I tried to be, but now she has a new man in her life. After all these years, she is getting married again."

"Do you like her betrothed?"

"Very much. And he adores her."

"That is wonderful. How are your sisters?"

"They are well. My oldest sister is married and has two children. The younger works in the bakery and always smells like bread. The suitors flock and it is my job to send them away. I tease her that it is only her aroma that her suitors love."

"And does she tease you in return?"

Thomas's eyes hold a decided gleam. "But of course."

"And what does she say?"

"Nothing that is appropriate to repeat."

"Truly?"

His face reddens a bit before he says, "She likes to tease me about my size."

I smile, but find I am thinking about his being an orphaned boy. "And what about the little boy who grew up without a father?"

"He grew big and strong and began hunting with the huntsmen when he was only twelve years of age. They looked after him. He had a dozen fathers teaching him to put meat on the king's table and his own," he says lightly.

"And he met an orphan girl in the woods and took pity on her," I add.

"It is not pity I feel for you, Grace. You have stirred my compassion, but never my pity. You are too strong for pity."

"I do not feel strong."

"Does the oak feel strong?" he says, indicating a massive tree that we are passing.

"I do not know."

"Whether it feels strong or not, it is."

I have no response.

We ride on in silence until Thomas says, "Thank you, Grace."

"For what?"

"For asking about my family. I have not spoken of my father in many years. It is good to remember."

"What was he like?"

"I am told I look just like him. He was large with the same curling brown hair. I remember a man who laughed a great deal and was gentle with his children."

"So, he was a good father."

"Yes, very. He was also a good huntsman."

"So you are just like him."

"I am not a father."

"No, but you are a good huntsman."

Thomas raises his eyebrows. "Why would you think so?"

"Tristam says you are. You will be a good father someday, also."

He blushes at the compliment, but then argues. "You cannot know that."

"But I do; you are gentle with the wounded horse, and with me. You kept your temper when Coltrane's brother fouled you in that Beebrong game three years ago."

"I just barely kept my temper."

"Well, he blatantly broke the rules."

"Imagine you remembering that; you were so young then."

"I was fourteen....At least we think that is how old I was then."

"May I ask you a question?"

"Certainly."

"You do not have to answer if you do not wish," he assures me.

I nod.

"Do you truly not remember your age or anything of your former life?"

"I remember just one event, an unpleasant one. My father was neither kind nor gentle."

"Men like that, I do not understand," he says, through clenched teeth. I see the muscles in his jaws bulge.

"They are filled with hatred. They are to be pitied."

"Perhaps, but I would prefer to punish them." His face is set in anger. I smile.

"Why are you smiling?" he demands.

"You are the third person who has told me they would like to punish my father. It makes me feel…cared for, though I would never want anyone to get hurt avenging me."

"No one can avenge you, because you cannot remember," he says and then pauses before continuing. "It must be strange to not even be certain of your age."

"I would like to know my given name, but I have grown accustomed to being called Grace."

"Do you think you will ever remember?"

"I try not to think of it. When I first came here, I was full of nightmares. I thought they were more than dreams. I wanted desperately to remember."

"And now?"

"The nightmares have passed. I have been here many years. I do not know if I will ever remember."

"Do you wish to?"

"Yes and no."

"I can understand that answer."

We ride in silence for a time.

"What are you thinking of?" I ask.

"I am thinking you will remember when the *yes* outweighs the *no*."

"Why do you say so?"

"I do not know. It simply makes sense."

"Well, that describes exactly how I feel."

"Tell me about not wanting to know."

"I fear there are horrors in store for me. The dreams are terrifying."

He is nodding. "And yet, part of you still wants to know. Why?"

"I would like to know my name, my age, and if I have a brother like you or perhaps a sister. I want to know if I left someone behind whom I loved."

Thomas is silent after my words. When I look at his face, his expression is difficult to read.

"Do you think of me as a brother?" he finally asks.

"I guess, in a way, I do. I also think of you as my friend, as someone I care for and count on."

"Very well, little sister, we must head back to the stables." There is a teasing note in his voice; he seems more distant than before.

I worry I have offended him somehow.

That very night, the nightmares return.

CHAPTER 69

TRISTAM

When I first began gathering information for the king, in the third year of his reign, the rebellion was not much more than disgruntlement. King Stefan solidified his power rapidly during those years. The dissatisfied faction was cautious. I had identified which noble houses were involved, but gathering evidence to accuse a man of treason is not easily done, especially when the conspirators speak only in veiled threats.

Lord Regis Tragoltha is the leader and I believe the entire Tragoltha family is involved. Their proximity to Traag enables them to slip across the border and lay their evil plans, especially as Regis has cleared lands to the north and east. The house of Beltran is also heavily involved; they have much to gain if the heir of Richard ascends the throne. Lord Dunbar is a reluctant participant and a weak man whom Regis bends to his will. Dunbar is too frightened of Regis to betray him, preferring instead to betray the king. Several other houses are involved, but fortunately the servants are largely loyal to the king. Many of them had served in the castle at some earlier point in their lives. Others simply do not like their masters. Every noble house has some servants who are loyal to their masters, but the rebels have far fewer than most. Set as they are on social advancement, they fail to take into account those they feel are beneath them. I easily built a network amongst the servants within the Beltran and Tragoltha estates, and I probably could have done it without the king's gold, so unhappy are these servants.

By the fifth year of King Stefan's reign, I knew every movement the rebels made. That year, they began communicating with the king of Traag, promising wealth, land, and plunder if he joined forces with them. Three years later, the Traag king continues to demand gold and supplies to fortify his troops before he will march against his neighbor. He is more than willing to invade Blinth if he knows he can be successful. His incessant demands hamper the rebels; they grow resentful, but they need the soldiers of Traag to attack King Stefan's guards for them.

I doubt the rebels fully consider the consequences of stirring up two opposing armies when their land lies in the corridor between the two forces, nor can I fathom how Regis and his cronies expect to control the forces of Traag, once they have been unleashed upon Blinth. The king of Traag has reigned for more than five decades; the man cannot be a fool. If Traag helps the rebels invade successfully, I believe they will put their own king on the throne of Blinth.

I do not fear the rebellion. Every rebel is known and watched when they visit the castle or come near our king, as my first order is the protection of King Stefan. I do fear a war with Traag, however. Traag has expanded her borders in every direction except southwest, toward Blinth, in my lifetime. For this, two things are responsible: the reputation of our warriors and the barrier of mountains. There is only one pass through which a battalion of soldiers can march. If Blinthian archers hold the high ground, they will wreak havoc upon the battalions as they come through the pass. I engage Brody to secretly map the mountains and the pass, looking for sheltered locations in which archers may be hidden from both the rebels and the soldiers of Traag. Brody finds three such locations on the northern side of the pass and four to the south. Some of these strongholds can hide as many as thirty archers from view in the valley below.

My friendship with Brody is often an excuse for my travels to the east. Many of my missions are accomplished in secrecy with Brody's help. Even so, comments are made about my frequent trips to this part of Blinth. Brody takes his widowed elder sister into his confidence, spreading the rumor that I come to court her. He also spreads the word that his sister is reluctant to move west and I am finding the courting of her to be difficult. Beatrice does not care that our duplicity makes her appear foolish for being reluctant to marry a wealthy landowner, and she merely laughs when I thank her for her service to the king.

"I care not what the rebels think of me," she smiles. "When they are exposed as traitors, I will be known as the wise one."

"Thank you for spending time with me, to assist me in keeping my secrets."

"It is a pleasure to spend time with a man of courage, if only I could love you…but you are much too young for me and remind me forcibly of my brother."

"And worse you can say of no one?"

"No, Brody is a good man, but both of you are too willing to place yourselves in the path of danger. I have no desire to be twice widowed."

"I do not fear for my life, or Brody's, in this venture."

"Then you are a fool. Regis is not as blind as you seem to think. He quizzes me about our relationship whenever he sees me. He suspects duplicity."

"Yes, he has made similar comments to me," I reply, sipping my wine.

"No doubt telling you you can do better for yourself."

"He said something to that effect, but the man cares not for character, only for land."

"What a flattering tongue you have, Tristam."

"Is it flattery to speak the truth?"

She shakes her head and laughs at me. "Save your charm for someone who can appreciate it."

I laugh out loud.

"You should also be more careful with your life."

"My Lady, you worry too much."

"And you do not worry enough."

In the end, she is the more correct.

CHAPTER 70

GRACE

Rumors spread that Tristam is wooing a sister of Lord Broderick, but he seems like a man heavily burdened, not a man in love. He continues to pour his love over me, his eyes glowing when he greets me after a separation.

"Ah, Grace, my only love," he says, returning one evening in midsummer.

"Careful, such speech will belie your supposed courtship."

His face grows grave. "What do you know of these things?"

"Rumors say Lady Beatrice is the reason for your travels….But I do not think you act like a man in love."

Tristam nods. "What else troubles you?"

"Other rumors say your travels are to observe the eastern landholders who may not be loyal to King Stefan."

Tristam is not pleased. I decide not to add to his burden by speaking of my nightmares.

"Those are the rumors I fear," I continue. "It would be like you to place yourself in harm's way, to serve the king."

"Have you had communication with the Lady Beatrice?"

"You know that I have not. Why do you ask?"

"Because you talk as she does."

"Is she worried for you?"

"Lady Beatrice is much too practical a woman to worry."

"But the second rumor is the correct one, is it not?" I ask.

"Do not ask me to tell you what I cannot."

"You need tell me nothing. I can read your face."

"Let us hope others are not as skilled."

"Most people are blind, but you should smile more and take gifts to

Lady Beatrice."

"Thank you, Grace. I will do so."

"You must be careful, if not for your own sake, then for mine. Without you, I…" I cannot finish my thought.

"You?"

"I would be lost…again."

"I have made provisions for you."

"I do not speak of wealth. I cannot imagine life without you."

"Then do not. All will be well."

I look as deeply into his blue eyes as the fading evening light will allow. "You believe the words you speak."

"I do."

"Very well. My trust is in you."

"Your trust is safe."

I want to believe him, so I do not persist. I know all I need to know. He will be careful and he is in danger.

After my first ride with Thomas, our rides together become a habit on the days when he is free from hunting. We often ride west, toward Langstonhorn, or north to the Boldengarth River. Sometimes we travel south, but we never go east.

We talk of all manner of things on our rides. I tell him of my loneliness when I first arrived in Blinth.

"I felt so lost. I kept thinking Tristam would tire of me and send me away. I used to come here for comfort."

"To the Wildcat Creek?"

"Yes, to this very place. I will show you."

Thomas dismounts and then leads Firefly to a log and helps me off her back. We give the horses a drink and then tether them to an oak. I lead Thomas onto a rock that protrudes out into the creek.

"I would come here and sit sometimes when Tristam thought I was in Tobias's garden."

"Really?"

"Yes, I have never told anyone this. I am not sure why I am telling you."

"You can tell me anything."

"Thank you."

"So what did you do here on this rock?"

"I would curl up with my knees to my chest, close my eyes and try to remember. I thought the water flowing over the rocks would help me."

"Did it?"

"Yes, but not in the way that I wanted it to. It soothed me, and it soothes me still."

"But it did not help you remember."

"No." I look down at the water. The dappled light reflects the green of the leaves overhead.

"You look sad."

"I am never sad when I am with you," I reply, reaching for a lighter note.

"Grace, there is something you are not telling me."

"There is something *you* are not telling *me*. I went looking for you the other day and the huntsmen said you were off working for the king."

I look up into his face, but he is looking away. He does not speak.

"You look just as Tristam did when we had this same conversation. You both are working for the king. I admire you, and I am afraid."

"What is it you fear?"

"I fear the loneliness I once knew in those woods to the north." My words catch me by surprise.

"Have you told Tristam of your fears?"

"I tried."

"What did he say?"

"He said I would be provided for, but that does not matter. I would be lost without him. He is my only family, yet I have no real claim on him."

"He would disagree."

I do not know what to say. I cannot express my feelings or my foreboding.

"Grace, is there something you want to tell me?" he asks, insistent.

At first, I shake my head, but then I change my mind. "Yes, be careful. Please, be very, very careful. I do not want to lose you, either."

"You will not lose me."

"Now you sound like Tristam again."

"Is that good or bad?"

"Both. Come; we should head back."

"Wait," he says taking my hand. "If you ever do want to tell me what is really bothering you, I will listen."

I blush and pull my hand away. "This business of the king is really bothering me."

"But that is not all. Do not ask me how I know and do not lie to me. That is no way to treat a friend."

I almost tell him about the nightmares, but I cannot.

CHAPTER 71

GRACE

After our conversation, I avoid Thomas for several days. Eventually, my guilt at ignoring Firefly takes me to the stables, but Thomas is not there. A young lad is tending the huntsmen's horses in his stead. I had been nervous about seeing Thomas, but find I am crushed that he is gone. Tristam is also away. Becca is working for her family. Catherine, Peter, and Trinicia have remained at their ancestral homes; they will come to the castle only for special gatherings now that we no longer attend classes. I break my promise to Tristam and ride to my rock on the Wildcat.

When I next ride with Thomas, I feel shy and awkward. I hide my discomfort and ask him questions.

"What would you do if you could do anything? Would you still be a huntsman?"

"In many ways the huntsmen are my family; they have been kind, but I would like to own a farm. I want to raise sheep. We already own several, but we need more land."

"How will you get it?"

"I will have to work for it." His face looks closed.

"I see. That is part of the reason for your secret work for the king."

"No, Grace, I do not serve my king for a reward."

"No, but you know how you will use a reward if you receive one."

He nods.

"What does your mother think of your plans?"

"She does not know about my work for the king. Only you know."

"What does she think about sheep?"

"She thinks they smell." His eyes are full of laughter and he pinches his nose.

We laugh together and I feel less awkward.

Several days later, on another ride, I learn that Thomas and his mother are very close. I learn that the eldest sister's two sons find their greatest pleasure in playing with their uncle, but I am not introduced to his family.

One day, when we are returning to the castle, two small boys come running at Thomas, calling out, "Uncle Thom, Uncle Thom!"

"Grace, be quick, pull up ahead of me," he says, slowing his horse's pace. I do as he bids.

"Lady Grace, may I greet my nephews?" he asks, in formal tones.

"Why certainly, Thomas," I reply.

I turn in the saddle to see a boy of about five summers pulling on Thomas's boot, while Thomas lifts a younger child in front of him onto the horse.

"Not fair!" says the older boy. "I want to ride with you."

"No, you shall have the privilege of leading a lady's horse, if she will allow it. Make your bow to Lady Grace, Scamp," Thomas replies.

The child bows, but he never takes his eyes off his uncle.

"Lady Grace, meet my nephews, Gerald and little Thomas."

"With pleasure," I reply. I notice a young woman watching us.

"Is that your mama?" I ask the older child.

"Yes, My Lady," Gerald replies.

The woman comes forward and curtsies low.

"My sister, Mistress Ruth," Thomas says.

"I am Grace," I say, reaching down to touch her hand. She has Thomas's golden-brown curls but her eyes are brown and her height is average. She blushes when I touch her hand.

"It is a pleasure to meet you, My Lady. The boys and I watched your archery competitions," she begins.

"You are amazing, especially that first year," Gerald interrupts. "You should have won. It was not fair."

"Now, Gerald, do not interrupt your elders," his mother chides him.

"That was a long time ago. You could not remember that, now could you, Master Gerald?" I ask the child.

"But I have heard the story many times and it was not fair."

"Life often is not fair. Is that not so, Master Gerald?" I reply.

"You are right, My Lady."

"But I think it *was* fair that I did not win that competition."

"How can you say so?" he asks.

"Well, I did not plan to shoot the hawk. He was too beautiful to kill for sport. But when he was wounded, he needed my help. He could not live if he could not fly. His heart called for my arrow and made it fly straight."

"Really?" The boy's eyes are round.

"That is how I feel," I reply, "though some would say I am fanciful to imagine such a longing from a hawk."

"I think you are right. On the ground, the hawk would have been eaten by a fox or vultures. That would have been worse for him."

"I think you are wise, Master Gerald."

I look up to see Ruth studying Thomas's face. She does not look pleased.

"Come boys, we must let Thomas do his work," Ruth says in a brusque manner.

"But Mother, I am to lead the lady's horse."

"And I would be honored to have it so, but your mother needs you."

"Mother, please!"

"Not today. Those market baskets need to be carried, young man."

"Another time, Master Gerald," I say, smiling into his face.

"Me too?" asks little Thomas.

"Yes, of course, when you are older," I reply.

Ruth is thawing a bit. "Thank you, My Lady."

"It was a pleasure to meet you and the boys," I reply, smiling. "They are wonderful."

"Do not let them hear you say so," she says, with barely concealed pride. "Supper is at sundown, Wee Thom. Do not be late."

"Yes, dear Ruth," Thomas replies.

When we reach the stables, I ask Thomas why his sister does not like me.

"She likes you very well," he replies.

"Well, there is something she does not like."

"That is true. At times, I wish you were not so perceptive."

"I am sorry. I will not pry."

"Thank you, My Lady."

"Oh, Thomas, I have told you I hate it when you call me that."

"But it is my role."

"When we ride together, you call me Grace."

"I forget myself."

"But you have my leave."

"I should not take liberties." His eyes are downcast. "My sister was reproving me."

I let out a heavy sigh. "Separating people is wrong; we are all the same."

"It is not my place to agree with you."

"If you believe that, then it is not your place to disagree with me, either," I joke, trying to lighten the conversation.

Thomas laughs at my sally. "I suppose that is true."

I grow serious. "Thomas, you know I believe nothing separates us?"

"I do know that, Grace. It is one of the reasons I find our rides so enjoyable. My sister is right, however; I need to remember my place."

"I do not like it when you speak of your 'place.' We are no different."

"Grace, you have the luxury of pretending that is true, but it is my job not to encroach. I must guard the line."

"I came to this country as a penniless orphan. You have a family and own land. Perhaps I am too far beneath you. Perhaps that is the line you need to guard. Plenty of noble families would say so."

"Never, Grace. I could never guard a line that separates us."

"But that is exactly what you are doing. The only difference is you are placing me *above* you, not below you. "

Thomas raises his eyebrows, nods slightly and looks away.

I see his jaw clench and wait for him to speak.

"Well, little sister, I am older and several hands taller, so perhaps I *am* above you," he teases, sitting up tall and smiling down at me.

I feel a strange sensation in my stomach. I cannot resist smiling up into his face, but my tone is serious when I reply, "Brothers and sisters ride side by side."

"Nevertheless, you will ride ahead of me from here to the stable."

"Now you want to give orders?" I tease.

"Yes, and you need to obey…for my sake."

I sigh as Thomas's horse slows and drops behind Firefly.

CHAPTER 72

TRISTAM

The end of the rebellion came rapidly. Everyone knows that the archers stopped the soldiers of Traag from ever setting foot on Blinthian soil. The peace treaty, signed by the king of Traag, is on display for all to see. Only three men alive know what preceded the end of the rebellion and one of them has been executed. There has been much speculation of foul play. The foul play was not on King Stefan's side.

I ride east in the early spring of the eighth year of Stefan's reign. By this time, my movements must be as well known to the rebels as their movements are known to me.

I am met by Regis and his oldest son, along with Beltran, two of his sons, and Dunbar. Their object is to prevent my passage to Brody's estate so I will not be close enough to the border to hear the troops assembling there. I believe their plan is to take me captive, but they have not taken Brody into account.

Brody rides to greet me and comes upon me just before the rebels surround me. Their swords are sheathed. For most of them, this is their last mistake.

Brody speaks in a jovial tone, "Well, gentlemen, what is your pleasure?"

"It is our pleasure to take you both captive as the first prisoners of the new kingdom."

I maneuver to get my back to the stone wall that lies alongside us. By pulling on Rufus's bridle, yet giving opposite instructions with my legs, I make Rufus give the appearance of restless sidling. He tosses his head and backs up against the wall. Brody is on my left side.

"Relinquish your swords and you will not be harmed. You are out-numbered," Regis says.

I pray Brody will not try to contradict him.

First, I throw down my dagger, then I make a show of reaching slow-ly for my sword. I catch Brody's eye. We draw our swords at the same instant.

Regis's hand is out, ready to receive my weapon. He receives it in the neck. The blade slices through and his eyes register a moment of sur-prise before his head lands on the ground next to the remains of Beltran, whom Brody has just killed.

Dunbar is backing away and throwing down his weapons. "I sur-render!" he cries.

The three younger men move forward.

"You are still outnumbered," says Regis's black-haired son. His sword is drawn and his eyes dart between us.

"What do you think, Tristam; are we outnumbered?" Brody asks.

"I sincerely doubt it," I reply. "Lay down your arms in the name of King Stefan."

Young Regis's sword arm draws back. As he thrusts, I block his sword blade with my own and do not pause, but press my sword straight on through his heart.

The Beltran brothers are trying to circle behind us as we have been drawn forward, away from the wall. Brody lunges and one of the sons reels back, a hand to his shoulder. His sword clatters to the ground.

"Quarter! Please, give quarter!" he cries, surrendering.

I face the last rebel. "Drop your sword, son. You will live to fight another day."

"No, I will be executed for treason."

"Not if you swear allegiance to King Stefan," Brody says.

He looks at Brody and then back at me. Suddenly, he lunges forward, spurring his horse, and crashes down upon us both. Brody is unseated and falls to the ground. Rufus, obedient to my hand upon his reins, moves sideways and I thrust through the boy's side, hating the need to do so.

I hear a scuffling sound and Brody shouting, "Tristam!"

The wounded man, who called for quarter, holds my dagger in his hand.

"That was my brother you killed!" he screams, throwing my weapon at me.

I dodge to the left and the dagger buries itself in my chest, below my right shoulder. I manage not to lose my seat on Rufus.

An arrow flies by me, catching my attacker directly in the forehead. The man is dead before he hits the ground.

"Who is your archer friend?" Brody asks.

I shake my head slightly.

"He called for quarter!" Dunbar is practically screaming; his voice is high and shrill.

"And then he resumed fighting," Brody states. "Look at Tristam's injury, you fool!"

Dunbar's eyes are wide. He is backing away from the two of us.

"Binds his hands, Brody." My voice sounds weak.

"How are you?" Brody asks while following my orders.

"I am losing blood. The dagger pierced no vital place. In my pack… get clean tunic…for bandage."

Brody tears the tunic with his teeth.

"We never were outnumbered, Tristam."

"Shh," I reply, nodding at Dunbar, who is becoming sullen with the passing of his fear.

"Archer, how far behind you are the king's soldiers?" Brody yells in the direction from which the arrow came.

A voice I recognize calls back, "Half a mile or less. I sent the signal and they are marching."

"Tristam, I cannot stanch this flow of blood." Brody sounds concerned. "Archer, I need your help!" he shouts.

Thomas rides up, dismounts, and kneels by my side.

"So, your mission for the king was following me?" I ask Thomas.

"Yes, Sir," Thomas replies.

"Thank you."

"My pleasure, Sir."

"Push harder on the wound, Brody, I am not a weakling," I say through clenched teeth.

As Brody packs the wound with strips of cloth, I begin to lose consciousness.

"Get word to Grace," I manage to say.

"Yes, Sir," Thomas replies. Those are the last words I hear for some time.

CHAPTER 73

GRACE

I have been restless for days and unable to sleep. Something dangerous is brewing; I feel it as one feels the approaching of a storm. When Thomas tells me Tristam has been wounded, I am almost relieved, for at least my waiting is over.

"What happened?" I ask.

"A dagger was thrown at him by someone who had already surrendered. Tristam dodged it, but it entered here," Thomas says, touching the hollow spot just below his right shoulder.

"He should be fine as long as he is carefully nursed," I reply, my voice brisk.

"Yes. I am to bring you and Lady Geneva to the estate of Lord Broderick. He says you are to consider their family's home as your own. He took Tristam there and sent me to fetch you."

"Thank you. Does Geneva know?"

"Not yet. I came first to you."

I give a wan smile. "Thank you, Thomas."

He reaches for me, but I turn away, pick up a bag, and begin packing. I am too brittle to be touched; if Thomas hugs me I will dissolve into tears.

"I will find Geneva."

I nod, but do not turn around.

We reach Lord Broderick's estate by nightfall. I had barely contained my frustration as Geneva packed herbs and bandages, but as we approach the manor I slow my pace, fearing what we will discover. The lengthening shadows do nothing to lessen my gloom.

"Courage, Grace," Thomas whispers.

"Word would have been sent if his condition had changed," Geneva says, hearing his words.

I clench my teeth and do not reply.

Lady Beatrice herself welcomes us and leads us to Tristam.

"How is he?" Geneva asks as Beatrice leads us down a corridor which opens off the entry hall.

"He has lost a great deal of blood, but he came to himself once. He asked for you, young lady," she says, turning to look at me.

I feel myself blush beneath her penetrating gaze.

"The two are very close," Geneva speaks for me. "Grace is probably too frightened to speak, My Lady. I am certain, when she finds her voice, she will thank you for your care of Tristam."

I nod. I cannot speak due to the lump in my throat; I feel as if hands are gripping my chest. I feel strength emanating from Thomas, though, and I borrow from his store.

We finally arrive at a large chamber. Lady Beatrice hands Geneva a candle and motions for us to enter the room ahead of her.

"I will wait here," Thomas says.

Tristam lies upon his back, his hands at his sides. His face is pale, whiter than I have ever seen it. He looks as if he has already left us and I draw a quick breath, freezing just inside the door. Geneva is stronger. She approaches, lifts his wrist, and feels for a pulse.

"Grace, remove those pillows from under his head. Place them under his legs. We want his heart lower, so the blood will flow there. When his pulse is stronger, I will check his wound."

"We propped him up to stop the bleeding," Lady Beatrice informs us.

"Were you successful?"

"Yes, but it took Brody a good while to get him here. He lost much blood."

Geneva nods.

We wait, both of us watching Geneva's fingers on Tristam's wrist.

"Grace, come here, child. His pulse is stronger. Hold his hand while I lay bare this wound."

I do as she bids me.

His hand is cool and his fingers are tinged with blue. I try to rub some warmth into them and not look at the wound Geneva is examining.

"He is very fortunate. The knife wound is clean and did not pierce the joint."

Lady Beatrice responds, "Brody said it was his own knife that was thrown at him by one of the traitors. The man had cried for quarter, which Tristam had foolishly given him." She is shaking her head. "I told him to be careful."

Geneva does not respond. She is mixing herbs and preparing to lay them on the angry red slash.

"What happened?" My voice does not sound like my own.

"Brody did not tell me very much, only that he and Tristam met six men and only one is a prisoner. An archer assisted them. Brody is unharmed, except for some bruises."

"That is well," Geneva replies.

"Who was the archer?" I ask.

"I do not know. Brody left immediately after delivering Tristam here, heading for the border, mumbling something about 'fire wood at the pass.' He did not relish leaving Tristam."

"He had his own job to do, no doubt," Geneva states, "and Tristam's as well, perhaps."

"Yes, My Lady."

"This will hurt him, Grace, but it will keep the green poison away. Keep holding his hand."

Tristam's eyelids flutter. He tries to pull away from Geneva.

"Be still Tristam; I am trying to help you," Geneva commands.

His lips move and I hear my name whispered. I squeeze his hand.

"She is right here, safe," Geneva says. "Talk to him, Grace. He can hear you."

"Do not leave me, Tristam. You promised," my voice is pleading and small.

"Always…keep my…promises," he whispers.

"You had best keep this one." My voice is no longer small. I dash an impatient hand across my cheek, wiping away a telltale tear.

I become aware of a silence in the room. Both Lady Geneva and Lady Beatrice are looking at me.

"That is right, my dear, tell him what to do. He is a fool to put himself at risk." Lady Beatrice is nodding, a knowing smile on her lips.

"He was doing the king's work," I say, defending Tristam.

"He is a fool, but he is brave and loyal."

"He is not a fool." My voice is loud and even.

"And he is not going to leave you, Grace." Geneva draws my attention back to Tristam. "He is breathing easier. Lady Beatrice, you did well by him."

"I have not your skills, My Lady, but I did what I could."

"You did very well. You and Lord Broderick saved his life."

"Let us hope he now values it as he should," she replies dryly.

I do not like Lady Beatrice, but I find myself agreeing with her.

CHAPTER 74

GRACE

When I leave the chamber where Tristam lies, Thomas is waiting outside the door.

"Thomas, you are the archer who protected Tristam." My words are not kindly spoken.

"Grace, I…"

"Do not try to deny it. I can tell by the look on your face."

"Who told you?"

"No one. This winter I noticed that your absences and Tristam's always occurred at the same time. I figured you were working together."

"We were not, and that is more than I am supposed to tell you."

"So Tristam did not know that you had been asked to follow him?"

"Grace, I protest…" he begins.

"Do not waste your breath. You were following the king's orders and are not yet at liberty to speak freely." My hands are on my hips and I am almost shouting.

His expression confirms my beliefs.

"I am glad to know the king took precautions for Tristam's safety," I sputter, sounding as sarcastic as Becca.

"So why are you angry?"

"Because you tricked me. Because Tristam is injured. Because…" Tears fill my eyes and I cannot go on.

Thomas reaches out to me and tries to pull me close, but I strike at him.

"Do not touch me! You had no right!"

"I *had* no right, or I *have* no right?"

"You have no right to touch me and you had no right to trick me.

What if you, too, had been injured, or worse?"

"So you are angry because I might have been hurt?"

"Yes! Yes, I am!"

"I do not understand."

"You should! I told you, on the day I showed you my special rock, how lost I would be if anything happened to Tristam."

"Yes, and I accepted the king's charge to follow and protect him. How can that not please you?"

"Ugh! You do not understand!" I cry.

"What do I not understand?"

At that moment, Geneva opens the door to Tristam's chamber. "Your voices are disturbing Tristam. He is asking for you, Grace."

"I must go to him."

"By all means," Thomas bows formally. His voice is like ice.

I turn on my heel and march away.

I have time, while sitting next to Tristam's bed, to sort out my anger. What I did not tell Thomas is that I would have preferred he stay safe while Tristam was doing the king's work. The thought that he was also in danger enrages me. I realize that my feelings for Thomas have grown deeper than I realized.

When Geneva comes to sit with Tristam, I ask her about Thomas.

"He left…"

"On the king's business, no doubt." My voice sounds petulant in my own ears.

Geneva looks at me with concern. "He left this for you," she says, handing me a piece of parchment.

I wait until I have left Tristam's chamber before unrolling Thomas's note.

Grace,
I am sorry for everything. I must leave.
Your Big Brother, Thomas

I crumple the parchment and march down the hall to the chamber I have been allotted. My intent is to throw Thomas's words into the flames, but I find I cannot. I smooth the crushed note so his strong writing is visible. I press his note to my breast and begin rocking. It is then that the tears come.

CHAPTER 75

TRISTAM

During my convalescence, Brody tells me the squelching of the rebellion went exactly as planned. Flaming arrows were sent from hidden vantage points into a pile of brush at the mouth of the pass. The horses at the front of the line shied and tried to move back while the warriors behind were pressing forward, eager to push through the narrow pass. Pandemonium broke out amongst the soldiers of Traag and they suffered many casualties as riders were knocked from their horses and trampled underfoot. I was the only Loyalist injured; all other Blinthian casualties are amongst the rebels.

The king's soldiers were never called forward into battle. The army of Traag eventually organized and retreated. Our guards moved forward and captured the rebels who tried to escape into Traag.

Lord Dunbar and the other prisoners were marched to the castle under armed guard. I missed their trials and executions, for it was close to four weeks before Geneva declared me fit to travel. I would have left for home a fortnight earlier, but Grace sided with Geneva and I was too weak to argue with both of them.

I am told that Lord Dunbar lost all semblance of self-control when he found himself a prisoner. He began talking to himself, muttering that an archer had killed a man after he had asked for quarter. Dunbar failed to mention that the man had almost killed me after laying down his arms. Dunbar's loose tongue did nothing to ease relations between the former rebels and their Loyalist guards.

I was not able to beg the king for mercy for Dunbar, though I doubt I would have been successful even if I had been granted the opportunity; King Stefan was angry that I had been wounded, and Dunbar was the only man alive upon whom he could vent his wrath.

Dunbar was granted a last request. He begged that his land not be divided amongst the Loyalists, but that at least a portion of it be given to his second grandson, Grace's friend, Peter. As Peter's parents are staunch Loyalists, this request was granted. Peter was given the entire estate.

Regis's land was divided among several Loyalist families, with Brody and his sister Beatrice receiving the western portions that adjoin their ancestral home. Thomas was awarded a fine parcel of land to the northeast, which is almost as large as Tristenhorn. I could not refuse the king's gift of land. I laughed when I learned my new property is in the far northwest corner of Blinth, bordering Traag and Lolgothe. King Stefan is asking me to guard the border. Fortunately, it adjoins Thomas's land so he can oversee it for me.

Regis's widow seemed to have had no notion of her husband's rebellious activities. She was questioned many times and, under the strain, the lady's frail health failed her. She died within weeks of the rebels' fall,, leaving Coltrane a landless orphan.

Coltrane had been sent, with a group of the king's guards, to the Polomian border the week before the rebels' attack. He had seemed reluctant to go, but had obeyed the orders. He was also questioned many times, as were those closest to him, under suspicion of having at least an awareness of the rebels' cause, but treason could not be proved against him. As he was young and in the service of the king, his life was spared.

King Stefan personally oversaw each of the nearly two dozen executions, but he had no taste for bloodshed. I found myself wishing that, in this one instance, he had not spared a rebel's son.

My only personal request of King Stefan was that Coltrane be watched by Loyalist knights. Coltrane, as a boy, had been conniving, and I have no reason to believe he has changed. He wears his bitterness over his losses like a badge, seemingly mourning the loss of the estate more than the loss of his entire family.

Coltrane was to have been knighted the year of the rebellion, but instead was given as a squire to one of Lord and Lady Tavenor's sons. The man is loyal and disciplined. Coltrane will not enjoy his assignment.

Lady Beltran and Melanie became residents of a property in Chantrell that belongs to the queen. I do not expect to ever again see them upon Blinthian soil.

CHAPTER 76

TRISTAM

Once I am out of danger, I become aware of Grace's coolness toward me. She never speaks of her feelings but retreats behind a film of ice when I try to discuss the matter with her. It is not until we resume her training with the dagger, several months later, that I begin to understand how deeply affected she has been by my injury.

At first, she refuses to resume her training at all, laying the blame on my weakened condition. She also questions the necessity, now that the rebellion is over.

"Grace, you have worked hard for many years to gain these skills. Blinth is at peace now, but who can say what the future holds? It is important to me that you are able to defend yourself. You still practice archery; why not practice also with the dagger?"

"I love archery."

"But not with a dagger?"

"You were almost killed with a dagger."

"No, I was merely injured."

"Have it your way," she replies.

"It would please me for you to resume your training, but I will not tease you to do it."

"Fine. I will do it to please you, but only twice in the moon's cycle. I do not wish to lose the skills I have, but I do not feel I need more."

"What you have is enough," I agree.

The first month we train, she holds back. In the second month, July, she fights with a new intensity and a barely suppressed rage that startles me. She wins the final practice battle, but continues attacking long after I would have been a corpse. Finally, I grasp her hands and pin them into the small of her back. She is twisting and writhing in my grasp, and she strikes at my foot with her heel.

"Let me go! I hate you!"

Her words surprise us both, and as I release her, she stops struggling. Her eyes grow wide and fill with tears.

"I am sorry. Forgive me. I did not mean…" she mumbles, not finishing her thought. She turns to run but I hold her wrist.

"Look at me, Grace." She keeps her eyes on the ground. "Do you hate me or are you angry with me?" I ask.

There is a pause. Grace is pondering my question.

"I do not hate you," she finally whispers.

"But you are very angry at me," I state.

Her eyes fly to my face. "You have been angry ever since I was wounded. We should have had this conversation sooner, but I thought you would tell me when you were ready."

She is shaking her head. "It makes no sense. You did not want to get wounded and you did not die. Why do I feel this way?"

"For the same reason that when a mother finds her child who has been lost at the fair, she hugs the little one close and then begins scolding. You hugged me when I awakened, but you have not scolded me. Scold me, Grace."

"No, you were obeying the king, doing his work."

"And I was not careful and I ran into a trap."

Her eyes blaze. "That is correct—" she begins, but stops.

"Grace, tell me!"

"My feelings do not make sense to me, so I do not know how to make you understand. When I tried to talk of this before, you merely talked about money."

"I will try harder to understand," I say.

She pauses, nods, and draws a deep breath. "You belong here. Everyone knows you, they knew your parents, your grandparents, and your brother. No one here knows anything about my past, my family, or where I belong in the world."

"You belong with me."

"Yes, and that is the *only* place I belong," she spits out. "What if you had gotten yourself killed?"

"Then you and Geneva would have lived on my estates."

"If King Stefan was in full power, but he cannot afford to extend himself for me. I am only important to him because I am important to you. He needs you, but I can do nothing for him; I can only cause him trouble."

261

I remain silent.

"Strategically, you know I am right."

I look away. She is right.

"When you were wounded, I fell down a black hole. I felt..." She looks away and bites her bottom lip. A tear slides down her cheek, but she brushes it away impatiently. "Alone... totally alone...as if I were back in the forest...hungry, cold, and injured."

"But you are here; I am fine."

"But I am *not* fine. The nightmares have returned."

I shake my head and close my eyes for a moment.

She turns away from me, shrugging my hand off her shoulder when I reach for her.

"When did they start?" I ask. My voice is low.

"They began last autumn, after a ride with Thomas. He asked about my past and I told him about the nightmares. When you were wounded, they stopped for a while, but when you were out of danger, they returned. I hoped they would stop when we returned to the castle."

"But they did not?"

"No, they did not."

"Can you tell me?"

"It is the same dream. It is dark. I am running through the forest. Someone is chasing me. I am running for my life."

I sigh.

"I am sorry to worry you with this," she says.

"Oh, Grace, when will you learn that you are not a bother? My sigh is because you are having these nightmares...because you chose to suffer alone...because I hoped you were free of the past."

"I will not be free until I can remember."

I nod my agreement. "I know you are right. Yet all these years you have been well and happy. I hoped perhaps you could escape without remembering."

"I am sorry."

"Grace, stop talking in that manner. You need not apologize. I am sorry that you suffer. We will handle this together. The only apology I will accept is when you apologize for not telling me immediately."

"But you were involved in the rebellion and then you were recovering."

"And you were angry. You retreated into silence. It is your way."

She hangs her head.

"I much prefer it when you attack. Attack me, yell at me, hit me... I do not care. But do not leave me."

"You should not leave me, either."

I find myself agreeing with her again. "You are right, and yet I did not choose to leave you."

"You chose to serve the king in a dangerous capacity. You chose to ride east alone when you knew the rebel uprising was near. You were too trusting when you gave quarter."

"I am guilty of all of those things. I will always serve my king in whatever way he asks, but I will be more careful for your sake. Also, I will never leave you voluntarily. When I am with you, I will always be right here, present."

She flushes at my words.

"That is the best I can promise you. Is it enough?"

She nods without looking at me.

"Can you promise the same?"

I wait a long time for her answer. Her hands cling tightly to one another and her knuckles show white. Her face is averted.

"You know that I cannot," she finally whispers. "I cannot stop myself when I go away inside."

"Are you certain that you cannot?"

"Do you think I do not attempt to fight against the inner pull?" Her voice is strident.

"I do not know; that is why I ask," I reply, lowering my own voice.

"I do try," she replies in a softer tone.

"And what happens?"

"I feel I am being pulled down, pulled under. I feel pulled into a darkness, an abyss, a place of solitude and isolation. I feel utterly alone."

"You are not alone."

"I was alone. I was very much alone"

I grind my teeth. "Yes, you were. I should like to kill the ones responsible."

Her eyes search my face. "A long time ago, Becca told me you wanted to avenge me."

"She is right. King Stefan forbids it and he is right to do so. It is better if they believe you perished in the forest."

She nods while a little smile plays at the corner of her mouth. She looks at my face for a moment.

"What is that smile for?" I ask.

"Nothing."

"Grace…?" my voice commands.

"It is nice that you want to avenge me, even if it is forbidden."

"Did you not believe Becca all those years ago?"

"It is just nice to hear you say it."

"Oh, Grace, do not doubt it for a minute. Come here, child."

She buries her face in my chest. I raise her face to mine, but she keeps her eyes lowered.

I kiss her forehead.

"I will try," she whispers.

"Try what, my darling?"

"To tell you when I fall into the feelings…when I get sucked down into the darkness."

Her eyes meet mine for a brief moment, before she buries her face in my chest again. I kiss the top of her head.

"I cannot talk when I have those feelings."

"You do not have to say anything, just come to me. Any time of the day or night."

"I will try. That is all I can promise."

"That is all I can ask."

I have pondered my own words many times since that day, in light of everything that followed. I have come to the conclusion that I would not unsay them, even if I could. She needed me. The child in her needed me. The woman did not.

CHAPTER 77

GRACE

It is as if Tristam's invitation for me to come to him when I feel small unleashes the demons that dwell within. The nightmares come more frequently and with greater intensity.

Now, instead of merely being pursued, I am captured. My wrists and ankles are bound to stakes. I fight like a cornered animal, but to no avail. I awake sweat-drenched and frantic, often shaking uncontrollably. At first, I cannot move. I long for Tristam, but cannot go to him. The next morning, I tell him of the dream and my inability to move. That much I can do, but no more.

Spring has flown, and I return to helping Tobias in the garden. I miss Becca. It seems strange that she and I are not training for the archery competition. I visit her when I am able, but she rarely has time to come to me.

I have not seen Thomas since the night we argued when Tristam lay wounded. I finally ask Becca about him.

"I have not seen Thomas since the rebellion ended. How is he?"

Becca eyes me with speculation. "What happened between the two of you?"

I do not say anything.

"Grace, answer the question. Last fall you and he went riding often. Now you never see one another."

"How do you know that?"

"Are you afraid he and I are keeping secrets from you again?"

I blush.

"He cares for you, Grace. He did not want to appear unlearned in front of you."

I blush more deeply. "I thought he did not want my help."

"You did not think. You felt hurt for no reason. I understand, though. You are so strong, yet your feelings bruise so easily."

"Will I always feel like an outsider here?"

"You are the only one who can answer that question."

"You sound like Lucinda."

"Good; she is wise. What happened between you and Thomas?"

"I was upset…" I begin.

"Yes?"

"It was the night Tristam got injured. I was stupid. I got angry. I did not realize how much I care for Thomas. I was afraid of losing Tristam… and of losing Thomas. I was angry that he was also working for the king."

"Tristam was wounded and you were angry at him, so you argued with Thomas?"

"Yes, and then he left. He never came back."

"He left without a word to you? That does not sound like him."

"He left a note."

"What did it say?"

"That he was sorry and he signed it 'your big brother, Thomas.'"

Becca wears a thoughtful expression. "Have you tried to contact him?"

"No…I do not know where he is. I have gone to the huntsmen's stables, but he is never there."

"Do you know about his reward for his part in the rebellion?"

"No."

"He was awarded land."

"So, he is busy sheep farming. That is wonderful."

Becca casts me a searching glance. "How do you know that?"

"He told me it was his dream."

Becca's face looks thoughtful.

"What are you thinking?" I ask.

"I am thinking that it is your turn to reach out to him."

"I cannot. I do not know what I would say. The nightmares are coming so often. They keep getting worse and worse. I find myself pulling back from everyone."

"He is here often. He still helps the huntsmen and watches over the horses. You could look there for him if you change your mind."

I shake my head.

"Are you seeing anyone? Are you spending time in the garden with Tobias?"

"Yes, and Tristam insists that I train with the dagger."

"When was the last time you rode Firefly?"

"I cannot remember."

"Oh, my Sweet One, come here." She pulls me into a strong embrace.

I lay my head upon her shoulder and try to hold back tears. "I do not know what to do. Will you talk to Thomas for me?"

"No, I will not. You will figure it out. Give yourself time."

"I cannot stand much more of this."

"Then it will happen soon."

I pray she is right.

CHAPTER 78

TRISTAM

Watching Grace suffer with her nightmares is agony. I feel helpless. Though I long to sleep in the antechamber adjacent to her room, I am not truly her father and gossip could ensue. Instead, I bring Bethany from Tristenhorn. She comes willingly and sleeps near Grace, with the door open between them.

Grace does not call for help or cry out in her distress. She cowers in bed with her eyes wide. I fear Bethany sleeps little at night. She trains herself to waken if Grace moves in her bed. When she finds Grace cowering, she comes to fetch me.

Grace does not know me when I enter her room that first night with Bethany. When I approach her bed, she flinches and watches my every move.

"Grace, it is I, your Tristam," I say. "Bethany will light the lamps," I continue, nodding to Bethany, who soon has the room filled with yellow light.

Some of Grace's fear seems to fade as the room brightens. I tell her everything I do.

"I am mixing Geneva's sleeping potion for you to drink. First, I must light the fire and warm the water."

"I can do that, Sir," Bethany says, moving toward the hearth.

"You must remember Bethany, Grace. She is here to help you."

Grace gives no response.

"Speak to her, Bethany."

"'Tis I, Lady Grace, your servant, Bethany. Come back to us."

Grace's eyes move from my face to Bethany's and back. She lifts her hand, extending it toward me.

I approach and fold her in my arms. She remains stiff for a few moments before softening.

I watch Bethany light the fire, pour water in the pot, and set it to boil.

"I will be in the next room, if you need me, Lady Grace."

When Bethany departs, Grace's tears come.

CHAPTER 79

GRACE

I seek out Lucinda in my distress and visit her at her cottage. I pour out the story of my increasing nightmares one May morning as we share a cup of tea.

"I do not know why they have returned," I tell her.

"When did they start again?"

"Well…it was September, or perhaps October."

"What was happening at the time?"

"Tristam was traveling a great deal, going east because of the rebellion."

"So they began when Tristam was absent?"

"Yes, I suppose so. I had been riding with Thomas. He asked if it bothered me that I could not remember my past."

"What did you tell him?"

"I told him yes, and no. He told me when the yes outweighed the no, I would remember."

"He has an old head on his young shoulders," she says.

I find myself thinking of Thomas, and Lucinda waits until I am ready to continue.

"It was the very night after I talked with Thomas that the nightmares came back."

"Have they been getting steadily worse since that time?"

"No, they ceased altogether when Tristam was wounded."

She nods her head and I wait for her to speak.

"It has been my experience that memories from the past do not intrude when the present is demanding. Now that Tristam has fully recovered, have the nightmares gotten worse?"

"Much worse. Do you think my dreams are really memories?"

"Your dreams are but dreams. I do believe they have a message for you, though. Only you can determine their meaning."

"I do not know what to think. I am so tired…beyond tired. I want to know what they mean."

"You will."

"How can you be so certain?"

"Because you want to know."

"I do want to know, but…I am afraid. What if the memories are…?"

"Whatever it is that frightens you, it is in the past."

"That is not how it feels."

"How do you feel?"

"I feel weak and small."

"You are neither."

"How can you say so?"

"Because the nightmares have come; therefore, you are ready. You are strong, Grace. Everyone who meets you knows this."

"Thomas and Becca say that, but I do not feel strong."

"Nor do you trust yourself."

I study her face but say nothing.

"Your mind, your body, and your spirit must work together. Fighting against yourself will not help."

"But I am frightened. No, I am terrified. I cannot sleep. I cannot be still."

"Can peace only be found on the other side of remembering?"

"Yes."

"Then the time is drawing near."

"Becca said the same thing. What must I do?"

"Have you tried remembering every detail of the dream upon waking?"

"No, I am so frightened that I am not thinking."

"Use your mind to help you."

I nod.

"Child, no one can take this cup from you. I would not, even if I could. There are gifts for you, not only pain. And remember, you are here. You are safe. You are loved."

"That is not how it feels."

"Nevertheless, my words are true."

CHAPTER 80

GRACE

I ponder Lucinda's words. The part of me that is afraid to know the truth seems very young, like the six-year-old who was defiled in the barn. I find myself talking to her, and not gently.

"What are you afraid of? You know you were defiled and abandoned. What is there left to fear?"

The child does not answer. She does not feel safe with me. She wants Tristam.

I find myself pulled toward Tristam by this desperate child in me. At the same time, I find myself trying to pull away from my dependency upon him. I feel at war with myself and therefore, at war with Tristam.

"I must be losing my mind." I do not realize I have spoken the words out loud until Becca replies.

"What makes you say so?"

"Where did you come from?" I demand. "I did not hear you approach."

"I came from the far side of the garden. Perhaps you did not hear me because you are so busy talking to yourself. Shall I leave you in peace?" Becca is grinning from ear to ear.

"No, please do not. I cannot find peace and would much rather stop looking."

She pulls me into an embrace and I cling to her just a moment too long.

"The nightmares still?"

"Yes, and I miss you," I reply. "Everything is vastly different now. I miss taking classes. I miss seeing you every day. How are you? Is your family well?"

"I miss you as well, though I barely have time to think of anything. I am helping several of the shopkeepers in the village with their accounts. They no longer have to come to the castle to pay the scribes to put their accounts into writing. My earnings are helping our family."

"They must be pleased."

"They are. Everything is going well. Tell me about you."

"It is the nightmares…and this idleness. I need work."

"So you are weeding the vegetables. Where is the gardener?"

"Tobias is ailing. I want to help him."

"That is kind."

"Not really, I need work."

"I remember that about you."

I smile, remembering the year of Benjamin's birth, and of working side-by-side with Becca.

"I find it difficult to believe that Benjamin is six years old."

"We all do," she replies, smiling. "He is growing up so fast."

There is a pause in the conversation and I know Becca is building up the courage to say something.

"What were you talking to yourself about?" she asks, picking up the weeds I have just pulled.

"I am not certain I can explain."

"Try, please. I am worried about you."

"I told Lucinda that there is a part of me that does not want to re-member what happened. That part feels young, like the six-year-old in the barn. I try to tell that part of me she has nothing to fear."

"She does not believe you, does she?"

"No, she does not."

"Were you kind to her?"

"No, I was…"

"Impatient?" Becca asks.

I nod.

"You are so gentle with the children when they get hurt or scared. Prissy and Lydia adore you, as does Benjamin. 'No one understands as well as Grace does,' is what they always tell me."

I smile.

"But to yourself, you are horrid."

"How so?" I ask.

"Well, I can see that you are exhausted just by looking at you, but instead of resting, you are working."

"I cannot rest. I cannot be still."

"And you cannot be nice to the six-year-old in the barn who was hurt and is still frightened. She is you. Without her, you cannot remember."

I heave a sigh.

"Why do you hate the child you were?"

"I do not hate her."

"But you would never treat Lyddie or Prissy the way you treat yourself, if they had been defiled. Why would you treat them differently?"

"Because it would not be their fault if they were defiled."

"So, it was *your* fault?"

"Yes, yes...I believe it was....I do not think I ever realized that before."

"How could it be your fault?"

"I do not know...I did not run away. I did not fight back."

"You were six years of age when you were dragged into that barn. You were probably smaller than Benjamin is now. And the man was your father!"

"I was so needy," I continue as if Becca has not spoken. "I was so hurt...betrayed...I had nowhere to turn."

"So you turned against yourself."

I nod, clenching my teeth. "I could not tolerate those feelings. If I had let myself sink into despair, I would not have survived. I would simply have died."

"But you did not die."

"No, I did not."

"So, you must have been very strong. We know you were strong enough to survive for many days alone in the forest when you were but eleven or twelve years of age."

"I do not feel strong."

"No, but you *were* strong and you *are* strong."

"I feel so weak."

"You can feel weak now. There are those of us who will protect you. Those who will draw close to you if you will let us."

"But I hate feeling this way."

"But does it make the little six-year-old Grace trust you a bit more, when you are honest about being hurt?"

I nod. "How do you know that?"

"I have lots of young ones at my house. I know how their minds work. They just want to be understood and cared for."

That night, when I awake from the nightmare, I do not need Bethany to fetch Tristam. My feet carry me swiftly to his room. The six-year-old child in me is fleet of foot and she throws herself into his arms. I do not chastise her when the tears come.

CHAPTER 81

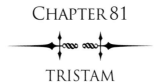

TRISTAM

Grace comes to me, shivering and drenched in sweat. I barely have time to leap from my bed before she is in my arms. Her terror is beyond words or tears. I stand holding her until her trembling ceases. I stroke her hair, her back, patting and soothing her, willing my strength to enter her body. I want my love to shield her, but I know it cannot; her demons are within, and I stand outside.

When her trembling eases, I build up the fire. She stays near me as I work. When my hands are finally free of tinder and tools, she takes one of them in both of hers and clings tightly. I hold her again until the tears come. At some point, we sit on the skins before the fire. The tears are followed by sobs and finally by a stillness which I mistake for sleep. When I shift her weight, intending to add logs to the fire, she clings again.

"I thought you were sleeping."

She shakes her head.

"How do you feel?"

It is several moments before she replies in a small voice, "I feel exhausted…spent."

I nod. "Can you tell me about the nightmare?"

"It ended, as always, with me running through a black forest. But this time, it included being led into the forest. This time, I saw them bind my hands and feet. I was staked to the ground."

"How did you free yourself?"

"I did not see that happen. The dream simply skipped from the staking to the running."

"I see."

We sit in silence for a time. I find my thoughts turning toward revenge.

"Do you have any idea who was staking you to the ground?"

"No; they are strangers, but they seem to be guards or soldiers. They are doing a job. I am nothing to them."

"You are everything to me." I speak without thinking.

Grace blushes and turns away, but she is not displeased.

"I must keep your fire going, My Lady. Have I permission to rise?" I reach for a joke.

"Why yes, My Lord," she replies, playing along. It is a good sign.

By the time the fire is again blazing, the grey light of dawn is entering the room.

"We must return you to your chamber," I tell her.

She does not speak.

"Turn your face to the flames," I order. "Unlike you, I have no antechamber in which to dress."

She gives a soft laugh and turns away. I dress quickly, wrap her in my cloak, and lead her to her room. She watches as I build up her fire. By the time I have finished, she is yawning.

"Can you sleep now?" I ask.

"I think so, but I am afraid. I do not wish to dream."

"Climb into your bed, child. I will fetch Bethany; she can stay with you while I go in search of Geneva. You need her potion to ensure a sleep free from dreams. Your body needs rest."

Grace looks as if she wants to argue against the potion, but she does not speak.

When I return, she swallows the draught without argument. I remain by her bed until she sleeps. When I leave her, Bethany takes my place.

CHAPTER 82

GRACE

The nights I run to Tristam in terror gradually come to outnumber the nights I do not. I have unleashed the process of remembering and cannot turn back. Every night, I dream the same dream. The details become clearer.

Five guards carry me upon a litter. I am taken to a clearing. I am passive until the men begin to bind me. I fight, but I am no match for them. One of them slashes my foot in anger. His cheek bleeds where I scratch him.

"Stop fighting, or the next slash will be to your throat," he promises.

"But Sir…" another guard begins, but the rest of his words are lost to me.

From the staking, the dream skips ahead to the time when I am running through the forest in the dead of night, just as I now run to Tristam's chamber.

I refuse to take the sleeping potion. I want to remember.

I thought it would make me free. I was a fool.

CHAPTER 83

TRISTAM

Grace's visits to my chamber become more frequent until there is scarcely a night she does not visit me. I choose not to speak to her of the proprieties. I can no more repulse her than I could have repulsed a terrified child, and she is a child, though in the body of a woman.

All subsequent visits follow the pattern of the first. She runs into my room, too frightened to speak. I hold her and, when she will allow it, build up a fire. Eventually, she sobs and, finally, sleep takes her.

I hope these nightly visits never become known to others. Assumptions would be made and gossip would surely follow. I do not alert Grace to this danger, for I trust myself to handle the situation, should it arise.

I see now, looking back, that I became weary. Fatigue engulfed me and clouded my judgment.

CHAPTER 84

TRISTAM

What happened that night should not have. I hold myself accountable.

I am sleeping the sleep of the dead when she comes to my bed seeking comfort. The nightmare again. I should have gotten out of bed and built up the fire, but I am in a fog and she is shivering and damp with sweat, so I simply pull her to me.

I hold her close, willing my warmth to stop here trembling. Finally, her shaking ceases and the tears come. When she finishes sobbing, she lies beside me, her face wet with tears. I kiss them away, like always: her forehead, her cheeks, and her nose. She presses her face into my neck, just under my left ear. I feel her lips brush my neck. She kisses my cheek. I lean to kiss hers, but she turns her head. Our lips meet. I am inflamed. I retain enough of my sanity to be gentle, to ask her permission before touching her. She is eager for my caresses, nodding yes to my questions, smiling and arching her back.

I could so easily have taken her as my own that night. Thank God some wiser part of me took charge.

Her arms are entwined about my neck when I come to myself. She clings as I pull away.

"Oh, my little one," I say, "we have worlds of time in which to explore each other. Let us go slowly." I smooth her hair back from her forehead. I kiss her eyelids.

She clings tighter. I cannot see beyond my own desire. I want to get away from her arms before I lose what little hold I have over myself.

I was not prepared for what came next. I was stupid enough to be blissful. That was the last time I was alone with Grace. She is now a prisoner.

I have played that scene over and over in my mind, looking for some clue, some hint, of what was to follow. Now I wonder: were her memories already breaking through when we were entwined? Was she trying to hold them at bay? Was her urgency more than simple desire? Was it a grasping at the present in the face of the deluge from the past?

I do not know.

I cannot ask her.

I failed her. That is the only clarity I can reach. I failed her.

I did not protect her, not even from myself.

I should have slept outside her door.

CHAPTER 85

GRACE

I wanted him. I do not remember how it began, but I wanted him. I went to his room seeking comfort, but when comfort became passion, I was not sorry. I wanted him to be mine. I wanted him to claim me.

I hide the flashes of memory that come over me as he explores my body. I see a flash of an evil hand upon my breast. I remember foul breath in my face and I remember turning away, only to be pinned in place by my wrists, but I push those flashes down.

I want Tristam, not the memories, but he stops us. He carries me to my bed. When he kisses my forehead, I move, trying to meet his lips.

He smiles and shakes his head, saying, "Patience, my Grace." He goes to the foot of my bed and, tenderly, he kisses the scars on my feet before departing.

Then he closes the door and I am alone with my memories.

He does not want me. He does not want me, runs like a refrain through my head. *He does not want me...I am damaged.*

The tears will not stop. The flashes of memory grow more vivid and terror consumes me.

I cannot seek out Tristam again; he rejected me. I lose sight of his tenderness. I let my knowledge of his love slip away. I am falling, falling into some bottomless well. There is nothing to hold on to.

I do what I always do when feelings overwhelm me. I run.

Not daring to risk running past Tristam's chamber, I take another route through the castle. I find myself in a twisted corridor that is unfamiliar. I search desperately for a doorway, craving the outdoor air and the feeling of being under the stars.

When I find a door, Coltrane is coming in through it. I try to push past him, but his arms go around me.

"Shh, slow down. What have we here?" he asks.

"Please, Coltrane. Let me pass."

"Grace, you look distraught, my dear. Come, tell Coltrane all about it." His grip on my arm tightens.

"Please, let me pass," I repeat. "I need to get to Geneva. Tristam is ill," I lie.

"Sharing a bed with Tristam, I see. Otherwise how would you know he is ill?"

My face flames. "Addie sent me," I lie.

"You are a terrible liar, Grace. Is that old man a good lover? Let us see how I compare." His hands are on either side of my face. He thrusts his tongue into my mouth. I fight with everything I have. I manage to get my right hand free and aim a blow at his ear.

"Oh, so the lady wants to play rough." His voice is oily. "I can certainly accommodate her." His first blow is to my left cheek. His second is to the soft place, just below my breastbone, that Tristam calls the center. I cannot breathe.

He propels me toward his chamber, marching me in front of him, grasping each arm just above the elbow. "I regret to inform you that my accommodations are not up to your standards. Sons of traitors are not accorded commodious living quarters. Still, I feel certain I can keep you well entertained." He whispers the words in my ear. When his lips touch me, I shudder.

He does not seem drunk, but the smell of mead is pervasive. I pray someone will pass us in the corridor, but my prayer is not answered.

His chamber is below ground, narrow and without a window. The stone walls are damp. The room is musty.

He strips me so quickly that he fails to notice the thin jeweled belt I always wear, the one that contains Tristam's dagger. I am thrown to the ground, and he flings my clothes off to the side.

I leave my body and watch the struggle from a corner of the ceiling. From that vantage point, I observe that my dagger is barely out of reach in the jumble of my clothes. I focus my attention on reaching it. My first goal is to slide my hand under my crumpled gown. Once my hand achieves this covering, it is easier to search undetected. My eyes, from the ceiling, assist me.

After much slow and careful searching, my fingers find the belt. I am lucky. I touch the wide part of the belt, near the hilt of the dagger. Slowly, painstakingly, my fingers work their way to my goal.

He defiles me. He is brutal.

When he closes his eyes above me, throwing back his head, I manage to grip the hilt in my dominant hand. In one stroke, I remove it from its sheath. He lies upon me momentarily, to gather his breath. I think about stabbing his back, but I cannot risk merely wounding him. If I strike, it must be fatal.

Had he freed me then, I would not have killed him.

I wait to see what he will do.

"So Grace, how does my prowess compare to the old man's?" he asks, looming over me.

I remain silent.

"Answer me, Grace."

I do not move or speak.

He strikes my face. My head snaps to the left. "Well, you stubborn wench, you will have another chance to figure it out."

Pinning me to the ground with his hips, he reaches for a length of rope. When he brings the rope to my left wrist, I snap. I am not thinking, only moving. I grasp the dagger firmly in my right hand in an under-handed grip. My eye hones in on his neck, just under his left ear. When he begins tying my left wrist, I strike.

My aim is true.

His eyes widen in surprise. He slumps on top of me, covering me in blood. I retch.

My only thought is to get clean. I want to slip past the guards at the western gate. I long to immerse myself in the Wildcat, but I am shaking too violently to be stealthy. I would surely be caught.

Instead, I make my way to the stables. Rufus and Firefly are upset be-cause they can smell blood. I wash myself repeatedly in the water trough, scrubbing at my skin with handfuls of hay until I bleed, trying to remove the filth of Coltrane.

Wrapping myself in a horse blanket, I hide in the corner of Rufus's stall. Now that I am no longer covered in blood, Rufus lips my hair and Firefly also comes over to me. They hover protectively. I do not cry, nor do I sleep. The nightmare comes to life and plays out before my eyes. I see my father, my mother, my brothers, and my sisters. I see our home, our gardens, and our poverty. I see my captors and learn that every part of the nightmare is true.

CHAPTER 86

TRISTAM

At dawn, Thomas finds Grace, blue with cold. He sends for me.
"What happened?" I demand, stripping off my jacket and wrapping it around Grace's shoulders.

"I do not know. She has not spoken. I found her clothes near the watering troughs, covered in blood, yet I see only minor injuries on Grace… nothing that accounts for so much blood."

"Grace, who did this to you?" I demand, gripping her shoulders.

She makes no response. Her eyes gaze blankly past my left shoulder.

"Grace, talk to me," I plead.

"Sir, I do not believe she can," says Thomas. "Shall we take her to her chamber?"

I nod.

"I have sent for Geneva," he informs me.

"Grace, we are going to carry you to your chamber. No one will hurt you," I assure her.

She makes no sign of comprehension.

Thomas stuffs her soiled clothes into a rucksack that he swings over his shoulder. We lift her carefully, keeping the blanket in place.

More than an hour passes before Geneva arrives. I fret and fume and build a roaring fire. Grace huddles before it. When I try to clean the wound upon her cheek, she pulls away.

When Geneva finally arrives I snap at her. "Where have you been?"

"Coltrane has been murdered," she whispers. "This was at the scene," she holds up a piece of fabric that matches the clothes Thomas stuffed in the rucksack. "It belongs to Grace, does it not?"

"My God!" I stagger back, leaning against the wall for support.

Grace submits to having her facial wound cleaned by Geneva. She will not allow Geneva to look beneath the blanket.

"She will not respond and the guards are coming to ask questions," Geneva says.

"You told them the fabric belonged to Grace?" I did not like my accusing tone.

"They presented me with it and recognition was written on my face. I could not hide it."

"I see…forgive me."

"I sent for Addie. We have to examine her. If Grace was defending herself from—"

"From an assault, she will not be charged with murder," I finish her thought.

"We do not know that she did it," Geneva insists.

"Thomas, give me that rucksack."

"Yes, Sir. I will be outside, if you need me."

My fingers find the jeweled belt. I pull it free and remove the dagger from its sheath. It is perfectly clean. "How did Coltrane die?"

"A knife wound in the neck," Geneva replies.

I close my eyes. The room slides away. I am in the stables with a much younger Grace, telling her of the fatal targets for a knife.

"Tristam?" Geneva speaks.

I shake my head and open my eyes.

"We need to examine her. They are sending an unbiased examiner, but they will allow Addie and me to be present."

"A female examiner?"

"I am the only one. They think I am too close to Grace to be unbiased."

"My God!" I explode, striking the wall.

Geneva flinches but does not step back. Her eyes hold mine. "It is out of my hands. They will let me do the exam, but he has to see the evidence himself."

"You seem certain there will be evidence."

Geneva nods.

"You know more than you are telling me."

She nods again.

A knock falls upon the door. "King's Guards, open up!"

I open the door a crack. Addie and a small, bald man of fifty-some years enter the room. I remember Theo from my days as a squire.

"We will wait out here, Sir," one of the guards says.

"Theo, I am grateful they sent you," I say, relaxing a bit.

He shakes his head. "I wish I did not have to do this. I am sorry, Sir."

"I understand," I reply before leaving the room.

Addie comes out a few minutes later. "She will not submit to the exam."

"Can she be drugged first and then examined?"

"She smashed the cup when Geneva held it to her lips. We need your help, Sir," Addie pleads.

"Am I to force her, then?"

"If you prefer, we can do it, Sir." The guard's tone is respectful, his eyes downcast.

"I prefer to let the child rest," I almost shout.

I feel a hand grip my shoulder. I turn to brush it off and find myself staring into Thomas's pleading eyes. "She needs you, Sir," he chastises me gently.

"I wish we could let her rest, Sir," the guard says. "This is an ugly business."

I sigh.

Thomas pats my shoulder as I turn to enter the room.

I hold Grace down while Geneva tilts the drug down her throat. She spits most of it in my face.

I pin her down during the exam.

I have never committed a more criminal act in my life.

CHAPTER 87

GRACE

I am not required to stand trial. I cannot speak of that night, or indeed of anything, so Headmaster is sent to me with quills and parchment and I write my statement while he watches. I am a prisoner in my room until my fate is decided. I want no one's company. The isolation does not bother me, but I still long to immerse myself in the Wildcat. I yearn to sink below the cool green water and meld with the fallen leaves on the bottom. I never want to surface.

I do not know why it takes so long for my fate to be decided. I know I am guilty. I do not learn until later that many women of all classes come forward and tell of Coltrane's attacks upon them. I become a hero to them. They leave offerings in the courtyard where I can see them, though I do not learn the meaning of these gifts for many weeks. These offerings of fruit, ribbons, and bits of cloth provide the only patches of color I see through my narrow window.

I am waited upon by servants I do not know, and guards bring my meals. Father Gregory is my only visitor. He hears my confession and I hear his words of absolution but remain steadfast in my refusal to receive communion. He does not know that it is not Coltrane's murder that tortures my soul. It is yet another example of my evil that I lose no sleep over killing my attacker.

Remembering my time in Tristam's bed is what keeps me awake at night. I am horrified that I expressed my longing, and doubly so that he rejected me. I should have told him about the flashes of memory. When he held me down for the examination, my betrayal was complete. I cannot reach out to him, or indeed to anyone.

I am down a very deep hole. I see no way out. I sleep as much as possible, but I am never rested.

CHAPTER 88

TRISTAM

Women of all ages and from every class crowd the courtyard the day Grace's verdict is read. I have heard of her support amongst the women, but this is the first time I have seen it. The chamber is filled with lords and ladies and every servant who can find an excuse to be present. A hushed expectancy falls upon those gathered when Grace is led before the king and queen.

Grace sinks into a curtsy before them and does not rise. Queen Laurel herself goes to my Grace and raises her to her feet. Grace's appearance is shocking. Deep circles, like bruises, lie beneath her eyes. She has always been thin, but now her bones are clearly visible beneath her flesh.

I catch my breath.

I have not seen her for six weeks, since the morning of her examination. My frustration at the slowness of the process of justice led to my banishment from court. King Stefan came to me in private.

"I cannot rush this process, Tristam; too much is at stake. Those close to Coltrane and his father are spreading rumors that the young man was murdered to avenge his part in the rebellion. If I show any signs of favoritism in this matter, a new rebellion may ensue. Do you understand?"

"Yes, Your Majesty." I bow.

"I am sorry for Grace and for you, but I must follow the protocol. I must go through the entire process. I do not expect you to be patient, that is not your nature, but I do command your obedience. Go to your estates until I send for you."

"Yes, Your Majesty."

True to his word, I have been summoned for the verdict. I long to go to Grace. I offered to stand beside her, but she refused. She faces her fate alone as I watch from my allotted chair in court.

She stands erect and silent as all charges against her are read. She stands erect and silent as the evidence is presented. She alone remains silent after the verdict of "not guilty" is pronounced. The cheering of the crowd in the courtyard is deafening. The lords and ladies erupt into conversation amongst themselves. Most people are clapping. Here and there, I see disgruntled expressions on faces of persons I suspect sided with the rebels' cause.

Court is adjourned. I make my way toward Grace, longing to take her in my arms, but she looks right through me and turns away.

I have not seen her since.

CHAPTER 89

GRACE

Not guilty. I have been declared not guilty. I am free to leave my chamber, but do not wish to. Visitors come, but I have nothing to say. He does not come. I tell myself it does not matter. I have a date planned with The Beast at the Boldengarth River.

I want to believe in Father Gregory's God, but a God of love is beyond my comprehension. Father Gregory says it is a sin to reject one's self. He says, "Jesus tells us to love our neighbor as ourselves. Jesus wants you to love yourself and your neighbor." I do not think that is what Jesus meant, but I cannot tell the good priest he is wrong. Father Gregory also says it is a sin to reject God's love. We have clearly established my sinfulness. These are but two more marks against me with the God of Blinth.

The Beast will be pleased with the sacrifice of my life. Father God will be displeased. It will be a third sin to the Blinthian God, who will no doubt send me to Hell, if He is real and not The Beast.

The only task that keeps me from my appointed meeting at the river is this writing. Most of my confession is preserved on parchment, but he—Tristam, not Father Gregory—deserves to know what I now know. He deserves to know the meaning behind the nightmares that drove me to his bed. When I am gone, he will be given these parchments; when he reads my words he will know all I have remembered about my past. I hope he will understand my appreciation for the wonderful years he has given me. I do not expect him to understand that I cannot go on. He would never give up. I am not giving up; I am still fighting, but he will not see it that way.

I prepare for The Beast, but I still sometimes pray to Father God, the God that Jesus calls Abba, a word meaning beloved father. I am not well in my mind.

Every day I sit at my table and write. Bethany waits upon me now, so I am no longer surrounded by strangers. Her rounding belly is proof of new life, but I am dying. I have not spoken since before I murdered Coltrane. I have fallen into the abyss and it has swallowed me.

I will meet The Beast on the night of the summer solstice; He is stronger than me, so I will use the light to my advantage. The Beast does not fear me, but neither do I fear Him. All my hurt, all my anger, all my rage, and all my pain will be thrown at Him. I can wound him and I long for that day, but there are tasks I must complete before I am free to execute my plans. There are letters to write, bequeaths to bestow, and loose ends which must be fastened into place.

Writing letters to the people I love is the most difficult task. I write Peter, Catherine, and Trinicia's letters first. The letters for Geneva and Lucinda take longer. Tristam's letter consists of four words—I love you, Grace—and I place it with the parchments I have written about my past. I struggle with my letter to Thomas, and find myself apologizing; he deserves to know that my caring caused my anger the night we fought. Becca's letter is impossible to write and I burn attempt after attempt. Becca's anger at me will know no bounds, and no words I write will reconcile her to my decision. If she believed in The Beast, she would rather go with me to meet Him fighting at my side than be left behind. However, she does not believe in Him, so she will always believe I threw my life away. In the end her letter is also brief. I tell her to marry Peter and always remember that I love her. I bequeath her many things, including the dagger that killed Coltrane, and ask her not to burn them in her rage. I will not write to Tobias, but will go to him to say farewell.

Bethany waits on me in silence but she longs to speak. The day I finish my letter to Becca, Bethany can no longer contain herself.

"Tobias is dying and he suffers, but he is waiting for you. Please… you must go soon!" she pleads.

"Yes, it is time," I agree. "Let us go tonight."

"I will arrange it."

"Please, I do not want to see anyone except Tobias."

"I understand," she replies softly, looking at the ground.

Near midnight, her knock falls upon my chamber door. "He is wakeful," is all she says.

I put on my cloak; my only adornment is my jeweled hip belt. The dagger is in my hand, not in its sheath.

By the time we reach Tobias's last earthly home, my breathing is shallow and quick, and my heart is pounding against my ribs. I stop Bethany as she raises her hand to knock on the door, signaling I need a moment. She studies my face closely.

"I will wait for you here," she says.

When my breathing slows, I enter the one-room cottage. A fire blazes as though it is the depths of winter, rather than early summer. Tobias lies propped up on a bank of pillows encased in linen. His quilt is finely made and he wears a bed jacket that I recognize as Tristam's. I find I am grateful to him for his care of Tobias. The kindness seeps past the rage that blocks my feelings toward the man I had once loved beyond reason.

I am unprepared for the change in Tobias. His face is pale and shrunken. His eyes are too far back in his head. His cheeks are gaunt and his skin appears thin as ashes. The veins are enormous upon the back of his hand when I raise it to my lips.

"Oh, child, I have been waiting for you." He speaks with effort, but his eyes hold a strong welcome.

I feel tears sting the back of my eyes. I have not cried since before… that night.

"Come closer," he says, reaching for me.

He places a hand on each side of my face and studies me in silence. I cannot meet his gaze.

"Oh, child, how you have suffered," he says. "Give it to me."

"I cannot," I manage to whisper around the lump in my throat.

"Grace, I am old. I have seen much."

I nod.

"People make their own choices."

His words surprise me and I do not understand their meaning. "Yes?" I whisper, stealing a glance at his face.

"Remember that when I am gone," he insists.

"Do not leave me!" The tears spill over and I sound like a child.

"It is my time, and I will never leave you. You must carry the memory of me, child. You will keep me alive. You are my only child."

Against such love I am defenseless. I break. All my anger, hurt, and rage pour forth from my eyes in the form of tears.

Though he is weak, he pulls me into an embrace. His calloused hand strokes my hair. I bury my face in his shoulder and lift a tentative hand to his whiskered cheek. Time stops.

"This is good," he says when I finally lift my face to look at him. "This is very good." He is smiling.

"I am sorry…" I begin, trying to dry my eyes and rise up from beside him.

"Stop," his voice is surprisingly strong. I stop and look down at him, his eyes hold steel.

"But…I came to comfort you…and instead, you are comforting me."

"You are also giving it. That is the way of this world…to give is to receive."

I have no words. My face crumbles and the tears return.

"I will be all right, do not weep for me. Someone is waiting for me," he indicates the corner near the ceiling, next to the left side of the chimney. "She wants me to come, as much as you want me to stay."

I see no one, but he clearly does.

"Who? Who is there?" I ask.

"She is my beautiful Isabella."

"Oh, Tobias, I am so happy for you."

"Grieve me not, child," he insists. "I take your burdens and leave my love."

"But…you cannot…take my burdens."

"Oh, my Darling One, of course I can."

"I do not understand," I say, and hear puzzlement in my voice.

"Understanding is not necessary, only trust. I can see further than you. Do you trust me?"

I cannot speak for the tears are pouring down my cheeks, but I nod.

"Trust is all that is required."

"I love you," I reply. When I kiss his forehead, my tears land upon his face.

"I love you, my Precious One," he replies before closing his eyes.

"Send Bethany to me," he whispers.

"Yes, my dear Tobias." I kiss his hand one last time and lift it to my cheek before obeying.

His lips turn up at their corners. "Remember, Grace…choices… choices and trust" are the last words he says to me.

I move quietly to the door and slip out onto the front stoop. My movements have been too stealthy to warn Bethany of my approach and I am startled to see that Thomas is with her. I draw back in surprise.

They both look guilty.

"He is here for our safety," Bethany begins. "You looked so frightened while we were walking here…I thought if we had an escort on the way back…"

"Thank you…thank you, both." I speak gently. "Tobias wants you, Bethany,"

Thomas hands me his handkerchief. "I will wait over here and keep watch," he tells me.

"Please, will you sit with me?"

His eyebrows go up in surprise. "Are you certain that is your wish?"

I cannot speak, but I look up into his face and nod.

He sits beside me on a wooden bench just outside Tobias's door. We wait in silence. The stars travel on their night paths. A silver moon rises.

Dawn is near when an owl flies silently overhead.

Bethany opens the door.

"He is gone," she and I say together.

CHAPTER 90

GRACE

Back in my chamber, I ponder Tobias's words. *Choices.* I did not realize I was making choices. My path felt prescribed. My rage led me to The Beast. Perhaps my rage *is* The Beast...perhaps The Beast has been feeding on me all these years.

Trust. I entrusted Tobias with my pain; I shared it with him. Although I can still feel it inside me, it has less power. He is taking it with him, as he promised. Some part of it will always be mine, but I can foresee a future in which I can say, as Lucinda does, that this pain is no longer of grave importance.

There is no stone wall in my mind. The stones are scattered and memories pour over them. I see my brother cutting my bonds and sending me south. I feel my little sister's arms around my neck as I carry her upon my back. The memory leads me to Becca's sisters, Prissy and Lyddie, who have also ridden on my back. I think of Becca and smile.

Flashes envelop me, but they are not evil. I see Geneva bending over to show me an herb in her garden. I smell Lucinda's sweet buns. I hear Headmaster's voice and think of Father Gregory, Peter, Bethany, Catherine, and Trinicia. I remember Tobias and the feel of the callouses on his hands. My mind goes to Thomas; dear, strong, gentle Thomas...and finally to Tristam.

I see Tristam lifting me onto his horse, carrying me to this chamber on the day we met. I see Tristam bending over me to show me how to string an arrow. I remember his arms holding me when I shook in terror. I remember his love, just as I remember the sun when it finally peaks out from behind dense clouds.

The fog is gone.

My plan lies shattered at my feet.

Tears pour from my eyes. I must get to Tristam.

I do not know where he is, but I will find him. I race down the corridor, nearly colliding with Geneva.

"Grace, you must stop. You cannot keep running away," she says, grabbing my arm.

"Dear Geneva, I am not running away. I am running to Tristam."

"Thank God," she breathes, releasing my arm. Her tears match my own. I pull her into a quick embrace.

"I just left him. He was going for a ride. Hurry!" she urges me.

He is saddling his horse when I arrive, breathless, at Rufus's stall. Suddenly I feel shy in his presence. I pause at the entrance of the stables, but he has heard my approach.

When he turns to face me, I am shocked at his appearance. His face is gaunt. He has aged, but then he sees me and the light returns to his eyes. His sun comes out from behind its cloud and beams upon me and I fall into his arms.

CHAPTER 91

TRISTAM

When I hear someone in the entrance to Rufus's stall, I think *another delay before I can ride*. When I turn and see Grace, I am not certain she is real. I have seen her many times in my mind's eye over the weeks of our estrangement. When she takes a tentative step toward me, I cannot move fast enough. I cover the ground between us in two bounds, wrapping my arms around her and lifting her in the old manner. I cup her face in my hands. Her cheeks are wet with tears, but she is smiling through them. My cheeks are not dry.

Placing one hand on either side of her face, I kiss her forehead, the tip of her nose, and each cheek in turn. My eyes devour her face. Words fail me.

Then Grace does something she has never done before; she reaches up and traces the wrinkles at the corners of my eyes and the furrow between my brows. She traces her fingers over my eyebrows, my nose, and my lips. I simply let my tears fall.

Grace recovers her voice first, "Oh, Tristam, can you ever forgive me?"

"I think I am the one who should be begging your forgiveness. I hurt you. I am not even certain how I hurt you…"

"It was my fault…all my fault," she insists.

"What happened inside you that night we were together? I fell asleep thinking of marriage."

She touches my face. "I am so sorry."

"Do not be. But please explain, I need to understand."

"I was seeing pictures from the past, as you were touching me. I thought….I was stupid."

She pauses.

297

"How so?"

"I thought if you took me as your own, it would erase those bad pictures. I just wanted you to hurry, to get it over with."

I reach for her, pulling her close.

"Oh, my Grace; I did not know."

"I did not tell you."

"Why not?"

"I am not certain. I think…I think I wanted to be in the moment, that moment, with you. I thought you could make the memories stop. When you left, I felt so rejected."

I shake my head. "That is difficult for me to understand. I kissed your feet…told you I adored you."

"I know…I know that now…but then I was not thinking, only feeling. I thought you had left me alone, abandoned me to my memories. I felt that you did not want me."

"I should have known. I was so full of passion. I was concentrating on controlling myself. I missed your needs."

She blushes a deep, rosy pink. I wait for her to speak.

"I did not know it was difficult for you."

"How can you not know that you are wholly desirable?"

She shrugs, still blushing fiercely.

I pick her up again in the the old way and kiss the top of her head before releasing her. My actions relieve some of the tension between us.

"It was difficult for me," I tell her.

"And I kept thinking, 'he does not want me; he does not want me.' I could not be still. I had to run. I had to outrun the memories and outrun your rejection."

I interrupt her. "The rejection that was not real."

"Yes, but the rejection *felt* real. Instead, I ran into Coltrane."

She stops talking. Her eyes move upward and to the left. She is remembering. I wait for what she tells me.

"Your training…It stood me in good stead." She pauses.

I wait.

"It was horrible…the blood, it was just like you told me it would be."

"I am so proud of you. You did a difficult thing."

"I do not think I could ever do it again."

"I pray you will never have to. I wish you could have killed him before he…" I cannot finish my sentence.

"Defiled me?"

"Yes."

"He punched me and I could not breathe. By the time breath had returned, my dagger was tangled up with the clothes he had ripped off of me. The whole time, I just concentrated on reaching it without distracting him."

"My God," escapes me, my fists are clenched.

"Still…I would not have killed him if he had let me go. But when he reached for a strap to tie me down, something fierce in me took over."

"Thank God! Thank God!" My words sound more like an oath than a prayer.

"Thank *you*; you trained me."

"But you did it. You protected yourself. Thank God for your ferocity."

She nods, "I wonder…"

"What do you wonder?"

"I wonder if that is why my memory returned, because I had protected myself…proven I was strong enough?"

"Is that how it feels?"

"Possibly….I had not thought of that before."

"You have certainly proven yourself in battle."

"All my memories came to me in a flood while I cowered in Rufus's stall."

"And here we are, in Rufus's stall."

She looks around and smiles. "Yes, we are."

"Do you want to tell me?"

"I want you to know. I have written it down, for I cannot speak these words."

"Do you want me to read them here?"

"No. There is a special rock by Wildcat Creek. The sun is warm today. Let us go out into the blue and yellow."

"As you wish."

CHAPTER 92

TRISTAM

We walk to her special place; a place she has never taken me before. She hands me several parchments and I begin reading her words.

I was not supposed to be The Chosen. My older sister was raised as The One. She led a life of privilege within our impoverished home. The best foods were selected for her. If someone got new clothes, it was only because there was fabric left over from a new gown for "The Chosen." Her name was Lilia, for the lily flower. She would be fed to the earth to make it fertile. Her life would be short, like a lily's.

My grandmother's name, Genevieve, was reserved for me, the second daughter.

"So that is your name, 'Genevieve.' It suits you."

"My name is Grace," she replies. "Keep reading."

I smile and do as she bids me.

My parents hoped Grandmother would be generous to me, her namesake, in her will, but that plan did not work out any better than the plan for Lilia's life. Grandmother became feebleminded in old age, and she left her fortune to a much younger man of no relation, who, I am told, looked like my grandfather when he was young; my grandfather died before my time, so I cannot judge.

Most of the time, my sister's special status was not something I coveted, but at the age of six or seven, The Sacrifice seemed far distant. When I was milking cows and mucking out horse stalls, Lilia was free to work on her stitchery. Manual labor would have ruined her fine clothes and pristine hands. I envied her that freedom, that idle time, for I had none. She hated tapestry work and I loved it, yet she was expected to produce it. Had I been more enterprising, I probably could have worked a trade. As things were, I finished her tapestry for the love of the needle and for her.

She had no future. As her womanhood began to flower, before she had ever been touched by a man, she would be given as a bride to "The Beast." She would be privileged to serve all Lolgothe, ensuring fertile crops, freedom from storms, droughts, and pestilence, by her sacrifice.

The Beast was not something I understood well. Sometimes when we misbehaved we were threatened, "The Beast is watching you. Beware of arousing his wrath." At other times, such as when a hailstorm crushed the wheat and oat seedlings, The Beast was the hail. It was said The Beast was raining destruction upon us for our evilness and greed. At those times, we sacrificed more to The Beast. Grain, fruit, vegetables, flowers, chickens, goats, even milk was poured upon the land for Him. His wrath was endless, as was His appetite.

Sometimes, The Beast inhabited a four-legged body of black fur, sharp fangs, piercing claws, and red eyes. His black tail ended in a sharp, pointed spade. At other times, he was embodied in the wind, the thunder, the blizzard, or the plagues that beleaguered our poor country.

Lolgothe is indeed a poor country, not only because the best of everything is fed to the ravenous Beast. The fields are full of stones and the soil is sandy. The winters are long and bitter. The north wind rips across the Northern Sea and rains a salt mist upon the land. The fields do not give good yield. The forests are full of pine; little hardwood grows in Lolgothe. Our pine houses burn easily when the cook fire leaps out of its hearth. Food is scarce; animals are lean. The people's disposition is not happy.

Illness is more common than health. People's teeth rot in their heads. It is not expected that a child will live long enough to be useful to his or her parents. The children who do survive are seen as a burden, another mouth to feed.

In the year of my ninth winter, before I reached my birthday in March, a particularly horrible illness was sent by The Beast. People sickened and died in three or four days. Boils erupted on their flesh, preceded by a high fever. At the time of death, blood poured from their eyes, their mouths, their noses, and their ears.

We lost Lilia and my mother both in a three-day period. I was now the eldest and therefore became The Chosen, but there was no leisure for me to enjoy my elevated status. I ran the household, cared for my younger siblings, and tried to avoid my father's displeasure. He always drank, but after Mother's death his drinking was no longer confined to the evening or rest days. He drank always, selling clothes, furniture, and even our dishes to maintain his inebriated state.

He began selling me. He had used me himself by then, of course; he had led me to the barn at the age of six. Now he led me to the barn and handed me over to other men. Money changed hands. He threatened, if I refused, to begin selling Delilah, my younger sister.

Samuel, my brother, knew what I suffered. We never spoke of it, but one day I saw his face through a gap in the barn wall. His eyes were wide. I silently mouthed the word "Run," and he did. But later, when I was released from the barn, my chores were already completed. A piece of bread was tucked into the kitchen corner where I kept my apron. It was Samuel who had done all this. I protected all of them. He protected me.

I began looking forward to the day when I would meet The Beast. All my rage was focused upon Him. I had no illusion that I would win the encounter. My goal was merely to extract my pound of flesh from His hide. To that end, I strengthened myself physically.

As the time drew nearer, I was given more privileges. A few of my sister's gowns were unearthed, though I thought they had all been sold. My hands had to be white and free of callouses. My arms soft and not muscled. I was no longer allowed to work. I was no longer sold in the barn. I was dressed and treated as something I was not: an innocent.

"But you are an innocent," I say to her.

"How can you say so? I have been defiled…many times."

"But Grace, you have never made love. That is a very different thing from violence and abuse."

"But the act is the same."

"No, Grace, that is not true. Did it not feel different when we were touching than when Coltrane was violating you?"

She blushes and looks away, but she also nods.

"You are a virgin, an innocent."

She is shaking her head.

"You do not have to agree with me. Just promise you will think about my words."

She nods and I continue reading.

For the first time, Samuel and I talked. I shared my plan. He was not reconciled to my sacrifice, thus he was more than willing to help me remain strong. He found thick leather gloves, God knows where, to protect my hands. He covered for me during the few hours each day that our father was sober enough to care about my whereabouts. I used the time to do the chores that would keep me strong.

Samuel came to me the day he saw Delilah being taken to the barn by Father. She was our only living sister. She was seven.

Samuel devised a plot. He used twine to trip Father at the entrance to the barn. He strategically placed the scythe for him to fall upon. The plan went awry, of course. Father was wounded, but not killed. Samuel was beaten almost to death for his carelessness with the scythe. I was able to remove the twine while Father was engaged in flogging his oldest son's flesh. Had Father seen the twine, Samuel would have been killed. I treated Samuel's wounds, which bothered him very little. Delilah was safe.

The green poison set into the injury upon my father's arm where the scythe had pierced his flesh. I nursed him. Samuel could not understand and I could not explain, but I was saving my rage for The Beast.

Father died suddenly one night. His pulse was fine at midnight, when I checked on him. The poison was receding and his appetite returning. He was calling for wine and ale. I gave him wine and went to bed. At dawn, he was stone cold. The wine bottle was missing. Samuel and I never discussed it.

I pause before asking my question: "Do you think Samuel poisoned your father?"

"It is likely. I would like to ask him."

Samuel assumed management of what was left of our lands and estate. Our brothers, Luke and Paul, were old enough to assist him, and I trained Delilah in my duties. We were not prosperous, but we were no longer constantly hungry. We knew a stretch of peace before they came for me.

The Sacrifice happens every seventh year. The year of Lilia's birth was one of the years in which lots were cast amongst all noble families with an infant daughter. The privilege fell upon our house. Lilia had exactly fourteen years to live. When she was seven years of age, she would watch the sacrifice of a child twice her age. If she died before reaching fourteen, our family would provide any girl-child between the ages of nine and fourteen. If I had died also, Delilah would have been spared. She was too young. The lot would then fall to the second house chosen and, afterwards, to the third. The lots had never gone farther than three families. All three daughters in those families would receive the best of everything, just as The Beast did.

Samuel was not resigned to my fate. I was not untouched by men. He could see no reason to end my life. As a sacrifice, I was worthless; as a sister, I was needed. I swore Samuel to secrecy about my defilement, arguing my life would not be worth living if I were known to be unclean. The men who knew I was unclean had their own reasons for remaining silent.

"Damn them! May God damn every one of them to Hell!" The words erupt from deep within me. Grace flinches and I change my tone. "You are not unclean, my darling. They are as unclean as swine in the fields."

"I feel unclean."

"You are not."

"It is hard for you to read this, is it not?"

"How could it not be for anyone who loves you?"

"Thank you for loving me."

"That is easy. Reading this is not."

"You do not have to read it."

"I want to know everything you have suffered."

"I think I understand. I wanted to know what you had suffered when you lost Constance and Faith," she replies.

I take a few deep breaths before I begin reading again.

The noblemen, surrounded by the king's guard, came for me the first day of March, just three days before my eleventh birthday. Had we resisted, or had I not been there when they arrived, our house would have been torched and no family member left alive. Knowing these conditions, I went willingly.

For three weeks, I was pampered like a princess in the castle. I was bathed. My hair was brushed. A wedding gown was fitted. My every whim was obeyed. I was fed whatever I asked for because I would feed The Beast. My requests were seen as coming from Him and I used this to my advantage. Not only did I request tapestry threads for those nights when I lay sleepless, I also demanded stones be placed in my bath. I convinced my maids that the stones were there to remove the rough skin, but at night, I lifted them, tied inside a blanket, to keep my arms and legs strong. I demanded time outdoors in which to look for signs of my bridegroom's approach. Once outdoors, I ran wildly, pretending I was seeking Him. The guards eyed one another, but they obeyed my requests. I was not even reprimanded for dirtying myself, as this gave the maids another opportunity to bathe me and soften my skin.

The March equinox was rapidly approaching. I was not the only one preparing.

CHAPTER 93

TRISTAM

The place of the sacrifice is unknown to all but the king; it is a secret handed down with the crown. The king selects his most trusted guards to deliver The Chosen to the altar of The Beast. In poor times, even good men can be bought. When a man's child is starving, he will trade information for bread. Samuel was resourceful. He found out which guards had been selected and which one's children lived in want. He used our small stores of grain to discover the location of the altar. He was there before me, hidden, on the night of The Sacrifice.

The ceremonies leading up to The Sacrifice are more elaborate than a royal nuptial celebration. I was displayed to the people, dressed in finery, for three nights. I was fed wine and rich food, though the wine was drugged. I felt a lethargic peace inhabiting my mind and my limbs after the first night of feasting. The second night, I ate less and only sipped at my wine. I lay awake all night without the drugs from the wine. By the third night, I was taut as a bowstring. Feigning lethargy was not an easy task.

On the most balanced night of the year, when daylight and dark are equal, The Sacrifice meets The Beast. Armed with a carving knife, I slipped from the feasting table, I was ready to meet my bridegroom.

I close my eyes and my hand moves to cover my stomach. I look at the moving water of Wildcat Creek before I continue reading.

At midnight, I was led to the king's private chapel. Only the noblemen were in attendance. There, I was placed on an altar in the center of the room and the men encircled me. In an elaborate ceremony, they drank deeply from a golden cup with two handles. Their arms were linked, and each man helped the next raise the cup to his lips. I was forced to drain the cup. Fortunately, little wine remained when the cup was finally passed to me.

A knock sounded upon the chapel door and five guards entered carrying a litter. I was laid upon it and carried to my groom.

I could tell the men did not like their task; I listened as I was carried deep into the southern woods. One was frightened. One felt pity for me. The leader was resigned and longing for his bed. The other two men said little as we traveled.

When they lifted me off the litter, I saw four stakes pounded into the ground. When they attached the leather bands to my wrists and ankles, I began fighting with all my strength. I kept thinking, I cannot attack The Beast if I am bound. *I was not easily subdued. I inflicted injuries upon them, though my knife remained hidden. In anger, the leader slashed my right foot with his sword after I was finally bound on the ground.*

"One more word out of you, and the next slash will be to your throat."

"But, Sir, she is to be alive and whole for The Beast."

"He will eat her, even if her foot is wounded. Trust me. I have done this before."

They left as soon as they could. I could not reach the dagger at my waist. Time passed slowly while I strained my ears to catch every sound. When I heard rustling footsteps approach, I prepared to meet The Beast. Perhaps I did. It was the leader of the guards, returning alone.

"No use letting The Beast have all the fun tonight. I doubt if he is particular about his bride's virginity." The man was undoing his belt and leering at me, a lantern raised in his left hand. My insides felt like ice. I could not move.

As I watched, his head seemed to snap to the side. One minute, I heard a slight sound of movement and in the next, a club slammed against my attacker's head. He crumpled.

Samuel used my knife to cut my bonds.

"Take this," he said, handing me a pack. "It is food and water. Head south. If it were not for the younger ones, I would go with you. Go, hurry!"

I tried to thank him.

"Go now! I have to make it look like The Beast devoured you, not this man. Give me your petticoat; that will help. They will be here to observe the sacrifice at two hours after midnight. There is not much time. I wanted to free you sooner, but this bastard was watching you. Had I known of his plans, I would have killed him sooner. Make haste...hurry!"

Without a word of thanks, I flew.

He risked every family member's life to free me. The picture of the guard's head exploding replayed itself in my head. The memory, like so many others, went behind the stone wall in my mind.

I finish reading, but do not speak.

After a passage of time, Grace lays her head on my shoulder. "I wish I knew what happened to Samuel," she says wistfully.

"Of course you do, Grace."

"Can we try to find out?"

"Perhaps we can. One of the king's men went to Lolgothe after the rebels were stopped at the pass. King Stefan wanted to warn them that Traag is armed and spoiling for war."

"Was Thomas the messenger?"

"That is not a question I can answer."

"He was," Grace replies.

I ignore her words and her smug smile.

"As a country, we are building alliances with Lolgothe. That could help us find Samuel, but protecting you comes first."

"Yes; if they know I am alive, they will kill my family."

Grace's face looks grave. I wonder if any of her siblings are still alive.

CHAPTER 94

TRISTAM

We sit in silence.

"Tristam?" Grace says softly after several moments have passed.

I shake my head, slowly.

"What is it?" she asks.

"I do not know what to say. I knew your burden was heavy, but I was not prepared for this."

"I never thought you would have to say anything."

"What do you mean?"

She pauses before answering, "I wrote all of this down for you to read after I was gone."

"You were leaving?" I hear the confusion in my own voice.

Grace hangs her head and nods.

"Where were you going?" I ask; my voice sounds demanding.

"You are not going to like what I am about to tell you." Her reply is barely audible.

"I do not like what I have already learned…" I begin.

She raises her eyes to my face. "But it turned out well, because you found me in the woods."

"But that does not remove the horrors you suffered," I reply, aching with the knowledge of her pain.

"No, it does not. That is why I was leaving. I thought if I went to meet The Beast, as was my lot, it would complete the cycle. I would have died fighting Him. I would finally have been the sacrifice I was meant to be. My death would end the horrors I had lived and carried within me."

"So you were planning to die?" My eyes are wide and my voice incredulous.

"No, I was planning to fight The Beast; I knew I would die in the fight."

I could not speak.

"Tristam, what is it?" her voice is small, like a child's.

"I do not understand your desire for death, nor how you would meet this 'Beast,' as you call him. Do you think he is real?" I find I am shaking my head in disbelief.

"In my inner darkness, He seemed very real. I was raised to believe in Him, just as you were raised to believe in the Lord Jesus Christ."

"But you have lived here and worshiped the Trinity. How could you believe in The Beast?"

"Coltrane had The Beast in him. So did the rebel who wounded your shoulder after receiving quarter. Father Gregory would call it evil. Evil and The Beast are one."

"Evil I understand. But how did you think you could simply walk out into the darkness and meet up with The Beast?"

"Evil has never been difficult for me to find," she states flatly, but I hear a hint of bitterness. "I was going to the Boldengarth River. All beasts must drink water, both two- and four-legged ones."

I have no words, so I simply shake my head once again.

"First you must realize I was not well in my mind or my body. I could not eat, nor sleep, nor work the tapestry. My mind was spinning, turning, mixing the past and the present. I could not make it stop. Geneva's herbs did nothing. I felt caged. I paced."

"Yet you were free to leave your chamber." My voice sounds confused.

"My body, the king had freed. No one could free my mind."

I nod slowly, taking in her words.

"I had a task to finish before I could go. I had to write down what I had remembered for you. I did not think it was fair for you to never know what I had uncovered."

"But it was fair to leave me?" I demand.

"No, it was not, and I am here." She takes my face in her hands. "Look at me!" She commands. "I am telling you of a plan I did not act on."

I release my breath, which I had been holding. "What changed your mind?"

"It was Tobias…something that he said."

"What did he say?"

"He used few words, but he wanted me to give him my pain. He planned to take it away with him. He called me his child and asked if I

trusted him. I wept…something I had been unable to do since before.…
But I had gone to comfort him and he was comforting me. When I told
him that, he said, 'to give is to receive.'"

She stops talking and I see her eyes gaze out at the horizon.

"The last thing he said was, 'Grace, remember you have choices…
trust.' It was as if he knew of my plan…yet I had told no one. Thomas
and Bethany took me back to my chamber. My mind stopped spinning
and my thoughts grew clearer. I remembered all the love that surrounded
me, the giving and receiving. Suddenly, I could not get to you quickly
enough."

She turns to look at me. My cheeks are wet. She reaches out her hand
to wipe my tears and I kiss her palm. She places a hand on either side of
my face.

When I can speak, I say, "I am glad that you are here…finally," I add,
winking at her.

She ignores my teasing. "This is where I belong," she replies.

I enfold her in my arms, lift her off the ground, and kiss her on the
forehead before releasing her.

"I am being selfish. There are others who long to see you."

"No, Tristam; I will not go see the others until our future is settled."

With these words, I sense danger. I look deep into her eyes. She returns my gaze without blinking or looking away.

I see before me an innocent young woman, strong, courageous, and
vulnerable. Love shines in her eyes.

I am the man who is most like a father to her. Her own father defiled
her and she believes she carries his filth. She will never believe in her own
innocence if my actions do not match my words.

I take both her hands in mine. Bending down upon one knee, I
choose my words with great care.

"Grace, I cannot imagine life without you. My love is yours. Would
you like to marry me?"

CHAPTER 95

GRACE

This is the moment for which I have been yearning since the day I met Tristam. I longed to marry him and truly belong to him, but I do not feel as I had expected to feel when I dreamt of this moment. My mind feels clouded. Tristam is still speaking and I force myself to listen.

"I do not ever want to hurt you again, as I did that night. If memories come, you must promise to tell me."

"I promise."

He smiles at me with such tenderness. He kisses my forehead and both eyelids, but a panting voice interrupts us before he kisses my lips.

"Sir Tristam, you are needed at the western gate immediately! Forgive my intrusion."

I know that voice. I bury my scarlet face in Tristam's shoulder.

"Thomas, what could possibly be so urgent?" Tristam asks.

Thomas is gasping for breath. "There is a young woman at the gates, begging for you. She says you are her father, Sir."

I watch Tristam's face turn ashen. His eyes search mine.

"Go to her!" I urge him.

"Take care of Grace," he says to Thomas before he leaves us.

I stare at the ground, waiting for the color to leave my cheeks.

"How did you know where to find us?" I ask Thomas, after a period of awkward silence.

"You brought me here once. You told me this place is sacred to you."

"And you remembered." The corners of my mouth lift slightly.

He nods. "I am sorry I interrupted you and Tristam. Am I the first to congratulate you on your betrothal?" His eyes are searching mine.

"Yes…no…I do not know. I feel…"

"You feel…?" Thomas prompts.

"I feel uncertain…confused. I need time to sort my thoughts."

Thomas says nothing and I continue. "I always wanted Tristam to ask me to marry him. I thought marriage would make me truly belong to him, and then everything inside me would settle into place."

"So he asked but you do not feel settled?"

I nod. "I feel even more unsettled. Maybe all those years I was wrong."

"Perhaps, or perhaps not. Maybe it is not a matter of right or wrong." Thomas smiles at me.

"What are you thinking?" I ask.

He shakes his head. "It does not matter what I am thinking. You will figure this out."

"So many things have happened so quickly. Perhaps too quickly."

"And perhaps you need time to sort things out."

"That is exactly what I need."

He smiles down at me. His dimples show.

"Why do I tell you things no one else knows about me?"

"You have asked me that question before. Perhaps it is because I am good at keeping secrets. Or perhaps because I am your friend."

"I thought you were my brother."

"Perhaps."

"Are you laughing at me?"

"Perhaps, or perhaps I am laughing with you."

"Can you speak a sentence without using the word 'perhaps'?"

"Perhaps."

I reach over and slap his arm. "Stop teasing! Which is it; brother, or friend?"

"I am whatever you need me to be. Remember that." His dimples are gone.

I pause before speaking. "Thank you, you are too good….I owe you an apology," I reply.

"For what?"

"For the night when Tristam was injured. I got so angry with you. I am sorry."

"You should not be."

"Why not? I was rude to you."

"Your anger told me you care for me."

This time, I punch his arm. "I do not care for you," I say, but I am smiling.

"Wonderful," he says, "perhaps that will change."

"Perhaps, if you stop saying 'perhaps,'" I reply, and we laugh together.

"Will you take me to Tristam and the young woman?" I ask.

His eyes search my face. "Are you ready?"

"Yes, let us hurry."

We run together as we did so many years before, when Becca's mother had the fever, only this time his pace outstrips mine. He waits when I lag behind.

"I am weak from too many days in my chamber," I pant.

"You are the strongest woman I know," he replies.

I have no words. I begin running.

We crest the hill near the castle gate. Looking down, I see a young woman dressed in rags. I watch as she melts into Tristam's embrace.

I stand rooted to the ground, not wishing to intrude, but Tristam turns, calling out, "Grace, I need you! Thomas, fetch Geneva! This is my Faith."

I run to him as Thomas leaves.

"I cannot understand her speech. I think she has been a prisoner in Lolgothe."

"Faith?" I ask her.

She nods, laying one hand upon her chest. "Faith," she repeats. Then she breaks into a flurry of speech. I am grateful for my lessons with Headmaster. Even with my studies of the language of my youth, I cannot understand every word.

Tristam's face is tortured. "What is she saying?" he demands.

I raise a finger, asking him to wait.

When Faith pauses to take a breath, I begin translating, knowing every word I speak pierces Tristam's heart.

When I finish, Faith is unsteady on her feet. Tristam lifts her, cradling her in his arms. I remember a different time, in a different place, when he lifted me onto his horse. My eyes are not dry and I turn away.

Thomas approaches with Geneva. I smile at him through my tears. I do not follow Tristam and Faith into the castle, but stand watching them until they cannot be seen.

She needs him. Just him. Geneva follows in their wake.

Something within me shifts and then roots itself firmly in place. The yellow sun peeks out from behind a cloud, lighting the sky a brilliant blue. I close my eyes and lift my face to its warmth. A rustling in the underbrush sounds like a stag.

My doubt is gone. My confusion evaporates. I belong to Tristam. I have belonged to him since the day he found me clinging to my Stag. He is my father. I am his child, no more than Faith, but also no less. Marriage between us would be wrong.

In that moment, I complete my journey the way it began, alone. Only this time, I can feel my strength, the strength I have always had.

"Grace?" I hear Thomas's voice, as if from far away.

I open my eyes and turn to him. I am smiling. "Yes?"

"There are a number of people waiting to see you."

"Really?"

"Yes, really. Not perhaps."

"Are you joking?" I look at him with a question in my eye.

"No; word spread that you had left your room. People care about you. Do not forget, to some of these women, you are a hero."

He leads me through the castle gates. The courtyard is filled with people, and a cheer goes up.

"Hail the Lady Grace!"

Becca grabs me and hugs me in her fierce way. Peter, Bethany, Catherine, and Trinicia are next. They are followed by Daniel, Sarah, Sally, and her sisters. Bethany is standing back, but I pull her to me and place my hand gently on the curve that holds her baby.

Benjamin latches onto my hand and will not let go. "You came back! You came back!" he hollers.

"No, Sweet Boy," I correct him, "I came home."

Acknowledgements

Acknowledgements were never something I read until I started writing. How do you thank the people who made you who you are and encouraged your creative endeavors? I'm not sure, but I am going to try.

My Family: Bill, if I listed everything you have done to help me, I would have to write another book. Our oldest, Tommy, you and your art are amazing. Thank you for capturing the feeling of this story on the cover and map. Our daughter, Meg, listened to me talk about this book for most of her childhood. Her input was invaluable and her comment, "Mom, Grace needs a friend," gave us Becca. Our youngest, Nick, came to my rescue on the title in the nick of time.

My mother, who taught me to love books and told me to keep writing. My baby sister, Carol, who grew up to be my dear friend. My big brother, Bobby, who loves me. My Father-in-law, Bill, who loves deeply. To my step mother, Clara, thanks for help in the formative years. To my Great Aunt Helen, who shared from her deep pool of wisdom.

The Healers: George, the first to hear, your gentleness brings tears. You taught me what a father could be. Jean, fierce momma bear, you pulled me back from the ledge and pushed hard for me to publish. Jerry, you were the first to ask and you were right; it is a big deal. Maggie, you taught me to pay it forward long before the phrase existed. Roger, you paddle a parallel path beside me and I can never be sufficiently grateful that you let me in. For Taylor, Candace, Joe, Amanda, and Ryan, healers all.

The Story Tellers: Many people have entrusted me with their personal stories of pain, sacrifice and survival. I am profoundly grateful, especially to the courageous children. I cannot list you, nor may I contact you, but you can certainly contact me if you wish. I carry you in my heart.

My Family of Choice: Kathy, Gery, Mandy and Lyndsay K., your house will always be my home. Di and Roger, who took me in without question. George and Nancy. Jim and Kim. Jerry and Sandy. Sheila and Michael. Maggie, Mo, Sally and Will, I'll always be a wanna be. P.C. and her girls, the Christmas with no heat was the best. Holly, who answered the phone in the middle of the night. If only a phone line could reach you now. Crenshaw and Stuart, and of course, Jo. Christina, sorry it took me so long to get here. I can't imagine a day here without you. I love all of you and am grateful for your presence in my life.

The Writers: My friend, Caroline, who told me to believe in my writing. She read the earliest versions that no longer exist. My writing group, especially Maija and Mary. They listened to every word and surprised me by wanting more. They made the story stronger and more real. They also spent hours editing when they could have been writing. I owe you and love you.

My First Readers: Kathy K. who read all the stuff I wrote that wasn't ready to be published and told me so with grace. When you said, "publish!" I was overjoyed. Kara, who doesn't even like this genre and gave me invaluable feedback, as did Robin, Annette, Kathy P., Amy, Hailey, Mary Beth, an expert on young adult fiction, Sally, Carol, Pat, Laura, Tommy, Bill and George, thank you. My niece, Audrey, devoured the first draft over Thanksgiving. I can still see you curled up in the chair with that big fat notebook. You warm my heart. Keep writing, Kiddo.

Publishing: Another Carol who introduced me to the people at Maine Author's Publishing and gave me advice and encouragement. To Sherry, my last minute hero, your editing made all the difference, especially since you teach high school English, love your students and give freely of your time and talents. Thank you to all the professionals at Maine Authors Publishing. Working with you is a pleasure.

Paddlers: Thank you to the paddlers of Indiana, who took me in, fixed my stroke, and encouraged me to race. Thank you to the paddlers of New England and all the Spring Training Camp paddlers, I could not have survived the move without you. I wish I could name you all, but I do have to mention a third Carol, my canoe partner. You, Yvonne and your family are precious to me.

I know I'm forgetting someone important. If it's you, please kick my butt and forgive me. Your name will be in bold print in the sequel.

Chocolate cannot be thanked enough and was absolutely essential to the creative process, as was the music of the Indigo Girls. Oscar, my fuzzy, four legged shadow, gave up many a walk for the cause.

Finally, profound gratitude to The Ground of All Being, for life, for the beauty of the earth, and for the grace to keep moving forward.

ABOUT THE AUTHOR

Cady Elizabeth "Betsy" Arnold is a Social Worker who believes in the healing power of narrative. In addition, she believes in the beauty of the world, and the meaning to be found in relationships. She has the great good fortune to have served as a counselor in an elementary school, at two colleges, and in various other settings where students have shared their stories with her while on the path to healing and wholeness.

Currently, she spends her non-writing time enjoying her family, kayaking, eating chocolate, and taking long walks in the New Hampshire woods with her dog, Oscar.

To learn more about the artist visit www.wtarnold.com.